DANCE
OF
STARS
AND
ASHES

BOOKS BY NISHA J. TULI

DANCE
OF
STARS
AND
ASHES

NISHA J. TULI

SECOND SKY

Published by Second Sky in 2024

An imprint of Storyfire Ltd.
Carmelite House
50 Victoria Embankment
London EC4Y 0DZ
United Kingdom

www.secondskybooks.com

ISBN: 978-1-83525-194-2
eBook ISBN: 978-1-83525-193-5

For every woman who's learning how to be unapologetically herself.

AUTHOR'S NOTE

Welcome back to Zarya's story! I am thrilled to share the next installment in the Nightfire series, where the adventure continues with more slow burn, angst—and get ready for some *heat* this time around. You ask. I deliver. And let's be real; it was always going to happen, as much as I love to torment you all a little bit. It hurts me, too, to make them wait, I promise.

I've been asked many times for a glossary and map for the series, and I've put a glossary together for you broken up by the characters, the world-building, and some of the extra stuff, which you'll find in the following pages.

If you want a map, great news—you can find one on my website at nishajtuli.com.

This story has a few content warnings, so if you'd like to read them, I'm listing them below. Otherwise, flip to the first page and head back to Daragaab, where some mysteries from book one will be answered while so many more are uncovered.

As always, I hope you love reading it as much as I enjoyed writing it.

Nisha

CAST OF CHARACTERS

Zarya Rai: Our heroine, Aazheri, wielder of night-fire, and in possession of the mythical sixth anchor. Will cut you if you piss her off.

Yasen Varghese: Zarya's BFF, lieutenant in the queen's army, rakshasa with silver hair and grey eyes. Not just a pretty face.

Vikram Ravana: Commander of the queen's army, future steward to Rani Amrita, rakshasa with some earth magic ability but not as much as you-know-who. Short dark hair and green eyes. We're not really sure where things are going with him yet.

Rani Amrita: Future queen of Daragaab, the last of the pure yakshi line. Dark hair and amber eyes, and Zarya's other BFF. Soon to become a tree, but she's ready for it.

Rabindranath Ravana: Also known as Rabin, Vikram's brother, most powerful rakshasa in Rahajhan with all the earth magic and the ability to shift into a dragon form. Broody, moody, and hot. Is starting to enjoy romance novels.

Row: Zarya's guardian and the man who kept her locked up for most of her life. Powerful Aazheri with five anchors. Long dark hair with braids, a stern expression, an all-around kind of scary dude.

Aarav: Zarya's sort of brother and pain in her ass. Apprentice to Row, Aazheri with two anchors. Decorated Khada soldier and boyfriend of Lekha.

Kindle: Agni from the region of Bhaavana, known for his fire magic and ability to alter emotions in others. A problem solver and the guy who can be counted on to comment sagely on stuff with ancient knowledge.

Suvanna: Merdeva from the queendom of Matsya. Has water powers and the ability to draw moisture from the air. Blue hair and almost blue skin, and she suffers no fools. The scariest bitch you'll ever meet.

Apsara: Vidyadhara from the region of Vayuu. Wielder of snow, ice, and wind. Has white feathered wings and long white hair. Beautiful and deadly, but nice when she wants to be.

Koura: A healer from the region of Svaasthy and powerful wielder of Niramaya—the magic of healing, channeled through the use of spirit. Dark skin, golden eyes. A gentle giant, but don't let that fool you when the stakes are rising.

Professor Dhawan: Former advisor to the crown in Gi'ana and former professor of languages at the university. Has retired to the forests of Daragaab to tend to his flowers. Really, really old.

Gopal Ravana: The nawab of Daragaab, powerful rakshasa, father to Vikram and Rabin. Looks like he boils baby monkeys for fun.

Jasmine Ravana: Third wife of Gopal Ravana, Vikram and Rabin's mother. We're pretty sure she doesn't like her husband all that much.

Rani Vasvi: Former queen of Daragaab. Amrita's mother. Very benevolent.

Tarin: Steward to Rani Vasvi. Sort of Amrita's dad. Looks like a small tree.

Aishayadiva (Asha) Madan: Zarya's mother and former queen of Gi'ana. Row's lover once upon a time, which is wild, right?

Raja Abishek: King of Andhera, the most powerful Aazheri in Rahajhan, and Zarya's father. Wants to steal her magic. Sounds like a bad dude.

Rahajhan: Name of the main continent, comprised of seven main regions: Daragaab, Svaasthy, Vayuu, Gi'ana, Andhera, Bhaavana, and Matsya.

Daragaab: Queendom of earth magic, lies in the southeast corner of the continent and is bordered by the Dakhani Sea to the south and the Nila Hara Sea to the east. The blight covers the southern portion of the region, while the rest is made of vibrant, lush forests.

Dharati: The capital city of Daragaab. Home to the Jai Palace.

Matsya: The underwater queendom of water magic. Lies in the depths of the Dakhani Sea.

Vayuu: The mountain kingdom of air and wind magic, residing high in the Pathara Vala Mountains.

Pathara Vala Mountains: Enormous mountain range in the northeast corner of the continent.

Bhaavana: The kingdom of love and passion, known for fire magic. Located in the northwest quadrant of Rahajhan, east of Gi'ana.

Svaasthy: The queendom of spirit magic and Nira-maya and the power of healing. Comprised of desert sands and residing on the southwestern shore.

Gi'ana: The queendom of knowledge and one of two regions that are home to the Aazheri. Located on the western shore.

Andhera: Northern kingdom and the second region known as the home of the Aazheri.

Dakhani Sea: Southern ocean of Rahajhan.

Nila Hara Sea: Eastern ocean of Rahajhan.

Ranpur Island: Small island off the southern coast of Daragaab and Rahajhan.

Premyiv: City located on Ranpur Island.

Other Creatures and Magical Things

Aazheri: Mage-like beings who use anchors that represent each element to create magic: fire, earth, air, water, and spirit. There is a sixth anchor known as the darkness, but it allegedly hasn't been seen in a while.

The Ashvin twins: Two powerful Aazheri brothers who used the darkness to bring misery upon Rahajhan and were banished away.

Vanshaj: The descendants of the Ashvin twins, relegated to positions of servitude and forbidden from using their magic by the application of a magical ring of tattooed stars around their necks.

Chiranjivi: Powerful beings that represent each region of Rahajhan—kind of like the Avengers.

Vidyadhara: Winged beings from the region of Vayuu, capable of wind magic.

Merdeva: Beings of water magic who come from Matsya.

Agni: Beings of fire magic from Bhaavana.

Niramaya healers: Beings from Svaasthy who use spirit to heal.

Rakshasa: Blood-drinking beings who use earth magic. Some can shapeshift into animals.

Khada: Elite force of soldiers whose job is to guard the wall around Dharati against the blight.

Fairies: Colorful beings with various skin and hair tones and known for their beauty.

Peri: Miniature versions of fairies.

Bayangoma: Magical birds that live in secret groves and bestow knowledge on those who are worthy in exchange for a drop of blood willingly given.

Naga: Snakes that live in the swamp, white and gelatinous and without eyes.

Ajakava: Giant bronzed scorpions.

Nairrata: Demon army that once did the bidding of the Ashvin twins.

Kala-hamsa: Red-feathered birds of varying size that are birthed from marble-like eggs that can hatch in the middle of the sky.

Dakini: Bipedal demons with black hides, big teeth, and long claws.

ONE

The soon-to-be queen of Daragaab snuggled peacefully in her massive green and gold bed, not the least bit aware that she was about to be kidnapped.

"She looks so sweet—just like a baby lamb," Zarya said, standing over Amrita. "It almost seems a shame to disturb her."

"This was your idea," Yasen replied, his arms crossed as he looked down his nose at Zarya before he directed his gaze towards Amrita. "You want to do this or not?"

Zarya nodded with a firm bob of her head. "I do. She deserves a chance to explore herself and live a little. None of this is fair. The seeding takes place tomorrow, and then—" Zarya mimicked a knife slitting her throat with a finger.

Perhaps Zarya was being a touch dramatic. Amrita wasn't actually dying, but in a few more days, her life as she knew it would be over. Amrita would undergo a series of rituals that would see her transition from the relatively everyday existence of a princess living in a palace to that of a sentient tree dedicated to the ruling of her queendom.

Zarya hated that Amrita had never been allowed the opportunity to have fun and let go. She'd been sequestered within these walls like a prisoner for her entire life. Forced to make herself small and retreat into the contained sphere of her reality.

What good was being a princess when you weren't allowed to have any fun?

She remembered when she'd first arrived in Dharati and met Daragaab's princess, believing Amrita's life must be so full of freedom and choice.

How very wrong Zarya had been.

Yasen shrugged as though none of this made a bit of difference to him—his signature move—and then jerked his chin towards the bed.

"So, wake her up. This night isn't getting any younger."

Zarya grinned and shook Amrita's shoulders gently. The princess mumbled something incoherent and rolled over to her other side, a tumble of dark curls falling across her face.

"Amrita," Zarya said, planting her knee on the mattress and shaking her harder. "Wake up."

Amrita groaned again before she rolled over, her eyelids fluttering open before they slid shut, and she continued sleeping like a baby, making a soft snoring sound.

Yasen snorted before Zarya tossed him a dirty look.

"Apparently, Her Majesty is a heavy sleeper," he said. "Maybe we should cut our losses before we're responsible for stirring up a continental incident?" He lifted a silvery grey eyebrow, his expression dripping with *I told you this was a bad idea.*

Zarya glared at him. "No, we're doing this. She'll thank us. Trust me."

Zarya climbed onto the bed and bent over Amrita.

"Wake up!" she said, louder this time, and shook Amrita firmly, who groaned again. Finally, her eyes peeled open, revealing the bright amber of her irises. She turned onto her back, her dark eyebrows drawn with confusion and the haze of slumber.

Amrita blinked heavily a few times before she frowned at Zarya and Yasen, obviously clueless as to what the pair was doing standing inside her bedroom.

"Zarya?" she asked, rubbing a hand against her forehead. Her eyes were red, and the skin around them swollen, like she'd been crying before falling asleep. "What are you doing here? What time is it?"

"It's the ungodly hour of eleven o'clock at night," Yasen said. "What time did you go to sleep? You're like a newborn."

Amrita frowned again, sitting up as she attempted to smooth down her wild tangle of curls. "I was tired."

"Perfect," Zarya said. "Now you've had some rest and are ready to come out with us."

Finally, the cobwebs of sleep cleared from Amrita's expression as she scanned her bedroom. "What on earth are you doing in here? How did you get past my guards?"

Yasen smiled. "We didn't. We entered by more unconventional means."

He gestured towards the balcony where they'd climbed up, using the vine-covered lattice that clung to the palace wall. Amrita's guards were stationed outside the door, and Zarya knew they'd never let her and Yasen take Amrita out of the palace without a hundred grizzled warriors surrounding them.

Given the traumatic events of the joining ceremony two days ago, Vikram and Gopal Ravana had both insisted Amrita remain inside the palace under all circumstances. Everyone believed the demon attack had been a maneuver designed to harm Amrita, knowing her magic could protect the city once she took her place inside the Jai Tree.

Amrita's eyebrows pinched together. "Perhaps it's time to hire new guards," she said. "Was no one watching that entrance?"

"Amrita," Zarya said, attempting to divert Amrita's train of thought to her plans for tonight. "It wasn't their fault. They're stretched thin right now, and we *might* have taken advantage of this convenient oversight in your security."

"Why?" Amrita asked, pulling her blanket up to her chin as though it were a sheet of cashmere armor.

"Because we're getting you out of here. Just for tonight."

"We're leaving the palace? Where?"

Though Amrita's eyes widened with concern, Zarya detected the note of excitement in her voice. It was just as Zarya thought—Amrita was desperate for an escape. Even if it was only a temporary one.

Zarya tipped up a mischievous smile. "It's a surprise. Come on. Get dressed."

"Vikram said I should stay here," Amrita said, her gaze moving to Yasen as though seeking the lieutenant's permission to defy his commander's orders.

"Don't look at me," Yasen said. "I'm not the one in charge around here."

"Amrita, if you don't want to go, we won't force you," Zarya said, clasping her hands under her chin. "But it's going to be fun."

When Amrita hesitated, Zarya took her hand and squeezed it. "Trust me. We won't let anything happen to you."

Despite Vikram's fears, Zarya was sure the city itself would be safe enough. The people of Daragaab were mostly busy dealing with the aftermath of the attack, repairing their homes and businesses, while the demons had withdrawn since that night, retreating into the swamp, where they'd remained relatively quiet ever since.

Ever since Zarya had used her nightfire to tame them.

She still wasn't sure if her magic had dismantled their hold on Daragaab or if they were simply biding their time and licking their wounds, gathering their strength for another attack.

Amrita must have seen something convincing in Zarya's expression because her face spread into a huge smile a moment later.

"Okay, fine. But it's just for a little while, right?"

"Right. A few hours at most. I'd never lead you astray," Zarya said, and Yasen snorted. Both women glared at him, and he held his hands up in surrender.

"What?" he asked with feigned innocence.

"Don't look at me like that," Zarya said. "You agreed to come along."

"Only under duress," he said as Amrita scooted off the end of the bed and crossed the room to her closet.

"I asked you *once*," Zarya replied as Amrita dug amongst the racks for something to wear.

It was true that Yasen hadn't been all that hard to persuade into indulging her scheme. She suspected it was because Yasen didn't agree with Vikram's tight hold on Amrita, either, though he wasn't in a position to voice those thoughts out loud. Even if they were friends, Vikram was still his commander.

"I suppose it's a testament to your impressive powers of persuasion. You should be very proud of that," Yasen said dryly as Zarya rolled her eyes.

"Put on something comfortable but festive," Zarya told Amrita. "Something that makes you feel like... you."

Amrita disappeared into her bathroom and came out a few minutes later wearing a pair of loose pink pants and a beaded white kurta. She'd freshly scrubbed her face and tied her curly hair on top of her head. Around her shoulders, she'd draped a sheer pink dupatta.

"How's this?" she asked, twirling from side to side. "Am I suitably dressed for whatever mischief the two of you have planned?"

"You're perfect," Zarya said, sliding off the bed where she'd been sitting. She wore her usual black leggings and a fitted sleeveless kurta of deep blue silk embroidered with silver stars at the hem. It had been one of Row's picks that she'd discovered in the haveli when she'd first arrived in Dharati all those months ago. "Let's get out of here."

Zarya took Amrita's hand, and the three companions exited onto the balcony that ran the length of Amrita's suite. Yasen hopped up onto the lattice attached to the wall first and shimmied down, disappearing into the darkness of the garden below.

Amrita peered over the edge before looking back at Zarya.

"We don't have to do this," Zarya said again. She really hoped Amrita wouldn't choose to remain in the palace, but Zarya didn't want to force Amrita to do anything that made her uncomfortable.

"No, I do," Amrita said with a determined set to her jaw. "In a few more days, a simple thing like climbing down a lattice will be... impossible."

Amrita's eyes shone with the threat of tears, and Zarya reached over to comfort her before the princess shook her head.

"I'm fine," she said before climbing up onto the railing and sidestepping onto the lattice with more agility than Zarya might have expected from the princess. Amrita slowly and carefully descended to the ground, and Zarya climbed down after her.

When they reached the bottom, Yasen held out a hand behind him, calling for silence as they listened to the distant sounds of the city. Zarya kept her senses on alert as well. Though she was confident they would be fine tonight, it was still wise to be cautious.

Despite the current calmness of the swamps, there had still been the occasional demon sighting. Vetalas with their clawed hands and teeth and their awkward limbs, along with kimpurusha, those lion-shaped apparitions that had once chased Zarya into the city.

But they were easily dispatched or frightened away. It seemed like some of their power had been leached from their bodies, and Zarya hoped she'd been somewhat responsible for that.

The Khada still faithfully patrolled the wall every night, though their work had been much quieter in the aftermath of the attack, much to everyone's relief.

No one was under the impression the demons wouldn't eventually rally again. After all, the blight still existed, but at least they had all been afforded a much-needed breather.

They only had to hang on until Amrita's transformation was complete. Once she took her place inside the Jai Tree, her magic would protect them with the full power of her gifts. Vikram had organized patrols to explore the swamps, searching for any changes or new threats so they weren't caught off their guards.

Yasen hadn't been exaggerating about their forces thinning due to the attack, and the army was working hard training new recruits amongst the city's populace, calling on every willing and able body who could find the correct end of a sword or spear.

Word about the blight was spreading across the continent now that things had taken such a dire turn, and an unexpected but welcome side effect was that people had been flooding in from other parts of Rahajhan, hoping to get a glimpse of the strange anomaly for themselves.

Many had stayed to help, stepping up to volunteer as fighters, builders, cooks, or healers, bringing in these new and much-needed resources. It was the help they'd needed for months, and Vikram seemed deeply relieved that it was finally arriving.

Zarya thought the smart thing would be to run as far away from the blight as possible rather than straight into it, but what did she know? She remembered Suvanna claiming the blight would eventually take over all of Rahajhan if they didn't stop it, and maybe those who arrived to offer aid understood that, too.

Whatever the case, no one in Dharati was complaining about the extra hands.

When Yasen was satisfied the garden was clear of hazards, he gestured for them both to follow as they wound past the stone fountains and raised flower beds. Despite her earlier reluctance, Amrita was beaming from ear to ear. Zarya was glad she'd decided to rope a somewhat reluctant Yasen into helping her carry out this endeavor.

"Tell me where we're going," Amrita whispered into the dark. "I'm dying to know. Can I guess?"

"No, I'm not telling you anything. Not yet," Zarya replied. "You'll see when we get there."

Zarya caught a movement in the shadows from the corner of her eye, right as someone stepped out in front of them, blocking their way.

They came to a halt as Rabin turned to face them, placing himself in the middle of the path like a big, grumpy boulder, folding his arms and spreading his stance.

"Where do you think you three are going?" he asked, his dark eyes flashing.

Zarya pressed her lips together in irritation. Of course, here was the last person on this earth she wanted to see. And he'd just caught them trying to escape.

Every time she thought about the way she'd practically thrown herself at him in the alley after he'd saved her life and accused her of being his father's spy, she died another humiliated death of mortification. She could barely look at him without feeling her insides twist like she'd swallowed a nest of burrs and had been doing everything she could to avoid being near him in the aftermath.

She was also doing her best not to think about him, but so far, wasn't having the best luck with that. Still, it was better than the reality of him standing in front of her, looking like every perfectly chiseled fantasy she'd ever had. The visions in her head couldn't seem to hold a candle to just how beautiful he was in the flesh.

It didn't matter. He was still the most insufferable, most overconfident, most cocksure man she'd ever met. And she couldn't stand him.

"That's none of your business," Zarya said, hating how her voice pitched up at the end of her sentence like she was asking for his permission. How dare he stand there, all solid muscle and fiery arrogance, and *question* her?

"I wasn't asking *you*," he growled, dropping his arms and approaching on sure steps. "I'm asking Her Majesty. You are supposed to be fast asleep in your room under guard."

"She's with us," Zarya said, pulling Amrita closer and staking her claim. "We're her guard for tonight, and she's soon to be the queen of Daragaab. She can do whatever she wants."

Rabin's eyes swung to her. "Is the *queen* unable to speak for herself?"

"Oh," Amrita said, her fingers coming to her lips as Rabin's fierce gaze fell on her. She flapped her hands, her forehead pleating with concern. "No. It's okay. I don't mind. Zarya's doing great."

Zarya smirked and folded her arms, gracing Rabin with a smug look.

"Rabin," Yasen said. "She'll be fine with us. We're just going for a little... tour of the city."

"Where?" Rabin asked.

"The Lotus Blossom," Yasen said.

A flicker of irritation deepened Rabin's bottomless scowl.

Zarya had asked Yasen to choose somewhere fun like the peri anada where she'd first kissed Vikram, and Yasen claimed he knew the perfect spot.

It took Zarya a moment to realize the low rumble she heard was coming from Rabin's throat.

"*You* are not going there," he said, his stance stiffening as he somehow managed to take up even more of the space around them. Though he'd been adamant he hadn't been speaking to

Zarya a moment ago, it appeared as though he was speaking directly to her now.

She curled her lip in disdain, matching his growl with one of her own.

She'd be damned if she *ever* obeyed a single one of his orders.

"Yes. We are," Zarya declared. This asshole wasn't seriously trying to tell her where she could and couldn't go? She grabbed both Amrita and Yasen's hands and stalked off, dragging them behind her.

Zarya heard the click of Rabin's footsteps as he followed.

She picked up their pace, forcing Amrita to scurry on her shorter legs. The princess peered over her shoulder in worry while Yasen let himself be tugged along, not caring either way.

"Then I'm coming with you," Rabin said. Zarya let go of her friends before she spun around, her nose flaring and her hands planted on her hips.

Rabin stopped just short of where she stood, his massive frame towering over her like a mountain blocking out the sun. She tried not to notice the way he smelled. That fresh, earthy aroma she remembered from her dreams layered with more grounded scents like the oil he used to sharpen his sword and hints of bitter coffee.

"You are *not* coming with us." Zarya spread her stance, hoping she looked intimidating, but was pretty sure she was about as menacing as a baby monkey.

"Then I'm going to alert the entire guard of Dharati that the princess is out on the loose."

"Oh, you would do something like that, wouldn't you?"

"Zarya," Amrita said. "It's fine. I'll just return to my room. You don't need to do this."

"No," Zarya replied, keeping her gaze pinned on Rabin.

Now, this had become a different challenge. One where she would not lose to him again. He'd already made a fool of her once, and she would die before she bent to his will. Now or ever.

"We're going. This is none of the *commander*'s business."

Zarya thought she caught the slightest flinch at those words.

While many of the palace soldiers had dropped to their knees in his presence the night he'd shown up, it was clear many things had been left unsaid surrounding his departure, especially given the way Vikram had reacted to Rabin's unexpected arrival.

She tucked that bit of ammunition away so she could make use of it—like driving a splinter under his fingernail—when the perfect occasion presented itself. If she couldn't intimidate him, she'd find more subversive ways to tip him off balance.

Zarya and Rabin stared at one another.

Gods, he was daunting. It was taking every ounce of her willpower not to curve her spine under the weight of his fury.

She hoped he couldn't sense the trickle of fear that crawled down the back of her neck. He looked like he could pick her up and crush her head like a paper lantern with one of those big hands. Then wipe it clean and sit down to dinner like nothing had happened. Maybe while cheerfully whistling a sinister tune.

He took another step until he stood so close she had to bend her neck to look at him. It was obvious he wasn't backing down, and he'd make good on his threat with the snap of a finger.

"Fine," Zarya said finally, hating that she had no choice but to give in. "Come with us, then. Just stay out of my way and keep your mouth shut. If you know how."

Before he could reply with another exasperating comment, she spun around and grabbed Amrita's hand, marching them towards the garden gate. Behind them, she heard the footsteps of the two men following. Zarya tried to shake off the dark cloud coalescing over her head. She'd wanted this to be a fun night for Amrita, but this overbearing commander was like a thorn wedged in the sole of her boot, leaving behind a trail of blood with every step.

She affected a bright smile, seeing the worry on Amrita's face.

"It's going to be great," Zarya said, hoping she didn't sound like she was overcompensating, and hooked her arm through her friend's. "And look, now we have an escort made up of two of Daragaab's most capable soldiers."

Zarya heard Yasen's snort but ignored it.

Rabin might be a dick, but it was obvious he knew what he was doing. As much as she didn't want him around, she had to concede they'd probably be a little safer with him watching their backs. Well, he'd watch Amrita's back. He'd just stab Zarya right through the heart and step over her corpse.

Finally, they approached a gate that deposited them into a narrow alley running alongside the palace. The street was quiet as they approached the end, where the bustling city was in full swing for the evening.

When Zarya saw the way Amrita's face lit up at the sights and sounds, she knew she'd made the right call in stealing the princess away for a few harmless hours. Amrita squeezed Zarya's hand as she scanned their surroundings.

"I've never been out here alone at night," Amrita whispered. "It's like an entirely different world."

Zarya grinned and then turned to Yasen. "Okay, lead the way."

He tipped his head, his gaze sliding to Rabin for a moment as if he wasn't sure what to do.

"Ignore him," Zarya said, spinning them around so their backs were pointed towards Rabin. "If he wants to play the role of our shadow, that's his choice, but he should remember that no one invited him."

Zarya didn't think Rabin was the kind of man who really

cared that he hadn't been invited, but it felt good to say, none-theless.

Yasen pinched the bridge of his nose. "Let's go, then."

He took the lead, winding them through the crowded streets as Amrita came alive. After the attack, she had spent an entire day crying. It had been all anyone could do to get her to stop or at least take a break.

It was hard to believe the attack had only been days ago as the streets surged with activity. There was evidence of the destruction all over—ruined buildings and piles of rubble and flowers laid out to honor the dead—but it hadn't taken long for everyone to settle back into normal routines. It wasn't due to callousness or any lack of affection for those who'd lost their lives, but rather, it was their way of coping.

By continuing. By existing in the face of whatever darkness hunted them all.

Zarya supposed the fact the demons seemed to have been cowed into relative submission had helped. People were very good at pretending everything was settled on the surface when it made it easier to get through their days.

Eventually, they arrived at a wide building with a white marble facade. Like many of the more ornate buildings in Dharati, it had been carved with an intricate pattern of flowers and leaves and vines.

Outside stood two giant rakshasas, bulging with muscle, who guarded the door. As Zarya and her companions approached, the rakshasas eyed their party, scanning them from head to toe.

Zarya noticed the moment they saw Rabin, their eyes widening a fraction before their chins dipped slightly in acknowledgment. Something about that annoyed Zarya. The way he commanded respect from everyone else.

She recalled a story Yasen had told her about Daragaab's former army commander, who had spent one hundred and fifty years fighting to expand their territory, and realized he'd been speaking about Rabin. She supposed all the falling to their knees made some sense in that case.

She kept her back towards Rabin so she didn't have to look at his smug, perfect face.

"How many?" one of the rakshasas asked Yasen, who held up a hand.

"Four of us."

"What is this place?" Amrita asked as the rakshasas stood to the side, allowing them in.

Zarya smiled at her friend and winked.

"This is where you get to live a little."

TWO

They entered the dim peri anada, blinking at the abrupt shift from the brightly lit street. Amrita clung to Zarya's hand as they pushed aside the beaded curtain, revealing a large circular room sectioned off with white curtains—some opaque and some translucent enough to reveal a very *specific* form of entertainment.

Through one curtain, Zarya observed a writhing silhouette —a woman straddling a man's hips as she rode him with her back arched and her breasts thrust proudly out. They moved in a practiced dance, churning back and forth like a toy boat tossed in the waves of the sea. The sight stirred something warm and liquid deep in her stomach.

"This is... different from the last place you took us," Zarya said to Yasen, who'd come to stand on her other side. She whispered the words softly as though she were afraid to draw attention to their presence.

"Vikram insisted on a tamer version of a peri anada that night. Training shoes, if you will. There are varying degrees of what an anada can offer. Some are just for dancing, while others allow you to explore all your dirtiest and most depraved fantasies."

Zarya bit the corner of her lip. "So, where is this place on the scale?"

Yasen's eyes sparked with wicked glee.

"Oh, this is where *anything* goes."

"Do you think this is a little much?" Zarya asked. "Amrita is a sheltered princess. She has no experience with... this."

Yasen's response was an amused look. "Are you afraid, Zee?"

"Why would I be afraid?"

"Because *you* are also a sheltered princess who has no experience with this."

She glared at Yasen, not appreciating the reminder.

"I'm fine," she said. "It's Amrita I'm worried about."

This place *did* summon one or two emotions that veered in the vicinity of fear, but Zarya would never admit that out loud.

Zarya turned to Amrita, who was watching Yasen with wide eyes, her mouth parted slightly with shock.

"Vikram wouldn't approve of this," she said. "Maybe this is a bad idea."

"Amrita," Zarya said, turning the princess towards her and clasping her shoulders. "You don't have to stay. And you absolutely don't have to do anything you don't want to. You can just watch or dance, but Vikram is not your keeper, and you aren't required to seek his approval on anything. Remember that *you* are the one who's going to be queen."

She could see Amrita weighing those words, her gaze studying their surroundings with a mixture of interest and nerves. This hadn't exactly been the evening Zarya had planned. She thought maybe Amrita could dance with someone she found pretty—maybe steal a kiss or feel their hands on her at least. But they were here now, and what else could they do but make the most of it?

"You're right," Amrita said. "Lead me to debauchery."

Zarya linked her arm through Amrita's and maneuvered her so they were facing the room. Not far from where they stood, a female fairy with pale yellow skin and sunny yellow hair sat atop an upholstered stool with her legs splayed wide while another fairy with iridescent blue skin feasted on her with eager strokes of her tongue.

Zarya stood transfixed for a moment, wondering what it might be like to do something like that with so many people watching. The two fairies didn't seem to notice they were the center of attention, wholly fixated on one another. Zarya cleared her throat, hoping to shield her nervousness from Amrita lest it bleed into the princess's confidence.

"You told me you've never experienced physical intimacy," Zarya said. "You deserve to have that chance before you never have the option again. If you want it."

Amrita said nothing as she watched the shifting bodies around the room. In a far corner, two male fairies had a female pinned between them, all moaning and thrusting in various states of bliss. In another was a rakshasa with his teeth sunk into a fairy's neck, both their eyes shuttered as a line of silver blood snaked down the fairy's throat.

Zarya hoped this wasn't too much for Amrita—she was going to kill Yasen. He could have easily brought them somewhere that wasn't quite so... feral.

"I do want it," Amrita said softly. "I want to know what it's like to..." she trailed off and looked over at Zarya, her cheeks turning pink.

"Which is a perfectly natural thing to wonder," Zarya said. "There's nothing wrong with that."

Amrita nodded, and Zarya noted the bob of her swallow.

"We can leave if you want."

"No. I don't want to leave," Amrita said, shaking her head. "Let's watch for a bit."

"Come on," Yasen said, waving them on. He led them through the crowd, past more curtains, some open to spectators and some firmly shut, though unmistakable sounds oozed through the fabric.

Amrita clung tightly to Zarya's arm, her eyes growing wider and wider as they moved into the club. Zarya couldn't focus, either. Though she was trying to keep a brave face, she really wasn't much more experienced than Amrita, and this place was a lot. She ventured a glance over her shoulder to find Rabin close on their heels, scowling at everyone they passed. More than one person caught sight of his thunderous expression and apparently decided they had somewhere else to be. He hadn't said a word since they'd entered, but Zarya could feel his eyes on her, disapproving and annoying.

When his gaze met hers, she quickly looked away. The hairs on the back of her neck twitched, and she rubbed at her skin, trying to dispel the feeling of his presence. Why did he have to show up tonight?

Finally, Yasen ushered them into another round room with ivy-covered walls and a ceiling dripping with an abundance of flowers. A long velvet-covered bench lined one wall, and they took a seat behind one of the small tables interspersed along its length.

A moment later, a fairy approached and took their drink orders before she sauntered away, her barely-covered hips swinging back and forth. With their arms still linked, Zarya and Amrita watched the bodies gyrating on the dance floor. The music was sensual and soft, with an underlying beat that lulled them into a swaying rhythm.

Soon, their drinks arrived. They were similar to those Zarya remembered from the first peri anada—bright and colorful and served in intricate crystal vessels. Hers was vibrant green and flavored with an intriguing mix of rosemary, mint, and passionfruit.

Yasen sat to Amrita's left, and after a few minutes, a male fairy approached him and offered a dance. Yasen didn't bother to check or even look their way before standing up and disappearing into the crowd. Zarya wondered where Rabin had gotten to as she scanned the room, acknowledging the nauseous drop in her stomach at the idea of him finding a fairy to enjoy in one of those curtained rooms.

She hated the relief that uncoiled in her stomach when she spotted him leaning against the wall with his arms crossed and one foot pressed against it as he glared at the crowd. A traitorous part of her ego hoped he'd look her way, but he kept his gaze firmly elsewhere.

She sighed, not really sure what she was expecting or even what she really wanted.

No, that wasn't true. She did know.

What she wanted was the same man she'd met in that dream forest. The one who'd looked at her with awe and wonder and not like he wanted to carve out her heart and slice up her organs for dinner.

She really didn't want to be in this place full of ripe bodies and the smoky scent of sex when her thoughts about him mirrored exactly what was going on behind those curtains.

"Are you having fun?" Zarya asked Amrita, pushing thoughts of Rabin from her mind.

Amrita nodded and grinned, her earlier nervousness having diminished considerably. "I'm having more fun than I've ever had in my entire life. This place is... intense."

Zarya smiled. "Good. I thought Yasen would take us somewhere a little more restrained."

Amrita nodded absently, her gaze clinging to the dance floor, clearly not paying attention to what Zarya was saying. She noticed Amrita was particularly intrigued by a pair of fairies—a male and female—both with lilac skin and bright pink hair—dancing with their scantily clad bodies pressed together.

"Which one catches your eye?" Zarya asked, leaning over and giving Amrita a sly look.

Amrita tipped her head and squinted as though she were trying to find a better angle to assess the scene. Her tongue poked against her cheek before she wrinkled her nose.

"Honestly? Both of them. I mean, I don't even know what I really like, do I? And they're both so beautiful. Is that too much?"

Zarya laughed. "No. Not if that's what you want."

The pair must have sensed their attention because they looked over before approaching, walking hand in hand.

"Care to dance?" the male asked Amrita. His bright hair curled against his carved shoulders, and his snug pink shorts barely contained the prominent bulge at his hips.

"We'll take good care of you," cooed the female. Long hair fell to her waist, the luscious tresses sort of covering her breasts, her tiny translucent skirt concealing almost nothing.

Amrita looked to Zarya as if asking for permission.

"Go on," Zarya said. "This is what you're here for. It's your night."

Amrita sucked in a deep breath and flipped her hair over her shoulders, perhaps in an attempt to assemble her courage. As she stood, the fairy pair each grabbed her by a hand, dragging her to the dance floor, where they pressed themselves up against her back and her front. The male's hand clamped around her hips, directing her into their seductive dance. Amrita's smile was as wide as the sea, and Zarya was feeling much better about Yasen's unconventional choice.

She'd wanted Amrita to dip a toe into the pool of desire, not go tripping off the deep end, but the princess was acclimatizing remarkably well.

"Zarya?" came a voice, and she looked over to find a male fairy with green skin and emerald hair giving her an expectant look. She knew that face.

"Amandeep!" she exclaimed, remembering him from their dance at the previous peri anada.

"I thought that was you," he said. "Mind if I join you?" He gestured to the bench, and she patted the spot next to her.

"Of course not." She slid over as he sat down and slung a muscled arm over the back of the seat.

"How are you doing?" he asked.

"I'm good. Do you work here, too?"

He nodded. "I like to cycle between a few places. Keeps things more interesting. Some nights, I'm just in the mood for... less," he said. "But this place pays much better than most."

He gave her a tight smile, but she could sense the underlying bitterness in that statement.

"I hope this doesn't sound... wrong," Zarya asked. "But are there other avenues of employment for fairies in Daragaab?"

Amandeep shook his head. "Not really. We aren't exactly regarded for our brains or our skills in any other trade. A few have carved out other positions for themselves, but it's rare."

"What about other realms in Rahajhan?"

He shrugged. "To be honest, I'm not sure. There aren't many of us outside of Daragaab."

Zarya frowned, and Amandeep shook his head.

"Most nights, I don't mind it. There's a certain freedom in knowing exactly what everyone expects of you. But there are days when I'd rather just be alone with my thoughts."

"I can understand that," she said.

"But enough about me. How have you been?"

"I'm good?" she said, not entirely sure how to answer that question.

How could she even begin to explain what had happened in the last few weeks? Between the recent attack on the city, Row's return, and all the revelations she'd learned about herself, it was everything she could do to keep herself grounded.

After discovering the sixth anchor in her heart, she'd been

sure the right course of action was to flee as far away as possible, where she wouldn't be a danger to anyone. But knowing her nightfire had stopped the demons two nights ago was rooting her to this spot. She wasn't sure what her plans were now, but that was something she'd need to figure out.

"That doesn't sound promising," Amandeep said.

"It's complicated," she replied, and he smiled.

"And *I* can understand that." Amandeep leaned over and said in a low voice, "But surely you can tell me why that incredibly gorgeous but very scary rakshasa is staring at us?"

Zarya followed the direction of Amandeep's gaze to find Rabin doing just that, his jaw so hard she needed an entirely new lexicon for the word "chiseled."

"Oh, don't mind him," Zarya said, glaring at Rabin and then turning back to Amandeep. "He's just a pain in my ass."

Amandeep snorted and leaned even closer, his mouth almost at her ear. "He looks like he wants to rip off my arm and beat me to death with it before he fucks you in a pool of my blood. If you catch my drift."

He peered up at her through his long eyelashes with a suggestive tilt to his lips. It was sort of hard not to catch his drift.

Zarya folded her arms as her expression turned petulant. "Trust me. He does not want that. Well, maybe the ripping off your arms part because he does seem to have a thing for violence, but not the rest."

Amandeep hummed and shifted closer so his bare, muscled body pressed against her. "Are you sure? Maybe we should make him a little jealous?" He dipped his head and ran his nose along the line of her jaw.

"Stop," Zarya said. "You don't have to do this."

He smiled. "I know. That's why I'm going to help you."

"Help me do what, exactly?"

"Just trust me. I know people. And I definitely know unrequited lust when I see it."

He raised his eyebrows in an impish gesture, and Zarya decided that whatever he had planned might be kind of fun. She was sure Rabin didn't care who she flirted with, but she *was* more than a little curious to test Amandeep's claim.

"Okay, fine," she said and threw a hand over her eyes. "Do what you must."

Amandeep grinned and leaned over, placing his hand on her knee. He squeezed it and then moved it up a few inches before he squeezed it again.

"This okay?" he whispered in her ear. From a distance, it would definitely look like he was saying something suggestive.

"Sure," Zarya said, her throat suddenly tight.

While she didn't have those sorts of feelings for Amandeep, anyone with eyes could see he was delicious, and something warm fluttered in the pit of her stomach as he lifted his hand and traced the line of her jaw with a finger. There was no question he knew precisely what he was doing when it came to the art of seduction.

He directed her face towards his, their mouths inches apart. He smiled, his eyes twinkling.

"Now what?" she asked breathlessly, pretty much ready to do anything he wanted at this point.

"Get away from her," came a deep voice as a shadow fell over Zarya. "*Now.*"

Zarya looked up to find Rabin standing over them, his arms still folded over his broad chest and his legs spread like he was ready to face down a stampede of feral tigers.

Amandeep blinked his long lashes.

"Is there a problem?" he asked, with a tilt of his head, and Zarya had to admire his lack of fear, given it really did look like Rabin was planning to tear off his arm and beat him over the head with it.

"You heard me," Rabin said, his voice as deep and dark as the bottom of a pit. Amandeep gave Rabin a cocky grin.

"Sure thing," he said. "I didn't realize the lady was spoken for. My apologies." Then, he turned to Zarya. "Have fun and keep in touch." He pulled a card from the pocket of his tiny shorts—where did he fit that?—and pressed it into her hand. "If you ever need anything, this is where to find me."

Then, he kissed her on the cheek, allowing his lips to linger longer than necessary.

Zarya swore she heard a growl from Rabin, and her brows pinched together with confusion. Something about this situation was pissing him off, but it couldn't be about her. He'd been perfectly clear when he'd told her he felt nothing for her in that alley.

She wouldn't allow herself to entertain any other hopes because it was all too depressing to contemplate otherwise.

Regardless, it was a delight to get under his skin, whatever the reason.

Finally, Amandeep pulled away with a quick wave. Rabin didn't move an inch as Amandeep stood, forcing him to squeeze past Rabin's bulk.

After Amandeep melted into the crowd, Zarya stood up, contemplating how foolish she'd look if she used the bench to try and mimic Rabin's height so it didn't feel like she was drowning under him. Likely quite foolish.

"What the fuck was that?" Zarya demanded, opting to stretch herself as tall as she could with little success. "He is my friend."

"You looked a lot more than 'friendly' there," he snarled.

"So what? That's what this place is for. What do you care?"

"I don't care," he said. "But the way you were acting—"

"*How* was I acting?" Zarya asked, arching an eyebrow and daring him to finish that sentence. "Do tell me. I can't wait to hear this."

She folded her arms, matching his stance.

They were so close she could feel his warmth. Their

surroundings couldn't help but make her wonder what it would be like to dance with him, his body pressed against hers. What would it be like to disappear behind one of those curtains and explore so many things she'd only imagined between the pages of her books and the private thoughts in her head? Her cheeks warmed, thinking of how she'd touched herself to those same kinds of fantasies at his family's estate just a few days ago. Perhaps on a bed where he'd once slept.

His eyes darkened, those golden flecks dimming into bronzed points of light before they dipped, scanning her from head to toe. His nostrils flared, and he opened his mouth, about to reply, when someone burst through the crowd.

It was one of the purple fairies Amrita had been dancing with.

"Please," she said, her eyes spread with alarm as she clutched at Zarya's arm, using it to maintain her balance as she crashed into her. "They've taken her!"

THREE

It took Zarya a moment to comprehend what the fairy was trying to tell her.

"The princess," Rabin said, already two steps ahead, the zing of steel filling the air. "Who?" he demanded of the trembling fairy. "Where did they take her?"

She blinked her big eyes, cowering under the weight of his questions. Her lips parted, but the only sound that came out was a high-pitched squeak.

"Answer me," Rabin demanded, towering over her with all the charm of a venomous snake. This wasn't going to get them anywhere. This poor fairy was too terrified to speak. Was this how he always dealt with people?

Zarya stepped in front of him, placing a hand at the center of his chest and *shoved*, putting some distance between him and the trembling fairy. It was a measure of his surprise because he actually took a step back. But he didn't look happy about it.

"Ignore him," she said, taking the fairy's delicate hand. "Please. Tell us what happened."

Though her stomach was twisting into knots, she tried to keep her voice steady. It would be one hundred percent her fault if something terrible happened to Amrita. "Who took our friend?"

The fairy's terrified gaze flicked to Rabin.

"Go find Yasen," Zarya barked over her shoulder at him.

He opened his mouth about to argue, but she glared, and he must have understood the sense in her command because he snapped it shut and stormed through the crowd, bodies leaping out of his way like tumbling leaves trying to escape a tornado's path of destruction.

His departure finally loosened the fairy's tongue.

"We went to one of the private rooms at the back. We were entertaining the lady," the fairy said. "And then they burst in."

"Who?" Zarya asked, oily dread slithering down the back of her spine.

"Vetalas," the fairy whispered as if she couldn't bear to say the word.

No.

Zarya hadn't even noticed Amrita leaving the dance floor. She'd been too absorbed in her pointless drama with Rabin, and she would kill him for distracting her. Except that she was entirely to blame for this.

A moment later, Rabin and Yasen burst through the writhing press of bodies.

"What happened?" Yasen demanded as he continued buttoning up his pants and straightening his top. Zarya quickly told them.

"Take us there," Rabin said, and the fairy nodded before she scurried away, gesturing for them to follow. They made their way to the back of the building to find several people gathered around a door ripped off its hinges, their expressions slack with surprise.

"This way," Rabin ordered, and Zarya and Yasen followed him out, spilling into the busy street, where they found another throbbing, pulsing mass of people, screaming and panicking, thanks to the monsters cutting through their midst.

"You! Did you see what way they went?" Rabin called to a guard standing atop a watchtower, who was busy lighting one of Dharati's emergency lanterns to signal a security breach to the rest of the city.

"Commander," the guard replied with a crisp salute. "They went that way."

He pointed, and Zarya and her companions took off running, skidding to a halt when they came upon a crowded plaza with at least half a dozen possible exits. Back-to-back, they all stood surveying the buzzing crowd.

"Which way did they go?" Yasen shouted at a group huddling together under a fabric awning. One of them pointed to a narrow alley with a shaking finger.

"Let's go," Rabin ordered, and then he bolted as Zarya and Yasen followed on his heels. Both Rabin and Yasen were armed with swords, while Zarya carried a dagger she'd been wearing at her hip.

After questioning a few more people, they were directed into a building that had clearly fallen victim to the kala-hamsa attack on the city. The top half had been cleaved off, leaving only a burned-out shell. They entered the dimness, pausing to survey their surroundings, when a muffled scream caught their attention.

"It sounded like it came from below," Zarya said, already running for the staircase. Every step was littered with soot and detritus, and she did her best not to trip on the way down. As she reached the bottom, more screams echoed against the stones.

At the far end, another door hung off its hinges, leading towards a dark opening. She stopped and peered into it as Rabin and Yasen approached on either side.

"What is this?" she asked.

"A tunnel," Rabin said. "They used to run under the city but were sealed off years ago when they became too dangerous to use."

"So, what you're saying is these monsters figured that out and unblocked this?" Zarya asked.

He nodded as his jaw hardened. "Or this one was missed when they closed them."

"And *then* they found it," Yasen said, somewhat unhelpfully, before they all exchanged wary glances as another scream barrelled from the distance. Rabin was already moving, and the other two followed, running in a single line down the constricted path.

"Where do these lead?" Zarya called from behind Rabin.

"Some lead to other parts of the city, and others lead into the forest beyond the walls."

As they ran, Zarya felt the path's gentle ascension like they were powering uphill.

"I think we're heading past the wall," Rabin called.

"How do you know that?"

"Because we're moving east."

He said nothing else as darkness closed in around them, making it impossible to discern shadows from substance. A moment later, a flare of copper light filled the tunnel. It was the same rakshasa earth magic she'd seen Vikram use the night the kimpurusha had chased them into the city.

Why hadn't Zarya thought of that? She was still adjusting to the idea that she had magic at all, let alone understanding all the things she could do with it.

The narrow tunnel filtered a thin blaze of light around Rabin's large frame, making their progress a little less treacherous. As they progressed, Zarya was trying not to think about the fact it had been several minutes since they'd heard Amrita scream.

"Light up ahead," Rabin said another minute later. They

stumbled for another few steps when Rabin ground to a halt. Zarya crashed into his back, her hands coming up to save herself from cracking a tooth on the cut of his muscle. He was very firm and warm and... *stop it.*

He peered down at her, his brows crimped with a look of incredulity.

"Before you go charging out the end of a tunnel, it's probably best to check no one is waiting to ambush you on the other side," he said like he was talking to a five-year-old, and she resisted the urge to stamp her foot just *like* a five-year-old. But he was probably right.

"Fine, do your surveillance, *Commander.*"

He sharpened his gaze and then eased towards the opening with his sword out. Slowly, Yasen and Zarya followed. They emerged into the open air, and sure enough, they were now somewhere in the blighted forest well beyond Dharati's walls.

"Keep your senses sharp," Rabin ordered as Zarya and Yasen scanned their surroundings from left to right while Rabin peered ahead.

"I don't think they're here," Yasen said.

They all held still, straining over the silence for a hint.

"Over there," Rabin said, pointing into the distance. Zarya couldn't make out what he was seeing, but Yasen also nodded. She squinted, but she wasn't gifted with the same rakshasa eyesight.

They took off running again.

As they drew closer, Zarya heard another scream before she saw the dark outline of shapes moving through the trees. It seemed there was a group of about five or six, and they were struggling to hold on to Amrita as she kicked and fought. They probably hadn't expected her to put up such a fight. Good for her. Too many underestimated this princess. Zarya puffed out a sigh of relief that she wasn't already dead. But what were they doing with her?

Rabin veered to the left, melting into the trees.

"Where's he going?" she asked, but Yasen didn't answer as they continued running.

"Hold up!" Yasen shouted, and a few of the vetalas looked over, their eyes growing wide before they let out a series of clicks and screeches that appeared to be their way of communicating with one another. A small group of vetalas broke off from the larger collection, turning around to face them, while the rest continued with a kicking, screaming Amrita clutched in their arms.

Zarya bent down to retrieve a second dagger from her boot before she and Yasen stalked towards the demons. She wished she had her sword with her, but this would have to do. The monsters ambled closer, their bony limbs too long for their bodies and their sharp teeth bared. They snarled with mindless abandon, and it took only moments for Yasen and Zarya to fall upon them, slashing and gutting them into a shapeless heap of limbs.

"Where's Rabin?" Zarya yelled, wiping a smear of blood off her cheek with the back of her sleeve. "We could really use his fucking help."

Surely, he hadn't just run off? He might be many things, but he didn't look like a man who backed down from a fight. But what did she really know about him?

She peered into the distance, despairing at the ever-widening gap between them and Amrita.

Yasen kicked into a run, and Zarya sprinted after him, racing over the dry plain, skipping over rocks and tree roots.

A roar from above drew their attention skyward as their view filled with an enormous black dragon rippling with a dark rainbow of iridescent scales. It flapped its enormous wings, stirring up a cloud of shadowy mist. She remembered it vividly from the night of the kala-hamsa attack. This was Rabin in his dragon form.

Zarya's pace slowed as she marveled at how he dove and looped through the sky when something struck her in the back. She went flying, landing on her hands and knees.

"Fuck!" she hissed as she rolled over just in time to evade the swipe of a clawed hand across her face. Her dagger flew up, slicing the vetala's palm deep enough to sever clean through its fingers. The monster squealed and stumbled back, clutching its wrist. A second later, a blade pierced through its chest as Yasen jerked it up before the vetala slid off his blade.

"Pay attention!" he said to her. "You almost got yourself killed."

"I am aware," she snapped as Yasen reached out a hand to pull her up before they launched back into the chase.

"Can't you use your thing?" Yasen shouted.

"My *thing?*"

"Yeah, the sparkly magic thing."

Zarya shook her head. "I still don't know how I did that. And what if I hit Amrita? I don't have enough control over it."

A dark shape dropped from the sky, swooping overhead. Rabin curved in a graceful arc, snatching one of the vetalas in his teeth and flinging its now headless body into the distance. A moment later, the head followed, plunging from the sky with an unceremonious thump.

Rabin flew up and made a wide arc across the sky, lining up to make another pass.

Zarya and Yasen chased down the remaining vetalas as two more broke from the main group, while the last two took off with Amrita still clutched in their pointy claws.

Their attackers only made it a few steps before a shadow grew from above, and Rabin scooped them both in his jaws, crunching through their bodies, letting the pieces fall to the earth.

"Help!" Amrita screamed as the two remaining vetalas ducked into a thicket of brambles.

Zarya growled as she dove in after them, wincing at the scrape of thorns ripping against her skin and clothing.

"Let me go ahead!" Yasen called as he hacked down the branches, clearing a path. "Why didn't you bring your sword?"

"Because I didn't think we'd end up confronting a pack of monsters in the middle of the city."

"You should always assume there will be monsters, Zee," he said, and she snorted a wry laugh as he squeezed past her.

"I'll try to remember that."

As Yasen chopped away, Rabin circled overhead, roaring into the sky. He swooped, his jaws snapping at the head of a vetala as if trying to pluck a flower of its petals. The vetala ducked, Rabin's teeth missing by a sliver as he lifted back up and circled again.

Zarya and Yasen squeezed through the thicket until, finally, they were almost on the creatures. Rabin dove again, curving so low the wind whipped up Zarya's hair. His jaws snapped, and he snagged his target, biting off its head with a tidy crack.

Black blood spurted from its neck as it remained upright for several seconds before collapsing to the ground. The second vetala screeched, dropping Amrita as it attempted to escape.

Yasen dove through the brush, spearing the demon through the back before it could get far. Then, he yanked out his sword and cut an arc through the air, lopping off its head.

Zarya skirted around Yasen and threw herself to the ground where Amrita was sobbing, wrapping the princess up in her arms.

"I'm so sorry," Zarya sobbed. "Are you okay?"

"I think so," Amrita said, her entire body shaking.

"Can you walk? Are you hurt?"

"No. Yes. I'm fine." Amrita sat back and held a hand to her forehead, her eyes closing as her chest contracted in and out with struggling breaths.

Zarya had made a huge mistake dragging Amrita out here tonight.

"We should get back behind the walls," came a gruff voice a moment later.

Rabin had shifted back into his rakshasa form and now stood over them, his hands hanging loosely at his sides, though tension hardened every line of his body.

"We don't know what else might find us out here."

"Okay," Amrita said, her jaw tightening. "Let's go."

Yasen and Zarya helped her up, and with Rabin leading, they made their way towards the city, its lights glowing brightly in the distance.

As they neared the wall, a battalion of soldiers took shape under the moonlight.

Zarya and Yasen exchanged a worried glance.

As they approached, Zarya could make out Vikram at the head of the group. When he spotted them, he broke into a run.

"Amrita!" he shouted as they drew closer. "Thank the gods."

"Vik," Amrita said, her voice strangled and breathless.

She dropped Zarya's hand and ran to him before collapsing into his waiting arms. He folded her into his embrace and then speared Rabin, Yasen, and Zarya with a look sharp enough to gouge out their irresponsible hearts.

FOUR

"What were the three of you thinking?!" Vikram shouted at Zarya, Yasen, and Rabin, his voice pinging against stone walls, lodging into the spaces between Zarya's ribs.

They stood in the courtyard at Ambar Fort, facing a line of Khada along with General Amjal and a furious steward, pacing back and forth.

Zarya stood with her hands clasped behind her and her chin up, understanding she deserved every bit of rage Vikram could hurl their way. They had fucked up—no, *she* had fucked up beyond forgiveness. This had all been her idea from the start.

Their dressing down was also witnessed by the Chiranjivi, including a frowning Row. Gods, how she knew that disapproving pinch of his features so well. She'd been avoiding his attempts to speak with her, having trouble reconciling his surprise return with everything he'd revealed. Overnight, he'd become a veritable stranger, and yet, she also felt like maybe she knew him better than she ever had.

Amrita stood with the rest, watching Vikram, her brow pleated with worry as she wrung her hands, bunching her dupatta between her fingers, leaving the delicate fabric wrinkled and smudged with perspiration.

"You could have gotten Amrita killed! It's not bad enough the city sits vulnerable and unprotected right now? If anything had happened to her, we would be finished for good! Without her magic to protect us, we are doomed! Do you understand that?"

Vikram resumed pacing back and forth, his hair framing his wild eyes. He'd been reciting the same accusations for several minutes, and the three on trial remained silent as he battered them with his verbal frustrations.

She watched as Suvanna and Apsara exchanged a meaningful look, but she couldn't decide what she read on their faces. Kindle was attempting to soothe Vikram's ire but wasn't having much luck.

Finally, Zarya couldn't keep quiet any longer.

"I'm sorry. It was my fault," she said, stepping forward. "It was my idea to take Amrita into the city, and I coerced Yasen into helping me."

"Yasen should know better," Vikram hissed. "He is a lieutenant in her army and understands how important her protection is. Do you have any idea what could have happened!"

"Vik, we—" Yasen said, and Vikram whirled on him.

"Don't! I don't want to hear it. This was reckless, irresponsible, and foolish. What were you thinking?"

Vikram turned and started pacing again, running a hand through his hair. Zarya rolled her lips together as guilt gnawed on the lining of her stomach.

He had every right to be furious. She had done an impulsive and idiotic thing by dragging Amrita out into the city late at night without her guard. And even worse, Zarya had let Amrita out of her sight because she'd been too busy having a pissing match with Rabin.

As if Dharati didn't already have enough problems, and

here she was causing even more. Zarya might have helped save the city during the attack, but that didn't mean she was exempt from the rules or the consequences of breaking them.

She exchanged a glance with Yasen, whose eyes shifted with guilt.

"And you!" Vikram said, whirling on his brother next. "What about you? You think you can just waltz back into Daragaab and do whatever you please, like you own the place?"

Rabin said nothing, his face an expressionless mask as he stared ahead, accepting his reprimand with an erect posture, just like the soldier he was.

"Vik—" Zarya said.

"You will address me as your commander," Vikram said, his voice bruised with ice. "You are a member of the Khada, are you not?"

Zarya bit the inside of her lip, willing the tears burning her eyes to remain where they were. Blubbering like a child in front of everyone wouldn't do her any favors. She had fucked up and deserved this vitriol. She'd never seen Vikram's eyes look so hard before.

"Commander," she said. "He... Rabin, he tried to—"

Rabin stepped forward with his hands clasped behind his back as he cut her off. "I was also responsible for our actions tonight. I thought I could keep the princess safe."

Zarya stared at him, wondering why he was shouldering these accusations. He definitely wasn't to blame for any of this.

"No—" Zarya said. "That's not what happened. He tried to stop us."

Rabin threw her a dark look she couldn't interpret.

"I don't want to hear any of your excuses," Vikram said. "I'm holding *all* of you responsible for this."

They held their tongues as Vikram resumed pacing, his hands balling into fists. No one else dared speak—the courtyard held its breath as everyone shifted uncomfortably where they stood.

"Lieutenant Varghese, you and Private Rai are assigned to night duty on the southern watchtower for the next week," Vikram said, addressing Yasen and Zarya, his tone now one of deadly calm.

Zarya wasn't entirely sure what that meant, but it was obvious from the hardness of Vikram's gaze and Yasen's slight flinch this wasn't a pleasant task.

"Yes, sir," Yasen said after a heartbeat of hesitation.

"That means you will also miss the seeding and the transformation ceremonies."

"No—" Zarya said, but Vikram cut her off with a sharp look. She straightened her shoulders. She couldn't miss these important events, not only because she was dying to witness them, but because she wanted to be there for her friend.

She exchanged a glance with Amrita, her pale face marred by dark circles ringing her eyes.

"Vikram, no," Amrita said, and he turned to her. "I don't want that. I want them at the ceremonies."

"They deserve punishment," Vikram said.

"I understand you think that," Amrita said. "But Zarya and Yasen didn't do anything wrong. They did me a favor tonight. I wanted to go with them, and I made no attempts to dissuade them. I could have said no—they gave me the choice—just like they gave me the choice to return to the palace at any moment. But I didn't, and I am responsible for what happened, too. Am I to be punished as well?"

"Of course not," Vikram said. "It's different—"

"Why? Because I'm not smart enough to hatch a plan like this myself? Because I'm too timid to go out into Dharati on my own?"

"Amrita," Vikram said, approaching the princess. "You know that's not what I mean."

"Then what do you mean? Vik, I've spent every day of my life sheltered from the world. I'm surrounded by riches and privileges that most people dream of, and I'm grateful for it all, but I haven't truly lived a single day of my life. Tonight, I lived. Tonight, I had the chance to feel what it's like to yearn for someone. To feel their touch and their skin against mine. To dance and to laugh and feel something other than this perpetual sense of duty and loneliness.

"They gave me that tonight. I know it was foolish and dangerous, and yes, the consequences could have been disastrous, but they weren't. All three of them came after me without a concern for their own safety. Those vetalas could just have easily found a way into the palace instead. There's no guarantee I would have been any safer where I'm kept under lock and key."

Amrita fell silent as everyone in the courtyard stared at her. Zarya wondered if those were the most words she'd ever spoken in their presence.

"Amrita," Vikram said softly. "I didn't mean you couldn't make a decision like this on your own."

"Then don't punish them. By keeping them from the ceremonies, you're punishing me, too. Zarya is my best friend, and I want her there."

Zarya let out a quiet huff of air at that statement, her tears pressing into the back of her eyes with alarming force. She willed them down. She would not cry. She also didn't dare look directly at Amrita, sure that would set off a flood of waterworks.

"Fine," Vikram said. "They can attend the ceremonies but are still on watchtower duty."

"Fine," Amrita said. "That is a fair and just sentence."

Zarya wasn't sure if they'd just won or lost this argument, but she was grateful she wouldn't miss anything important. And spending time on the watchtower with Yasen didn't sound like the worst punishment.

Vikram then turned to his brother, and the tension in the air grew so thick it pressed against the back of Zarya's throat.

"You are not a member of Daragaab's army," Vikram said to Rabin as he came to stand in front of his brother. Rabin had a few inches on him, and the older brother looked down, his dark eyes unblinking and his expression neutral. Zarya wondered if she caught a slight hitch in his frame at Vikram's cutting reminder. "So, it is not in my purview to punish you, but understand, brother, that you disappeared from my life decades ago, abandoned your duty, and then walked back in unannounced to interrupt one of the most important days of my life, only to be here for two days and nearly get *my* future queen killed."

Rabin and Vikram stared at each other, both clearly warring with some internal battle, but neither free to express what they were thinking.

"What I can do is convey my deepest regret and disappointment not only for your actions tonight but also for the disrespectful and unceremonious nature of your return. You should have stayed wherever you were with your tail between your legs like the coward you are."

This time, Zarya definitely noticed the slight wince in Rabin's steely demeanor, but he continued to hold his tongue as Vikram stepped back.

"She is my queen, too," Rabin finally said, his voice low and rumbling. His meaning was clear. He regretted what he'd done and understood they had all nearly lost her, potentially hastening the fall of Dharati once and for all.

Vikram shook his head.

"No. You lost the right to call her that when you left. *This* is no longer your home, Rabin."

Zarya felt the sharp collective intake of breath around the courtyard at the bitterness in his words. Vikram took Amrita by the arm before addressing a group of guards standing off to the side.

"The princess is now under twenty-four-hour watch until the transformation ceremony. She doesn't go anywhere or see anyone without my permission."

Vikram's gaze found Zarya, reminding her she was included in that group, and she nodded. She watched Amrita's face crumple with sadness. Her leash had been shortened all because of what Zarya had done. She hoped what Amrita had experienced tonight made up for some of it.

"Come on," Vikram said, pulling Amrita with him. "We're going home."

Then, the future queen and her steward left, surrounded by a circle of guards, leaving Zarya and the others standing under the starry night sky and the punishing weight of Vikram's disapproval.

FIVE

Thump. Thump. Thump.

Zarya groaned as her eyes peeled open. She didn't think she'd slept more than three hours last night. Why was she already awake?

Thump. Thump. Thump.

It took several murky moments to clear away the haze of exhaustion, realizing that a knocking sound had shoved her out of a deep sleep.

Oh. Oh. Oh.

Thump. Thump. Thump.

What *was* that?

She lay still, trying to parse the sounds, when she heard a grunt and a soft cry followed by more thumping. Not thumping. Banging. As in the headboard of Aarav's bed in his room directly above hers.

"Oh gods," Zarya moaned, covering her face with a pillow, trying to drown out the noise of Aarav fucking Lekha upstairs. Ever since the joining ceremony, she'd become a constant presence in the haveli, and they couldn't keep their hands off one another. It was sickening.

"Kill me," she whimpered when the noise continued to perforate layers of cotton and feather, her entire room shaking like she'd been dropped into the middle of an active volcano. Was this house made of toothpicks?

She could easily have slept for twelve more hours, but there was absolutely no chance of that now. She rolled off the bed, falling to the floor in a tangle of sheets, where she lay staring at the ceiling.

Now, it was quiet. Maybe they were done?

Thump. Thump. Thump.

Oh. Oh. Oh.

"So gross," she mumbled as she staggered to her feet and then retreated down the stairs to the main floor, where, blissfully, the noise didn't reach. Someone had put on a pot of coffee. She gratefully poured herself a huge mug and took a fortifying sip, wincing at its bitterness.

Strong. Strong enough to stand a spoon in it. Just the way Row had always liked it.

It was weird having him around after all these months of him living here like a ghost. Always on their minds and in their memories, but now, he was painfully, excruciatingly... here.

"Zarya," came a deep voice from the living room. "Is that you?"

She hesitated, wondering which was the lesser of two evils —listening to Aarav having sex or enduring the inevitable conversation with Row.

It was a toss-up, really.

She knew she'd have to talk to him eventually, but she wasn't ready yet.

"I know you're up," came Row's almost amused words, and she glowered.

Since when was he *amused* about things?

Finally, he appeared in the doorway. He was already dressed, wearing his usual long black jacket that fell past his knees, belted with a wide strip of leather wrapped around his waist and tied off at his hip.

"How are you?" he asked, and she shrugged.

"Tired."

He tipped his head, studying her.

"Are you going to lecture me about last night?" she asked.

"I think you already understand the consequences of your actions."

Zarya huffed and sipped her coffee, grimacing again, before she went in search of some cream to temper the taste.

"I was hoping we could talk a bit," he said. "About everything."

She turned to face him, bracing her hands against the countertop behind her. "Yeah. I guess we should do that."

"Should we go outside?"

His gaze flicked towards the stairs, where the faintest sounds of Aarav and Lekha hung in the air like a swarm of buzzing mosquitoes.

"Seems like Aarav has... been busy," Row said, and Zarya laughed in spite of herself.

"You could say that. And yes, please, for the love of the gods, let's go outside. I'll gag on my stomach lining if I have to listen to that any longer."

Row raised an eyebrow. "Glad to see nothing has changed around here."

He said it in a weary sort of way that made Zarya fall silent instead of responding with her usual sarcastic remark. Had he expected some kind of epiphany to transpire between her and Aarav in his absence? True, they weren't at each other's throats quite as much, but they still had a ways to go before they could call each other friends.

Row turned and headed back through the living room, opening the door to the balcony outside. It hung suspended over the ocean, offering a view of the palace and the street below on their left.

"This house is really beautiful," Zarya said. "Weird that you never mentioned it before."

He pressed his lips together. "I needed somewhere to stay when I visit the city," he replied, ignoring the subtext of her comment. "The palace is too confining for me. Too many eyes and ears and silver tongues trying to dig up every secret."

"You have a lot of them, don't you?" Zarya asked. "Secrets, I mean."

Row ignored that comment, too, and settled on one of the divans under the pergola, gesturing for her to do the same. Zarya did, gripping her coffee between her hands and tucking her feet up under her.

They sat in silence for a few minutes, listening to the city rise with the sun. A moment later, the sounds of grunts drifted overhead, and Zarya looked up towards Aarav's open window.

"Hey!" she shouted, tossing a pillow that failed to reach its target and landed on the patio with a soft thump. "We can hear you! Close your damn window!"

The sounds stopped, and a moment later, an arm reached out and slammed the window closed.

"At least someone is enjoying themselves," she muttered to herself.

Maybe a small part of her was envious of Aarav. She thought about last night and the atmosphere inside the peri anada. The way Rabin had reacted when she'd been talking to Amandeep.

Had Rabin been jealous like the fairy had claimed? He'd told her he felt nothing for her. Unequivocally. In the most devastating way possible. She wondered if Rabin had Aarav's stamina... and *no*, she was not wondering that. That was not a productive thought.

"I was wondering if you had any questions for me," Row

asked, breaking through Zarya's inner monologue and *maybe* the graphic image of Rabin lying in bed naked, his muscles glinting in the morning sunlight and his long hair tousled against crisp white sheets.

"What?"

"Questions? For me? About everything you learned? Maybe about your magic?"

Zarya focused on Row and then sat up straighter.

"Yeah. My magic. I only know what I learned from a book that Professor Dhawan wrote about Aazheri magic. But I'm lost. I don't know how I created the nightfire, and I'm not sure how to do it again."

"Five Anchors," Row said, "that represent the five elements —air, water, fire, spirit, and earth. You already understand this part?"

Zarya nodded. "I do. I have them all."

He nodded. "You would have to in order to possess such a rare gift."

"Nightfire really hasn't been used in all those years?"

"It's true," Row said.

"And all this time, you actually thought I might have it?"

He shrugged his wide shoulders. "I couldn't be sure, but it made sense with everything else I knew."

"What about the thing I could do with the stars?" she asked, referring to the benign way she could draw starlight from the sky when she lived at the seaside cottage. "You always seemed so interested in it but also scared of it."

"I wasn't sure what nightfire was exactly," Row said. "I'd never seen it before, nor could I find anyone who had. The books describe it as an absence of light, but I hadn't realized how much it *looked* like the night sky. In retrospect, your strange gift was most certainly another clue, but it wasn't confirmation of my fears."

"And this is why you didn't want anyone ever seeing or knowing about it."

"It was. That's why I was scared. It obviously wasn't typical Aazheri magic—but I couldn't be sure of what it was."

"Why—" Zarya stopped. She wanted to ask why he couldn't have told her any of this. He'd explained himself upon his return—that her mother had been hiding her from her birth father, the northern king of Andhera, who might be angling to steal her magic—but it still didn't feel like a satisfactory answer. She wasn't sure she'd ever receive an explanation that felt like enough.

"Zarya—"

She lifted a hand. "You told me, and I won't pretend I understand. But I wish you could have trusted me."

"It wasn't that I didn't trust you," he said. "It was everyone else. I didn't know who I was protecting you from."

"Okay," she said, brushing past it, for now, feeling yet another wash of tears pressing in her throat. It would take time to get over this—to move past the lies she'd been fed for so long. "Tell me more about the anchors. Five of them."

Another question burned on her tongue, but she didn't dare voice it out loud.

What if there are six?

Both Row and Dhawan seemed so sure that only five were accessible. That the sixth was lost. Koura was so sure the darkness had been banished forever. What did it mean that she could touch it?

Row had claimed nightfire was a way to control the darkness, but Zarya had the disquieting sense it was capable of much more than that. If she could control it, then did it have some part of the darkness itself? And why did Row and Dhawan not see that? She was sure that being captured by the giant winged demon had been the catalyst that forced her nightfire out—they were connected.

This was why her magic had called the naga in the swamp. They, too, were born of that same dark magic and must have been responding to a kinship with those ribbons of starlight, even in its inert form.

As she'd lain awake last night, still pumped full of adrenaline, she'd discovered she could push the sixth anchor behind the others. Lock it away by lining it up behind her fire anchor so a perfect five-pointed star remained.

Darkness. It whispered to her with a seductive purr.

"Every Aazheri has a unique signature," Row said, following up on her question about the anchors. "Their anchors manifest themselves as images or avatars."

"What's yours?"

"It's generally considered rude to ask that amongst Aazheri." Row gave her an amused look.

"Oh, sorry. I didn't know." She hated how little she knew about everything.

"In my case, they're animals," he said. "A whale for water, a bear for earth, a serpent for fire, an owl for air, and a maiden for spirit."

"That's incredible," Zarya said, her eyes widening. "Mine is a star."

Row inhaled a sharp breath.

"Your mother saw stars, too."

"She did?" The question piqued something hopeful in that empty space behind her heart. For the first time ever, she belonged to someone. Even if her mother was gone, a piece of her lived inside Zarya. That knowledge was the greatest gift Row had ever given her.

"I want to know about my mother," Zarya said. "Tell me what she was like."

Row smiled with the corner of his mouth, some fond memory passing over his gaze.

"She was fierce. And strong and very brave," he said. "You remind me so much of her."

"You mean stubborn and pigheaded then," Zarya said, and Row laughed.

Who was this man with this easy posture and this soft chuckle? Was this who he'd always been, but she'd been too angry to see it? Had he changed in these past months? Or maybe she was the one who'd changed.

"She loved to dance," he said. "And sing. She had a beautiful voice. I think if she hadn't been a queen, she would have sought out the theater. She also loved to paint, though she never had time once she took the crown."

Zarya liked hearing that. "Did she like reading?"

Row shook his head. "She did, but not as much as you."

"I suppose she had a real life to live and didn't have to invent one in her head," Zarya said.

She wanted to ask Row more about his relationship with her mother and the love they'd shared but assumed it would be too personal. Maybe in time, he'd trust her with those stories, too.

Row gave her a long look and then cleared his throat. "Aazheri sense their anchors in different places in their bodies, too," he said. "I see mine in my head."

Zarya placed a hand over her chest. "Mine are in my heart."

"I wouldn't expect anything else."

"I'd say the same about you."

They exchanged a look edged with something new and soft, like the seeds of a dandelion, delicate and easily dispersed. But maybe they could capture them and build a relationship where they might tease one another and behave like equals. Like family, instead of a man and his captive.

She hadn't forgiven him yet but was also growing weary of the grudge she'd worn like a stain for so long. The acidic taste of resentment burned through her tongue. She wanted to be better than this. Without the walls of the cottage pressing in on every side, maybe their relationship could find room to breathe.

"All Aazheri magic follows the same principle," Row continued. "Every spell is a combination of elements drawn together at varying strengths to create the desired effect."

He lifted his hand, and a blue flame burned in his palm.

"For example, I can create this with a combination of fire and air, conjuring a fire hot enough to melt through even the most impenetrable materials."

Zarya watched as he concentrated on the flame, making it turn green before it exploded into a shower of leaves that tumbled into his lap.

"Add in a little earth, and you get something entirely different," he said. "It's hard to teach because everyone's magic is so different. There's a lot of trial and error involved in the process. After all these years, I still discover nuances and tweaks that help refine my power."

"How old are you, anyway?" she asked.

He tilted his head, studying her. "You've never asked me that before."

The statement felt almost like an accusation. It was true she'd paid little attention to her guardian beyond what his actions had always meant for her.

"I'm asking now."

"I'm four hundred and thirty-seven," he said.

The answer didn't entirely surprise her. There was no question Row had lived through a lot.

"What's that like? Living for so long?"

He lifted his shoulders. "It's the only thing I've ever known." He paused, considering his words. "But the weight of near immortality can be heavy. There's a reason magical species tend to stick to their own. Forming bonds with people you know will have to leave you long before the end can be unsettling."

"How long do Aazheri live?"

"That is a matter for debate. Hundreds of years. Maybe a thousand? No one can say for sure."

Zarya nodded. "Okay, teach me some magic." She placed her mug on the table and pushed up her sleeves.

Row then ran her through a series of common anchor combinations as Zarya tested them against his magic. While the proportions differed, she began to decipher its patterns and could see how she might use this knowledge to continue practicing.

"Try mixing a bit of spirit and water," he said.

She did so, producing a rainbow that arced from the palm of her hand and disappeared over the edge of the balcony in a shimmering riot of color. She grinned, weirdly proud of herself.

"That's always been one of my favorites," he said.

When they'd had enough, Zarya stood. Something had been weighing on her conscience ever since she'd escaped the cottage. "Hold on for a second. I have something I want to give you," she said. She tiptoed into the house and paused, but it sounded like Aarav and Lekha had tired themselves into silence. Maybe he'd hit his head so hard that he'd finally passed out.

She made a mad dash to her room and retrieved Row's sword lightning quick, just in case Aarav and Lekha woke up and resumed their activities.

When she returned to the balcony, she held it out to him. It felt like a first step to peace.

"I'm sorry I stole this after you went missing. I was only thinking about myself at that moment."

Row took the sword. His fingers traced the etched patterns in the leather. "I'm glad you've had this with you. These runes are protective."

"What kind of magic is that?"

"Some Aazheri have magic that is unique to only them, like your nightfire. Mine works through symbols, like the ones I used to protect us from the swamp and to keep you there. It's called rune binding." He was silent for a moment before he handed the sword back to her. "But you should keep this, Zarya."

"It's yours."

"I want you to have it. Let it keep protecting you. It would give me some peace of mind. Whatever happens, a part of me will always worry about you. I know you don't believe me yet, but I only ever wanted the best for you. You aren't my daughter by blood, but understand that I've always thought of you that way."

She'd spent months wondering if Row was her father, and when he'd told her he wasn't, a part of her had shriveled away like a flower in winter. She was so angry with him, but he'd also been the only home she'd ever known.

"What about my father?" Zarya asked. "My real father." She shook her head. That description didn't feel right. "I mean the man who fathered me."

Row's shoulders slumped as though he'd been dreading this question.

"Your father," he said slowly, "is a complicated man."

"Evil," Zarya said, thinking of the few things she'd learned about Raja Abishek. Namely, when Yasen had told her about how he'd murdered all those vanshaj and that he wanted to steal her magic.

"He's... driven by the desire to see Aazheri as the irrefutable source of power in Rahajhan," Row said. "And sometimes that makes him do things many would question."

"That sounds like you're making excuses for him."

"No, I'm not trying to, but it's more complex than that. I left Andhera because I disagreed with both his treatment of the vanshaj and the ways in which he chose to assert his dominance. It all became too much, and while I understood some aspects of his vision, I couldn't agree with his methods."

"What vision?"

"The power of the Aazheri has dwindled in the past centuries. When Aazheri mate with non-Aazheri, our magic becomes null. It only happens to us—no other magical species is bound by this limit of nature in the same way, and, as a result, there are fewer of us than ever."

"That sounds a lot like yakshis," Zarya said, remembering what Vikram had told her about keeping their magic pure.

"Not exactly. Yakshi magic remains—it just mixes with the other side. It was their prejudice that led them to decide that wasn't good enough for them. Their offspring may be less powerful in yakshi magic but not necessarily overall."

"Well, that seems rather shortsighted."

"Indeed," he said. "But for Aazheri, our magic just dissipates into almost nothing."

"And that's why Raja Abishek is so interested in magic?"

Row nodded. "He's been trying to find a way around this constraint for a long time, and sometimes that pushes him to make the wrong choices."

"How does taking my magic help, then? Aren't I Aazheri?" It still felt weird to say it.

"Yes, but he would see you as a necessary casualty for the greater good."

Zarya scoffed. "It sounds like he just wants all the power to himself."

Row tipped his head. "You aren't wrong about that."

"So, is he bad?" she asked, and Row gave her a long look.

"I don't know how to answer that, Zarya. He's... just what he is."

She chewed on her bottom lip, sifting through everything he'd just said.

"When did you leave Andhera?"

"Over a century ago," he said. "He was angry when I told him I was leaving, but he let me go. I haven't seen or spoken to him since."

She frowned.

"Why are you telling me all this now? You've had years to do it. Where's this emotional side of Row coming from now?"

Row shook his head and ran a hand down his face. "There's always been a distance between us. I know why, but I've never liked it. When I left the cottage, I vowed that I'd do better to bridge this gap on my return. You and Aarav are the only family I have left in the world, and I want us to act like it."

She considered those words, realizing something else she'd maybe known all along. She didn't only belong to a mother she'd never met. She belonged to Row, too. As much as she'd fought it, she always had. He'd protected her and kept her alive to the best of his ability. He'd been handed only hard choices when it came to her upbringing, and he'd made so many mistakes, but wasn't everyone entitled to a few?

Maybe a part of her regretted the years that had been lost between them. Years she'd wasted being angry when she could have had a version of the family she'd so long desired.

Zarya clutched Row's sword to her chest, accepting it as the offering it was. A first step on a pockmarked road towards forgiveness. "Thank you. For this and for finally telling me everything."

Row patted her on the knee with a hopeful look in his eyes.

"I'm sorry it took me so long."

SIX

After Row left, Zarya remained on the balcony, sipping her now lukewarm coffee, which hadn't improved the flavor at all. She made a note to wake up earlier so she could brew it, then caught herself. That felt a little too much like their routine in the cottage, where she had often been the first one up, making breakfast for everyone. If Row beat her to it, it was usually because he was either gone for the day or out in the garden training with his weapons.

She hadn't always minded it. When he was done with his tasks, he'd come inside and help, sometimes offering to prepare the food. They'd talk a little, but they'd also stew in silence that wasn't necessarily awkward but had always been tainted with the secrets that lingered between them.

She sighed and placed her mug on the table before walking to the far side of the balcony to study the palace. Many sections were in ruins—its delicate white towers snapped off like stems. The garden was littered with detritus, where an army of dutiful vanshaj were busy cleaning up.

Zarya's gaze drifted to the chasm that had been the first harbinger of disaster all those months ago. It had ripped through their lives at the time, but now it was barely noticeable in the surrounding destruction. Just another obstacle to navigate on this road they were traveling without a compass.

Gopal Ravana hadn't made any further progress in sealing the chasm since she'd last seen him. Rumors were circulating that he'd refused to help unless he was granted a tract of land on the northern border of Daragaab, and the former queen hadn't seen fit to acquiesce. Zarya imagined that with Amrita soon taking her place as queen and Vikram as her steward, he'd find a way to secure his wish.

But maybe Zarya could do something about the rift now that she had access to her magic. Professor Dhawan's earth anchor hadn't been strong enough, and she wasn't sure if Row had already tried. She wondered where she fell on the scale of strength compared to the two older Aazheri. Given Aarav only had two anchors, she knew she was at least more powerful than him. The thought didn't bring her as much satisfaction as it might have a few months ago.

Either way, this might be a good opportunity to see what she could do.

Feet already moving, she headed through the haveli and down to the boulevard. Even before the attack, the rift had found a tentative place in the lives of the Dharatis as they maneuvered around it, skirting the ropes that cordoned off its treacherous borders. It had become a part of their daily existence in a seamless way that spoke to the resilience of the human spirit.

Still, it was a hazard, and Zarya wanted it gone. The more the blight festered and wormed its way into Dharati, the more she wanted to eradicate every trace of it. As she walked the length of the rift, Zarya came to a stop at the end where a guard stood watch, ensuring no one accidentally wandered into it. She contemplated her next step after asking the guards stationed nearby to ensure everyone kept their distance.

Remembering how Rabin had placed his hand on the earth during the kala-hamsa attack, Zarya mimicked the movement, bending down with one knee on the ground and her palm flat to the sun-warmed surface.

Her sixth anchor was locked away for now, and her five-pointed star spun, almost like it anticipated her intentions. It seemed to sense her thoughts and emotions, growing agitated when she was upset or enthusiastic when it knew she was about to use her magic.

Focusing on her earth anchor, she drew on it. It shuddered as the ground underneath her started to vibrate. Taking that as an encouraging sign, she focused on closing the rift, imagining the sides pulling together. The chasm walls shifted a fraction as the earth groaned in protest. Rocks and shards of stone tumbled into the void as the ground continued shaking.

She squeezed out another fraction of movement while sweat beaded on her forehead. As her vision tilted from the effort, something nudged inside her rib cage, trying to get her attention. The sixth anchor peeked out from behind the fire anchor, begging to be noticed, and Zarya clenched her teeth. She would not touch it. She'd already decided that. Whatever enticing power it held, she would not wield anything that called itself the darkness without knowing what it meant.

Zarya let out a sound of frustration and let the earth anchor snap back into place as the rumbling street settled into stillness like the ripples of a puddle smoothing out.

She cursed under her breath, standing up.

"Looks like you could use some help, Princess."

The air in her lungs stalled. *That voice.* The way it made her ribs compress and her stomach twist.

A shiver rolled down her spine as she turned to glare at Rabin.

He stood with his impressive arms folded across his equally impressive chest and his head tipped with a smug expression on his face. She wanted to punch him in his perfectly straight nose. How did an army commander with this much attitude manage to go this long without someone repeatedly breaking it? Taking in the breadth of him, she suspected few would have the guts to punch him, though.

"I'm fine," she said and then sucked in a sharp breath, wanting to clear her conscience. "Actually, I did want to thank you for sticking up for me last night with Vikram. You didn't have to take the blame for my mistake."

Rabin's eyes narrowed as they dragged down the length of her body. He said nothing as the silence stretched and stretched.

"Hello?" she said. "I just said thank you."

He blinked as the corner of his mouth curled up in a snarl. "That isn't necessary," he finally replied, his voice full of derision.

Zarya opened her mouth and then closed it, at a loss for words. What an absolute jerk.

"Fine. Never mind, then."

She turned away, attempting to gather her focus and concentrate on the rift.

Now, he was watching her, which made her too self-conscious to try again.

"Do you need something?" she asked, peering over her shoulder. "Feel free to find someone else to bother."

He sauntered closer, scratching his chin as he peered into the chasm. Zarya tried not to notice the bit of shadow on his face that made him look even more dangerous and totally and utterly... lickable. Good gods, what was wrong with her? He'd made it clear he detested her, and this mooning was officially pathetic. So, he was handsome? So what? There were plenty of handsome men around Dharati. He wasn't anything special.

"Doesn't look like you're fine, Princess."

"Don't call me that."

"What? Princess? Isn't that what you are?" He smirked and came to stand next to her. "Move over."

"Excuse me?" Zarya's cheeks heated with anger and a traitorous hint of something stirred from the heat churning in her stomach. She rolled her neck, willing herself to calm the fuck down. He really wasn't *that* good-looking.

He was just an irritating man.

"I need some room," he said in a tone that implied it should be obvious. The intense look he gave her shot fire straight between her thighs. Her lips pressed together as she tried to ignore it, wishing she could get control of these rebellious urges.

She made an exaggerated show of stepping out of the way, bowing down in a deep, mocking curtsy.

"*Oh.* By all means. *Commander.*"

Now, it was her turn to smirk at the flicker of irritation in his gaze.

"Did that bother you, *Commander*? You aren't the only one who can make use of empty, meaningless honorifics, are you?"

Rabin ignored her comment, bending down and placing a fist against the earth. She watched him focus his gaze as the chasm walls began to rumble again, vibrating with far more enthusiasm than they'd managed for her.

Clearly, Rabin's earth magic was much stronger, which made sense, given he was a rakshasa, and this was their purview. She remembered Apsara telling her there was only one rakshasa with the strength to close the rift, and Zarya now knew it was the one currently making every nerve in her body tingle.

Of course, it was.

"Wait," Zarya said, grabbing his arm as a lightning bolt of electricity speared up through her fingertips. He stopped and looked at her hand around his arm before his gaze met hers. She dropped it and wiped her palm on her kurta, hoping he hadn't noticed how sweaty she was.

"What?"

"Don't just do it. Tell me how to do it."

His eyebrow arched, his gaze sweeping over her from head to toe. It felt like a finger running up the inside of her thigh, swirling the warmth in her belly.

"I can't. My magic is different from yours."

"Oh," she said, stepping back. "Of course. I didn't think about that."

He gave her one last lingering, if disdainful, look before he concentrated on the street again.

"Keep everyone away!" he shouted to the guards, who were all watching the pair. A crowd of curious onlookers had gathered a few feet from the edges.

Rabin's gaze focused on the chasm again, his large fist against the ground. The earth rumbled, the sides of the chasm groaning inwards like a thread pulling a ripped seam into a straight line.

The walls shifted bit by bit until the sides lunged at one another, slamming together and sealing the gap. The spectators gasped as a few of them stumbled from the impact. Zarya spread her feet to prevent herself from toppling over.

Then, Rabin twisted his hand and shifted his focus as a line of magic ran along the crack, dusting away the edges until the street was completely healed, as though nothing had ever happened.

Zarya was beyond impressed, but she'd die before ever admitting that.

"Not bad, Commander," she said, pretending to scrutinize the chasm. She squinted. "Did you miss a spot there?"

She pointed in the distance.

"I did *not* miss a spot, Princess," he said, his jaw hard as he stood.

She folded her arms and shrugged, deciding she couldn't let him have the last word. She thought about the Ravana estate and the beautiful gardens. The plants and creatures and flowers that had been bursting everywhere.

What if it had been Rabin's magic, and not Gopal's, that had been responsible for all of that?

"I guess that was somewhat impressive," she finally said. "But can you make flowers?"

That devastating eyebrow arched again, and she swore she saw the slightest hint of amusement dance in his gaze. It harkened to their days in the dream forest when Rabin had been someone else. Someone entirely different. Someone she actually liked.

"Flowers?"

"Yes. Flowers. You know, the pretty colorful things that smell nice."

Again, his gaze swept over as he made a slow circle around her, one confident step at a time. Then, he stopped directly in front of her and held up a fist.

"I can make flowers, Princess."

His hand opened, and a shower of pink and white blossoms tumbled gently over Zarya's head. She smiled as she looked up, the soft, velvety petals caressing her cheeks.

"I can even make them smell nice," he said.

Then, with one last look she felt straight to her toes, Rabin turned and stalked away.

SEVEN

"What exactly is so bad about patrolling the watchtower?" Zarya asked Yasen later that evening as they leaned against the wall in one of the Jai Palace's smaller entertaining salons. Thanks to Amrita's intervention the previous night, Zarya and Yasen were waiting to attend the seeding ceremony that would soon begin. "Why are we being sent out there as punishment?"

"Because it's the most boring and unpleasant place to stand guard all night."

Zarya considered that. "That really doesn't sound so bad."

Yasen smiled. "I have a feeling he was going easy on us. It's about a loss of honor more than anything. The watchtower is usually reserved for the discipline of young, fledgling recruits getting up to mostly harmless mischief, and that in itself was meant to embarrass me."

"How can that possibly embarrass you? You don't care about things like that."

"This is true," Yasen said, taking a sip of his wine. "Like I said, he was going easy on us. Vik has always had a soft heart."

"He was furious."

"I know, but I'm his best friend, and you're the girl who..."

"I'm the girl who what?"

"Honestly, I don't know. What are you two, anyway?"

Zarya shook her head. "I don't know, either. We're nothing. I think. Maybe. I don't know."

"Okay, well, as long as you're sure." Yasen took another sip as he surveyed the crowd.

The room was filled with high-ranking nobles dressed in an array of glittering clothing and jewels, including the Ravana family, who were notably absent one growly former commander. Row was also here, conferring with Kindle and Dhawan on the far side of the room.

Nearby, she saw Apsara and Suvanna leaning together with their hands clasped. They were dressed in their usual attire—the winged woman in white leather and Suvanna in varying shades of blue and green to complement the shifting hues of her hair.

Apsara was laughing at something the merdeva had said.

"Are those two an item?" Zarya asked, tipping her chin towards the pair.

Yasen watched them and shrugged. "I think they've got a casual friends-with-benefits thing going on. I'm not really clear on their relationship status."

Zarya watched the two women, noticing the spark in Apsara's silver eyes. Zarya didn't know much about love but didn't think Apsara's feelings seemed casual. She cupped the back of Suvanna's head and leaned down, whispering something in Suvanna's ear that nearly made the merdeva smile, which was notable since Suvanna was hardly the smiling type.

"How much longer till this starts? What exactly happens inside?"

"I don't know, but apparently, there's something in a pool of water. Tarin does some woo-woo stuff, and then they go in, and somehow that plants the seed inside Amrita."

Zarya recalled Amrita's nervousness about this event, given

it took place in the nude. Zarya hadn't had a chance to talk to her friend after the events of last night, and she hoped the princess was doing okay.

"Woo-woo stuff?"

Yasen grinned. "I'm pretty sure that's the technical term."

Zarya snorted before a thought occurred to her. "You don't think it like... swims inside her or something? I'm imagining a tadpole now."

Yasen tipped his head, the corners of his mouth turning down. "I guess that might make sense. Is it really that different from the more conventional method?"

Zarya shuddered. "Yes, it is. That has got to be the least romantic thing I've ever heard. Poor Amrita and Vik."

"There are worse things," Yasen said.

"Like what?"

He grimaced. "Give me a minute. I'm trying to think of something."

"See?" she said. "It's awful."

At that moment, the doors at the far side of the room swung open, and everyone was beckoned towards it. Yasen and Zarya followed the crowd, walking down a set of stairs behind Koura, who looked over a broad shoulder and smiled.

"How are you doing?" he asked in his rumbling voice. He wore a yellow kurta that set off his deep brown skin. "No more adventures in the city tonight?"

Zarya huffed out a dry laugh. "Never again."

His golden-eyed gaze softened as they wound down the staircase. "For what it's worth, I think you did the right thing."

"Thanks," Zarya said. "I hope so."

The stairs transformed from the palace's white marble into grey stone as they went deeper. Eventually, they all emerged into a cavern hewn from the rock. The space was filled with hundreds of small statues depicting beings that were part animal, part human. Zarya and Yasen stopped near one that was half elephant and half man that came to the height of her knee.

"What are they?" she asked him.

"The gods," Yasen said. "Their likenesses are only permitted in the most holy of places."

In the center of the high room was a pool lit from within. At the edge stood Dharati's former steward, Tarin, clasping the head of his cane while Vikram and Amrita flanked him, both wearing loose and ornately decorated robes embroidered with a myriad of tiny round mirrors and beads.

The crowd of about fifty people gathered in the room, positioning themselves along the walls and between the icons, taking care not to disturb them. Zarya waved at Amrita, hoping to offer a bit of comfort and confidence, and Amrita nodded, though her face was pale and her smile tight.

Once everyone was settled in the room, Tarin began to speak. He recited from a book in a language that Zarya didn't comprehend. His words had a mellifluous quality, like a song or a poem, and seemed to calm everyone as if they were a spell.

When Tarin was done, he gestured to the pool, where a set of stairs had been carved into each end. Vikram and Amrita moved to stand before each. They untied the knots around their waists and dropped the robes, exposing themselves entirely to the crowd.

No one else seemed surprised by this, and Zarya watched as Amrita lifted her chin proudly. She'd been afraid of getting naked in front of just *Vikram*, but had she known she'd have to do it in front of *everyone*? Amrita blinked, looking only at Vikram's face, and Zarya admired her bravery. She wasn't sure she could do this without crumpling into mortification.

Vikram and Amrita then descended the steps into the pool, and Zarya let out a breath of relief as the water camouflaged their bodies. Tarin began speaking again, more of the same words recited in some ancient language that began stirring the water inside the pool. The light within grew brighter and brighter as the water moved around them, swirling and churning.

Amrita and Vikram joined hands, and much like in the joining ceremony, a thread of light surrounded them, twisting around their bodies and between their hands like they were being tied together. They looked into each other's eyes, focused entirely on one another.

The lights in the pool began to change color, flashing in a rainbow, dancing and moving like fireflies or falling stars. The water continued swirling, gaining speed until there was a bright flash right before the cavern descended into darkness.

Zarya held her breath, and it seemed like everyone present was doing the same when she couldn't hear a peep. A moment later, the pool lit up again with a soft light, throwing everyone into shadows.

Amrita and Vikram still held hands in the pool, and they looked up at Tarin, who was giving them a benevolent smile.

"The seeding has been completed," he said in his rumbling voice. "The future of Daragaab lives on. Please proceed out of the cavern, and the queen and her steward will join you shortly to receive your congratulations."

At that, everyone filed out of the room and back up the stairs before they filtered into the same salon, where vanshaj were circulating with trays of food and drinks.

Zarya accepted a glass of sparkling wine and joined Yasen. A moment later, Vikram and Amrita appeared at the doorway. Their skin was glowing and damp, their hair curling in soft tendrils along their hairlines. They looked relaxed and at ease, and Zarya was relieved. Maybe things hadn't been as awkward as Amrita had feared.

More servants waited for the royal couple with trays laden with drinks and sweets. Vikram and Amrita accepted both with polite nods as the partygoers surged forward to offer their blessings.

Zarya wanted to ask Amrita more about what exactly had happened inside that pool. She realized she'd have to do it soon if she wanted to ask her directly and not have to speak through Vikram, and that notion dropped her into a deep wave of melancholy. Amrita had called Zarya her best friend the other night, and Zarya didn't have many of them to spare. The idea that she was essentially losing one sat in her stomach like a rock.

She also wondered what it would be like to have someone voicing your every thought. And more importantly, having to share everything with someone else. No more private conversations ever again. Amrita had said she trusted Vikram with her life, and Zarya hoped that would always be the case.

Vikram and Amrita continued to mingle with their guests as they made a circuit around the room. When they came upon Yasen and Zarya, Amrita broke into a smile and wrapped Zarya in a tight hug.

"How are you doing?" Zarya asked.

Amrita pulled away. "I'm good. That was fine. Did it look fine?"

"Yeah. It did. Maybe a little... weird?"

Amrita leaned in closer. "A little bit, but Vikram was very supportive."

"I'm glad. How are you after last night? I'm so sorry about what happened."

"It's okay. I think that was something I needed to do. It clarified some things for me."

Zarya squeezed her friend's hand. "I'm very happy to hear that."

Zarya saw a flash of sadness pass behind Amrita's eyes for the briefest moment before the princess shook her head and then beamed a smile at her.

"So, please don't be sorry. I'm glad you did it." She leaned in closer. "I'm trying to convince Vik to drop your punishment."

"You don't have to do that," Zarya said. "It was still reckless."

Amrita didn't have a chance to answer her as some noble courtier tapped her shoulder and then hugged her. Zarya stood back, watching the room. In a corner, Apsara and Suvanna were getting closer to one another, and Zarya smiled. She loved seeing people express their feelings openly. Maybe love was on the horizon, no matter what Yasen said about it being a casual relationship.

Row was chatting with Aarav, who had his arm slung over Lekha's shoulders. Zarya prayed they wouldn't be coming back to the haveli later tonight. Didn't his girlfriend have somewhere else they could do their business? Preferably somewhere Zarya would never have to think about it ever again.

"Zarya." She turned to find Vikram beside her. "I was wondering if we could speak for a moment. Alone?"

"Sure," Zarya said.

Vikram wrapped his hand in hers, his skin warm and inviting.

He tugged her out of the crowded room and into a quieter alcove down the hall where they might converse in private.

"What's going on?" she asked as he moved in, leaving only a small space between them.

"Zarya, I wanted to talk about last night. I was very hard on you, and the guilt has been eating me alive."

Zarya pressed her lips together. "It's fine. You are the commander of Daragaab's army, and soon you will be its steward. What I did was thoughtless, and your anger was justified. No matter what Amrita says about enjoying herself, I shouldn't have put her in danger like that. Not just her but the entire city. If anyone should feel guilty, it's me."

He shook his head. "I let my temper get the best of me. You know that you're special to me," he said. "And I—"

"It's fine," she said. "Really. You treated me the same as you did Yasen, and he's your best friend. I would have been more annoyed if you'd been too lenient with me, to be honest."

The relief in Vikram's expression was palpable. "I could barely sleep last night," he said. "Thinking about how I'd spoken to you."

He appeared so distraught that she felt the need to offer comfort. She wasn't angry with him.

"How are you doing?" Zarya asked, hoping to move past this. "With everything. With your brother's return and with the joining?"

Vikram sighed and ran a hand along the back of his neck. The top of his loose robe shifted to reveal his chest underneath, muscled and firm from all his hours of training. She wondered idly if he was still completely naked under there and decided she probably shouldn't be wondering that.

"As well as I can be," he said before he turned to face her again and took her hand, holding it up to his chest. He flattened her fingers against it so she could feel the pulse of his heart. "I wanted to ask you something else, too."

She tipped her head in a question.

"When we spoke in the library at my father's estate... we discussed potentially pursuing this thing between us."

"Yes?" Zarya said, the word coming out a bit more strangled than she intended. She'd given a lot of thought to that conversation and everything that had happened since. She still wasn't entirely sure where she fell on the idea of pursuing a relationship with Vikram, given all of the strings that came with it. But maybe he was about to cut her loose and take the decision away from her. Part of her welcomed it.

"I'd still very much like to continue what we started," he said. "Have you given more thought to it?"

"I have," she said carefully, realizing he was not letting her down at all. "I'll be honest, I'm still not sure. Don't you want some time to settle into this role and feel things out before making big decisions about your life?"

His expression hardened. "Zarya, we almost died a few nights ago. That attack pressed upon me the importance of seizing the moment. We might not have that time left, and what would be more tragic than not grasping at every pleasurable opportunity while we can?"

He reached up and tucked a piece of hair behind her ear, his meaning clear.

"I think..." she said, stalling for a moment to sort through her thoughts.

The truth was, she *had* felt something for him, but she'd come to realize those feelings were gone. Or at least, they'd diminished. Whatever bright-eyed wonder she'd experienced had been about the exhilaration of her freedom when everything had been fresh and new and exciting. He was the first man to ever pay her any attention in that way, and she'd turned towards it like flowers drinking in rays of sunshine.

He didn't make her knees weak like she'd always imagined when she'd read about it in her books—at least not anymore—but she wondered if she was being foolish. Believing in a fantasy that might never be real. Those were stories. Those weren't life. Still, she didn't feel she could say yes to what he was asking.

"I think I'm not sure yet," she said, cursing herself for her cowardice. She was avoiding the question, and she knew it. "I need to be honest with you about that. You wouldn't want me doing something I'm not one hundred percent comfortable with."

She said the words as the question they were, hoping they'd allow her a bit more time to process.

Vikram's shoulders slumped, and he ran his fingers through his damp hair. "Of course not. I'm sorry. I shouldn't have cornered you like this again."

"It's okay," she said, squeezing his forearm. "I didn't feel cornered."

Vikram dropped her hand and took a step back. "I should return to the party. Can I see you soon? Maybe we can spend some time together, just the two of us?"

"Sure," Zarya said, though she wasn't certain she wanted that, either. What she did know was that she didn't want to be responsible for that wounded expression on his face again.

"Wonderful," he said with a smile before he leaned down and pressed his lips to her temple, allowing them to linger for a moment. Then, he gave her one more look before he turned and left.

Zarya counted off a few seconds and then followed, emerging from the recessed alcove before coming to a stop.

Rabin stood in the middle of the hall, his stance rigid.

She watched as Vikram passed his brother, their gazes focused on one another. Neither of them spoke, but a thousand undeclared accusations echoed through the hall, anyway.

After Vikram passed Rabin, he turned to enter the salon with a last glance back in Zarya's direction. She stood frozen in the hall as Rabin's gaze creaked to her. Her cheeks warmed, and she wasn't sure why she suddenly felt like she'd been caught doing something illicit.

Rabin took a slow step towards her, but she retreated, raising a hand.

"No," she said. "You—stay away from me."

He stopped, his large frame hunched towards her like a jaguar waiting to pounce. He seemed to vibrate with the effort of holding still.

Then, Zarya turned and walked away, casting one look over her shoulder to find him still in the same position, watching her with an expression like thunder. She rounded the corner, relieved to be away from him and very much noticing how her knees were so weak she could barely stand.

EIGHT

Zarya knocked on the door to the queen's apartments. After a scuffling sound on the other side, it swung open. A woman in a green sari beaded with silver bowed with her hands pressed together before she turned and gestured for Zarya to follow.

They entered a brightly lit salon filled with female courtiers dressed in their most ornate clothing. Beads and crystal and luxurious fabric, along with a heavy cloud of perfume, hung in the air like curtains.

In the center sat Amrita, her left hand stretched out while a vanshaj woman, wearing the white salwar kameez of the palace servants, traced intricate details on her palms using a tube of dark brown paste made of henna.

"Zarya," Amrita said, her expression dreamy and distant. "Come. I've arranged for you to have your mehndi done. This is an important part of the transformation ritual."

"For me?" Zarya asked, settling onto a pillow beside Amrita and holding out her hand as a second vanshaj woman took it and immediately set to work.

"Well, no," Amrita said. "For me, but it's also traditional for those closest to the queen to have theirs done. Plus, it's fun and pretty, and I want you to have some, too."

Zarya smiled and settled back as someone handed her a small glass of wine. She sipped while she surveyed the room, noting faces she recognized. Many of the nobility chose to live at Jai Mahal when not at their country homes. Some had also lost them to the blight, and there had been no opportunity to rebuild.

"How are things going?" Zarya asked.

Amrita shrugged, and Zarya sensed there was something different about her friend, though she couldn't put her finger on what.

"How did you feel during the seeding last night?" Zarya asked. "Was it okay for you in the end?"

Amrita nodded with a vacant smile. "It was. Vikram put me at ease, and it was really no big deal. Once I was in the water, I realized how silly I was being. He's now the most important person in my life, and I will have no more secrets from him."

Zarya pressed her lips together but said nothing. She thought that sounded like a horrible fate, but she didn't want to make Amrita feel bad by saying so.

"I'm glad it was okay. That you're okay," she said instead, and Amrita smiled. "How are you feeling now?"

Amrita tipped her head as if considering the question thoroughly. The silence stretched, and Zarya leaned over. "Amrita?"

"Hmm?" she asked, turning towards Zarya. "Yes?"

"I asked how you were feeling," Zarya said.

"Oh. I feel... different."

"Different how?"

"Like I'm less... present."

Zarya waited for Amrita to expand on what that meant, but the princess was humming to herself as she watched the mehndi artisan trace a floral pattern down the line of her index finger.

"Amrita?" Zarya asked again. "Are you okay?"

Amrita nodded. "Of course. I'm ready," she said. "This has always been my destiny. Now or ten or twenty years from now makes no difference."

"Are you sure?"

Amrita's mouth pinched into a sour pucker, the strange loftiness in her expression settling.

"Yes, I'm sure," she replied with her voice harder now. "This is done and set into motion. I must protect the city, and it's time to step into the duty I was brought into this world for."

Zarya leaned away, taken aback by Amrita's sharp tone, but supposed her friend was undergoing a lot of stress right now. It only made sense the princess was anxious about her future.

"Your Majesty." Before them stood a rakshasa female, decked out in gold and jewels, wearing a vibrant yellow sari. She dropped to her knees with her hands pressed together. "Is there anything you need? More sweets? Perhaps more wine? Is your pillow fluffed to your liking?"

Amrita shook her head. With that same dreamy voice as before, she gestured to Zarya.

"No, I'm fine, Priya. Perhaps Zarya wants something."

Priya's lips fused together as she tipped her head towards Zarya, who wasn't sure what she'd done to earn this woman's ire. She considered asking for something outlandish just to see her reaction but decided to pretend she was mature.

"Thank you, but I'm fine," Zarya said, and Priya nodded, again pressing her hands together before she shuffled away and joined her friends, all of them casting furtive glances their way.

"What... was that about?" Zarya asked.

Amrita frowned as her amber eyes darkened.

"They've suddenly remembered I exist," she said. "Now that I'm close to becoming queen, they're attempting to curry favor. That one," Amrita said, pointing with her free hand in a way that was so obvious that Priya had the grace to blush and look away, "wants me to grant her a massive estate sitting empty along the coast because the blight swallowed hers."

"Oh," Zarya said. "And you don't want to do that?"

Amrita looked at her with a small smile before she lowered her voice.

"I haven't decided yet, but right now, I don't need these nobles consuming resources and manpower to decorate their fancy houses. I need everyone here to help rebuild the city and the wall. This is our priority, but these nobles only care about their selfish desires."

Amrita raised her voice at the end of her sentence, speaking loud enough that several heads turned their way, guilt passing over their expressions. Zarya covered her mouth, trying not to laugh, though part of her was concerned by these abrupt shifts in Amrita's demeanor.

"What's gotten into you, my friend?" Zarya asked.

Again, Amrita transformed, her expression turning smooth and stoic as she stared across the room at some point in the distance. "Perhaps I've realized that I do hold more power than I think. Vikram helped me see it," she said. "Last night, we talked after the seeding, and he said some things that made me realize I don't have to be docile and agreeable all the time. *That* is not my job."

"Well, I like it," Zarya said, leaning over in a conspiratorial whisper. "Though I think you've quite shocked them all."

Amrita blinked slowly. "That part has been rather fun."

"Why was Priya so sour with me, then?" Zarya asked. "What did *I* do?"

"They know I actually like you," Amrita said, raising her voice again. "Zarya was my friend before she knew I could do things for her."

This time, Zarya saw more than one courtier turn red before they turned away to focus intently on their wine glasses.

"Amrita!" Zarya said, shocked.

"I think Priya is convinced I'm giving that house to you," Amrita said, and Zarya widened her eyes.

"And why does she think that?"

"I might have hinted at it," Amrita said, and Zarya snorted on her drink. "Don't worry—it's just to keep her on her toes." Amrita slid her glance Zarya's way. "Unless you want it, of course?"

Zarya waved a hand. "No, that's quite all right. I don't think I'm quite in the 'estate management' era of my life just yet."

"Well, if you change your mind," Amrita said as though she'd already forgotten about the conversation, her voice trailing off.

"Noted."

The woman who had been decorating Zarya's hand finished and indicated that it was time to switch. Zarya examined her handiwork, mesmerized by the swirls and arcs, the flowers and scallops that formed the ornate design.

She placed her glass next to her and held out her blank palm.

"You left the seeding early last night?" Amrita commented, now on her second hand as well. Her markings were far more intricate, winding all the way up her arms and covering her feet and ankles.

Zarya wrinkled her nose.

"Is this about Vikram?" she asked, still speaking with that strange, breathless voice like she wasn't entirely here. "I saw you two sneak off together."

"Amrita—"

"It's okay," Amrita said, gently nudging Zarya with her shoulder. "Truly. I know how he feels, and I do not have those feelings for him. It's fine. I promise."

"He was asking if we could give things a go," Zarya said. "He wanted to pursue what we started before I knew who you were to him."

"And what did you say?"

"I said I wasn't sure," Zarya said.

"But, you are sure." Zarya flicked her gaze to Amrita. "I'm not on anyone's side here. I just want you to be happy."

"You want him to be happy, too."

"I do," she said. "But only with someone who wants to be with him. He deserves that."

Zarya blew out a breath. Everyone in the room was engrossed in their conversations, though their glances occasionally slid to Amrita and Zarya. She noticed the Ravana wives seated under the window, chatting with a group of fawning courtiers.

She studied the beautiful Jasmine Ravana—Vikram and Rabin's mother—seeing the resemblance to her sons in her face. The angled eyebrows and the strong jaw. Jasmine had the same gold flecks in her dark eyes as Rabin, though hers were less pronounced.

Jasmine looked up, and their gazes met for a prolonged heartbeat.

"Why don't you want to pursue things with Vikram?" Amrita asked, noticing the silent exchange between Zarya and Jasmine. "Is it only because of the steward thing? Because I meant what I said—the demand for celibacy is an archaic constraint, and few would judge him for pursuing a relationship."

Zarya peeled her gaze away from Jasmine to look at Amrita.

"No. It was that at first, but I think I've realized I don't feel the way he wants me to feel about him. That I don't feel..." she trailed off. Could she reveal the whole truth to Amrita?

But the princess was perceptive, and she picked up immediately on the thought Zarya had failed to complete.

"Don't feel what? Is there someone else who you have these feelings for?"

"No," Zarya said entirely too quickly, and Amrita raised an eyebrow.

"Oh, yes, that was very believable," she said with a roll of her eyes that felt more like the princess she knew.

Zarya smiled. "There might be."

"Who?" Amrita asked, her eyes spreading wide. "I haven't seen you talking to anyone other than Yasen, and I know it's not him. Wait—" Amrita narrowed her eyes. "Rabin. When he came with us the other night, there was a weird tension between you. Is it *Rabin*?"

"No! Of course not. That's ridiculous," Zarya said. "Will you keep it down?"

But Amrita ignored her. "But you just met him. Oh, was it love at first sight? What does he think about this? Have you talked? Have you kissed? Tell me everything." Amrita was talking a mile a minute, and Zarya resisted the urge to reach over and clamp a hand over her mouth. She would ruin all the hard work of the henna artist.

"Stop it," Zarya begged. "I'll tell you. Just keep your voice down."

"Okay," Amrita said, ducking her head. "Tell me."

"I didn't just meet him."

"What do you mean?"

Zarya then relayed some of what had happened in the dream forest, following it up with his less-than-warm reception at the joining ceremony.

"So, I know he doesn't feel the same way," Zarya said. "But I still can't seem to organize my thoughts when I'm around him."

Zarya glanced at Amrita, who was staring at her hand. She waited for her to respond, but it seemed like Amrita had drifted off again.

"Amrita?" Zarya asked.

The princess looked over, her brows furrowing and her mouth flattening.

"Does Vik know about this?" she asked in a sharp tone.

"No," Zarya said, taken aback by yet another quick swing in her character. "No. Absolutely not."

"Does Rabin know about your past with Vikram?"

Zarya paused and shook her head, feeling a bit like she was being scolded now. She thought about him standing in the hall last night after her discussion with Vikram. Had he heard them talking? Did it matter?

"I don't know," she answered truthfully.

"You're going to have to tell him. Vikram, I mean," Amrita said. "He cares for you."

"There's nothing to tell," Zarya said. "Nothing is going to happen between me and Rabin."

"But you said you feel something for him, even if that's the case."

Zarya blew out a breath.

"I will," she said as Amrita eyed Zarya up and down.

"I know you'll do the noble thing, Zarya." Amrita said the words pointedly, like she expected nothing less. Zarya winced at the idea of having to come clean with Vikram, but she knew Amrita was right.

Amrita had returned to watching her mehndi application, that impassive expression once more in place as she hummed to herself. It seemed the seeding really had changed her, and Zarya wondered if she was already losing her friend.

NINE

The sun was sinking over the horizon when Zarya and Yasen headed for the southern watchtower the following night. As they left the city, they nodded towards the line of Khada soldiers guarding the perimeter wall.

"You know," Zarya said as they approached the forest, "this seems a little dangerous, doesn't it? You and me out here all on our own?"

Yasen shrugged a shoulder. "You wanted to join the Khada. If you'd listened to me from the beginning, you could be snug in your bed right now while I suffered alone."

"Hmm," Zarya said.

"It's okay," Yasen said. "You can just admit I was right."

"Over my dead body."

Yasen chuckled as they fell into a comfortable pace, their horses' hooves picking over the grass.

"Don't worry. The watchtower isn't actually inside the blight," Yasen said. "It just offers a view of it from up high. And we're not completely alone—we'll be relieving the earlier watch."

Well, that was reassuring.

"What trouble did they get up to that earned them this punishment?"

"They added food coloring to the toothpaste of a rival squad, turning everyone's teeth lime green for days."

Zarya huffed out a laugh and covered her mouth. "That's actually pretty funny."

Yasen smiled as they continued.

"It's been quiet, though," Zarya said. "Out there."

"It has. Ever since that night." Yasen gave her a side-eyed look that wasn't judgmental, but it was curious.

"Since I obliterated them with my weird ancient powers, you mean."

"I always knew there was something off about you, Swamp Girl," he joked, and she gave him a wry smile. Somehow, he always knew the right thing to say to dispel the pressure cresting behind her ribs.

They turned east, heading towards the shore, and then rode along the beach, staring out at the water. By now, the sun sat low across the ocean, a million points of light reflecting off the waves while the moon and stars peeked out from above.

"How much longer until we get there?" she asked. "Does someone come out to the watchtower every night?"

"Not much longer, and yes, it's rare there isn't someone who hasn't been sentenced for some misdeed."

Zarya snorted at that as Yasen came to a halt.

There it stood in the distance, a tall tower made of white stone that rose many feet over the forest surrounded by blackened trees and bushes, the ground beneath turned to the mushy bog she'd traversed so many times.

"Not inside the blight, hey?" Zarya said softly.

"Not anymore, I guess," Yasen said, studying the narrow structure.

"What should we do?"

"It's quiet, like you said. Let's just check things out. We

don't have to stay long. I don't think Vikram was angry enough to ask us to risk our necks."

He trotted forward, and Zarya followed.

"Last night, he apologized for yelling at me," Zarya said. "Said he couldn't sleep because of the guilt."

"Well, how nice for you," Yasen said. "I've been getting the silent treatment. But then Vik doesn't want to get into *my* pants."

"Shut up," Zarya said. "That's not—"

Yasen snickered as she broke off her train of thought because that was precisely what it had been about. Why did that thought bother her so much?

"Listen, use your advantages where you get them, Zee. The world is hard enough."

Zarya made a noncommittal noise. "Well, he doesn't want me badly enough to get me out of coming out here with you, it seems."

"I bet if you had let him inside those pants, you'd be home in bed right now," he joked.

"What makes you so sure I didn't?"

"Because after your little talk, he returned in a foul mood, only stayed at the party for another few minutes, and then left in a huff."

"Oh," Zarya said.

"Don't feel bad. That's not your fault."

They arrived at the tower, stretching their necks to trace its full height. After tying up their horses, they entered the door at the bottom and made the ascent.

"This is another reason this task is reserved for miscreants," Yasen said. "All these fucking stairs."

Zarya laughed but decided to save her energy as they wound up and up.

"How many are there?" she asked.

"You know, I've never counted," he said in a deadpan voice that suggested that was a ridiculous question to ask.

"Right. I guess not."

After what felt like a very long time, they arrived at the top to find it empty.

"Where are the soldiers we're supposed to relieve?" Zarya asked. "I just realized there weren't any horses tethered downstairs."

"Good question," Yasen said, his eyes narrowing as he peered into the swamp over the crenelated wall that bordered the circular roof deck.

Zarya turned around, observing the glowing city of Dharati in the distance, the expanse of ocean on one side, and the shadowy slice of swamp. It sat to the south like a dreary blot of ink, the darkness nearly impenetrable.

Zarya studied it as Yasen came to stand next to her.

"Do you see them?" he asked.

She shook her head.

"You don't think they went out there? Why would they?"

"Maybe I should go look for them," he said. "You stay here."

Yasen turned, and Zarya grabbed his arm. "You are not going out there all alone. We're staying here. Maybe they got bored and returned to the city."

She wasn't sure why, but it didn't feel safe for either of them to wander any deeper into the blight. Something in the air felt off.

"But maybe they didn't."

"Then what good will it do to go out there on your own and get yourself lost or worse?"

His brows drew together as he relented.

"We'll give them a few minutes to see if they turn up. If they returned to Dharati before the end of their shift, I'll have them stripped of their rank."

"You do that," Zarya said as she once again surveyed their surroundings.

"I can't believe Row kept you living out here in the wilds, with this field of death spreading all around you," Yasen said.

"The area around our house was protected," she said. "And it was quite lovely if you forgot it was basically a prison. But yeah, it didn't make for the most welcoming environment."

"What did you do all the time?" he asked.

"I read a lot of books," she said, and Yasen laughed.

"Right. I should have guessed."

"It was all I had," she said softly, and he wrapped an arm around her shoulders and tugged her closer.

"Then I'm glad you had them."

She looked up, blinking back the threat of tears.

"But please don't cry again."

"I'm not," she said, wiping the corner of her eye.

He dropped his arm and leaned forward, resting his elbows on the ledge.

"We'll have to let Vik know this tower has been compromised when we get back. It must be recent."

His eyes wandered towards the city, the light of worry reflecting in their stormy depths. She knew what he was looking at—the creeping border between the blight and the untouched plain beyond the wall.

The dark side and the light side.

The line between safety and ruin.

This vantage made it even more apparent just how little space remained between the blight and Dharati.

"How long do you think we have until it reaches the city?" she asked.

He shook his head. "Not long enough. I don't think it will ever be enough."

"What will we do, Yas? Where will we all go?"

"I'm not sure. Evacuate Daragaab. Leave it to the monsters? Try to fight back until no one is left?"

"It won't stop here," Zarya said, certain of that.

"No, it won't," he agreed. "I'm hoping that we can actually fight back with Amrita as queen."

"What do you mean?"

Yasen gave her a wry look. "While Rani Vasvi was very benevolent and all, she wasn't good for much beyond blinking her eyes and bestowing everyone with patient smiles."

"Yasen! That was your queen you're talking about."

"I know," he said, not sounding at all sorry about it. "But she was a figurehead. She had to be dragged into any sort of action."

Zarya remembered Amrita sharing similar sentiments.

"But Amrita is much smarter," Yasen said. "And wants to put her mind to helping Daragaab. Once she's in her place, I'm confident she'll put all of the queendom's resources into action."

"You know about her wishes?" Zarya asked. She'd never gotten the sense that Yasen and Amrita were close.

"I asked," he said. "I wanted to know what sort of queen we were all waiting on. I think she was so grateful that anyone cared that she told me everything." He pressed his lips together. "Nearly talked my ear off. I had to fake a migraine to get away."

Zarya laughed. "I'm sure you loved that."

"I kind of did. Ever since, she finds me occasionally to ask about my thoughts or opinions on an idea she has. We aren't really friends, but we have a mutual respect for each other."

Zarya stared at Yasen.

"What? Why are you looking at me like that?"

"You have many layers," Zarya said, and Yasen laughed.

"I'm not just a pretty face."

She smirked and then tapped his cheek. "Shame. It is just *so* pretty."

They both fell silent as they stared out over the blight,

simmering in its eerie stillness. It draped in the air like thick velvet, muffling her senses.

"How are you feeling?" Yasen asked. "With Row back? You haven't talked much about all the things he said."

She took a moment to consider her answer.

"I feel overwhelmed," she finally said. "Of all the wild reasons I'd imagined for why Row kept me locked away, none of them came anywhere close to the truth."

"What did you think?"

"Oh, I don't know. Maybe he didn't want to subject anyone to my terrible singing voice? My horrible morning breath? The way I can't make a proper samosa to save my life?"

Yasen smiled. "Or maybe because you cry so much?"

"Shut up," she said, playfully punching him in the arm. "I do not."

"You do. Look, you want to cry right now."

"Because you're so *mean* to me," she said, and they both laughed.

"No, really," Yasen said. "Tell me how you're doing. I want to know."

She shrugged. "I finally know who my mother is, and while I always knew she was dead, maybe a small, tiny part of me always hoped that Row had been wrong or was lying about it. But that hope is gone now, and I'm having trouble reconciling that. I lost something I never even had."

"But you have a father."

"I do. Who's apparently a murderous tyrant. So that's... certainly something."

Yasen snorted. "Drama does seem to follow you wherever you go."

"Only recently. My life was as boring as dry rice until a few months ago."

"Would you ever want to go back to that? I mean, not the captivity part but the quietness of it? The solitude?"

She shook her head. "No. That was never the life I wanted. Despite everything, I am grateful for how it all turned out. Meeting you and Amrita and Vik and all the others. That's what I've always wanted."

"Hmm," Yasen replied. "A quiet cottage by the sea sounds like a nice kind of life."

"Yeah, I could see you there. Maybe one day you can have that. As long as you let me come visit you sometimes."

He gave her a small smile. "It's a deal, Swamp Girl."

She looked out on the blight again and then squinted. Something was moving in the trees. Maybe it was the missing soldiers.

"Do you see that?" she asked, pointing into the distance.

Yasen leaned in, following the line of her finger.

"See what?"

"There. You don't see something moving?"

She gripped the stone railing, quickly realizing it wasn't the guards.

It looked like a large mass sweeping along the earth, like a huge wave rolling over the ocean but dense and made of shadows.

Yasen shook his head.

"I don't see anything. Just the forest. Are you sure?"

Zarya continued watching as it moved, pooling across the ground like thick puddles of smoke.

"I... maybe it's nothing."

She stared at their surroundings as the mass began to take shape, drawing closer. She realized it wasn't a singular entity but hundreds of bodies moving together. But that made no sense.

"Zee, what is it?" Yasen said, his gaze moving between Zarya and the point where she was staring.

The foreign presence kept moving until it hit the treeline, moonlight spilling over it and revealing an army of demons with horns, razor-sharp teeth, and long, deadly claws, all wearing beaten black metal armor.

"Zee? What's going on?" Yasen asked her, and she shook her head.

"I don't know. You don't see that? Please tell me you see that." She clutched his arm, squeezing it hard.

"See what? Zee, you're scaring me."

She lifted her hand to her throat as the army ground to a stop. They weren't quite solid where they stood but had the consistency of apparitions or ghosts. She noticed the way the wind made them ripple like they were made of the softest silk.

What were they, and why was she seeing them?

The demon army halted at the edge of the blight and waited, just staring at Dharati's distant walls, making no attempts to move closer. She should do something. But what? Could she call on her nightfire? She still didn't know how to use it but vowed she would practice—starting tomorrow. Hopefully, Row or Professor Dhawan could help her.

"Zarya!" Yasen said, wrapping his arm around her. "What is it?"

"I see..." she said. "There's an army."

"What?" he asked, alarm coloring his expression.

"There's nothing there, Zee."

Her mouth gaped. "I don't know how to explain it, but there are hundreds of them." She swallowed hard and then whispered, "I see them."

"You're sure?" he asked, and she nodded slowly. Was she sure? Was this just in her head?

"Then we need to alert the Khada immediately."

She finally tore her gaze away.

"Let's go," Yasen said. "Zee, we need to tell them."

Zarya slid down against the wall, wrapping her arms around her knees and bowing her head against them.

"I just need a moment," she said into her folded arms. "I can't breathe."

"Okay," he said softly, and then she felt his hand wrap around her forearm as he held on, letting her sort through her thoughts.

"Can you tell me what's happening?" he asked after a minute.

"I don't know," she whispered.

This had to be connected to her sixth anchor. She needed to unburden herself with the truth, but she couldn't stand how Yasen might look at her if he knew what she was carrying inside her heart. He might think she was a monster herself. Maybe she was.

"I've been under a lot of strain." She wiped a tear from the corner of her eye and then stood up. The army still waited, completely silent, staring at the city. Prickles climbed over her scalp, and she rubbed it before she scrubbed a hand over her face.

"You still don't see them?" she asked.

"Sorry. I don't."

"Then let's go. We need to tell Vik and the others right away. This is a warning. Something is coming."

TEN

Zarya and Yasen rushed back to the city, pushing their horses as fast as their hooves could fly. Her heart thudded in her ears as she continued to cast looks over her shoulder. The silent army stood and stared at the city, making her skin crawl with an eruption of gooseflesh.

What were they? Why couldn't Yasen see them? Why could *she*?

She tried not to think about what it meant.

Maybe this was all in her head. She would almost welcome it. Better for her to be losing her mind than the alternative.

They burst into the palace and thundered towards the steward's quarter, where Vikram had recently taken up residence, overseeing his duties as Daragaab's commander along with a list of new tasks as its steward. He looked up from a pile of papers on his desk. Seeing the looks on their faces, he stood, pressing his hands to the surface. "What is it?"

Yasen waited for Zarya to offer an explanation. She opened her mouth and closed it, having no idea where to begin.

"We saw something in the forest," she said finally. It was a woefully inadequate description for the horror lurking in the trees.

"What? Tell me," Vikram demanded, looking between the two of them.

"I'm not sure. An army," Zarya answered. She sounded insane.

"A what?"

She went on to describe everything as the color leached away from Vikram's face. Zarya and Yasen's sudden entrance had called everyone's attention because several others had also been drawn to Vikram's study while an eavesdropping crowd of servants gathered in the hall.

"Zarya, what's going on?" Row asked, coming up beside her. She explained again, turning to face Dhawan and the other Chiranjivi, who had also arrived.

"And you couldn't see it?" Kindle asked Yasen, who nodded. Yasen looked at Zarya with an expression that suggested he was sorry for letting her down, but this wasn't his fault.

"We need to investigate," Row said. "Find out what it is."

"We'll gather the queen's guard immediately," Vikram said.

"You can't just send them out there," Zarya said. "There were hundreds of them."

"Gather all the Khada, too," Yasen said. "Sound the alarms. We'll need everyone."

"But what if it's nothing?" Zarya asked. She was starting to panic now. "What if it's all in my head? What if it's a diversion or a trap? We could be running straight into it."

"What if it isn't in your head?" Apsara asked. "Row is right. We need to understand what we're up against."

Zarya nodded reluctantly, and Kindle laid a hand on her shoulder before he squeezed it.

"If it's nothing, then it's nothing. The worst that happens is we lose a few hours of sleep. But if it's a threat, we'd be remiss not to take every precaution we can."

"Sure," Zarya said, but she wasn't convinced.

Any lingering reservations were brushed aside as everyone sprung into action. She noticed Rabin had also entered the room at some point during the discussion, but she turned away, ignoring the gust of warmth in her stomach. She wouldn't allow herself to be distracted by him anymore.

Outside, the city's alarms blared to life, shrieking through every door and window. Zarya headed with the others through Dharati's panicked streets to arrive at the massive iron gates that guarded the city. A throng of armed soldiers had already gathered, and they shouldered their way to the front as they waited for every available body to assemble behind them.

Their army was well-trained, and collecting their forces didn't take long. But could one made of bone and flesh contend with one cut from shadows that only she could see? From her vantage point on the ground, it was hard to be sure, but Zarya was certain this wasn't enough to give them the edge they needed.

Zarya spotted Aarav weaving through the crowd. He made his way to where Zarya stood between Yasen and Row.

"What's going on?" he asked, and they filled him in. He gave Zarya a strange look, and she expected a callous remark about how she was losing her mind, but he said nothing before he focused on the gates that were now slowly dragging open.

Zarya pushed to the front and exited the city. She felt it was her job to be the shield between these monsters and everyone else.

Suvanna stood to her left, while Yasen stood on her right, forming a line with Vikram, Kindle, Koura, Rabin, and Apsara. Behind them, the army waited for their cue as everyone stared at the forest in tense silence.

"Do you still see them?" Yasen asked.

She nodded. Not only could she still see them, they'd moved even closer while remaining immobile and silent, but for the subtle shift of their forms in the breeze. Her nerves stretched, and shivers spread over her scalp.

Row approached her.

"Zarya, tell me what you see."

She described it as accurately as she could as the puzzled furrow between his brows grew deeper and deeper.

"What is it?" she asked in a whisper.

"Nairrata," Row said, sending another ripple of apprehension twisting in her gut.

Zarya remembered the name. The Ashvins' demon army. The twin brothers who'd unleashed the darkness on Rahajhan a thousand years ago.

"Your description sounds almost like those found in ancient texts, but I don't remember them being spirits. They were always described as corporeal," Row went on.

"What should we do?" Vikram asked. "How do we attack an army none of us can see? How do we even know they're there?"

Vikram's gaze slid to Zarya, and seeing the look on her face, he said, "Sorry. But we need to be sure."

She shook her head and pressed her lips together. Of course he was right to question her claim. Everyone was staring at her now. What if there *was* nothing there, and this was all in her head? Was she losing her mind? She might have dragged half the city out here for nothing.

"Wait," Apsara said a moment later, holding up a hand. "I hear a noise."

"Everyone quiet!" Vikram yelled as all conversation around them dried up.

Zarya listened intently, trying to pick up on what Apsara was hearing. It took a moment to notice the tremors that vibrated up her body from the earth.

"I feel something," Zarya whispered, and she couldn't begin to describe her relief when several others nodded in agreement.

"It's coming from the forest," Yasen said. "It sounds like... whispers."

Zarya still couldn't hear anything, but she put it down to his superior rakshasa hearing. Yasen stalked forward, pulling out his sword and staring at the screen of darkness that spread across the horizon. Then, Zarya heard it, too. Whispers were a good way to describe the sound, but it was crisper than that. It was sharp and metallic, interspersed with clicks and high-pitched squeaks, like someone dragging a steel bed frame over a rough surface.

While part of her was relieved that she hadn't convinced everyone out here for no reason, a much more significant part was terrified about what was coming this way.

She stared intently at the forest and the ghost army that remained unmoving.

Suddenly, two mounted figures wearing the uniform of the queen's guard burst through the darkness, screaming.

"Run! They're coming!" the guards shouted, and Zarya realized these must be the missing soldiers they'd been meant to relieve on the watchtower earlier.

The guards stampeded towards them as the eerie sounds of the forest drew closer, and the vibrations under Zarya's feet intensified.

The guards careened to a stop as they approached the line.

"What is it?" Vikram shouted.

The soldiers' faces were pale, their eyes rolling with terror.

"Monsters," one of them whispered, and the word expanded over the gathered assembly like a curse. They turned to face the forest as the shadows of the army parted like a curtain, revealing the horror that lay beyond.

"Good gods," Kindle said as he stepped back.

"What the fuck are those?" Yasen asked.

Zarya made a low noise in her throat at the line of giant bronze scorpions that now stood facing them, their tails arched and poised to strike.

"Ajakavas," Apsara said, her voice raw with dread. If Apsara was frightened, what chance did the rest of them have?

"Let me guess?" Zarya asked, her voice shaking more than she would have liked. "Another creature of myth that shouldn't be here standing in front of us right now, ready to tear us to shreds?"

Apsara nodded grimly. "Precisely that."

"Great," Zarya said with a wry huff. "That's just perfect."

The ajakavas assembled along the treeline, assessing their opponents. Maybe the only comforting thing about their entrance was the fact that her ghost army had melted into the ether. Had they been here to warn her? Or had they been responsible for bringing these monsters to their door?

Zarya didn't have any more time to wonder because that same whispering they'd heard from the trees churned into a discordant melody akin to the chitter of insects. Gods, she hated bugs. This was a literal nightmare come to horrifying life.

As a unit, the scorpions began to get louder, their tales snapping and their pincers clicking. Zarya could have sworn they were laughing at their pitiful army gathered at the wall, white-knuckling their meager weapons.

A row of bronze shells gleamed in the moonlight like fortified caverns designed to protect a horde of treasure. Zarya already suspected they wouldn't stand a chance against them.

And then the monsters charged.

"Ready!" Vikram yelled, holding up his sword. "Show them no mercy! Attack!"

Their line surged as Zarya and Dharati's army ran across the open plain that spread between the city and the forest, her arms pumping and the wind blowing her hair.

They came upon the ajakava in a clash of swords and screams.

Zarya estimated there were about fifty scorpions, and while their force numbered in the hundreds, it became quickly apparent it would take a small battalion to bring down each one.

Screams echoed in the air as the scorpions' tails swung, biting into the backs of the soldiers, piercing easily through their armor with sharp stings as fighters screamed, foaming at the mouth before their eyes rolled into their heads and they collapsed to the ground.

Ahead of her, Aarav and Yasen fought an ajakava along with a group of soldiers as they surrounded the demon, trying to reach its bronzed shell.

Zarya approached from the side, swinging her sword, vibrations numbing her arm as it glanced against the monster's carapace, leaving a long scrape like a diamond scratched over a mirror. But it was obvious the creature hadn't felt a thing.

Aarav ducked as the demon swung out a pincer, attempting to sever him in two. Yasen fought on the other side, aiming for its face where it seemed like it would be most vulnerable.

A flash of light caught Zarya's attention, and she saw Rabin shooting beams of copper light towards the monster, the magic bouncing off its shell and ricocheting into the sky.

Row sent alternating bolts of fire and lightning towards the monsters as he lifted an arm and made a slicing motion before a forked bolt of lightning hit an ajakava in the head, right through the line of its many eyes. The scorpion screeched and flipped over on its back from the force of the blow, its horrible needle-like legs scrabbling in the air.

Rabin sprinted for the fallen creature, leaping in the air and landing on its stomach in a crouch before he used both hands to spear it with the point of his sword.

The demon writhed for several seconds before it finally stopped moving, caving to death.

"The heads and stomachs! That's where they're vulnerable," Rabin called from his perch atop the lifeless creature. "Aim for the heads and stomachs! Flip them over. Get underneath!"

"Zarya!" Row called to her. "Use your nightfire. It worked on the demons last time."

Right. With her sword gripped in one hand, Zarya concentrated on her anchors, trying to remember how she'd called it up the night of the kala-hamsa attack.

Her five-pointed anchor spun in her heart, and she pulled them together, sending out a bolt of fire that slammed into the side of a scorpion. The force sent it flying, and it rolled over and over until it stopped on its back. A swarm of soldiers launched themselves on top, spearing it through the middle like Rabin had done.

Okay, that wasn't entirely what she'd planned, but it would do.

Not sure why her nightfire hadn't surfaced, she made do with another blast of fire as she moved down the line in the opposite direction of Row, trying to knock over as many as she could, leaving the soldiers to finish them off.

Apsara, her long white hair and feathered wings spattered with blood, also used her powers of air and wind to pick them up, flip them over, and pin them to the ground.

They were making good progress, systematically taking turns, knocking the monsters over, and then gutting them through.

Zarya chanced a glance into the forest, still wondering about the silent army of soldiers. Were they gone, or just biding their time? Had these demons been sent to wear them down before the real nightmare swept in?

She squinted into the darkness, noticing low shadows moving between the trees.

"No," she whispered, spinning around. "More coming!" she screamed. "More coming!"

Sure enough, dozens more ajakava emerged from the forest, descending in a storm of clicks and chitters.

The night became a blur of magic and fire, the glint of steel and bronze, and the shrieks and cries of soldiers and demons as each side traded blows.

Covered in red and black blood, Zarya staggered along the earth, passing the foaming corpses of the fallen army, her body spent, not sure which direction was up or down. She alternated between fire and air, noticing her strength slowly dwindling as she channeled more and more of her power. Nevertheless, she persisted, doing whatever she could to immobilize the demons while the others moved in for the kill.

Periodically, she searched the crowd, ensuring Yasen was okay. She looked for Row, and Vik, the other Chiranjivi, and even Rabin—breathing easily when she saw him, also covered in blood as he leaped onto another scorpion and finished it off with a plunge of his sword and a fierce gleam in his eyes.

The way he moved was magnificent, and Zarya found herself staring as he whirled between skirmishes like he practically had wings. She wondered why he hadn't transformed into his dragon. As if feeling his eyes on her, he glanced over her way, their gazes locking for a heartbeat before a cry summoned her attention.

Aarav was on the ground, a scorpion stalking towards him as he scrabbled back on his hands. Zarya noticed he was no longer holding a weapon, his sword lying several feet away.

Zarya ran towards them. She gathered her fire anchor, prepared to blast the beast away, but too many soldiers crowded around it, hacking away at its impenetrable outer shell to no avail.

"Move!" she screamed. "Move out of the way!" But they were too engrossed in their task, and her voice was drowned out by the noises of the fight.

"Move!" she screamed, sprinting closer. She grabbed the arm of a soldier, seizing his attention.

"You all need to clear out of the way!"

The man seemed to understand immediately, and he nodded before shouting at his companions to clear some space.

Aarav inched back, caged by the legs of the ajakava. A soldier moved in, and the scorpion swung out a pincer, snapping around the woman's waist and snipping her clean in half like she was nothing but a satin ribbon.

The parts of her mangled body dropped to the ground, and Zarya let out a cry and covered her mouth as bile basted the back of her throat.

Aarav had figured out how to stay out of danger for the moment. There wasn't much the demon could do where he lay positioned directly under its mouth. Its claws didn't bend in a way that allowed access to Aarav, and its mouth posed no threat. It crept along as Aarav scrambled back—it was working for now, but that wouldn't hold the demon off for long.

Finally, there was an opening, and Zarya took it, sending out a blast of fire, but something was wrong. Instead of a steady stream, it was a weak, thin line of magic. She had used too much. The fire hit the scorpion's carapace, knocking it sideways but without enough force to turn it over.

It screeched as it slid, its legs scrabbling in the grass, but worst of all, Zarya had caused Aarav to lose his safe position under its head, and he was now within pinching distance. The ajakava snapped a claw, cinching Aarav around the waist before it lifted him up, tossing him side to side.

Aarav screamed as his legs kicked. Zarya screamed, too, remembering what it had just done to the woman a moment ago.

She had to do something. She couldn't let Aarav die like this. She pulled her sword from her back and, hoping the thing was distracted, she ran, skidding underneath its body.

Then, she lunged up with her blade, spearing the beast through its stomach between the joints of its shell. She felt the shudder as she drove the sword in deep, a cascade of black blood drenching her. She gagged as it filled her nose and mouth while she twisted her blade.

Blinded to her surroundings, she felt the demon go still and had just enough presence of mind to roll out from under it before it collapsed onto the earth with a heavy whump.

Zarya wiped a hand over her eyes and then lay in the grass, panting, unable to move as the sky swirled above her. She heard her name, and Aarav appeared in her vision, positioned on his hands and knees. "You saved my life, Zarya. Can you get up?"

"I'm not sure," she said, her voice and throat raw. "Are you okay?"

"Yes," he breathed. "I almost wasn't. Gods, that was close."

In the distance, Zarya could hear the fighting. They weren't done yet. She struggled to her feet.

Koura spotted her and came running over.

"Are you hurt? Do you need healing?" he asked them both, scanning Zarya and then Aarav from head to toe. It was hard to tell where she began, and the demon's blood ended.

"I'm fine. Just winded."

Koura clamped a heavy hand on her shoulder. "You're sure?"

"Yes. I just need a moment."

The healer nodded and then jogged off, seeking out anyone who might benefit from his gifts.

They continued fighting, losing track of the hours and minutes until the strength of the assault began to cease. Zarya and Aarav fought together as the last scorpions were dispatched, their army ragged and covered in blood.

Finally, the sun rose above the horizon, and the last of the ajakava skittered away and melted into the darkness of the trees.

Zarya watched them as everyone left standing on the battlefield stirred inside this hollow victory.

She turned to find the plain surrounding the city littered with fallen soldiers and dead ajakava. It was a massacre, but at least they'd kept them from breaching the wall. Dharati might not survive another attack.

She spotted Vikram in the distance, shouting orders with Yasen at his side, and breathed out in relief. As she approached them with Aarav in tow, she quickly searched for the others, finding everyone safe, if a little battered, as tears rolled down her cheeks.

"Zarya," Aarav said, clapping a hand on her shoulder. There was a time she would have shaken him off, but she gave him a weary smile. "You saved me. I don't know how to thank you."

"You would have done the same for me," she said, and they watched each other.

A moment later, he nodded. "I would have. Zarya, I would."

The corner of her mouth tipped up.

"I know, Aarav. Come on. Let's go see if they need our help."

ELEVEN

Battered and bruised, the citizens of Dharati collected themselves once again in the face of the dangers that were closing in on them, bit by bit. As the sun rose the following day, the city spiraled to life, honoring the dead and stepping back into the threads of their days. They'd grown used to chaos, understanding how to pick up the pieces, though they all wondered how many more times they would do this before everything unraveled once and for all.

Zarya and Yasen were commended for their role—if they hadn't been assigned to the watchtower that night, then the city might not have been warned of the impending attack. Despite her unease about the ghost army being visible only to her eyes, Zarya was glad it had at least prepared everyone for the ajakava.

Row and the other Chiranjivi had questioned Zarya endlessly about what she'd seen, trying to puzzle out the mystery of her vision. She didn't know how to answer any of them.

The two guards who'd run out of the trees to warn them had both perished in the fight, and no one could ask what had possessed them to abandon the tower and enter the forest that night.

It was one puzzle after another.

Vikram promoted Yasen to interim commander of Dara-gaab's army, acknowledging he could no longer manage the position given his new duties as steward. As a result, Yasen had been busy at the fort, and she hadn't seen him much since the attack.

But it was finally time for the concluding phase of Amrita's transformation, and it couldn't come too soon. Until she took her place, the city wouldn't be safe.

Zarya dressed for the ceremony in the haveli, donning a pair of light blue pants accented with silver beads, along with a matching sleeveless choli. Over them, she layered a sheer, flowing jacket that reached to her ankles and buttoned just below her bust line. She left her hair loose, hanging down her back in soft waves.

When she was ready, she made her way to the palace, intending to see Amrita one last time before she changed forever.

Zarya recalled their last conversation and wondered if the princess had already changed, though. It was obvious the seeding had begun the transformation even before Amrita was fully relegated to her position inside the Jai Tree.

As Zarya crossed the plaza, she contemplated the strange events of two nights ago. Had she imagined those ghosts? She would have an easier time believing they weren't real if they hadn't preceded the arrival of the ajakava. The two events had to be connected.

She entered through the side garden, finding the palace bustling with its usual level of activity. Several vanshaj scurried past, laden with food, towels, and other items required to attend to the palace's residents. Most of the nobles would be at tonight's ceremony and likely had numerous pampering 'emergencies' cropping up.

She knew her way around much of the palace by now and easily found Amrita, who was preparing for the event. Zarya was admitted to a small round room with windows on all sides, draped with flowers and vines. In the center, Amrita stood wearing a simple white sari, the hem dusting the tops of her bared feet.

Attendants brushed her dark hair until her curls were as smooth as polished onyx, while another dusted her face with powder. Thick lines of kohl rimmed Amrita's amber eyes, making her appear older and more serious—a direct contrast to the blank and emotionless look on her face.

"Amrita," Zarya said as she entered, and her friend's head swiveled slowly like she was moving underwater. Amrita blinked, but her eyes remained vacant and distant. "How are you?"

"Zarya," she said in a breathy voice. "How nice to see you. You're so kind to see me off like this."

Zarya frowned as she moved closer, and the attendants moved away, finished with their tasks. Amrita slowly pivoted with her arms stretched out like a child showing off her party dress. Like she was a statue on a pedestal placed there for everyone to admire.

"Amrita," Zarya said, her throat knotting up with tension. She hated seeing her like this.

"Yes?" Amrita said, blinking her big eyes and tipping her head in question.

"I... I'm going to miss you."

"Oh. Well, that's very nice."

Zarya moved closer and took Amrita's hand. "You're sure that this is what you want?" Zarya had no idea if there was any way to undo what had already been set into motion, but she had to ask, anyway.

The mask of Amrita's expression crumpled for a moment before it solidified again. "Of course. What a silly question."

Zarya nodded, holding in everything she wanted to say. Of course, Amrita had to fulfill her duty. She just wished she didn't have to lose herself entirely in the process. "At least you'll be able to do all those things you wanted to improve Daragaab, right?"

Amrita's gaze drifted off, pointing to nothing Zarya could discern.

"Amrita?" Zarya asked, tugging gently on her hand.

"What? Oh yes." Amrita smiled and patted Zarya's hand. "Thank you for coming. Everything will be well."

"Okay," Zarya said, noting the flurry of activity happening around them. The ceremony would begin soon, and this would be done. Zarya drew Amrita into a long hug, though Amrita didn't seem to know what to do with it, her arms hanging limply at her sides.

She pulled away and watched the princess, who peered back with the same almost manic smile. There was nothing more she could say or do. This was Amrita's fate, and Zarya would have to accept it.

Quickly, she turned to leave, unable to look at the hollow shell of her friend a moment longer. Lost in her thoughts, she came up short when someone stepped in her path—a vanshaj woman with a white dupatta draped around her head.

"Please, miss," the woman said as she pressed her hands in front of her.

Zarya stopped and studied the woman who stared at her wide-eyed. When the woman said nothing, Zarya tipped her head.

"What is it? Can I help you with something?"

The woman stepped forward, glancing from left to right to check they were alone.

"My sister. She saw them, too," she said, her whisper so soft that Zarya barely heard her.

Zarya shook her head. "Saw them, who?"

"Out there," the woman gestured in the direction of the city gates. "I was in the hall when you were telling the steward, and my sister, she fought against the ajakava. She said she saw them, too."

Zarya's hand shot out, wrapping around the woman's wrist. "The ghost army? She could see them?"

The woman nodded. "I thought... You seemed upset. I thought you might want to know."

"Is your sister vanshaj?"

"Yes," the woman said. "Of course."

Zarya stared at the woman, her gaze drifting to the line of stars tattooed around her neck as a premonition nudged in the back of her head.

"Zee!" She turned to find Yasen approaching, and she dropped the woman's wrist. He looked relaxed but regal in a cream kurta and slim burgundy pants. The woman stepped back, putting distance between them.

"I've been looking everywhere for you," he said, his gaze flicking between the two women. "Everything okay?"

"Yes," Zarya said. "Let's go."

She took his arm and looked at the woman.

"Thank you," she said.

"Of course."

Then, Zarya left with Yasen as they wound their way through the palace.

"What was that about?"

"Hmm?" Zarya asked, her thoughts a million miles away. "Oh. Nothing."

Then, she asked, "Have you seen Amrita since the seeding?"

Yasen nodded. "She's... different."

"What if it was never Rani Vasvi's temperament that made her so complacent but rather an effect of the transformation itself? What if it... dulled her?"

Yasen's mouth pulled at the corner. "I guess we'll find out soon enough."

They exchanged a look, and she nodded. Daragaab needed a strong ruler. Someone to stop the blight and remedy the many ancient ills of this queendom.

They entered the central courtyard, which glowed softly in the falling dusk. Lotus blossoms cradling candles filled turquoise pools, reflecting warm light. A host of fruit trees planted in white wooden boxes had been spaced around the perimeter, and hundreds of points of light hovered in the air, almost like the stars had descended from the heavens just for this occasion.

The charred Jai Tree stood in the middle of the otherwise cheerful space, lost and forlorn, absent of light and color and life.

Piles of cushions and low, round tables sat on top of thick embroidered rugs laid out on the stone floor. Several were occupied by nobles, courtiers, and high-ranking officers, their polished and decorated uniforms signaling their positions of importance. Yasen and Zarya snagged an empty table and slid into the plush cushions. A bottle of sparkling wine sat in the center, and Yasen poured two glasses.

Zarya sat back and sipped, trying to relax. In just a few more hours, Amrita would be the official queen of Daragaab, and the enchantment on the wall would return to its place. Dharati would be safe once again—or as safe as possible, considering the circumstances.

She couldn't get the conversation with the vanshaj woman out of her head. What did it mean that her sister could see the apparitions, too? How much did anyone know about the caged magic of Rahajhan's most vulnerable citizens?

Aarav sat nearby, his arm draped over Lekha's shoulders. The pair had been going at it like rabbits in the haveli again last night, and Zarya wondered if he'd consider taking his girlfriend somewhere else in exchange for saving his life. They were driving her nuts. And it wasn't only because Zarya's own love life was currently as prickly and starved as a dried cactus. Maybe she should have taken up Vikram on his offer the other night. But she was pretty sure that wouldn't help scratch this incessant itch she couldn't reach.

Aarav grinned over at Zarya as their eyes met. In spite of everything, he'd become much less of an idiot lately. He'd fought bravely during the city's attacks, and she'd grown to respect his fearlessness during his time with the Khada. It was a different side of him. One that she found she liked. She didn't know if they could ever be friends, but maybe they could veer in that direction.

The Chiranjivi all sat together, including Row. They appeared deep in conversation, casting furtive glances first in Zarya's direction and then towards a certain black-haired rakshasa warrior. What were they gossiping about? Her gaze wandered to the edge of the courtyard, wishing she hadn't noticed him, but she was drawn to him like a very stupid moth hovering around a very hot flame.

Rabin stood leaning against a wall, looking like his usual moody and restless self. His sleeveless kurta showed off the impressive cut and breadth of his arms, as well as the tattoos that ran their length—dragon scales, Zarya realized. They shimmered in the light, catching various jeweled colors against the midnight-black ink.

He'd recently shaved, leaving only the barest shading of stubble, and Zarya tried her best not to stare. Poorly.

He didn't even try to pretend he wasn't staring back. Only his was less of an awed glimpse than a glower clearly meant to melt the marrow right out of her bones. She let out a huff and then turned away as heat flushed up the back of her neck before draining half of her glass in one long sip.

She could still feel his eyes on her, and she resisted the urge to turn back. What did he want? Why couldn't he just leave her alone? Was he still convinced she was his father's spy? What a ridiculous notion.

Speaking of which, Zarya also found the nawab seated on the far side of the courtyard with his wives. They were closest to the Jai Tree in a place of honor. Professor Dhawan and Tarin also sat near the front, their heads bent together, lost in some deep and likely profound discussion.

Maybe she could corner the professor later and talk to him about what she'd seen in the forest. After the vanshaj woman had confirmed this hadn't been just in her head, she felt more confident about trying to find the source of the vision. It had to be real if it hadn't been only her. She wondered if anyone else had seen it. Other vanshaj?

A hush fell over the crowd, and Vikram and Amrita emerged from the palace amidst a ripple of soft murmurs, their arms linked together. Amrita's expression was still wooden and distant, and Zarya inhaled a deep breath, missing her friend and the brief but meaningful times they'd shared together.

Hand in hand, Vikram and Amrita began to walk through the courtyard as she picked fruits at random from the trees surrounding the perimeter. She passed each one to Vikram, who peeled and opened them and then handed them back to her. She took a single nibble from each fruit: a pear, a banana, a mango, a lychee, a pomegranate.

"What is she doing?" Zarya asked, leaning towards Yasen.

"Imbibing the fruits of the forest. It will start her transformation. The trees are hundreds of years old and are brought out only during a queen's transformation into the Jai. They are sacred, tended by a hand-picked crew of rakshasa gardeners with an especially gifted affinity for growth magic."

Zarya regarded the trees with their bright green leaves and slender trunks. Juices were running down Amrita's chin, staining the fabric of her sari. When they were done, Vikram and Amrita approached the blackened Jai Tree, entering through the doors and disappearing inside.

Tarin, who waited at the entrance, followed behind.

"What happens now?" Zarya whispered to Yasen.

"Now, we wait. The transformation is a private affair."

"Have you seen this before?"

"No, Rani Vasvi was alive before I was born. We're actually very fortunate to be witnessing this." He said it with reverence, and Zarya was surprised to see this rare show of emotion.

As the door to the tree closed, the guests resumed their chatter. Platters of food were brought out on round silver plates, each ringed with a dozen depressions filled with a multihued variety of curries and chutneys, a stack of hot buttered roti and naan waiting in the center. One was placed in front of Zarya and Yasen in a cloud of spiced aromas.

"If one didn't know any better, I'd say you're rather moved by this whole thing, Commander," she teased.

"Don't call me that," he said before his eyes widened, and he shook his head, running a hand down his face.

She sat back, bemused by the outburst.

"Sorry," she said, touching his arm. "I... why not? What's wrong, Yas?"

"Nothing."

She watched him for a moment as he tore off a piece of bread and scooped up a mouthful of lentils. Obviously, something about his new role was bothering him.

"Do you seriously expect me to believe that?" she asked before he looked over at her and then returned to his food, ignoring her question. She knew there would be little point in forcing him to talk about it. He'd close up tighter than an underwater vault. She'd have to coax it gently out of him like winning over a scared bunny rabbit.

"So, are you going to tell me why Rabin is staring at you like he either wants to spank you or fuck you?" Yasen asked, his eyes flicking to the back of the courtyard, very clearly trying to change the subject as Zarya choked on her wine. She picked up the napkin lying across her lap and dabbed at her wet chin.

"He is not. Stop that."

"He most certainly is," he said, grinning. "So, you can tell me yourself, or I'll go over there and ask him."

Zarya widened her eyes. "You wouldn't."

Yasen offered her a smirk that dared her to try him.

"He isn't interested in either. Trust me." Zarya's face flamed as she buried it in her glass.

"Why? What happened? Don't make me go over there, Zee."

She couldn't bring herself to meet his gaze as she mumbled, "Because I practically threw myself at him, and he made it very clear he is *not* interested."

She definitely didn't add the part where she'd not only thrown herself at him but couldn't stop thinking about him. Okay, not just thinking *about* him but thinking about what it would be like if he touched her. Gods, she hoped he didn't have some secret mind-reading rakshasa magic she didn't know about.

Yasen's eyes widened, and he burst out laughing.

Zarya grabbed a pillow and buried her face in it.

"It was mortifying. I'm such an idiot."

Yasen was still laughing, his entire body shaking.

"It's not funny!" Zarya said but found herself smiling at him.

"These Ravana men are certainly your weakness, aren't they?" Yasen wiped a tear from his eye.

Her laugh was dry. "Tell me they don't have any more

brothers. Or a handsome cousin I could make a fool of myself with."

Still snickering, Yasen was now enjoying himself immensely.

"No more brothers that I know of, but there is a sister. As for cousins, I'm sure there are dozens scattered about. Maybe you're best asking for detailed family histories before you throw yourself at anyone else."

Folding her arms tightly, she slumped down in the cushions and pouted. Just a little bit.

Yasen glanced over at Rabin. "For what it's worth, he was the one who flew into a rage at Gopal when he had me and that vanshaj woman beaten."

Zarya recalled the horrid tale Yasen had shared with her the night Rani Vasvi had died. "He did?"

"Yeah, he was furious. He called Gopal an immoral piece of shit who was too in love with himself to hold the position of nawab right to his face. I thought Gopal was going to pop a vein."

She covered her face with her hands and groaned.

"So, you're telling me under that gorgeous but scary exterior is a man with a heart of gold?"

Yasen grinned. "Well, I didn't say that. But he is gorgeous, isn't he?" Yasen looked over to where Rabin was still staring at them. "I swear he got even better-looking while he was away."

"That isn't helping, Yasen." Zarya gave him a pointed stare, and he drew her in with an arm, giving her a squeeze.

"Also, he lied. He absolutely wants to do both."

"Whatever," Zarya mumbled, but something lightened in her heart.

"I'm right. I know that look. Trust me. He's ready to name his sword after you, and I don't mean the one on his back." As he turned towards Rabin and raised his glass in salute, Zarya picked up a pillow and smashed it into Yasen's face, spilling his wine down the front of his shirt.

"Hey!" he cried, reaching for a napkin to dab at himself.

"You deserved that," Zarya said.

Yasen shook his head, still chuckling.

"Didn't you once tell me that moody and brooding wasn't your type?"

"Oh, shut up," she said, and he laughed again.

At that moment, a hush fell over the courtyard as all eyes returned to the Jai Tree. The foot of the tree was no longer black. Whatever Amrita, Tarin, and Vikram were doing had started to take effect. The ruined trunk split and cracked, then fell away, leaving smooth, white bark behind. The dead pieces tumbled off and turned to dust.

White bark climbed up and up, spreading across the branches. As ash blew on the wind, flowers bloomed. Silver, gold, copper, and bronze. Huge, glossy, luminous blooms reflected in the moonlight. Hundreds of them burst to life, their fresh, sweet fragrance sweeping over the courtyard on a perfumed breeze.

After several minutes, the transformation was complete; the tree was even grander and more magnificent than before. Everyone in the courtyard burst into applause, tears streaming down faces, arms reaching out to embrace one another. Music began to play, and some of the attendees stood up to dance.

As everyone celebrated, the tree began to glow with silvery light before a cloud of translucent ribbons spun out of the floral canopy and lifted into the atmosphere. Zarya craned her neck to watch Amrita's magic swirl in the air before the thread broke apart and spread across the sky, spearing for the edges of Dharati and touching the city's walls. The net of silvery light illuminated their upturned faces.

The queen's magic grew brighter, small points of light racing along the ribs that formed the barrier of protection before they dimmed and then melted into the air. Everyone cheered as the protective magic surrounding them settled in place. The city was shielded once again.

"That was the most amazing thing I've ever seen," Zarya said.

Yasen blinked and turned to her with his usual sardonic grin. "I give it an eight out of ten."

With an eye roll, she leaned back into the cushions, watching the ongoing celebrations, but couldn't relax. Energy hummed along her bones. She sensed Rabin—that tug she always felt when he was near. He could deny it, but she wasn't imagining it. Zarya scanned the back of the courtyard to where he stood. Heat flared in her chest as their eyes locked, and Zarya wondered if Yasen might be right.

TWELVE

The sky-blue doors to the courtyard stood open as the citizens of Dharati streamed in on a river of joy. There was much to celebrate today. They had a new queen, and the protections over their city were back in place. Everyone could rest a little easier when they closed their eyes at night. The threat of the blight was still a constant presence, but Amrita had just provided them with some breathing space.

Everyone, perhaps, but Zarya, who couldn't get the strange image of that ghost army out of her head. Nor the conversation with the vanshaj woman who'd confirmed her sister had seen them, too. Something told her it was all connected to that forbidden sixth anchor. It all made her wonder if there were things about the vanshaj that had either been forgotten or conveniently repressed. They were, after all, the descendants of the Aazheri twins who'd once used the darkness with impunity.

Who could she ask for more information without drawing any undue attention to herself? Maybe she could talk to Row, though she was sure he would have told her if he'd suspected she carried the darkness. He'd laid all his cards on the table now, and there would be no reason to keep this from her.

She needed to do some research on her own. Now that her magic had been exposed and everyone knew she was Aazheri, perhaps she could ask permission to read the magic books kept inside the palace library. Maybe she'd talk to Amrita when fewer visitors besieged the queen's attention.

She surveyed her jubilant surroundings, the mood lifting the cloud that had been hanging over her for weeks. The courtyard had become a sight of merriment and celebration as the citizens of Dharati arrived to pay their respects to their new queen. They brought offerings of flowers and incense, gold and jewels, pieces of art, or whatever token they could afford, no matter how small. Their gifts gathered in piles along the walls, creating a mountain range of treasure.

Palace servants passed through the crowd, bearing trays of drink and food, while children screamed and laughed as they wove through the lines. It was a beautiful sight to behold. After the past week's events and the city's devastation, seeing people happy again was a welcome relief. At least for now.

Zarya did her best to enjoy the event as she wandered amongst the crowd, attempting to revel in the pleasure of their smiles and their joy. Despite the circumstances, this was a happy occasion, and everyone wanted to celebrate.

She also did her best not to notice another figure arrowing through the crowd with much more purpose, looking like he was searching for someone to interrogate over a fiery pit full of vipers. Rabin marched along wearing the same sleeveless leather kurta as last night, weapons strapped to his back and hips. Something about how he was staring everyone down like he owned this place set off a ripple of irritation.

"Will you stop it," she said, storming up to him. He came to a halt and looked down his nose. He was easily a head taller, and she did her best to stretch to her full height, consciously aware of how much bigger he was.

"Is there a problem, Princess?" he asked, his voice low and dangerous.

"Yes. Stop walking around here scaring everyone. These people have done nothing wrong."

"Who am I scaring?" he asked, sweeping out a hand just as a trembling family backed away, clearly trying to escape his notice.

"Those people." She pointed to the family, whose eyes widened as if they couldn't believe she'd just singled them out.

"They're not scared," Rabin said. "Are you scared?"

He stepped towards them, and they backed up, the mother picking up a small child that had just started wailing as if a hideous fanged monster had crawled out from under his bed.

Rabin turned back to Zarya, and she gave him a pointed look, drawing out a scowl.

"I'm ensuring the new rani and her steward are safe," he said, folding his arms over his chest. "And the nawab. Anyone could just walk in here, meaning them harm."

"You hate your father," Zarya said, not entirely sure if that was true, but she surmised it was a good guess after all of Rabin's accusations.

"That's none of your business, Princess," he snarled.

"Stop calling me that."

"What? Princess? Does that bother you?"

"You know that's not what I am."

"Hmm," he said, eyeing her up and down. "No, you're definitely not that."

"What is *that* supposed to mean?"

His mouth stretched into a smile, but there was nothing amused or friendly about it. It was the self-satisfied smile of a predator stalking a mouse across an open field.

"Nothing," he said before he turned and walked away, effectively dismissing her.

Zarya huffed and then turned in the opposite direction. She needed a break from the crowd and the heat of the sun, anyway. She entered the palace and made her way through the cool halls, finding herself in the garden where she often practiced fighting with Yasen.

Today, it stood empty. She pulled out the book she'd tucked into the back of her pants, deciding an adventure into her favorite story might help settle this constant churn of worry in her gut. She settled on a fountain edge and flipped it open, losing herself in the comfort of the familiar words.

Though she'd probably read it at least a hundred times, it was still her favorite. She became too engrossed to notice the footsteps approaching until he was upon her, a shadow darkening her page. Zarya flinched as she looked up, finding Rabin with a deep glower on his face.

What the hell was he doing here? Did he follow her? She looked down and tried to continue reading, hoping he'd take the hint and go away. She would do everything she could to feign disinterest, as though her entire body wasn't reacting to his presence.

Refusing to acknowledge him, she flipped the page with enough force to nearly tear it out.

"What are you doing?" he asked, but she continued ignoring his looming presence. When he didn't appear to be taking the hint, she slapped the book on the ledge and stood, folding her arms over her chest.

"What does it *look* like I'm doing? What happened to keeping your precious father safe? Shouldn't you be in the courtyard terrorizing another poor family?"

The sizzle of his silent glare practically singed the hairs on her arms.

"Argh," she cried and threw up her hands, storming past him.

"Wait," he called. "You forgot this."

She whirled to find him now holding her book, a triumphant gleam filling his eyes.

"Give it to me," she said, holding out her hand, but he backed up, flipping the pages.

"Give me that!" she screeched, knowing she sounded shrill, but she didn't care. "What are you? Five?"

"His hand slipped under the silk of her nightgown, his fingers burning trails up her thighs," he read in his deep voice. *"Her breath hitched in her chest as her nipples turned into peaks of ecstasy."*

He raised an eyebrow and looked at Zarya with a smirk.

"Is this what you're reading out here?"

"That is none of your business," she said, folding her arms and straightening her shoulders. She had nothing to be embarrassed about.

He flipped the page and continued reading. *"His tongue slipped over her heated sex, swirling over her nub of pleasure, making her moan."*

Zarya swallowed the knot in her throat as a gush of heat flared between her thighs at his deep voice reading those words out loud. She was not imagining his tongue anywhere in her heated-nub-of-pleasure vicinity. No, she was not.

"*Nub* of pleasure? This is very scandalous, Princess," he said.

She placed a hand on her hip and made a dismissive gesture. "I didn't know what it was about. I just picked it up somewhere."

"This is underlined and highlighted, with little stars and hearts," he replied. "And, look, your name is written inside the front cover."

"Oh, shut up," she snapped. "Give that back immediately."

He circled around the back of the fountain, still reading.

"I think I'm enjoying this, though."

He flipped the page. *"His enormous member felt like a rod*

of iron silk," he read. "*He thrust it inside her wet channel as she let out a breathy sigh.*"

Zarya growled low in her throat from anger and irritation and also an inconvenient flare of arousal. Somehow, her daydreams had never included someone *else* reading these passages to her.

Fine. She'd take it if he wouldn't give it back. As she withdrew her sword, the zing of steel drew his attention towards her.

"Give it to me," she said, pointing it at him.

He closed the book and tucked it into the back of his pants.

"Care for a friendly duel, Princess?" he asked, baring his teeth in the least friendly way possible. "If you win, then I'll return it?"

"And if you win?"

"Then you'll tell me how you created the dream forest."

She rolled her eyes. He was obsessed with this. Obviously, there was no way she could back down from this challenge. There would be no living with him if she did. Not that there was really any living with him, anyway.

She lowered her sword and eyed him down. "You think you can handle me?"

"Oh, I'm pretty sure I can," he said, cracking the knuckles of his left hand.

He didn't give her any more warning before he yanked his sword from where it was anchored on his back and launched, but she was ready. If there was anything Row had taught her, it was to always be prepared for an attack when a man looked at her like that.

Steel clashed in the silence of the garden, the satisfying sound ringing in the air. Their blades met with enough force to send vibrations up her arm.

Not surprisingly, Rabin was quick as lightning as they parried, his movements smooth as smoke. Zarya ducked and lunged, trying to evade the slicing edge of his blade.

"Are you trying to kill me?" she hissed as their blades crashed against each other so hard it nearly threw her off balance.

"I thought you'd been trained," he said, swiping out and narrowly missing her thigh.

"I have."

"Then prove it, Princess."

He continued attacking, giving her no space for breath as his sword moved like it had a mind of its own. It was so fast she could barely see it.

She grunted as she dropped, feeling the swish of his blade so close to her ear a few small hairs sheared away, scattering in the air. Moving around the garden, they fought, neither of them willing to concede or give up the advantage.

But he was larger and stronger and obviously knew what he was doing.

He forced her back, but her steps were quick and sure, and she managed to press him in the opposite direction for a few beats. He snarled and advanced, forcing her to retreat, their blades moving like liquid as they countered back and forth.

Zarya was tested to her limit. She'd been training almost her entire life, and while it was clear she still had things to learn, she would not let him take the upper hand. She would not go down without fighting with everything she had.

Rabin pressed harder, his movements almost impossible to track, until she advanced, ducking as he swung his blade. She thrust, and her blade met flesh as she nicked him on the bicep, paring through his skin.

The draw of blood stilled their movements, his gaze falling to where it oozed down his arm, and Zarya did her best to contain her triumphant smile. It wasn't proper to celebrate injuring your opponent.

"I thought you could handle me," she said, trying not to

sound winded. Her chest expanded with tight breaths; her fore-head beaded with sweat.

Rabin rolled his neck and then arched a dark eyebrow before he launched at her, and she swore he was moving even faster now.

"Bring it, Princess," he snarled, and why did that cause a conflicted shiver to erupt in the very pit of her stomach and between her legs?

He spun around and swung as Zarya caught his blade, the crash echoing off the pavers and slicing through the quiet morning. They moved around the garden, dodging over flower boxes, fountains, and benches, trying not to trip.

Still, they fought, and Zarya was starting to tire, wondering how long they'd keep at this.

"How did you create the forest?" he asked again. "How did you bewitch me into coming there?"

"I don't know!" she said. "I didn't do any of that!"

"You're lying," he said.

"I'm not. Why would I lie?"

"Because you're hiding something," he snarled, and then Rabin struck, catching her in the thigh. His blade sliced through fabric and skin, and she gasped as she stumbled, her heel catching the edge of a flowerbed.

Rabin circled her sword, knocking it from her hand, before she tripped over her feet, crashing into the garden wall. He was on her a moment later, his front pressed to her back and her palms flat against the surface.

Neither of them moved as their breaths sawed in and out. She felt every inch of him against her—his hard chest and thighs. The slab of his stomach. The heat of his breath tickling the hairs on her neck. She was frozen in place, ignoring the ache in her leg, feeling the warmth of blood dripping down her knee. The sensation was nothing but a sneeze compared to the intensity of his body lined with hers.

"Do you concede defeat?" he asked.

"I concede nothing." She gritted her teeth as he moved in closer, forcing her cheek against the stone.

"Yield," he said, his voice a strained snarl, his hand bunching under the yoke of her braid, his fingers lightly digging into her scalp.

"Never," she said as she pressed against him. He was too strong for her to move out of his hold, and even if she did, how far would she get? "Let. Me. Go."

"You're already hurt," he said. "And you will never best me. *Yield.*" The command in his tone nearly made her relent. Something about the way he was so damn bossy made her thighs clench as she imagined them in this same position but maybe with far less clothing between them.

Gods, what was wrong with her? He'd stolen her book, threatened her, and literally just sliced open her leg, but he also hadn't coddled her. He'd treated her like a worthy opponent, and she would prove she'd earned that title.

"I'm fine. What do you care?"

He said nothing for a moment before he dropped his hand, his fingers wrapping around her hip as they dug into her bone. Her stomach flipped as she suppressed a groan borne of a confusing combination of aches. The sweep of his thumb over the sliver of her exposed skin nearly had her knees buckling. Thank the gods she had this damn wall holding her up.

"You want to keep fighting, Princess?" he asked, speaking directly in her ear, so close that his warm breath snaked down the line of her throat and crept lower.

"Yes," she squeaked, hoping he didn't notice the way this was affecting her. "I want my book back. And I want an apology for stealing it in the first place."

"You're okay?" he asked, and she frowned. He said the words with anger like he was mad at himself for asking them.

"I'm fine."

There was another paused breath before he finally pulled away, releasing her from the sphere of his overwhelming presence. Maybe a part of her was disappointed, but she wasted no time, diving for her sword and then pointing it at him.

Their blades clashed again, and they fought until Zarya nearly collapsed with exhaustion. She sunk on the edge of the fountain, her chest heaving in and out, a stitch pinching her ribs.

"Fine," she panted. "I yield."

She clutched her chest and let her blade fall to the ground, her head hanging between her legs. Sweat ran down her temple and dripped off the edge of her nose.

Rabin stood over her, and she looked up, expecting to find him gloating, but he watched her with an emotionless expression, his dark eyes sparking with those dazzling golden flecks.

He reached behind him and dropped her book on the edge of the fountain.

"Get that cut on your leg examined by Koura," he ordered before turning on his heel and storming away.

"Yeah, fuck you, too!" Zarya yelled at his back.

THIRTEEN

Zarya stood in front of the mirror in her bedroom, examining the patch of blue and purple mottled skin spreading over her hip and thigh. The slice where Rabin had cut her had been bandaged and still ached. She hadn't bothered with the infirmary, maybe for no other reason than to be contrary to his demand. She could decide for herself what injuries needed tending.

Instead, she'd limped back to the haveli, cleaned up her leg, and collapsed on the bed.

Some kind of primal energy had taken hold of her during their fight, scorching through her blood. She couldn't stop. She wouldn't stop. They'd thoroughly bludgeoned one another, and she hoped Rabin was in a similarly bruised state. Unless he was made of iron, he had to be wearing some evidence of their fight.

She'd used every single trick Row had taught her, holding nothing back. It rankled that she had been the one to yield first, but she'd had nothing left.

She could still hear his random accusations of her so-called deception. The demands to know how she'd created the forest, over and over. Asking how she'd brought him there. If only she knew the answer to any of those questions. Was it her? He seemed so sure.

Or was he trying to trick her? Maybe he had been the one to create all of it. That didn't seem possible, though—he was so angry about it.

Zarya gently prodded the bruise and winced. Her muscles screamed as she limped to her bathroom, gasping in agony as she stripped off her clothes, now stiff with dried sweat. She wrinkled her nose at her own filth, but she hadn't been able to move after she'd collapsed on the bed last night.

She ran a hot bath, hoping to loosen her tense muscles. When she was done, she dressed in her light Khada training uniform and went to raid the kitchen. She was due at Ambar Fort but hadn't eaten since yesterday, and her head swam with lightheadedness.

The house appeared empty. Row and Aarav were off doing whatever they did when they weren't home. *Home.* It was strange how quickly they'd fallen into this new routine. She'd spent her entire life with them keeping tabs on her, and now they were finally treating her like she was her own person.

She noted the new runes marked at various spots around the house, on the walls and doors, realizing that while Row might have cut her noose, he was still very much aware of where she was. She was warming to the idea that his protection was less about caging her and more about caring for her. Maybe she could learn to live with that. It's what a parent would do, after all.

Once she'd eaten, she headed through the bustling streets of Dharati and towards Ambar Fort. Zarya's gaze traveled up to the canopy of flowers courtesy of Amrita and the magic protecting them all. She sensed a lightness in the city's mood they hadn't felt in a while.

The fighting yards emanated the same carefree aura, the

sounds of laughter and chatter mingled with the strike of steel and the grunts and sighs of a strenuous bout of training.

Given the aching in her body, she skirted past the fighting rings, wincing at the idea of holding a sword. When she spotted a group of rakshasas practicing their magic, she headed in their direction.

She studied their target practice for a few moments as they sent out streams of that same coppery light she'd seen Rabin and Vikram use. Another faced the wall with her hands held up as thick vines crawled down from the top edge.

Professor Dhawan sat along the wall on a crate, his hands resting on the cane positioned between his legs. She walked over and leaned against the wall, sliding down to the ground to watch the rakshasas train.

"Are there no Aazheri in Daragaab's army?" Zarya asked a moment later, and Dhawan glanced down at her.

"No. Only a handful have made homes at this end of Rahajhan."

Zarya watched as a rakshasa male placed his hand on the earth, concentrating until it began to rumble, and a tree sprouted up from nowhere, cracking through the ground a moment later.

"Wow," Zarya said, and Dhawan chuckled.

"I presume you are here to practice as well?" he asked, and she nodded.

"I am, but I'm not sure where to begin. During the ajakava attack, I tried to use my nightfire again, but my magic sort of tipped, and the only thing I could do was summon regular old fiery fire."

Dhawan smiled and then gestured for her to stand. "Then get on your feet. Let's see what we can do."

Zarya did as he asked, dusting off the back of her pants. "Is it okay to do here? What if someone sees it?"

"They've all seen it," he reminded her, and she nodded.

Dhawan heaved himself up, and the pair walked to the center of the training area. He faced her and wrapped a hand around one of her shoulders.

"Close your eyes," he said, and her lids fluttered closed. "Imagine your magic like a series of building blocks, one stacking on top of the other. You want to feel the pieces of a puzzle falling into place. Not all the blocks are the same size, though. If you want to douse a flame, you might have a larger box of air and a smaller one of water."

Zarya's brows pinched together as she tried to envision what he was describing, but her magic felt nothing like blocks. It was fluid and formless, more like ribbons tying together.

"Are you sure about that?" she asked, opening one eye. "My magic doesn't seem to... go that way."

"Of course I'm sure," he said with the confidence of an old man used to being listened to. "I've trained hundreds of young Aazheri."

"I thought you were a language professor. And a diplomat for the royal family," she said.

"I've lived many lives, girl."

She didn't care for the condescending twist in the word "girl," but she let it slide. He was trying to help her, after all.

She attempted to do what he asked but had no idea how to shape her ephemeral whisps of magic into something as rigid as blocks. As she kept trying, he encouraged her with tips and tricks that were anything but helpful.

She let out a breath of frustration.

"Professor, I really think my magic is different. I thought Aazheri used different patterns to channel their magic?"

"Not in this case," Dhawan said. "While that's true, the fundamentals are the same. You want to avoid developing bad habits, or you'll regret it when you move into the more complicated spells."

She chewed on her lower lip, trying again, but everything felt awkward and off-kilter.

"Try aiming there," Dhawan said, turning her to face one of the targets the rakshasas had been using.

"But I—"

"Just try," he insisted.

She nodded, still attempting to do what he asked, but she distinctly remembered balling her magic into a knot when she'd used her nightfire. Perhaps her memories of that night were clouded, though. She hadn't been thinking straight. And besides, when she'd tried the same thing on the ajakava, it hadn't worked, so maybe he had a point.

A blast of magic shot from her hands—another bolt of fire that struck the target and bounced off, hitting the wall. It ricocheted across the training yards, skimming over everyone's heads as people shouted, "Duck!" and "Watch out!"

Suvanna, who stood on the far end of the courtyard, rescued the soldiers with a splash of water, dousing the flame into a sprinkle of harmless mist. Everyone turned to see who had nearly lit them all on fire, and Zarya wished she could crawl into the ground like a worm.

"Sorry," she whispered and then waved like a complete fool. They turned away a moment later to resume their training, but not before Zarya nearly perished from mortification.

"I'm not sure this is working," she said to Dhawan, who laid a hand on her shoulder.

"Keep trying. You'll get it soon enough. I'm happy to help you any time—just send for me in the palace."

"The palace? You're not living in your cottage anymore?"

"I thought it best to be closer to the library so I'm able to continue looking for information about the blight."

Zarya glanced towards the busy fighting yards, feeling a few lingering stares directed her way.

"That makes sense," she said, turning back to Dhawan.

"I'll only be leaving to tend to my garden from time to time," he said.

"Your garden?" She wondered what was so important about a few flowers when the world was falling down around them.

The corners of Dhawan's eyes crinkled with his smile. "My flowers are very important to me. They've kept me company through many lonely times." He clapped her shoulder again. "Get yourself something to eat. I hear they're serving paneer pakora."

Dhawan gestured towards the fort and the small canteen that served the soldiers coffee, tea, water, and other various snacks throughout the day. Her stomach rumbled as the smells wafted towards her.

She stepped over the threshold and surveyed the room full of soldiers, taking a break at small wooden tables.

"Ooh. Ooh. Steward, I see an arrrrrmmyyyyy..." came a mocking voice, and Zarya's attention turned to a member of the Khada, recognizable by his uniform, with his back to the door. "They're made of ghooosts."

He held up his hands and wiggled his fingers, and everyone around him burst out laughing. It took her a moment to realize they were mocking... *her*.

"Oh, oh," continued the Khada, "I can't control my magic." Then, he feigned someone stumbling as they threw out a hand, mimicking her earlier mistake with her fire.

Rooted to the spot, her ears grew warm, her neck flushing with heat. Her gaze met with a soldier who sat in a chair, looking up at her. He wore a line of tattooed stars around his neck, and she saw something reflect in his eyes. A secret code that transmitted between them. He'd seen the ghost army, too.

The room had fallen silent as every eye turned towards Zarya, guilt coloring their expression.

"You idiot," someone snarled, and she turned to find Aarav stalking towards the bully. "Shut your mouth." Aarav grabbed the man's collar and dragged him towards the door. Zarya stepped out of the way as Aarav hurled the soldier to the ground. "This is not the behavior of a Khada."

Aarav spat on the ground, narrowly missing the man's head. "Get out of here before I explain to the general what a disgrace you are."

The soldier scrambled back as Aarav hunched over him with fury in his eyes. Then, he flipped over and scurried away as Aarav straightened and turned to Zarya.

"Sorry. I hope you don't mind. He's always such a little prick. He had that coming."

Zarya nodded slowly. "No. It's okay." She bit her cheek. "Did you... just defend me?"

Suddenly, Aarav seemed embarrassed by his actions as he rubbed the back of his neck. "Yeah, I did." He shrugged and grinned. "You would have done the same."

She would have. Maybe not once upon a time, but things had changed for them.

"I would have kicked his ass until he was black and blue," she said with sincerity. "I guess we'll call this even for the ajakava attack."

Aarav turned serious. "Zarya, you saved my life that night. This doesn't make us even at all."

She nodded and swallowed, trying not to cry. Yasen would be mortified.

"Thank you," she said, meaning those words more than she ever had in her life.

"C'mon." Aarav slung an arm around her neck and directed her back to the canteen. "Let's get some pakoras before they're all gone."

FOURTEEN

After her humiliation in the fighting yards, Zarya requested a leave of absence from her Khada duties for a few days. Not because she couldn't face the others, but because her mind was filled with too many opposing thoughts, and it was obvious her training was suffering from a lack of concentration. She wouldn't do anyone any favors until she sorted some things out.

Today, that thing would be the presence of the demon army plaguing her dreams. The young vanshaj man in the canteen had seen them, too. She was sure that's what she'd read on his face.

She had to find the woman who'd confronted her after the ajakava attack. When she entered the palace, she asked around until finally, someone directed Zarya towards her.

When the woman saw her approaching, she stood, regarding Zarya with wariness.

"I'm sorry to bother you," Zarya said. "Can I speak with you alone for a moment?"

The woman nodded as she tightened the dupatta over her head, and the two of them retreated to a private corner.

"I didn't ask your name last time," Zarya said.

"It's Mahi."

"It's nice to meet you, Mahi. I'm Zarya."

The woman blinked, clearly on her guard.

"Will you tell me where your sister lives?" Zarya asked, and Mahi's face drained of color.

"Why?"

"Because I'd like to ask her about what she saw."

The woman shook her head, opening her mouth, but Zarya cut her off.

"Please. I won't tell anyone else, but I need to speak with her. I promise not to get her into any kind of trouble."

The woman hesitated, and Zarya waited, hoping Mahi would sense her desperation and her sincerity.

"You swear not to hurt her?"

"Of course I do. I wouldn't let anything happen."

"Fine," the woman said, digging out a scrap of paper and a pencil from a pocket. She scribbled an address on it and handed it to Zarya. "Her name is Meera. Tell her I sent you."

"Thank you," Zarya said.

She took the paper, scanned it, and then nodded to Mahi before she went in search of Yasen. She had to talk to someone about this, and wouldn't mind some company during this task.

She found him at Ambar Fort, overseeing the day's training.

"Can you take a break?" she asked. "I need you to come somewhere with me."

She handed him the paper with Meera's address, and his eyebrow arched.

"What do you need in the vanshaj quarter?"

"I'll explain on the way."

Yasen blew out a breath, rubbed a hand down his face, and then pushed himself away from the post where he was leaning. He shouted some orders to a lieutenant to take over.

"Okay, let's go."

"Thank you," she said as they headed into Dharati's streets.

While they walked, she explained to him what had happened with Mahi.

"And what does this have to do with anything?" he asked. She hadn't told him about the sixth anchor yet. She wasn't ready to reveal it to anyone—even someone she trusted.

"I'm not sure," she said. "But I need to talk to someone else who saw them. It might be important."

Yasen shrugged as though he wasn't sure about that, but he led her towards her goal, anyway.

"This way," he said as they turned a corner and passed under a stone archway. Zarya wasn't surprised to find the vanshaj quarter in a state of dilapidation compared to the rest of the city. Here, narrow wooden buildings that looked like they might topple at the slightest breeze sagged against one another, everyone living stacked like crates in a cellar.

She wondered why anyone thought this was acceptable. She wasn't sure if Amrita intended to do something about this, but surely she didn't condone it? Signs of poverty were evident everywhere, rail-thin children running about wearing little clothing, their bones as sharp as razors.

"This is..." Zarya said softly, trailing off.

"I know," Yasen said.

"Why don't they do something about this?"

"Old prejudices run deep," he said.

She gave him a sharp look. "Surely, people aren't that blind."

They wound through the run-down streets, unable to avoid the haunted eyes of the passers-by.

"The nobility barely considers the vanshaj as human. I don't think it even occurs to them to do anything about this."

"Did Amrita never voice her desire to do something about this during your talks?" Zarya asked.

"She did, but she's different now that she's queen."

"You mean she's just like Vasvi."

He nodded. "That is my fear."

Zarya pressed her lips together but said nothing as they continued.

Yasen consulted the note from Mahi.

"Over there," he said, pointing to a tiny house made of weathered grey boards, built with no fanfare—just a tiny box with bare, uncovered windows.

Zarya knocked on the thin plank door and waited with Yasen a step behind her. She heard a shuffle on the other side before the door popped open.

A young woman wearing the uniform of Daragaab's army opened it, her gaze narrowing as she looked Zarya over.

"Yes?" she asked.

"Are you Meera?"

Her gaze tapered at the question.

"Why?"

"Your sister told me where to find you."

"Why would she do that?"

Zarya looked around, ensuring no one was listening.

"She told me what you saw. Nairrata. The demon army."

Meera growled low in her throat, but it died out as her eyes widened when she looked over Zarya's shoulder.

"Commander," she said, bowing her head. "I'm sorry. I didn't see you there."

"It's fine," Yasen said, the lines around his mouth tight. "This is a... social call?"

He looked to Zarya for confirmation, but she wasn't really sure how to describe the reason for their presence.

"Please come in," Meera said, obviously reluctant.

"I'm sorry," Zarya replied. "We'll only be a minute."

The tiny home was depressingly bare. A pallet on the floor. A tiny kitchen with a few battered pots hanging on hooks. A single small table with three chairs, where another soldier sat, eyeing them with mistrust.

"That's Hari," Meera said as she gestured towards him. "Have a seat."

Zarya gingerly took an empty chair, afraid the rickety frame would collapse under her weight.

"Commander," Meera said, gesturing to the third one.

Yasen waved a hand. "I'll stand. You sit."

Meera clearly didn't like the sound of that, either, but she acquiesced, settling into the chair.

"I'm Zarya," she said. "And that's—" She waved a hand, suddenly nervous. "You know who he is, I guess."

"Yeah," Hari said. "Who are *you*, exactly?"

"I'm—" She wrinkled her nose and looked at Meera. "Is it okay to talk about this?"

"Oh, you mean him?" Meera said, gesturing to Hari. "Yeah, he's cool."

Zarya nodded. "I wanted to ask about what you saw," she said.

Meera clasped her hands on the table, looking down at them.

"It was... an army," she said. "But... they weren't solid. I don't think they were real."

"Anything else? Did they move? Or say anything?"

She shook her head.

"No. They just stood there, staring at the city. Did you see something else?"

"It was the same for me," Zarya said, dejected by Meera's response. "Have you ever seen anything like that before?"

Meera rolled her neck. "Sometimes, when I'm on patrol in the swamps, I see things the others don't."

"You do?" Zarya leaned forward. "What?"

Meera shrugged. "Monsters. Demons. But they're like that army—not entirely there. More like shadows of what they might be."

Zarya swallowed the tension building in her throat. A

memory surfaced from many years ago when the blight had started spreading. She'd been with Row, examining the rot, when she'd seen something in the bushes.

She'd pointed to it, but Row had claimed he'd seen nothing, and when she went to search, it was already gone. Part of her thought her mind must be playing tricks, but now she wondered if there had been more to it. Over the years, she spent plenty of time alone in the swamp, exploring as far as her tether would allow, but had she seen things others couldn't?

"What about you?" Zarya asked, addressing Hari. "Do you see things, too?"

"No," he replied. "I haven't seen anything."

Zarya considered Meera's claim. What did this mean? Zarya stared at the line of tattoos ringing Meera's neck. The mark that was supposed to keep her magic contained.

"Do you ever feel... something?" Zarya asked, lowering her voice as though someone might hear her.

"Something?" Meera asked.

"Magic." Zarya breathed the word, which hung suspended in the air like a beacon and a warning.

"I don't know what magic feels like," Meera said, though Zarya sensed Meera wasn't being entirely truthful about that.

Zarya touched her chest. "It's like a burning here." She then moved her fingers to her forehead, remembering what Row had said about Aazheri feeling their anchors in different places. "Or here."

Meera placed her hand flat against her heart. She blinked her dark eyes once, twice, three times like her eyelashes were coated in mud.

"Maybe," she said, so low that Zarya could barely hear her.

Yasen made a sound of surprise, and everyone looked at him.

"You can't tell anyone that," Yasen said, his expression

fierce. "If anyone knew you could feel magic, your life would be over."

"I know that," Meera said, her eyes going dark. "I don't know what my sister was thinking when she told you this."

"It's okay," Zarya said. "We won't tell anyone. I promise. Your secret is safe with us."

Yasen nodded his assent, but Meera's shoulders remained hunched to her ears.

"Can you tell me what you feel?" Zarya asked. "Please."

Meera shrugged and then picked at a splinter on the rough wooden table.

"It's nothing much, but sometimes it feels like it's... sparkling inside me? I can't think of any way else to describe it. It feels like something is trying to break free."

"Can you perform any spells?" Zarya asked. "Have you ever tried to use it?"

Meera's gaze shifted between Zarya and Yasen, her brow lowered.

"It's okay," Zarya said. "I swear that nothing you say here leaves this room."

"I have," she replied, her voice shaking. "I know I shouldn't, but it burns inside me. Sometimes, it hurts." Tears began to fill her eyes, and Zarya reached over to clasp Meera's hands.

"I'm sorry. I wish... there was something we could do," Zarya said as she eyed the tattoos around the woman's neck. Here was another mystery to solve—had anyone ever success-fully removed these marks? Were there vanshaj who had escaped this noose?

"What do you think it means?" Meera asked. "That I saw them, too?"

Zarya shook her head. "I'm not sure, but I'm determined to find out."

"Why?"

"Someone kept me from my magic once, too. And there's a reason that you and I can see it."

Meera pressed her lips together and nodded. "Are you... like me? Vanshaj? How did you escape this life?"

"I'm not sure," Zarya said. "I don't really know who I am."

Meera studied Zarya's face as if searching for a lie. When she didn't find one, she nodded.

"Can I ask you something else?" Zarya asked.

"What?"

"May I touch it? Your tattoo?"

Surprisingly, Meera didn't appear taken aback at the invasive suggestion.

"Go ahead," she whispered and lifted her chin.

Zarya reached out and gently touched the side of Meera's throat, her fingers tracing the line of stars. Her magic stirred in her chest, simmering like it was luxuriating in the heat of a sunbeam. It stretched towards Zarya in the most disconcerting way, like it was trying to claim something it had lost.

"At night, when I lie awake, it grows warm," Meera said. "It tingles. Sometimes, I wonder if it's... alive."

Their eyes met, the moment churning with bottomless depths of... what? An understanding and a connection that neither of them understood but invariably bound them. Zarya pulled her hand away as she rubbed the tips of her fingers together.

"Thank you," Zarya said. "I'm sorry we interrupted your day."

"If you discover anything, will you come back and tell me?" Meera asked. There was a thread of hope in her voice that made Zarya's heart twist. She hoped she hadn't put ideas in this woman's head that could never come to pass.

"Of course," Zarya said.

After they said their goodbyes, Zarya and Yasen left the house and headed towards the palace.

"What do you make of all that?" Yasen asked.

Zarya looked over at him. "I don't know. I wonder who else can feel what she does?" She told him about the man in the canteen, as well. "Those two guards who abandoned their posts on the watchtower that night. Were they vanshaj?"

"One of them was," Yasen said, and that further confirmed her theories.

But theories of what, exactly?

"That might explain why they left." Zarya scanned the people passing by as though she might be able to tell simply by looking at them. "Have you ever heard of anything like this before?"

"No," Yasen said. "But any vanshaj who feel a connection to magic would keep that secret."

"What would happen if someone found out?" she asked, already knowing she would hate the answer.

Yasen's expression was grim. "I imagine they'd be killed on the spot."

Zarya said nothing to that as they wound their way through the streets and exited the vanshaj quarter. She chewed on her lip, spiraling into her thoughts. A shop caught her eye when they were a few blocks from the palace.

She stopped, staring at the open storefront that sold a variety of fighting leathers. She'd abandoned all her training gear when she left the cottage all those months ago and had never owned anything as nice as this.

"We're going shopping?" Yasen asked, catching the direction of her stare.

She approached the store, running her fingers over the soft leather of a black, corseted vest. "They're beautiful."

"Can I help you?" asked the man behind the counter.

"I'd like this," she said, pointing to the garment she'd just touched. "And those." She pointed to a pair of leather pants.

"Of course. Would you like to try them on?"

Zarya followed the shopkeeper into a dressing room while Yasen grumbled about having to wait.

"Then leave," she said through the curtain.

"It's fine," he said, and she heard him sit in the chair positioned outside with a thwump. "Just hurry your ass up, Swamp Girl."

"Keep it up, and I'll try on every item in the store. And then do it all again, just for good measure."

He chuckled, and she exhaled a deep breath, focusing on sliding on the boots she'd chosen, trying to shake off the worst of the creeping apprehension after her encounter with Meera. The woman could feel her magic, even if it was rooted deep, and that meant something important. She was sure of it.

Finally, Zarya was dressed. She stepped out of the changing room and spun in front of the mirror, admiring herself.

"What do you think?" Zarya asked, and the corner of Yasen's mouth lifted.

"Not bad, Zee. You look like you might be able to beat me in a fight wearing that."

She rolled her eyes and then dug into her old clothing, procuring some coins she'd earned from her job with the Khada.

"I'll just wear them out," Zarya said before she turned to look in the mirror again, smoothing her hand over her stomach and feeling the weight of these mysteries squatting heavy on her shoulders. They were winding around her, forming a labyrinth of dead ends and dangerous traps. Could she find her way through?

After they were finished, they entered the street, walking side by side.

When they passed Ambar Fort, Yasen gestured to his right. "I'd better get back." The look on his face was grim, like this wasn't a task he was looking forward to.

"What's wrong, Yasen?" she asked, stopping and touching his arm. "Is this about your new role?"

She didn't want to push him, but he looked so unhappy right now. He sighed.

"Nothing. I'm fine."

"Very believable," she deadpanned, and that won her a small smile.

"It's only temporary, right? Until he finds someone better to fit the position. That was our agreement."

"You know you're more than capable of doing this, right?" she asked.

"Maybe. But the point is that I don't *want* to." He thumbed behind him. "Anyway. Where are you off to?"

"To see Amrita," she said. Zarya wanted to investigate everything she'd learned further, and she had a good idea of where to start. "I want to ask for access to the magic books."

"Be careful, Zee," Yasen said. "If anyone finds out what you're doing, it could mean trouble."

"I'm always careful, Yas. You know that."

He rolled his eyes before she gave him a salute and turned to walk away, determined to chart a path through this maze.

FIFTEEN

Today, the Jai Palace courtyard stood empty, the gifts and tributes to Amrita scattered across the ground like the aftermath of a gilded avalanche.

These offerings would remain for another few days before anything that could be salvaged would be distributed to people in need, while the flowers would be tossed into the sea as an offering to the gods.

Zarya stood outside the high green doors, studying the stunning array of flowers and branches. While a level of normalcy had returned to the palace, it was only normal on the surface. A bandage over a festering wound. How long could they reasonably rely on the queen's magic to keep them safe?

She opened the door to the tree and stepped inside. The throne room had transformed, too. Instead of the mossy green of Rani Vasvi's domain, the floor was now black and white tiles, the walls made of white iridescent marble that shimmered in hues of soft purple and pink.

Up ahead was the dais where Amrita had now taken her place. Here, too, was a change—instead of brown branches and green leaves, there was shimmery white bark and foliage rendered into metallic pink and green and gold. The effect was stunning.

Vikram stood facing Amrita, and Zarya noted the handful of courtiers lounging in the space, seated on the divans pushed up against the rounded walls where food and drink sat on low tables surrounding them. They spoke in hushed tones, their conversations halting mid-gossip as they watched Zarya approach the queen.

"Hi," Zarya said, stopping behind Vikram, who turned and smiled.

He spread his arms in a warm gesture. "Zarya, it's nice to see you."

His gaze swept over her in a way that suggested it was more than just nice.

"How are things with you... two?" she asked, trying to ignore it. She didn't want to come between this steward and his queen, even if they claimed their relationship wasn't based on any romantic feelings. It felt wrong and... weird.

"We're doing well," he said. "Have you come to say hello?"

Zarya nodded and gazed up at Amrita, who was watching her now. Her big amber eyes held the same bright vacancy as before her transformation. What had happened to her? Had Rani Vasvi been this way? Still, everything about Amrita was overwhelming.

"Hi," Zarya said, suddenly shy in the presence of such a magnificent sight. Amrita was so wholly other from what she'd been. She stood so tall, just like Vasvi, her body one with the roots and branches that surrounded her. But she was still Amrita in her own unique way. Zarya could see the shape of her face and the warm expression she had come to know.

"How are you doing?" Zarya asked.

"She says she's doing well," Vikram said, and Zarya started, forgetting that Amrita couldn't actually answer her. "She's happy to see you."

Zarya stared at Amrita, thinking of the last conversation they'd had. Had Priya gotten her hands on that estate, or was Amrita still holding out? She wanted to talk to Amrita about Rabin and the wild encounter in the garden yesterday, but now, she couldn't.

She hadn't revealed anything about her connection with Rabin to Vikram and wasn't ready to do so yet. She wasn't sure what she owed him. They weren't technically involved and really never had been, but for a few kisses that had all happened under a cloud of secrecy.

Still, if she considered Vikram her friend, then she would have to reveal she had feelings for his brother, even if they weren't reciprocated. Realizing she could no longer confide in Amrita, Zarya brushed past these thoughts, getting to the matter that had brought her here in the first place.

"I was wondering if I could have your permission to access the magic books in the palace library?"

Amrita blinked, and there were several seconds of silence before Vikram asked, "Her Majesty would like to know why."

Zarya looked around the room, noticing the curious stares directed her way. She recalled Yasen's warning about vanshaj magic and knew she had to keep this confidential.

"Because I'd like to learn about my abilities. I'm hoping I can find out more about what... I'm capable of."

This part wasn't a lie, even if it wasn't the entire story. She sidestepped the phrase "nightfire," conscious of the need to keep it, if not secret, then at least hold some of the mystery from anyone outside the handful of people who already knew the truth. There were ears in this room, and she had no idea who was trustworthy.

Again, there were several beats of silence, and then Vikram answered, "Her Majesty agrees you may access the books for the purpose of learning more about your magic. She does ask that you not interfere with the efforts to learn more about the blight."

"Of course I won't," she said, offended by the insinuation. "Why would I do that?"

"It's important to the queen that all efforts are focused towards eradicating its presence."

Zarya looked up at Amrita, seeing something flash across her eyes. Pain?

"Does it hurt her?" Zarya asked. "To maintain the protection on the walls?"

"It can cause her some discomfort. She's still learning and sometimes has trouble holding onto the barrier," Vikram replied. "Thus, the sooner we find a solution, the better."

"So, we're still vulnerable?" she asked. Was it an oversight that Amrita's difficulty with her magic hadn't been mentioned earlier, or were they deliberately keeping this information from everyone?

"We're fine," he said. "Don't worry. They are but temporary breaches and are easily re-established."

"What about helping the vanshaj?" she asked. While Zarya didn't want to bring up vanshaj magic, she did want to address the deplorable conditions they'd witnessed earlier this afternoon.

Confusion flashed across Vikram's face. "What about them?"

"The vanshaj quarter is in pretty rough shape. Surely, you know that?"

He rubbed the space between his eyes. "Zarya, what is the point of this?"

She opened her mouth and then closed it before she found her voice. "The point is, Amrita said she wanted to make improvements on her mother's rule. This would be a good place to start."

"As I've just explained, we are busy with the blight, and

Amrita is focusing her energies on the city's protection. There has been an increase in attacks on the southern wall. The army is busy and already stretched thin, as are all our resources."

Vikram's eyes flicked to Amrita, and it was obvious they were conversing silently. Zarya resisted the urge to launch into an argument.

"Her Majesty agrees," he said a moment later. "You are not the first to come to us with this request, and we will address it when the time is right. For now, we must deal with the immediate threats to Daragaab's safety."

Vikram paused once again, listening to Amrita, while Zarya felt heat rising up her neck. Was Amrita already turning into her mother?

"She suggests you continue your weapons training and work with Row on your magic. That is how you can be most useful to her."

He then scribbled something onto a piece of paper and handed it to her. "This will give you access to the magic books in the library. Give it to the archivists."

Zarya stared up at Amrita, unable to believe her ears.

"That's it?"

"That is what she desires," Vikram said.

Amrita's expression remained neutral as she watched Zarya, but she had to know Zarya was angry with this inadequate response.

"Fine," Zarya said, accepting the note and shaking her head before she turned to leave.

"Zarya!" Vikram called, and she stopped.

"Can I come see you later?"

Zarya's lip curled. He was asking this right in front of the queen? In front of everyone watching them, waiting for a juicy tidbit to pass around like over-ripened fruit?

"No," she said curtly, feeling no need to add anything to temper her harsh response, and then turned and left the room.

* * *

Zarya strode through the palace, heading for the library, attempting to put the encounter in the throne room out of her head.

She needed to read more about the anchors and, more importantly, the dark magic that hummed inside her chest. She checked for her five-pointed star, assuring herself the sixth anchor remained safely tucked away.

The library was a swarming hive of activity when she arrived. Immediately, she spotted Professor Dhawan seated at a table surrounded by open books, his nose nearly touching a page that occupied his focus.

Dhawan looked up at her approach, sitting back.

"Zarya," he said. "What brings you here?"

She held up the note Vikram had handed her. "I've been granted permission to access the magic books. I was hoping I could learn more about my abilities."

He scanned her over as he folded his hands across his stomach. "Have you been practicing your building blocks?"

"Yes," she lied. There had been little opportunity to practice since his lesson, and she'd snuck in whatever time she could, but not the way he'd instructed her. Instead, she'd focused on the ribbons of her magic and had managed to channel small streams of nightfire. It wasn't perfect, but it was progress.

"Good, good," he said, nodding. "I'm glad to hear it. Let me know when you'd like to practice again."

"Sure," Zarya said.

"Have a seat," he said, gesturing to the table across from her.

She did as he asked, scanning the books laid out. Her eye snagged on a book of fables sitting open, and she dragged it over. She scanned the page, absorbing the familiar lines of the story of the Bayangoma birds.

"This was always my favorite story when I was a child," she said, flipping the page. This edition had been beautifully illustrated in splashes of color and edged with gold paint. "Row used to tell it to me all the time."

"Ah," Dhawan said, peering over. "That is a magical tale indeed. I've always liked the idea of the birds revealing secrets only to those who are deemed worthy. It seems very noble, doesn't it?"

"I wanted them to tell me who my parents were."

"You know there's a grove less than a week's journey from here?"

"I thought it was only a story," she said.

"It is not," he replied. "So few are successful in proving themselves worthy that the Bayangoma have been elevated to the status of myth."

Zarya breathed out a long sigh. All this time, it had been so close. But no matter how much she'd wanted it, Row would never have taken her, anyway.

"*A* grove? There's more than one?" she asked.

He nodded. "Indeed. There are a handful throughout the continent, though their exact locations are secret unless you know where to look."

"Do you know?" she asked, not sure why it mattered anymore. She knew who her parents were, and a twinge of nostalgia surfaced for this thing she'd craved so much throughout her childhood.

"I do," he answered.

"Maybe I'll visit someday."

"I think you should."

She looked over to meet Dhawan's understanding gaze and forced a tight smile. Sitting back, she eyed the narrow hallway where two attendants flanked the entry that guarded the magic books. These must be the archivists Vikram had mentioned.

"I'm going to go look around," Zarya said, and Dhawan

nodded. She approached the archivists and handed over her permission slip. One of them inspected it before gesturing her through.

She wandered into the narrow hall, scanning the titles. She didn't know what she was looking for but hoped something notable would jump out. Numerous titles about yakshi and rakshasa magic were interspersed with the occasional work about Aazheri, vidyadhara, and merdeva magic. On any other day, she'd be tempted to start from the beginning and read through every single one, but today, her search focused on answers about vanshaj magic. Perhaps unsurprisingly, she found nothing on the shelves.

At the end of the hall stood an iron gate molded into ornate lattices and secured with a massive lock. Beyond it were more books lining the walls. She approached it, pressing her face against the bars, peering into the dim alcove.

And then she heard it. *Whispers.* Something was calling her. She remembered the same sounds in the forest prior to the ajakava attack. They seemed to purr with the cadence of her name, beckoning her closer. Her hands wrapped around the bars, and she shook the door, rattling it on its hinges.

"Hey!" came a sharp voice—one of the archivists was peering down the hall. "Get away from there."

She spun around. "What are those?"

"*Those* are not for you," the archivist said.

"But I was granted access to the books of magic."

He snorted. "Not those you weren't."

Then, he turned away, dismissing her. She stared at the books behind the gate a bit longer before one of the archivists snapped his fingers, telling her to move it along. She huffed and continued scanning the remaining shelves, hoping something useful would present itself.

Professor Dhawan appeared in the archway, placing a book back on the shelf before selecting another one.

"Can you hold this for me?" he asked, flipping it open.

She nodded and held out her arms, and he laid the book across them. He then held up his hand and pulled a small dagger hanging from his belt. He dug the point into his finger as a drop of blood swelled on the tip.

Then, he placed it on the page and concentrated intently before a swirl of magic surrounded him. The words on his page melted away to be replaced by another set.

"What did you just do there?" she asked.

"Ah, translated the text," he said, retrieving the book from her. "This was written in a dialect I'm a bit rusty with."

"You can do that?"

"Yes," he nodded. "A drop of blood woven with a bit of spirit and some earth for the trees the pages are made of. Perhaps a bit of fire if it's an especially exciting tale."

"But I asked if you could translate a book for me when I visited your cottage."

"You did," he said, tapping the page and then flipping it. "But the effect is only temporary, and without magic of your own, it wouldn't have been much use to you. At the time, I didn't know you were Aazheri, so it did not occur to me to suggest it. Do you want me to show you how to do it now?"

Zarya thought of the book she always carried in her bag—the one containing her mother's picture that she'd stolen from Row all those months ago.

"No. I think I got the measure of it," she said, not entirely sure she wanted his help after that so-called training session with her nightfire. She would try to translate it herself.

Dhawan continued reading the book in his hand. Again, she heard the whispers, and she spun around, but of course, there was nothing. What lay beyond those gates?

"Can I ask you something?" Zarya asked, tearing her eyes away to face the professor again.

Dhawan's forehead pleated with a question. "Yes?"

"Can you tell me more about vanshaj magic?" she asked, and his frown deepened even further. He slapped his book shut.

"Why would you want to know about that?"

"I'm just curious," she said, carefully dancing around the questions she really wanted to ask. "If they were connected to the Ashvins, would they have some of their gifts? Are they Aazheri, too?"

"Why are you asking such questions?" he asked, his voice full of admonishment and maybe a touch of rage. "The vanshaj are forbidden from using their magic and are certainly *not* Aazheri. Who is putting these ideas in your head?"

"No one is. I can think for myself. And I know all that, but don't you think—"

His hand reached out to grab her wrist, gripping it tight enough that she winced.

"Do not speak of such things, girl," he said, his eyes flashing. "These are dangerous ideas that will get you killed. The vanshaj are broken. Wicked. Do not for one moment let their docility fool you into thinking otherwise. Their kind tore apart this world once, and if given the freedom, they'd do it again."

Now, Dhawan was shaking, his grip growing tighter on her arm.

"Okay," she said. "Professor. You're hurting me."

Immediately, his hold slackened, and he ran a hand through his hair.

"I'm sorry, my girl. I just... Please, be careful. Forget these ideas. This is not something to toy with. Do you understand me?"

Zarya rubbed her wrist and nodded, not sure what to make of his strange behavior. His eyes were warm and concerned now.

"Good," he said before flipping his book open once again. "Is there anything else I can help you find?"

"No," she said. "I've had a long day. I'm going home."

"Very well," he said. "I'd like to invite you for dinner one night so we might discuss your magic further."

"Sure," she said, still a bit shaken by the way he'd just reacted but didn't want to stoke his ire by turning him down.

"Excellent."

Dhawan turned, burying his nose in his book as she made her way to the exit. Before she left, she turned back.

"Professor?"

"Hmm?" He looked up.

"How are your flowers?"

He blinked and then smiled. "They're doing quite well. Thank you for asking."

She returned his smile and then left the room.

SIXTEEN

As Zarya headed for the haveli, she pulled the book with her mother's image out of her bag and flipped it open as she entered the house and slammed the door behind her.

Dhawan's reaction to her questions about the vanshaj hadn't been completely a surprise, given everything she knew, but that manic light in his eyes had thrown her off. Why was everyone being so... belligerent about this? Did people truly believe the vanshaj might cause them harm? Or was everyone too rooted in their prejudices to think logically?

Though her visit to the library hadn't turned up the answers she'd sought, she had at least learned something that might be useful. She placed Row's book on the counter and pulled a dagger from her boot. She pierced the tip of her finger to draw some blood and then concentrated, weaving a bit of spirit with a tendril of fire and earth, as Dhawan had explained.

Carefully, she touched her finger to the page of the book and watched as the words transformed, melting away and reforming in the common tongue. She let out a breath of surprise. She'd done that. All on her own. She was even more surprised to find the words were written in someone's neat scrawl and not printed, like a textbook or her beloved novels.

This was someone's personal diary or journal. Whose? She's stolen it from Row, so maybe his? Or what if it was her mother's?

"Zarya?" Row called from the other room. "Is that you?"

Shit. She hadn't realized he was home. She opened the nearest drawer and stuffed it inside just as Row appeared.

She spun around, hoping she didn't look as guilty as she felt.

"Hi," she said, her hands gripped behind her back.

"You okay?" Row asked, studying her quizzically.

"Sure." She pushed back the hair that was sticking to her sweaty forehead. "Just a little tired. It's been a wild few days."

"Of course," Row said. "You should get some sleep."

"Good idea."

Zarya waited, and Row watched her. Was he going to keep standing there?

"Anything else you need?"

"No." She folded her arms. "Are you going to bed soon, too?"

"Not yet. Apsara and Suvanna are headed over, so we can catch up for a bit."

A knock sounded at the door, and Row moved past her to open it.

"Come in," Row said to Apsara and Suvanna, and Zarya greeted the two women with a tight smile. After they settled around the kitchen table, Row poured them all a drink from the decanter in the middle. Zarya willed her gaze away from the drawer where she'd stuffed the stolen book. How was she going to retrieve it now?

"Are you joining us?" Apsara asked when Zarya still hadn't moved. Gods, she looked like a fool standing here. Row was going to suspect something was up at any moment.

"No," she replied. "I was just going up to bed."

"Okay," Row said, and Zarya lingered for another moment. His brows furrowed as he glanced at her again. Could she be any more suspicious? "Well, good night?"

"Yes. Good night," Zarya said to everyone and then went slowly up the stairs.

After entering her room, she undressed and lay down in her camisole and underwear, still sore with the aches and pains from her fight with Rabin in the garden. Thankfully, she hadn't seen him since, though that did nothing to suppress the irritation of that entire encounter. What an asshole.

Laughter floated from downstairs, and she wondered how long Apsara and Suvanna would remain here. After another hour of chatter and the distinctive pop of a new bottle of wine opening, it was clear they didn't plan to head home anytime soon.

Eventually, Zarya drifted off to sleep, and when her eyes snapped open again, she found herself in the dream forest, feeling the tickle of grass against her bare arms and legs.

"Fuck," she grumbled.

She no longer craved this place like she once had—now, it was just an annoyance. What was she doing here again? Someone was just trying to torment her now.

She sat up, surveying her surroundings. The forest remained as it always was, with its lush dark trees and that violet sky so dense with stars it was like she could scoop out a handful and tuck them in her pocket.

She stood and shivered, gooseflesh pulling up on her skin. Rubbing her arms, she took a few steps. The grass was soft under her feet, like walking on velvet. She gazed up, wondering if someone was up there. A puppet master, pulling her strings. Intent on making her squirm.

When it was clear that no response was coming from the sky, Zarya looked around again. The forest was empty, save for herself. Maybe that was it—she had been the one to create this, and tonight, it would be only her. Now that Rabin hated her, this would become yet another place where she wandered alone forever.

Leaves tickled her fingertips as she trailed her fingers along the bushes. If she had created the forest, then what was she supposed to do here? Was this a sanctuary into which she could retreat? Or was there something waiting here?

The cool breeze chilled her skin, and she shivered again. Could she learn to control this if this was a manifestation of her own mind? Was this typical of Aazheri magic, or did it have to do with the secrets she harbored?

She circled the clearing, peering into the depths of the dark trees, telling herself she wasn't disappointed about being here alone. She'd been here alone before. The day Vikram had taken her to the Maya Quarter, and she'd seen this place in the mirror. She hadn't been asleep then, so that wasn't a requirement. She'd also been awake when she'd first met Rabin after she'd touched the egg that had fallen from the sky.

What was the connection between all these seemingly disparate events?

Regardless, she knew she belonged here. She couldn't explain why other than she felt a gnawing hunger in its shadows, like they were trying to consume her and make her one with every blade of grass, every buzzing dragonfly, and every spark in the sky.

Then, she felt *him*.

Like a craving churned from the very depths of her starving soul, she felt him. It drew her into some central force of gravity like she was a moon and he was her planet. She couldn't have pointed to the specific direction it towed her, only that it felt like water seeping into her lungs, trying to drown her.

She stopped and listened for a rustle in the leaves that signaled his approach.

When nothing happened, she took a few more tentative steps.

"I know you're there," she called in a sing-song voice. "I can feel you."

Her hands brushed the leaves again, creating a soft whisper.

"What kind of warrior are you?" she taunted. "Hiding in the trees? Afraid that I'll beat you at sparring again?"

She couldn't really claim she'd won that day, but that was hardly the point.

"Don't worry. You're safe. I'm not carrying a weapon tonight." She looked down, realizing just how obvious that was, given the scant presence of her undergarments. Finally, a movement caught her eye, and she halted.

Rabin emerged from the trees across the clearing, and her breath seized in her chest.

Apparently, he'd also been pulled from slumber because his top half was bare, and he wore only a pair of loose black pants that hung low on his waist, revealing the cuts of muscle angling along his hips.

Whatever pithy comment she had planned withered on her tongue as he tipped his head and studied her, his penetrating gaze lingering on her face and then her shoulders, sliding down the length of her torso and legs. She felt it all intimately, like he was running his hands carefully over every inch of skin, ensuring he didn't miss a single spot.

A pulse throbbed between her thighs as his gaze snapped up to meet hers.

"You did not beat me," he said, taking a few steps forward. Gods, he was magnificent. All hard muscle and smooth planes over warm brown skin contoured by the soft glow of starlight. Iridescent dragon scales continued up his arms and over the rounded caps of his shoulders, meeting at a point at the center of his chest.

On his ribs was another tattoo—this one of a black dragon

perched mid-flight, meticulously drawn with the same iridescent ink that reflected blue and purple and green.

"I definitely made you sweat," she said, then bit her tongue,
realizing how that sounded. As he shifted, she noticed a line of
silvery scars—dozens of horizontal lines bisecting the branching
rivers of his thick veins—laddering up his left forearm.

"That you did," he said, his voice low and rumbling.

He stalked closer to her, and she gripped the tree behind
her for balance, worried her knees would melt out from
under her.

He stopped a foot away, and she took the opportunity to let
her gaze wander over him, drinking in the view.

"The dragon?" she asked, tipping her chin at his ribs. "Do
you have a picture of yourself tattooed on your body?"

He frowned, his dark eyebrows drawing together. "It helps
control my transformation. Magic can be tricky, as you know."

She blinked, surprised he'd offered that glimpse into his
vulnerabilities. She *did* know, recalling how he'd released her
magic in the forest when she'd been suffering.

"Why did you help me that night? You've actually saved my
life twice now."

"The binding on your magic wouldn't have killed you," he
said. "Not technically. Though you probably would have
wasted away to nothing eventually."

She hooked up an eyebrow. "I'm trying to thank you, and
again, you're rebuffing me?"

"Was that a thank you? That wasn't what it sounded like,"
he asked, and she sucked in an angry breath.

"Is that what you're mad about?"

"No. Don't be ridiculous. I already told you once that you
didn't need to thank me."

"Then what is your problem with me?"

His jaw hardened, his dark eyes flashing. "I don't have a
problem with you."

She laughed, the sound tearing out of her. "You've got to be kidding me."

He rubbed a hand down his face, and for a moment, he appeared uncharacteristically flustered. "I thought you were a spy for my father."

"So you said. Do you still think that?"

He shook his head. "I'm not sure."

She folded her arms and looked up at him. "So, who am I, then?"

He tipped his head as if considering. "Maybe a spy. Maybe sent here to torment me."

She scoffed. "Torment *you*?"

"Yes," he said, the word a growl practically ripped from his throat.

"I haven't done anything other than *exist*."

His eyes darkened, the gold flecks sparking like fireflies spinning through shadows. "I am *aware*."

"What... is that supposed to mean?" she asked, narrowing her gaze. Gods, he was confusing and irritating, *and* he was moving closer.

Suddenly, there was no space left between them. Her breath hitched as she looked up, noting every minute detail of his face. The scar through his eyebrow. The way the corners of his eyes turned up the slightest bit at the ends. The dusting of freckles over the bridge of his nose and the pale scar slicing along his left cheekbone.

Her gaze drifted lower, voyaging over the lines of his throat and the arc of his shoulder, the powerful scaffolds of his stomach, and the fine trail of dark hair that disappeared into his waistband.

She exhaled a breath, her lips parting as he stared down at her like he was trying to peel her open.

"What do you want from me?" she whispered, the words scattering on the breeze.

He said nothing as he wrapped a strong arm around her waist and pulled her against him. Their bodies lined up, her soft curves meeting with the hard ridges of his torso and thighs.

She felt him then, the way he thickened against her. Her stomach flipped, and her insides stretched with molten heat, a needy ache building between her thighs.

"I..." he said before he cut himself off and then pushed her back so she pressed against the tree behind her. "I need to do this."

The words came out strangled with longing as he dipped his head and ran his nose up the line of her throat, his arm cinching around her waist. Her head fell back as she arched into him before he gently nipped the skin just below her ear, his warm breath curling around the column of her throat.

She thought of sharp teeth and those elongated rakshasa canines sinking into her heated flesh while he fucked her against this tree with his big hands gripping her thighs.

But maybe she was getting ahead of herself.

His hand slid up her back, cupping her head as he journeyed down the length of her throat, his lips dragging over her skin. She whimpered a desperate plea when his other hand found her ass, his fingers digging into the flesh, and he pulled her harder against him. There. Oh, gods. She could feel the length of his hard cock against her stomach, and there was no mistaking the effect this was having on him. She didn't have much to compare it with, but it felt... generous.

He then slid both hands to the backs of her thighs and lifted her up, her legs wrapping around his waist as her back hit the tree. Now, she could feel him between her legs, the steely length of him pressing deliciously against her clit. She ground against him, wishing for the release she'd been craving for months.

He thrust his hips against her, the friction making her groan. She could feel everything. Her entire body was on fire, every nerve ending exposed, and excruciatingly aware of his touch and his heat and his scent.

She gripped his shoulders, sliding her hands down his arms, her fingers exploring the grooves and ridges of his magnificent brawn before she slid them up his back.

Her breasts crushed against his chest, her sensitive nipples sending tingles over her skin as his hand slid up the fabric of her camisole, his large palm scalding hot against her ribs. He opened his mouth and sucked on her neck so hard that her entire body felt like it was going to turn itself inside out.

The scrape of teeth against her collarbone nearly had her flying out of her skin.

He pulled up and looked at her, and their gazes locked, two stars finally colliding in the empty void of space.

Slowly, he lowered his head, and her lips parted as she licked them. His hungry eyes traced the movements of her tongue like a monster preparing to devour her body and soul.

They both paused, breathing in each other's air, the tension alive with static. Zarya inhaled a deep breath, ready, so fucking ready for this.

She leaned in, but... Rabin pulled away, his expression hardening to stone before he lowered her to the ground and stepped back.

"I'm sorry. We shouldn't do this," he said, the words falling from his mouth and plunging to the earth with a thud.

"What?" she asked, blinking furiously as she used the tree for support, the abrupt change in tension leaving her dizzy and close to collapsing.

"Forgive me."

Then, he turned around and disappeared into the trees.

Zarya woke up in her bed with her skin flushed and her heart galloping in her chest. What the fuck was that? Had he just... What had he just done? Made her think he was about to kiss her and then just... stopped? *Forgive him?*

She shoved her hand into her soaked underwear, her fingers roughly circling her clit as she curved off the bed, coming apart almost immediately. But it wasn't enough. That *bastard*. Once again, he'd done this to her, only this time, he'd hooked a chain around her neck and yanked her to the ground before he'd tossed her back.

Fire kindled under her blood, so she rolled off the bed, marching through the haveli and down to their private section of beach.

She dove into the water, underwear and all, sighing at the cool water slipping over her fevered skin, letting the adrenaline drain out of her fraying nerves.

What had that been about? Why did he touch her like that only to back away? Why shouldn't they do this? She'd never been so irritated and pissed off in her entire life.

She rolled onto her back, floating in the water with her arms and legs spread out as she stared at the sky. She thought of him again, of the way he'd felt against her. Of his rough hands and his soft mouth when he'd kissed her neck.

The way his cock had thrust against her, clearly wanting this as much as she had.

She ached for him, bereft of that electric and damning touch. Why couldn't she let go of this?

Empty and unsated, she slid her hand over her stomach, plunging her fingers inside her body as she again made herself come to the devastating image of the man who would surely be the death of her.

SEVENTEEN

Everything progressed from bad to worse as Zarya descended into the foulest mood she'd experienced in months. Not since before she'd escaped Row's cottage had she felt such paralyzing frustration.

Over the next week, the palace became her own personal jungle, festering with venomous stares and awkward silences as Zarya tried to avoid Rabin. If they ended up in the same room, she pretended he was no more interesting than furniture.

But he was making it impossible. Despite the fact he had been the one to walk away, his gaze followed her everywhere. *He* seemed to follow her everywhere, his expression wavering a line between regret and expectation. Zarya had no idea what it was supposed to mean, and it was only making her angrier. And more confused. And completely miserable. And it certainly didn't help that he kept on being so damned beautiful.

At night, she tossed and turned, thinking of him, doing her best not to give in to what her body craved. She wasn't sure what she was holding out for. To prove something to herself or to him? He'd never know what she got up to alone in her room.

What had he *meant* when he'd said they shouldn't do this?

Why not? Was this about what had happened with Vikram? Had Vikram told his brother to back off?

Zarya hadn't even considered that until now. She still needed to talk to Vikram. He'd sent her notes more than once, asking if they could meet. She kept dreaming up some excuse or another to hold him off. She was sure she didn't want him. Not only because of his ties to Amrita, but because, after experiencing what she'd felt with Rabin, she knew Vikram wasn't the one.

Unfortunately, it wasn't Rabin, either, but that was fine. At least now she knew what she was waiting for. Someone who made her feel that way but didn't screw with her head in the most infuriating way.

Gods, every time she thought of how he'd been the one to approach her. *He'd* been the one to put his hands on her, and then he'd just... stopped.

Fueled by restlessness, Zarya couldn't sit still. She marched over to the palace, looking for Yasen. She pounded on his door, and he opened it.

"Where is the fire?" he asked.

"I need to train," she said, dispensing with any niceties.

"Okay. Lovely to see you, too."

She ignored him, barging into his small room. As a soldier, he wasn't privy to the same opulent suites found in the rest of the palace. She noticed he hadn't moved into the larger quarters reserved for the army's commander but decided not to bring it up, hoping he'd talk about it when he was ready. She paced the length of the space, but it was too small, and the lack of movement left her unsatisfied.

Much like a lot of things lately.

She stopped. "Please. Can we go and hit things? I need to expel some of this... energy."

"What's this about, Zee?" he asked as he retrieved his sword.

"Nothing. I'm fine."

"Okay, let's pretend I believe that."

"Good," Zarya said, brushing past him back into the hall as he followed her towards the central courtyard. It stood empty today, the air cool and comfortable thanks to the shade of Amrita's shimmering leaves.

Zarya drew her sword and then turned to face Yasen. He pulled his blade free and tossed the sheath to the ground before they began sparring. Their blades flashed as the sound bounced off the stone walls.

Zarya fought furiously, but Yasen matched her speed, fending her off until she swung, nearly missing his ear and shearing off a lock of his silver hair. It floated to the ground, landing on the pavers in a way that suggested it was also judging her erratic behavior.

"Whoa!" he cried. "That's enough! What is with you?"

"Nothing," she snapped.

He raised his arms in the air and dropped his sword on the ground with a clatter before he folded his arms.

"I'm not training with you anymore until you tell me what's going on. You've been feral for a week, and I'm tired of you snapping at me. What's wrong, Zee?"

Genuine concern laced Yasen's question, causing Zarya's shoulders to slump.

"I'm sorry." She rubbed a hand over the back of her neck, guilt twisting in her stomach. She had been peevish with him and everyone around her lately, and no one deserved this treatment. There was only one person who did, but she was doing everything she could to keep her distance from *him*.

Yasen waved it off and gestured to a stone bench on the edge of the courtyard.

They sat down, and Zarya leaned against the wall, tipping her head back.

"It's Rabin," she said before she looked at Yasen.

His eyebrows drew together. "Rabin? As in Daragaab's former commander and Vik's brother? The one who showed up here unannounced after disappearing for years?"

Zarya let out a small huff of breath. "Yes, that one."

Yasen leaned in, his shoulder bumping hers as he lowered his head and said, "Did he do something to you that I need to kill him for?"

Despite herself, her mouth turned up in a half-smile at Yasen's protectiveness.

"That's violent and sweet, but no. Technically, not."

"Technically? Does this have to do with throwing yourself at him?"

She wrinkled her nose. She hadn't told anyone this story in detail yet. Even with Amrita, she'd kept it vague enough for plausible deniability if anyone were to go digging. But she needed someone to talk to, and Amrita was no longer an option.

Zarya gave Yasen a sidelong look. "You remember when I got so sick, and I told everyone a stranger came and lifted the binding curse on my magic?"

"Yes?"

"Well, I wasn't entirely truthful about who the stranger was."

"Excuse me?" Yasen asked.

Zarya looked away, staring at the Jai Tree's wide trunk and flowering branches, not sure why she couldn't face him.

"It was Rabin."

She sensed Yasen's surprise before she turned to gauge his reaction. "But I didn't know that. He told me his name, but I had no idea that he was Vikram's brother."

Yasen's brow furrowed. "I don't understand."

"Honestly, I don't, either. It's been happening for months. Ever since I left Row's cottage. One night, I found myself in this dreamlike forest, and he was there. At first, it was just a glimpse, but as time passed, we began to talk and get to know one another. And Yas, there was this incredibly strong emotion between us. A connection. It was so vivid."

Yasen's mouth hung slightly open. He leaned forward and held out his hands, moving them up and down as he spoke. "Are you telling me you've been having dreams about Daragaab's most legendary commander for *months*? And you didn't tell me?"

Zarya nodded, feeling contrite about the whole thing. Maybe it had been foolish to keep this from everyone all along. Rabin could have been dangerous, and she'd told him exactly where to find her. While he hadn't physically harmed her, she still couldn't be sure of his intentions.

"I didn't understand what it meant—I still don't. And more importantly, I had no idea who he was. For a while, I thought I was hallucinating or losing my mind. But then, when he showed up at the joining ceremony, I understood he was real."

Yasen bit his lower lip, his expression thoughtful. "I'd forgotten, with everything that happened afterward, but he said something to you right before that giant bird dropped from the sky. Did it have something to do with this? I should have suspected something was up because how could he have known who you were?"

Zarya nodded. "He was furious with me. Somehow, he got it into his head that I'd been working with his father to spy on him. He accused me of bewitching him and creating the forest. But the thing is, I wasn't entirely sure if what he was saying wasn't true."

"What do you mean?"

"Not the spying part, of course. That's ridiculous," Zarya said. "But the other part. I know so little about my abilities. Until a few weeks ago, I had no idea what I was. What if I did create it? What does it mean, and why does it bring him to me?"

Yasen shook his head, not that she was expecting an answer.

"But then he saved me during the kala-hamsa attack," she

said. "When I was falling, he was in his dragon form, and he saved my life, just like he did when he lifted the curse on my magic."

"I didn't know that about the night of the attack," Yasen said. "Why didn't you tell anyone?"

She shrugged. "We both woke up in the middle of the ruins of some building, and then he tried to carry me." She snorted. "I got so mad because he was being such a dick that I refused. I could barely walk, but I made him nearly drop me."

"Sounds about right," Yasen said.

"Then, he dragged me into an alley and accused me of spying, and *that's*... when I kind of threw myself at him."

Yasen rubbed a hand over his face. "Very smooth, Zee."

"Shut up," she said and then laughed wryly. "I wanted him to admit why he'd come. The last time I'd seen him, I swear he almost kissed me, and then he showed up and was so... rude. When I asked him to admit what he felt, he told me in unequivocal terms that he felt nothing, and then he walked away. That's when I ran into you."

"Wow," Yasen said. "Okay, so you seemed fine after that. What happened to set you off now?"

"It turns out the dream forest still exists. A few nights ago, we both ended up there again, both of us wearing our night-clothes." Zarya dropped her face in her hands and let out a groan. "Have you *seen* him without his shirt?"

Yasen's eyes grew wide as she looked back at him. He nodded sagely. "I have, and so far, this is a very good story, Zarya."

She snorted, grateful for his humor.

"Anyway, we talked a bit, and he kept making these cryptic statements, and then he..."

"What? Tell me."

"Then, he approached me, and he put his arm around me, and I could feel that he—"

She cut off, feeling her cheeks heat.

"What? His dagger was happy to see you? His dragon was stiff? His phoenix was rising?"

Zarya burst out laughing and covered her face with a hand.

"Yes. Oh, my gods. You are so embarrassing."

"Then what?" Yasen asked, perched on the edge of his seat.

"He lifted me up, and he was kissing my neck and—" She stopped again, the heat of her memories overwhelming.

"Do not stop now, Zee. I forbid it."

"He kissed my neck, and it was so passionate and—"

"Hot?" Yasen supplied.

"Yes. *So* hot," Zarya breathed. "He was about to take things further. I'm pretty sure. No, I'm very sure. And then he just stopped. Pulled away. Told me we shouldn't do this and left."

"He did *what*?" he asked.

"I *know*."

"That's *it*?" Yasen was wild-eyed. "Who does that?"

"You see why I've been in such a mood?"

"You were right, he does deserve to be killed."

Zarya snorted. "Now, I can't get away from him. He's always around me and looking at me, and he's so brooding and so beautiful, and I have all these conflicting urges, and I don't understand what he wants. It's making me crazy."

Zarya flopped over on Yasen's lap, burying her face into her arms.

He chuckled, stroking her hair softly.

"Oh, my poor Zee. Look at you. What a fool that man is."

"Don't say anything nice to me. I don't deserve it. I'm sorry I've been so mean."

Yasen tipped Zarya back up, wrapping an arm around her.

"I'll forgive you this time. After hearing why, I can't really blame you. What a dick."

She gave him a teary smile. "Yasen, I know I'm not very

experienced with this stuff, but this seems significant. No offense, but it's nothing like it was with Vikram."

"Good, I'm glad this isn't how you felt about him. Vik would have broken your heart. And you don't need experience to recognize that." Yasen pointed a finger, placing it on her heart.

"Thank you. I actually feel a little better."

"That's what I'm here for," Yasen boasted. "You really do need to get laid, though."

She snorted. "Shut up."

EIGHTEEN

Zarya flipped through the notebook she'd stolen from Row, seated on the divan in the haveli's living room. After the incident with Rabin in the forest, she was having trouble rousing herself from her funk, so she retreated into herself, turning to her oldest companion—books.

She'd retrieved the 'borrowed' journal from the drawer where she'd hidden it and was now deciphering the script. Upon closer inspection, this wasn't Row's handwriting. It didn't sound like him, either, so it must be her mother's, given her previous relationship with Row. Or maybe Zarya was grasping for a connection with the woman who'd borne her, and this wasn't hers at all.

But the picture of her mother was there, along with the very prophecy Row had recounted upon his return to Daragaab. The one predicting Queen Aishayadiva of Gi'ana would be the one to birth a child who would wield nightfire. Zarya traced the words with her finger, tasting the bittersweetness in the lines. They were an answer to a question she'd been asking all of her life but were also a nexus to a thousand more.

She continued studying the picture, remembering what

Row had said about her mother being an artist. Had she drawn this image of herself, or had someone done it for her? Zarya touched the pendant dangling around her mother's neck, the same as the one Zarya wore. After performing the translation spell, additional marks of ink had appeared around the jewel, dark swirls curling in the air.

Flipping through the pages, Zarya realized her mother had been documenting both the magic and history of Aazheri.

Zarya landed on a chapter about paramadhar—conduits who acted as tethers for powerful Aazheri. The text described them as something like a magical servant or squire. Paramadhar had the ability to not only enhance the magic of their master but they could also take on their injuries or sickness and make them their own. In some cases, they could even heal their master, communicate through their minds, and sense each other's feelings.

Beyond just magic, paramadhar could also amplify their master's speed and strength. And when the Aazheri died, so did their paramadhar. The relationship was born from a deep emotional connection, though it wasn't romantic in nature.

She chewed on the corner of her thumb, devouring a passage about how destined pairs could sense or even speak to one another across continents. Sometimes, finding each other in unlikely ways, often in the worlds existing between physical planes.

The seedlings of an idea took root in her mind.

The dream forest. It wasn't a part of this world. Of that, she was sure.

Would that explain how she'd found Rabin? Did they hold some kind of strange connection? *Something* had drawn them together. The book also said the bond wasn't romantic, and though she was loath to admit it, her feelings for him were definitely not ones of mere friendship or companionship. But maybe it explained why he didn't return those feelings.

She sighed, realizing she would really have to get over him.

She read a few more pages about the Ashvins and their dark magic as the book recounted some of their worst sins. Mind control and stealing souls and using the threat of their raised demon armies of nairrata to enslave and threaten anyone who tried to defy their wishes.

A knock interrupted her reading, and she considered ignoring it, wanting to be alone to stew in her thoughts, but the pounding persisted.

She waited, hoping that Row or Aarav would answer it, but neither was home as usual. Finally, Zarya hauled herself up and opened the door to find Yasen with a smile on his face.

"What?" she asked, letting him in.

"I see you're still in a sparkling mood," he said, and she grunted before she headed for the kitchen, hoping to find something strong to drink to numb her brain.

"I've come to rescue you from this spiral into self-loathing," Yasen declared.

Zarya rummaged around in the cupboard, producing a bottle half-filled with dark liquid.

"Aha," she said, finding a glass and pouring herself a measure.

"Come on. The begums Ravana are throwing a fancy supper in the courtyard, and we're going," Yasen said.

Zarya made a noncommittal sound before she downed the drink and then coughed at the burn searing up her throat. Yasen slapped her on the back, probably a bit harder than necessary. And also, she wasn't actually choking.

"You can't sit in here wallowing forever. There will be lots of wine. Good stuff. Not this swill." Yasen picked up the bottle and sniffed it, pulling a face. "This could strip paint off the walls."

"Fine," Zarya said, wiping her mouth with the back of her hand. "But don't stop me from drinking it all."

"I wouldn't dream of it."

She turned to face him, and he scanned her up and down.

"Is that what you're wearing?"

Zarya looked down at herself. She'd been lying on the sofa most of the day in her wrinkled kurta, the hair piled on top of her head sharing many characteristics with a rat's nest.

"I have to get changed, too?" she asked, and Yasen rolled his eyes.

"It's a nice thing with fancy people. Yes, you need to change. You can't show up there looking like something a cat dragged in."

"You're making this seem far less appealing," she said. "What if I want to wallow here in my filth?"

"You can do that tomorrow. Tonight, you're pretending you're a civilized member of this city."

He reached over and scraped a spot near the corner of her mouth with his fingernail, dislodging a crust of food that had pasted itself to her skin.

"Revolting," he said, flicking it to the floor with a shudder.

"Fine. Point taken. Give me a few minutes." She poured another glass of the liquor and then thrust it against his chest. "Have a drink while you wait."

"Take your time," he called after her before she heard him dump the contents in the sink. "You're going to need it."

A short while later, she'd done her best to clean herself up. She'd brushed her hair and cleaned her face, put on some makeup, and changed into a fresh kurta and pants made of soft green silk embroidered with silver flowers. A pair of dangling silver jhumka and a coordinating necklace made it look a little less like she'd just pieced herself together.

"Better?" she asked when she found Yasen sitting in the back garden overlooking the ocean. He'd found something more palatable to drink, a glass in his hand.

He looked over and scanned her up and down. "Better."

"Then let's go. This better be fun."

"Everything is fun with me," he joked, and she smiled.

"You know. That's kind of true."

"Don't get sentimental on me, Swamp Girl."

He held out an elbow, and she looped her arm through it before they walked to the palace, entering through the courtyard doors.

A long table ran through the center, laden with golden plates, crystal goblets, silver flatware, and centerpieces bursting with white flowers and greenery. Dozens of delicate wooden chairs lined the table, already filled with courtiers. Zarya spotted Row sitting with Kindle and Dhawan, while Apsara, Suvanna, and Koura occupied the seats across from them.

When Zarya and Yasen appeared, they looked their way and nodded. Row smiled at her, and she returned it. They had been having dinners together the last few nights, their conversation less stilted and awkward. She was learning to forgive him. Slowly.

A servant greeted them and walked Yasen and Zarya past Row and the others to a pair of empty seats.

"No," Zarya said, grabbing Yasen's arm and dragging them both to a stop.

Rabin sat next to his mother, deep in conversation. Zarya had never seen Jasmine—Gopal Ravana's third wife—so animated. Gone was her usual vacant expression as she gazed lovingly upon her eldest son. Clearly, she adored him, and the realization made Zarya's heart twist with a curious sense of longing.

Two empty chairs opposite the pair were clearly meant for Zarya and Yasen. This was not what she had signed up for.

"I'm going back to my nest of blankets and cheap booze," she said, backing up, hoping to escape before he noticed her.

But Rabin and Jasmine chose that moment to look over, and now it would be far too obvious if she ran. Besides, Yasen was already hauling her towards the table with his hand clamped around her elbow.

"Yasen," Jasmine exclaimed. She wore a teal sari and a mountain of gold jewelry, her dark eyes rimmed with rings of kohl. "Do sit down and join us. I feel as though I haven't seen you in so long." She gestured to the empty seats.

Zarya's lips and fingertips went numb as they approached, and Rabin studied her with his penetrating gaze. It was obvious that Yasen was enjoying this immensely as he shoved her towards the chair in front of Rabin while she tried to maneuver herself to the other. But Yasen smoothly dodged around her and sat down, leaving her no choice but to sit across from Rabin.

She scowled at Yasen as she dropped into the seat.

"I will kill you," she hissed under her breath.

Yasen gave her a simpering smile before he clapped his hands together.

"Jasmine Aunty, everything looks splendid. You and the wives have truly outdone yourselves this evening."

Jasmine's shoulders wiggled as she preened at the compliment.

Zarya did her best to look at anything other than the man across from her, but she *felt* his attention, and their eyes met. Heat shimmered between them before Zarya looked away, her neck flushing in a way she hoped he didn't notice.

She used the opportunity to study her surroundings. Vikram sat at the head of the table next to his father and Diya, another of the Ravana wives. Gopal lifted his wine glass to his lips and threw Zarya a scathing look over the rim.

Apparently, her elevation from mere human to Aazheri hadn't altered his opinion of her. To think Rabin thought she was *his* spy. It was laughable. Wait until he found out that Rabin might be connected to her through a magical bond. That would make for fun dinner table conversation.

Zarya looked back to find Rabin studying his father as well, a line creasing his dark brows. When he noticed her stare, his gaze met hers again.

She huffed and picked up her wine glass, burying her nose in it. Maybe if she got drunk enough, this meal might be tolerable. Of course, there was the possibility she might make a fool of herself again, but she'd take that chance in exchange for inebriated bliss.

A flicker overhead drew everyone's attention skyward towards a large translucent dome made of pale golden light, flickering in and out of focus. Zarya squinted, realizing it was Amrita's magical barrier struggling to remain in place. Her gaze went to Vikram, who was staring up at it, too, as the table broke into a flurry of whispers.

After a few more seconds, the dome flashed away, leaving the sky clear once again.

Vikram looked at the crowd and raised his hands. "Nothing to worry about," he said, and Zarya wondered if she was imagining the strain in his voice. "Sometimes, Her Majesty grows tired, but everything is fine now. Please continue your dinner."

The guests did as instructed, slowly resuming their conversation.

Zarya exchanged a glance with Yasen.

"Is that normal?" she asked.

"I'm not sure," he replied. "I haven't seen that happen before."

"Shouldn't we do something?"

"Like what? Hold up the magical barrier in the sky with our hands?"

Zarya rolled her eyes, picking up her wine while continuing to stare at the sky. How could someone tell if the magic was actually in place? Wouldn't it look the same if it were gone? Vikram had sounded confident everything was fine, though.

"So, Rabin," Yasen said, with his glass perched in his hand. "Had any good dreams lately?"

Zarya choked on her wine and kicked Yasen under the table, but the angle was awkward, and it glanced off rather than being the sharp jab she'd intended. Yasen ignored it entirely as he bestowed Rabin with an innocent smile and a curious tip of his head.

Rabin glared fiercely at Yasen, then at Zarya.

Since the question had been asked, she had to admit she *was* curious to hear the answer.

"Tell us," Jasmine said, turning to Zarya, having apparently missed the previous exchange, "I'm so curious about where you came from. Why did you spend your life living on the shore instead of here in the city?"

Zarya turned to her, wondering how much anyone outside the Chiranjivi knew. It was obvious there was some discussion about her origins, or Jasmine wouldn't be asking the question.

"Because that's where I was comfortable," Zarya said sharply. Her temper was on edge, and she didn't appreciate Jasmine's prying. After everything Row had revealed about her parentage, Zarya had to be wary about who to trust. This was getting exhausting—secrets upon secrets tied up with lies and half-truths. Would she ever have the freedom to trust the people she met?

"It's very mysterious, isn't it?" Jasmine continued. "Who did you say your parents were?"

"I didn't." Zarya took a long drink of her wine. "Dead. Both of them."

Jasmine tutted. "That *is* a shame."

Her expression seemed knowing as her gaze flicked to her son, his eyes still pinned on Zarya.

She stuffed a large piece of roti into her mouth, ruing the day she'd ever laid eyes on a single Ravana. This entire family was far too involved in her business, never giving her a moment's peace.

She chewed slowly, grateful when Jasmine's attention was

diverted to the person seated on her other side. A servant leaned over to refill Zarya's wine glass. She swallowed the food and then took another long gulp.

Thankfully, the alcohol was taking effect, and her brain was now buzzing pleasantly. In fact, this was the most relaxed she'd felt in days. What was in this stuff? She'd have to buy some bottles to keep at the haveli.

Crossing her arms, she leaned back in her chair, staring at Rabin. He was now intensely interested in his food, mopping a piece of roti through a pool of gravy over and over again like he was trying to punish it for existing in his presence.

"I think it's got enough sauce on it," Zarya said, arching her neck to peer at his plate and squinting like she was having trouble seeing it.

The wine was definitely making her bolder. Or more foolish. Sometimes, it was a fine line, wasn't it?

Rabin looked up from his food as her stomach dipped in response. It was that same heat she'd felt the other night. Suffocating and life-giving at the same time. Enough to drown her and consume her. She didn't want to feel any of this. She wanted to forget about him. Move on to someone who wouldn't leave her standing alone in the middle of a strange forest in her underwear after *he'd* initiated an almost kiss.

She bit her lip, and his eyes zeroed in on her mouth, his pupils spreading. She didn't understand what game he was playing, but she was sure something was affecting him, too. She couldn't have imagined all of that. She shifted in her seat, thinking of his hard cock rubbing between her legs and the tenderness of her nipples as they brushed his firm chest.

Well, now she knew what she'd be doing tonight once she returned to the solace of her bedroom. She wasn't proud of it, but she couldn't help the way he made her feel. She'd get over it eventually. In the meantime, she'd have to make do with her hand for company.

Rabin's golden-flecked eyes raked up her frame as a shiver rolled down her spine.

He leaned forward, and he opened his mouth. She couldn't decide if she wanted to hear what was about to come out of it. Probably something else to remind her that while he might be the most beautiful man she'd ever seen, he was also a huge, massive dick.

But at that moment, a soldier ran shouting into the court-yard, pulling every eye towards him.

He stopped and then scanned the table. When he caught sight of Vikram, he headed straight for him.

"Steward," the soldier said with a bow, "the blight has breached the southern wall. It's—"

He glanced at the faces surrounding him, turning pale.

"We must evacuate immediately. The blight is *consuming* the city."

NINETEEN

Chaos erupted as Vikram began shouting orders, while Yasen leaped up to ready the palace soldiers. Zarya pushed up from her seat, staring at the sky. That same dome they'd seen minutes ago blinked in and out until a bright light flashed, and the sky cleared once again.

"The queen's magic has failed!" Vikram shouted. "Call her guard to the walls!"

Warnings blared in the air, signaling the emergency.

Zarya then exchanged a look with Rabin. Row and the others were already bolting for the gates, and she wasted no time following.

As she emerged into the street, a wave of chaos surged in the opposite direction. She'd already lost sight of Row in the churning sea of bodies. Rabin stood next to her, and they shared another look before he nodded, and they both took off running. Zarya was shoved left and right as they pushed through the throngs of panicked Dharati citizens fleeing for safety.

Rabin took the lead, his wide shoulders struggling to cut a path through the confusion. He stopped and raised his arms as the tide diverted around him. A moment later, an earthen ramp rose up from the ground, forming an elevated runway. Zarya marveled at the construction offering them a clear path.

Rabin looked over his shoulder, his expression telling her to follow. Though they were now a few feet off the ground, Zarya still couldn't see what was driving everyone this way. It took them several minutes to reach the southern gates where she had first entered Dharati after escaping the swamp.

It was then she finally realized what was happening. No gates, no matter how tall or strong, would stop the taint decimating the city. Around them, screams echoed against stone and concrete because the soldier hadn't been far off when he'd said the blight was consuming the walls.

Black rot seeped up from the bottom, spreading like ink tipped over pristine cotton. It scaled up the mortar and bricks, staining their golden glow with decay. For several seconds, Zarya watched, unable to comprehend the horror of what she was witnessing.

"Do you hear that?" Zarya asked.

Rabin nodded as he stared at the infection crawling over the ground, edging closer to where they stood. His jaw hardened. "I do."

Chewing. Gnawing. Crunching.

The blight was literally *devouring* the city and everything in its path. Soldiers were shouting orders, attempting to usher people through the streets while trying to maintain some semblance of order. There would be no point in trying to rescue anyone if they were trampled in a stampede of fleeing bodies.

"To the northern forest," the soldiers shouted. "Take cover in the northern forest. Now!"

"What do we do?" Zarya asked Rabin as Yasen came thundering up behind them. She reached for him. "Yas?"

They all watched in horror as the blackness continued to chew its way forward. Zarya backed up, step by step, watching as it crept closer to the tips of her shoes.

"This has never happened before," Yasen said. "It's always moved so slowly."

"What if it doesn't stop?" Zarya asked, looking towards the palace. "What do we do about Amrita? She'll be trapped."

"Your nightfire, Zee," Yasen said. "It stopped the demons. Maybe it would work now?"

She watched the blight, hesitating.

"What's wrong?"

"I'm not sure how. It was an instinct. I haven't practiced it enough. I've been trying, but I don't know how to control it." She took another several steps back as the rot inched forward. The screams of the city slithered into her consciousness. Everyone would die if they didn't stop this.

"Just close your eyes," a low voice said in her ear. Rabin stood behind her now, his hands clasping her shoulders. She tried to ignore the heat of his palms as they burned right through the fabric. "Concentrate on slowly pulling each of your anchors one at a time, like towing in fishing lines."

"Okay." She closed her eyes, forgetting what Dhawan had told her. Rabin's advice was more in tune with the way her magic behaved. The five points of her anchor flared to life, warming her from the inside like a sparking flame.

"Slow and steady," Rabin said, his breath tickling the shell of her ear. "Don't draw it too fast, or you'll burn yourself out."

Zarya took a deep breath as the glittering star inside her sparked and spun. The rot had climbed the top of the walls now, and she took a few more steps back as it advanced along the earth, Rabin moving in sync with her.

He didn't release his hold, his steady presence calming her thumping heart.

Earth. Air. Fire. Water. Spirit.

She checked each of them off as she drew a small bit of each while a force swelled inside her chest. Her magic pulsed as it surrounded her heart, encasing it in gilded light.

Drawing more, her magic expanded, filling her up and surging through her limbs and then her fingertips as a rush of nightfire exploded from her hands. Its deep glittering blackness slammed into the ground and began racing towards the rot.

It clashed with the blight, forcing it back several feet, forming a semi-circle of untouched stone where Zarya and Rabin stood.

She cried out in relief and almost jumped for joy. "It worked!"

"Good girl," Rabin said, a note of pride in his voice as his lips brushed the edge of her ear. "Try it again. It will become easier each time."

She called up the glittering star inside her with more ease as nightfire blasted forth again, sending the blight into retreat.

But then something went terribly wrong.

A deafening roar preceded the sight of the entire southwest corner of the city beginning to crumble, blackened buildings toppling on top of one another. Ash and dust billowed into the atmosphere as screams tore through the air, growing louder and morphing into freewheeling panic. The crowd surged in every direction, seeking safety.

"I think I pissed it off," she said as dread curled in her stomach.

"Yeah. I think you did," Rabin replied as more buildings toppled in the distance, leaving nothing but puffs of smoke in the skyline.

They stood rooted, the destruction advancing faster and faster. Soldiers shouted, urging people to move quicker as pandemonium descended in every direction and their foundations shook.

Two soldiers brought up the rear of a group of women and children as they sprinted forward. Shadows leaped, cresting over the men's heads and slamming down like a tsunami, swallowing them, their screams echoing as they disappeared into the darkness.

"Gods," Zarya whispered as waves of shadows swelled up around them, leaping, jumping, snatching people as they ran from it, trying to escape the cold fingers of death.

"We need to move," Rabin declared as he grabbed her by the hand, and they started to run. Screams echoed everywhere as more and more people were guzzled into the blight. Buildings crumbled overhead as Zarya and Rabin dodged hunks of stone and falling debris. She had to do something. Amrita would die if the infection reached the palace. She couldn't let that happen.

A blink of light flashed overhead, and they watched as Amrita's magic blitzed in and out. After a few seconds, the sky cleared.

"Do you think it's back in place?" Zarya shouted. It was impossible to tell, and given the extent of the destruction, it was likely a moot point at the moment.

"I have no idea," Rabin said.

Zarya tugged on his arm. "Wait," she said, bringing them to a stop.

He didn't question her—nothing but complete trust written on his face.

"What is it?"

"I have an idea. I don't know if it will work, but I need to try."

Her gaze flicked to the palace where the Jai Tree stood, its colorful flowers spreading across the grey sky, and Rabin nodded.

"Tell me what you need."

She nodded and fell to a knee, placing her hand on the rumbling stones. With her eyes closed, she reached for the source of her magic. Now wasn't the moment for restraint, and she wrenched on each of her anchors with all of her force.

She felt them spear into the center of her heart, where they collided in a glittering crush before nightfire sprung from the tips of her fingers, the lines shooting out and then merging to form a wave that raced over the stones.

It crashed into the edge of the blight, bursting through it like water against a rocky shore. It was an absence of light, its darkness blacker than the blight itself, broken only by the points that sparkled in its yawning density. The blight resisted her efforts, clawing back at her nightfire, trying to consume it, too. It didn't want to be restrained. It wanted to run free.

Zarya hung on, shaking as it overwhelmed her fire, and she feared she didn't have the strength to stop it. That's when she noticed the sixth anchor had broken free from the cage where she'd tried to keep it contained.

Forbidden and seductive. A demon wreathed in silk. Fire built from whispers.

Zarya wanted to resist its lure.

Darkness.

She didn't know what it would mean if she took its hand and allowed it entry into her life. If it would change everything.

But the city was crumbling around them, and she had to protect Amrita. Maybe she had no choice. Maybe everything she'd been through, from her captivity to the revelations of her past and the people who created her, had all been leading to this moment.

If she leaned into the sixth anchor, it might be a step from which she could never return, but she had to take that chance. Hoping it wasn't a mistake she'd regret forever, Zarya channeled the darkness into the heart of her anchor, and her magic exploded in a shower of sparks, flowing out of her in tumbling waves.

Nightfire raced over the blight, soothing it, stroking it, seducing it into a trance. It slowed and stilled, her senses reaching out to discover what called. A wave of shadow crested and tumbled down on her head, enveloping, embracing, caressing. Darkness danced around her as black smoke swirled in her nose and lungs.

It wanted her. Her breath. Her life and heart and blood. It didn't want to be soothed. It wanted to claim her as its own. It pulled, trying to extinguish the flickering light in her heart, but she held on, gritting out her resolve.

Thankfully, her fire was stronger. *She* was stronger.

Zarya felt her magic draining, pulling through her veins as waves surged out of her, spilling in torrents, tumbling over everything in its path. Sweat dripped into her eyes, and her muscles trembled as she clung to the unimaginable flood of power.

Just when she wasn't sure she could hold on any longer, a hand, large and warm, engulfed hers. With a tight squeeze, a gush of strength billowed into Zarya as her flickering flame flared with renewed brightness, feeding her more power. Finally, the blight's strangle loosened a fraction. She sensed its surprise at her resistance.

Zarya closed her eyes, digging deeper into the magic inside her. The blight retreated as she forced it back. It drew away. Down the streets, past buildings and slain bodies, through the gates and over the walls, and deep into the swamp.

Zarya finally released her trapped breath, letting go of her six anchors. The darkness whipped away from the rest, retreating to its cave. Her fire expended for now, it left an absence in her heart, like a piece had been hollowed out.

The blight rolled off as her vision cleared. Rabin hunched down next to her, one knee to the ground, his hand still gripping hers. Slowly, he looked up, and their gazes caught.

The city was quiet. Blackness surrounded them on all sides, everything in ruin, but the blight had stopped advancing, at least for now. And it hadn't reached Amrita.

Unsteady on her feet, Zarya stood, black spots bursting her

vision. She stumbled, but Rabin caught her, wrapping his arms around her. He pulled her in close, resting his chin against her forehead.

"Zarya," he murmured into her hair. "I lied. I feel it, too."

She looked up at him, and everything went black.

TWENTY

Zarya woke up inside the palace, lying in the same bed where she'd slept before. Her surroundings were quiet except for the dull roar of crashing waves outside. Her body didn't so much ache as it felt like it had been drained of everything.

She recalled the last thing she remembered. Looking up at Rabin as she fainted in his arms. Had she imagined those words he'd said?

I lied. I feel it, too.

What did that mean, and why had he chosen that particular moment to enlighten her and fuck with her head a little more?

She slid out of bed and slowly stood. Her limbs felt hollowed out like someone had removed all her bones and piled them into a corner. She padded over to the mirror, noting the dust that coated her hair and clothing.

She looked the same. A strange sense of relief flooded through her. What had she expected? Horns or a tail to sprout now that she had embraced her darkness? But even with no visible change on the outside, she couldn't quell the thoughts running through her mind. A truth that had been scraping at her subconscious for some time now.

The blight wanted her and had been chasing her for months. Not months. Maybe years. The magic she once believed benign and useless was inexplicably tied to the entity plaguing Daragaab. She was sure of it.

Did this mean she was the one who could stop it?

Did Row and Dhawan know this was possible?

After what she'd just experienced, she didn't think she'd be strong enough on her own. Yes, she'd forced it to retreat, but it had nearly destroyed her. If it hadn't been for Rabin... She shook her head. Everything was piling up, making it impossible to clear her thoughts.

She slipped on a pair of shoes left by the door and padded through the palace halls. Today, they were quiet, absent of their typical bustle. Only the palace servants moved about their duties with less zeal than usual. She'd never seen it this empty in all her months here.

Zarya walked to the courtyard, where the door to the Jai Tree stood ajar.

Inside, Row stood with the rest of the Chiranjivi as well as Rabin, Yasen, Vikram, and Aarav. Everyone was talking at once—or rather, arguing. The topic of discussion was clear. This had been the most aggressive attack on Dharati yet, and they were running out of time and options.

Vikram assured everyone that Amrita's barrier of protection was once again in place and that she'd learned from this mistake. But her enchantment had been compromised, and her magic wouldn't protect them forever.

The queendom had to be evacuated, and the blight had to be stopped once and for all.

Rabin leaned against the wall, his keen eyes quietly observing the conversation. He spotted Zarya first, standing straighter when he saw her. They exchanged a private look, and she studied him from head to toe. When he'd taken her hand, her nearly-spent magic had recovered, surging up with enough force to beat back the blight.

Paramadhar. The ancient word echoed in her head like a lost song dusty with neglect. Rare. Almost as rare as her night-fire, her mother's writing had said. If Zarya was possessed of one impossible gift, then why not another? Nothing about her life made sense anymore.

He returned her scrutiny with a thorough perusal of his own. She felt it touch that empty space behind her heart, heat blooming in her cheeks.

"Zarya," Apsara said, coming up and placing a hand on her shoulder. "How are you feeling?"

"A little weak and shaky, but I'm fine. My magic—it's so small." It simmered faintly below her skin, reduced to only a pinpoint of light. Zarya tried to call it up, but it stuttered, slipping away.

"I think you must have used a lot of your power," Apsara said. "But you didn't burn out if you can still sense it. It will come back."

"Burn out?"

"It can happen if you expend too much at once. You need proper training. There hasn't been time. We could have worked with you if you'd told us when you first discovered it."

Plagued with guilt for all the lies she'd told, she caught sight of Rabin as he mimicked Apsara's stern expression. Zarya stifled a smirk, reminding herself she was still angry with him.

"How is everyone? How is the city?" Zarya asked, ignoring Apsara's chastising glare.

"Almost a third of the city is gone," Row said. "The guards are trying to locate bodies. We don't know how many died. What happened? What did you do?"

Zarya described her idea to channel the nightfire through the earth instead of attacking it head-on, not sure where the notion had come from, but it had felt right, and her instincts had been correct.

"You could have died," Row said. "You aren't ready for this."

"What did you want me to do? Let it take the entire city?"

Row flattened his mouth, anger flashing in his dark eyes.

"Don't pretend like you're worried about me now. You had years for that."

Row's shoulders slumped, and she didn't miss the hurt in his eyes, but a few dinners and concerned glances wouldn't wipe out nineteen years of captivity and secrets. She was trying to forgive him, but he had a lot of trust to earn.

"Besides, we'd probably all be dead if I hadn't tried."

She looked at Rabin again and nodded slightly. *Thank you for your help.*

"We need to evacuate the city," Vikram said, dark circles under his eyes.

"And go where?" Row asked.

"What about Amrita?" Zarya interjected, gesturing to the queen.

"She agrees an evacuation would be most prudent," Vikram said.

"We can't leave her here to die!"

"I agree," Apsara said, arms crossed over her chest, her white feathers ruffling. Zarya looked at her gratefully.

"But we don't know how to stop this!" Suvanna said, looking even more angry than usual. Her blue-green hair floated around her, its movement as agitated as she was. "How do we destroy the darkness?"

"She's right," Zarya said. "My magic only seems to hamper it, stun it for a little while, but whatever is in those streets is very much still alive and will try again."

Zarya chose her words carefully. The blight hadn't been beaten or hampered. She'd soothed it, persuaded it to retreat, and it had obeyed as well as any trained soldier. Nightfire was a way to control the darkness—Row hadn't been wrong about that —but she suspected he'd meant it in a different way than she was experiencing. Her control came through obedience rather than through force.

"I may have some insight to offer," said a voice coming from the Jai Tree entrance. Professor Dhawan stood with a book in his hand.

He entered the room as everyone followed his movements. He stopped in front of Zarya and peered at her.

"Something about your magic was bothering me," he said. "It's a rare gift, yes, but there was something else I was forgetting. A memory I couldn't quite grasp."

Dhawan shuffled forward, coming to stand in the center of the majestic chamber.

"I don't know why I didn't see it earlier. The five of you came here to fight this plague."

He looked at Row, Kindle, Koura, Suvanna, and Apsara, studying each in turn.

"The Chiranjivi have existed for as long as anyone can remember. Magical beings representing each of the realms. Selected by destiny. Of course, the borders of kingdoms and queendoms are merely a convention. They change, they shift, they grow, they die, but the gifts tied to the land do not change. No matter where they've lain over the centuries, each realm has fostered a unique gift bestowed on only one worthy being.

"Often, those gifts are regarded as rare by those around you, but tell me, Apsara, have you actually ever met another vidyadhara who can wield ice?"

Apsara shook her head. "No, most of my kind can only work with wind."

"Not most. All. Only *you* can wield ice." Apsara's eyebrows drew together.

"Suvanna, your ability to draw water from air is also a unique gift, otherwise unseen amongst your people."

The merdeva nodded in acknowledgment.

"Koura, you don't just heal—you can restore life. Name someone else who can do that."

Koura also nodded.

"Kindle, your gift of controlling emotions is extraordinary. While most agni can influence them, you can do much more than that, can't you?"

Zarya shot Kindle a dark look, remembering when he'd assured her he couldn't alter a person's feelings.

"It's not something I choose for people to know. It would make me a target," Kindle replied. Dhawan gave him a knowing glance.

"Row, you are gifted with runes. Only your abilities were strong enough to hold back the blight from your home all those years."

Row's expression was nonplussed, clearly distrusting the place Dhawan was leading with this information. Five sets of eyes regarded each other across the room.

"The Chiranjivi were formed at the end of the Hanera Wars to act as stewards. They were to serve as a reminder to never stray into the darkness again. To never be tempted by its power. And for a thousand years, they have done that.

"Your unique powers have passed through generations as Chiranjivi have died and been reborn. But your creation was so long ago that most people don't remember why they even existed.

"And, of course, that originally, there were seven."

Dhawan's gaze went to Rabin. "Five came when they were called. But one did not. Now, the sixth is here, and I can't help but wonder what forces brought you home."

Zarya looked at Rabin, as did everyone else, while he stared at Dhawan with a look she couldn't interpret.

"Some powerful rakshasas have the ability to shift into animals, but you are the only dragon to exist. Isn't that right?" Dhawan asked, touching the side of his nose, his eyes sparkling. "And everyone knows that to be dragon-touched is to have the luck of the gods on your side."

Rabin nodded as well, his dragon-scale tattoo visible through the opening in his kurta.

"You said there are seven," Apsara said. "Why does this matter?"

Row's gaze flicked to Zarya, full of apprehension, and she stilled.

Dhawan turned to smile at her as she wore the weight of everyone's curious stare.

"The seventh gift, of course, is nightfire."

"No," Row whispered, his shoulders sagging. Zarya cut a glare at him.

"I still don't understand," Apsara said, her gaze jumping around the group. "So, there are seven of us."

Dhawan regarded Apsara with an enigmatic expression.

"The seven of you are together. Whole. Joined for the first time in almost a thousand years, Apsara. There have always been gaps—births, deaths, times when you were scattered across the continent and beyond. And, of course, the missing nightfire kept you from ever being whole.

"But the seven of you are here now—in the same room. And I would bet my very long life on the notion that together, you will be able to defeat the darkness."

Voices erupted in a thousand questions. Zarya quietly digested Dhawan's news, her eyes meeting Rabin's across the room.

"But how?" Suvanna asked. "This knowledge is useless without a plan."

The room fell silent, lost in their thoughts.

"The Bayangoma," Zarya whispered, and every set of eyes snapped to her.

"Zarya, that was just a story I told you," Row said.

"No, they're real. They exist. Right, Professor?"

"They are," he said. "A hidden Bayangoma grove resides less than a week's journey from here. That is true."

"Then maybe that's it," Zarya said. "Maybe that's the answer."

Dhawan nodded slowly, an auspicious light shining in his eyes as he looked at each of them in turn. "Maybe it is. After all, what could be more worthy than the Chiranjivi united after a thousand years, seeking a way to destroy the darkness?"

Several heartbeats of silence suspended everyone in stillness.

"This is nonsense," Apsara cried a moment later. "You can't be serious. A bird is going to tell us what to do about that?" She gestured vaguely in the direction of the swamps.

Koura, calm like a pillar in a storm, laid a hand on Apsara's arm. "What choice do we have but to try?" he asked, his deep voice rumbling. "We are almost at the end. We have no other options. Nowhere else to turn."

Zarya wasn't entirely convinced, either, but she noticed Kindle and Row nodding as they looked to the healer, his golden eyes acknowledging their support.

Suvanna stepped forward, a hand planted over her heart.

"We came here to stop this. It doesn't matter anymore who was right." She glared at each of them to remind everyone it was her. "All that matters is that we save Daragaab and, in turn, all of Rahajhan. This thing won't stop at its borders, and all of our homes are in danger. If there is any chance this is the answer we've spent years seeking, we have to take it."

Rabin strode next to Zarya, his elbow gently brushing her arm. He gave a short bow to Dhawan and the rest of the group to indicate his accepted role in the plan.

Apsara turned to Zarya, seeking out an ally.

"Apsara, I think we have to try," Zarya said. "For Amrita."

Apsara's jaw hardened, her gaze circling the room as everyone else nodded their assent.

"Fine," she said, throwing up her hands. "Make the necessary preparations. We leave first thing in the morning."

Then she stalked off.

TWENTY-ONE

After Apsara's abrupt departure from the throne room, Zarya remained to plan their excursion with Dhawan and the rest of the Chiranjivi. First thing tomorrow, they'd set out on what might be a fool's mission, but no one could deny how many of their hopes were riding on this.

During the conversation, she sensed attention from both Vikram and Rabin, and while she was sure of what the former wanted, she had no idea what to expect from the latter. What she did know was that she had no desire to engage with either, and as soon as they were done, she made a swift exit and went to search for Yasen. She knew she'd have to confront Vikram soon, but she was doing the mature thing and completely avoiding it.

What she needed was a stiff drink and something to distract her until tomorrow. She was once again being forced to reconcile the pieces of herself she hadn't known existed until someone chose to enlighten her. Every time she thought she understood who she was, someone came along to peel away another bruised layer, exposing the raw nerves beneath.

Row had kept this from her, too. She'd seen the look on his

face and the defeat in his posture when Dhawan had revealed how her magic made her a part of the Chiranjivi. What had Row's plan been? To just hope she would never find out? Why had he chosen to do this again when they'd been making such strides in their relationship?

When Zarya found Yasen, he was in the palace ballroom, lounging at a table with a drink in his hand. Massive crystal chandeliers dripped from the ceiling, reflecting soft light off walls covered in jewel-toned silk.

As she slid into the seat next to him, a server immediately placed a drink in front of her. Weren't they short-staffed right now?

"What is going on here?" Zarya asked, referring to the dozens of courtiers chattering with crystal glasses perched in their hands. "Is this a party? Right *now*?"

Yasen pulled a wry face. "I'm almost sure Vik's father arranged the joining with Amrita so he could throw parties like this using the royal coffers. And why not?" He waved his glass over the scene. "It isn't like half the city was devoured by the blight mere hours ago. Why let any of that get in the way of a good time?"

He had a point, but as she surveyed the room, sparkling with conversation and jewels, she wondered if he was being too hard on them. This situation was stressful for everyone.

Though as she watched the nawab sink his teeth into the pink flesh of a fairy's exposed neck, she thought maybe it wasn't all that stressful if you were rich. Perhaps Gopal Ravana saw himself as untouchable.

"What's new with you?" Yasen asked, leaning over and pressing his shoulder against hers. "Any brooding warriors catch your attention lately?"

Zarya flushed and threw Yasen a *would you shut up* look.

She hadn't had the chance to tell him what Rabin had whispered to her before she collapsed in his arms, and she was hesi-

tant to read anything into it. She would die before she called
him out on it and made a fool out of herself again. Besides, she
was still angry about how he'd been treating her, and she hadn't
reconciled how she felt about that yet, especially as she was
increasingly certain that he was magically tethered to her
somehow.

"You're one to talk," Zarya said. "That rakshasa in the
corner can't take his eyes off you."

Sure enough, a ridiculously handsome male was looking in
their direction. His hair gleamed a pale shade of blonde, his
brown skin dusted with gold to match his sherwani that
stretched very pleasingly over his lean frame. Yasen glanced
over, a rakish grin on his face. The rakshasa, sensing the invitation, began to walk over.

His eyes passed over Zarya before focusing on Yasen.

"Is this seat taken?"

Yasen patted the spot next to him. "It is not."

The male sank into the seat when a voice she recognized
sounded behind her.

"Zarya," Vikram asked. "Could I speak with you alone for a
moment?"

Zarya repressed a sigh as she twisted in her seat to face him.

She had a feeling she was about to be cornered again, but
this was good. It was time that she cleared things up. She looked
at Yasen, maybe hoping he'd rescue her from this conversation,
but he was already engrossed with his new friend.

"We'll give you some space," Zarya said. "Enjoy. And be
good."

"You too." He waved at her absently, not looking her way.

Vikram then directed her through the room. They exited a
set of narrow glass doors leading out onto a small balcony that
overlooked the gardens. Partially repaired after the kala-hamsa
attack, they glowed merrily in the twilight. The ocean crashing
on the nearby shore drowned out the sounds of music and

chatter inside, making it feel like Zarya and Vikram were in a world of their own.

"I was hoping we could talk," Vikram said, standing beside her at the railing. "Have you thought about what I asked you the other night?"

"I have," she said. "I'm really sorry, Vik, but the answer is no."

"But why? No one will care, and damn the people who do."

"It's not that," she said. "I mean, it's partly that, but it's more, too."

"What?" he asked, stepping closer.

"I'm just not ready. I've only just started exploring my life and this world, and I want the chance to be on my own for a while."

"I'd give you all the freedom you want," he said. "Whatever you need."

"No, you can't do that. Not if you want what I suspect you want from me."

His lips pressed together, but now she was starting to get annoyed. A "no" was enough. She didn't have to explain herself. He was the one who'd lied to her to start with. He was the one who'd been deceitful, and she needed to remember that.

"Vikram, the answer is no. Please don't ask me this again."

She said the words firmly, hoping they would make her meaning clear. He narrowed his eyes, studying her face as though trying to puzzle out the pieces of her expression.

"Is there someone else? Is that it?"

She was officially losing her patience with this conversation now.

"That is none of your business."

She paused, letting the silence stretch between them until she said, "I'd like to remain your friend, but I must ask you to respect my wishes. I am not, nor will I ever be, interested in pursuing a romantic relationship with you. You lied to me and made a fool out of me, and I've forgiven you for it on a level of friendship, but friends are all we're ever going to be."

At the ominous flash in his gaze, she put a fraction of distance between them.

He noticed her movement, the corner of his mouth curling into a sneer. "What do you think I'm going to do to you?" he asked.

She remembered being in the dining room at the Ravana estate, seeing Gopal up close and thinking she could never picture that sort of malice on Vikram, but she recognized something now—something buried within the depths of his eyes that filled her limbs with lead.

"Nothing. I'm hoping you'll respect my wishes," she said.

He moved to fill the space, and she took another step back.

"Please don't come any closer. You're making me uncomfortable."

Vikram let out a sharp huff of breath and then braced his hands against the wall where she found herself trapped.

"Vik—" she said, her tone threadbare with impatience. If she had to use force, then so be it. "Don't do this. This isn't who you are."

"What's going on here?" interrupted a deep voice.

Rabin now stood in the doorway, his elbow propped against it, his loose posture suggesting casualness, but she noted the bottomless rage simmering in his eyes.

Great. This entire family would be the death of her.

Vikram spun around, and Zarya used the distraction to edge away. Of course, that put her directly between the two men she was doing everything to avoid.

"This is none of your business, Rabin," Vikram said.

"It sounded like the lady was asking you to leave her alone."

Rabin pushed himself away from his nonchalant lean and folded his arms, his posture now oozing with aggression.

"We were just having a conversation. Right, Zarya?"

Vikram looked to her for confirmation, but she wouldn't be siding with him. Her gaze moved from brother to brother, and then she saw Vikram's expression morph into something else.

"Is this... the someone else?" Vikram asked, pointing to Rabin. "This is why you're rejecting me. For him?" Vikram glared at his brother. "You haven't taken enough from me?"

"No. Absolutely not," Zarya said, finally finding her tongue. "None of this has anything to do with either of you."

She stormed towards Rabin and stopped when he blocked her way.

"Move," she said as he peered down at her with an arch of his brow. She glared with the heat of a thousand suns, and after a moment, he stepped aside.

She passed him and then looked back.

"And for the record, I don't need you to rescue me," she snarled at Rabin. "Both of you leave me the fuck alone."

TWENTY-TWO

Zarya stormed through the ballroom, catching sight of Yasen, who was still talking to the rakshasa she'd left him with. She was furious, and she needed to get as far away as possible from every Ravana within cannon-fire distance. She couldn't believe she'd have to travel with Rabin to the Bayangoma grove tomorrow. Avoiding him was going to be impossible.

But she was done. She'd had enough of this family and of him. She burst out of the ballroom and strode down one of the halls, sucking in a sharp breath when she heard her name.

She recognized Rabin's voice, but she continued walking. Could no one take a damn hint around here?

His footsteps sped up, and she considered breaking into a run, but how silly would it look to have him chase her through the palace? She refused to give up the last shreds of her tattered dignity for *his* sake.

"Zarya, please," Rabin said, grabbing her arm and bringing her to a stop. "I'm sorry."

She whirled on him.

"Sorry, about what, exactly? You have a thousand things to be sorry for!" She shook him off. "Leave. Me. Alone."

"No," he said, grabbing her wrist and tugging her closer. "Please just listen to me."

He maneuvered them so she was crushed against the wall with him looming over her, but she wouldn't allow herself to feel *anything*. She'd spent enough time thinking about him and wouldn't give him another moment.

"I'm not interested in this," she said, pressing her hands against his chest, trying to hold him at a distance. "Whatever you have to say, it's too late."

She attempted to scoot under his arm, but as she broke free, he pulled her against him, her back hitting his chest as his arm banded around her waist.

"One minute," he said in her ear. "I beg of you. Then, I'll let you go."

Her hands balled into fists as she thrust her hips, trying to dislodge his hold.

"This is... Let me go," she said, but he pressed harder into her, the air in her lungs turning to mud.

"Once you hear me out."

She growled low in her throat. This bastard.

"I told you to—" she snapped as his hand pressed under her collarbones, his fingers spreading and his mouth brushing the shell of her ear. Her entire body reacted with a flush of heat, slicing off her words and scattering them like motes of dust.

She squeezed her eyes shut, her thighs flexing and her stomach falling through her feet. Why was this turning her on? What was wrong with her? The way he overwhelmed her—his scent filling every corner of her brain. He had her trapped in his strong grip, but she wasn't afraid. No, that wasn't entirely true. She was afraid, but not for her safety. It was fear of the way he made her feel. Like she was tumbling into a pit with no bottom, and it was the most exhilarating rush she'd ever felt in her life.

This wasn't anything like when Vikram had cornered her a

few minutes earlier. This was oceans colliding in a war for dominance, but she was already losing.

"Let go of me," she said, resisting every urge to melt into the blazing heat of his big body. "*Now.*"

There was a moment of hesitation before he complied, releasing his hold. She spun around to face him and opened her mouth, prepared to tear him into bloody strips, but he cut her off.

"I'm sorry for everything," he said, pressing a hand to his chest. "I made a mistake. When we were in the street facing the blight together, I realized I've been a complete and utter fool."

Her hands balled into fists, and she ground her teeth, searching for a suitably withering reply.

"And an ass," she said.

That wasn't exactly what she'd been going for, but it would do.

He nodded sagely. "That too."

"And a dick." She was sort of on a roll now.

"I'm everything you want me to be."

He leaned closer, creating a tense space of nothing between them.

"Where is this coming from?" she demanded. "You've been behaving like you can't stand me for weeks!"

"I can explain everything," he said.

She folded her arms, willing defiance into her expression.

"I want a lot more than an explanation."

"I'll say it with my mouth," he said. "And I don't just mean with words."

She arched an eyebrow.

"You think I'm going to just let you touch me again? After everything you've done?"

He smirked in a way that suggested he knew she absolutely was going to let him. She couldn't decide if that made him more attractive or if it just infuriated her. Either way, she scowled for good measure.

"Don't pretend you aren't aching for me," he said.

She swallowed against the sudden dryness in her mouth and attempted to scoff, hoping it sounded convincing. "You sure think a lot of yourself. I am not," she said, but the words sounded like the hollow lie they were. He chuckled then, the sound vibrating down the length of her spine. He'd always been so serious; she didn't know he *could* laugh.

"I see it," he said. "Those perfect lips parting so prettily. The way your pupils spread. Those delicious panting breaths when I do this."

He reached out a finger, finding the spot where the edge of her top exposed a bare sliver of skin, his warm hand sliding up her ribs. She practically bit through her tongue, trying not to react to the touch as it roared through every nerve in her limbs.

Zarya huffed. "That doesn't mean I want anything to do with you," she spat.

"You don't deny it?"

"It's just physical. It *means* nothing. I feel *nothing*."

She hurled his carelessly tossed words back at him, and fuck, did that feel good.

"I think you're lying."

"You're the liar," she said.

He shifted closer, pressing into her space so his entire body felt like it was consuming hers, his warmth and all his hard muscles nearly touching every part of her.

"You're right, Zarya. I did lie. I was an idiot to tell you otherwise. I feel it, too."

He leaned in closer, his hands planting on the wall on either side of her head as he whispered in her ear.

"I feel it when I close my eyes and think of you spread out on my bed, begging me to fuck you until you can't walk straight."

Zarya was losing the thread of why she had been angry as desire clouded her brain.

"I hate you," she said, just because the words felt good to say.

"I can live with that," he said. "Just let me apologize to you. Let me show you just how sorry I am."

Zarya had to admit she was curious, but she couldn't just give in to him, could she? He'd been insufferable for weeks. What kind of fool would she be to let down her guard at the first offer of... What exactly was he offering, anyway?

His hand dropped, once again finding the waistband of her pants, his fingertips hooking over the hem before his thumb swept along the plane of her stomach. Her lungs went tight as she exhaled.

"Yes," he said with a sense of self-satisfaction. "That right there. That adorable little breath that tells me you feel it, too."

Gods, could he be any more full of himself? She refused to admit it.

He leaned down and ran his nose along her throat. Her head tipped back as she let out another involuntary groan, and the fingers against her stomach dug in, sending a burst of heat exploding below her navel.

What did she want right now? To allow him to continue? A moment ago, she'd said she was done. But now, with his presence and her undeniable need, it was harder to be sure.

"I want to kiss you," he said. "Tell me you want it, too."

"Absolutely not."

The smile on his face spread into a feral grin.

"Is that how it's going to be, Spitfire?"

She narrowed her eyes. "Oh, very clever."

Their eyes met, and it was everything she could do not to arch towards him. She wanted to kiss him, but she wouldn't unless she could trust him first.

He leaned down, but she turned her head, and he stopped.

"Very well," he said, stepping back as her suffocating lungs finally expanded with air. "But don't think I'm done with you. I'll see you soon."

He smiled, revealing the point of one sharp canine before his tongue flicked over the tip. The action nearly made her entire brain seize in her skull. Then, he scanned her from head to toe before he turned to walk away.

She clung to the wall at her back, watching him leave, waiting for the pounding in her chest to settle. She wasn't sure she could even walk right now.

When she finally got her bearings, she headed for the haveli and chugged up the stairs before she stripped out of her clothes and into her nightgown.

She paced the room for several minutes, replaying that moment with Rabin over and over. She couldn't deny everything he made her feel, but he was going to destroy her. She didn't know why she was so sure, but he'd already kicked her heart once, and she was determined not to let him do it again.

That had been too much. All of this was too much. She was spinning out. She didn't know how to deal with all of these conflicting emotions or the complexities of these relationships she'd never had to navigate before.

As much as she'd hated living at the seaside cottage, at least things had been simple. The only people she had to please were Row and Aarav, and since she really didn't care about pleasing either of them, it hadn't mattered all that much.

She climbed between the crisp sheets, hoping to lose herself to the blissful embrace of slumber, but found herself tossing and turning for what felt like hours.

Eventually, she must have drifted off because she opened her eyes and cursed.

She lay in the grass in the dream forest as she groaned, "No, not tonight."

Maybe he wasn't here, but she was positive her luck wasn't that good.

She pushed up, looked across the clearing, and huffed.

He stood with his arms folded, leaning against a tree, all bravado and confidence, half-naked like a fucking gift from the gods. Celestial light highlighted his brown skin, including the swells of his biceps and tapers of muscle that disappeared into the low-hanging waist of his loose black pants.

She groaned again as he smirked.

"I told you we weren't done yet, Spitfire."

"Did you bring us here tonight?" she asked, and he cocked his head.

"You know as well as I do we have no control over this."

She tapered her gaze. "Oh, *now* you're sure about that, are you?" She stumbled to her feet and added, "Well, *I'm* done."

She looked up as if seeking an escape from the heavens, spinning around. She turned again and then squeaked when Rabin appeared directly in front of her.

He took a step, and she backed up, her calves hitting a large rock behind her. Where had that come from?

"Zarya," he said, his voice filled with an authority that reminded her he was used to commanding an army of thousands. "Sit."

Her legs melted out from under her as she collapsed onto the rock.

Dammit. How did he do that?

He surprised her by dropping to his knees.

"I wasn't done apologizing," he said. "In fact, I'd barely started."

She huffed out a strained laugh. "And you're going to do it from your knees?"

He arched a dark eyebrow. "If that's what it takes."

"I... uh..." She rubbed her face. Why couldn't she think straight?

He pressed in closer, and she shut her eyes, trying not to become distracted by the way he smelled or the way he felt against her. She was angry with him. He'd been terrible, and he would have to grovel first if he wanted anything else.

His hands gripped her ankles, and he uncrossed her legs before he moved between them, the insides of her thighs pressing against his warm torso. Waves of heat rolled up her limbs before pooling low in her stomach.

"I still don't understand this sudden change," she said, her breath coming in short pants. "You were so sure we shouldn't do this."

"I was wrong," he said. "You and I both know this forest means we're inevitable."

He had a point.

She knew she should stop him. That she shouldn't let him get any closer, but she was paralyzed and couldn't seem to react. He slid his large hands up the sides of her legs, slowly, so agonizingly slowly. He pushed up the edge of her nightgown, exposing the top of her knee, and then leaned down to press the sharp tip of his tooth to the delicate skin on the inside of her thigh.

She shivered and gasped, her skin pulling up gooseflesh and her nipples peaking.

"I'll do whatever it takes to earn your forgiveness. And your trust," he murmured against her.

"You've got a long way to go," she said, trying to sound determined, but it was clear he wasn't deterred.

He shifted and dragged his hands higher, gripping her hips, sending a burst of butterflies in her stomach.

"I will never give you a reason to doubt me again," he said. Then, he leaned down and kissed her shoulder, his lips warm and soft. It sent another tremble climbing up her back as she squeezed out a reflexive moan.

"Tell me you lied," he said, peering up at her through a fringe of dark lashes. "Tell me you feel it, too."

"Of course I do," she whispered. "I already told you that."

He licked his lips—his full, perfect lips—and moved closer as his hands slid higher under her nightgown, his palms curling over her ribs.

"Does that mean I can kiss you?"

"No," she said. "You pushed me away. Remember? Left me standing alone in an alley after I nearly *died*."

The gold flecks in his eyes fused into dark bronze points, and she caught a moment of contrition flash across his face.

"Then I have an idea," he said. "One I haven't been able to stop thinking about."

"What?" she asked.

"Your book," he said. "The one that described tasting the... 'nub of pleasure,' was it?"

Zarya sucked in a sharp breath. "What about it?"

"There are other places I can kiss you."

"What do you mean?" she asked, pretty sure she understood but wanting to hear him voice it out loud.

His mouth arched into a half-smile that did erratic things to her heart. Things that might literally kill her.

"I want to taste your pussy and fuck you with my tongue, Zarya. Is that clear enough?"

She nearly choked on her own tongue. "Is this your apology?"

He leaned down to press his mouth to her navel, his warm breath permeating the thin fabric covering her stomach.

"It is. But only part of it."

Zarya swallowed. Hard. She'd never had someone do that to her, though she'd thought about it plenty of times.

"I don't know if that's appropriate," she said, but her voice was so stretched it was painfully obvious she was barely holding it together.

"Has anyone tasted how sweet you are, Spitfire?"

She didn't want to admit her inexperience. He was too damn sure of himself.

"Of course. Loads of times," she lied.

"Oh, did you have many suitors locked away by the sea?"

She almost laughed at her ridiculousness. Of course, her lie was too easily disproven. They all knew her history.

"I don't think that's any of your business," she said, and his eyes went black.

"I don't like the idea of anyone else touching you," he said.

"Well, that's too fucking bad," she said, lifting her chin. "I am my own woman."

He hooked his hands behind her hips and then jerked them forward so her ass was perched on the edge of the stone.

He lifted one of her legs with his hand under her knee and ran his nose along the length of her thigh, stopping just short of her center before he dragged it in the other direction as stars burst in her vision.

With his other hand, he shoved up the hem of her night-dress, exposing her underwear. He smiled as if to himself, as those golden flecks in his eyes sparkled.

Then, he leaned down and pressed his nose to the wet fabric between her thighs. She gasped, her head falling back as she arched into him.

"Beautiful girl," he murmured. He closed his mouth over her, his tongue pressing into the silk, building friction against her clit. But it wasn't enough. Her hips bucked, and he let out a low, dark laugh. He hooked his fingers into the sides of her underwear and yanked them down roughly. After tossing them away, he tugged her closer, her legs spreading wide for him.

"Unless you tell me to stop, I'm going to devour this wet pussy. Do you understand?"

She whimpered and nodded right before he lowered his

head. Before he could touch her, she grabbed a fistful of his hair and yanked his head back up.

"This doesn't mean I forgive you," she said, and the light in his eyes gleamed with the sadistic pleasure of a new challenge he had every intention of winning.

"When I'm done, you'll be the one on your knees begging for forgiveness."

She tried to scoff, but he didn't give her the chance as he licked her from back to front with a filthy slide of his tongue. She groaned as her hands found purchase on the rock behind her, her fingers digging into the unyielding surface.

The tip of his tongue swirled against her, causing her legs to jerk with a pitiful whimper.

"Oh gods," she whispered as he continued licking and tasting her.

A moment later, she felt a pressure at her entrance and then the slide of his thick finger working its way into her. As he continued to suck and tease her clit, he pumped his hand in and out.

"Gods, you're so tight," he moaned. "Do you think you can handle more?"

"Yes," she said, not even sure what he meant, but she did want more. More of anything he was giving her. Gods, she was so stupid for doing this, but this felt so good.

She felt him slide in a second finger, and she inhaled sharply at the intrusion, the way she felt so achingly full and stretched. He curled his fingers, and she clutched the stone, feeling like she was falling.

"That's a good girl," he whispered as he continued pumping in and out. "Fuck my fingers like they were made for you."

Zarya's eyes fluttered closed as she reveled in every sensation. Every twitch of her body and roll of pleasure that spiraled through her limbs.

"Open your eyes," Rabin ordered. "Look at me when you come."

She did as he asked, unable to resist that voice that commanded her to do his bidding like the helpless, silly butterfly she was. His tongue found her core again, and he continued sucking and biting gently as he watched her from under the fringe of his dark lashes.

Slowly, he dragged her closer to the edge as her toes pointed and the muscles in her arms and legs shook. But she held on, wanting to experience this moment for as long as she could. It was exquisite torture wrapped up in the release of a breath she'd been holding for far too long.

Another rough circle of his tongue had her head spinning, her vision sparking with points of light, and then she blew apart, her cry echoing against the trees and leaves and still night air as wave after wave of cresting warmth bloomed from her stomach.

Rabin moaned as he continued tasting her, his face buried between her thighs like he was a man starving for water. When she stopped shaking, he pulled away, and she watched as he licked his fingers clean, savoring the taste of her in his mouth like it was the sweetest wine.

"Do you forgive me yet?" he asked, and she pinned him with a glare.

"Never."

He grinned and flashed his sharp teeth, running his tongue along them.

"Then it looks like we're going to have to do that again."

TWENTY-THREE

When morning arrived, Zarya's eyes blinked open with a haze of exhaustion. She couldn't have gotten more than a couple of hours of sleep. She wondered if her body rested while she was in the forest or if it had the same effect as being wide awake?

Because gods, she'd never been more awake in her life.

The last thing she could recall was Rabin's smug expression after he'd made her come so hard she'd forgotten her own name for several seconds.

She slapped a hand over her face. Maybe she shouldn't have let him do that. He'd probably be completely insufferable in an entirely different way now. But that had felt so good and so *right* at that moment. Like every second they'd shared over the past months had been leading up to this. She had wanted more then, and she still did, but she would be damned if she wasn't going to at least try to make him work a little harder for it.

She had her dignity, after all.

Sort of.

After lugging herself out of bed, she dressed in the leather armor she'd purchased with Yasen and cantered down the stairs.

Aarav sat at the kitchen table eating breakfast. A large

platter of spiced eggs and potatoes sat in the center, and he gestured towards a chair.

"Eat up," he said. "You've got a long journey ahead of you today."

Then, he peered behind her as if waiting for something.

"What are you looking for?"

He shrugged. "Just wondering if you had someone up there with you last night."

Her face flushed with warmth.

"Why would you think that?" she asked.

"Because you were making some very... audible noises last night."

Oh no. She'd been moaning in her sleep. Her face turned even hotter as Aarav's face stretched into a mischievous smile.

"There's no one up there," she said. "There was no one up there."

He cocked his head in an amused question, and she realized that didn't sound any better.

"I mean... Ugh, it's hard to explain."

He held up his hands in surrender, his fork clutched between his fingers.

"Hey, it's none of my business how you satisfy your urges."

She tossed him a dirty look. "Oh, like you're one to talk." She stomped to the table and dragged out a chair. "Where is Lekha, anyway?"

"At work in the infirmary," he answered.

She dropped into her seat and pulled a plate towards her. "I guess you'll be glad to have this place to yourself while Row and I are gone."

He grinned.

"It's going to be clothing optional in here for a few days," he said with a wink.

"Gross," Zarya answered as she spooned eggs onto her plate,

and he chuckled. She took a bite of eggs—they were delicious. "You cooked me breakfast?"

Aarav shrugged. "I figured you've done it enough times for me."

Zarya looked at him, stunned for a moment, without any idea how to respond. "I... Thank you."

"Don't mention it," he said and then, after a short pause, added, "Zarya, I want to say something."

"Yes?"

"I want to tell you I'm sorry."

She sat back in her chair.

"For what?"

"I was jealous of you."

Her brows furrowed, and she folded her arms across her chest.

"You were?"

"Row sometimes talked about how powerful you would be someday," Aarav said as he sat forward and rested his hands on the table.

She let a heartbeat pass between them and then said, "You knew?"

Aarav nodded. "That you were Aazheri, yes. But not your lineage. I didn't know, either, why he kept you there, but he told me that if he could find a way to unlock your magic, you'd be powerful beyond his imagining."

"But you didn't stop him from keeping me there."

Aarav's shoulders slumped heavily. "I've always known my power would be limited. My parents weren't especially gifted. They sent me to study with Row, hoping I'd amount to something. They were old friends of his. I wanted what he had. What a powerful Aazheri could be. And you had it. And you had Row's admiration, even if it might not have seemed like it to you. He's always respected your courage. Even I could see that, and I hated you for it. It was childish of me." He stopped. "*You* were a child."

"An orphan, in fact," she added, unable to resist.

The corner of his mouth tipped up in a wry smile. "An orphan, in fact," he agreed.

"Are you saying all this because I might die out there," she joked.

He laughed. "Can you let me have one moment instead of cracking jokes?"

She found herself smiling in spite of everything. "Thank you, Aarav. I probably could have done my part, too. I wasn't the easiest kid to live with."

"That you were not," he said, and she made an indignant sound as his shoulders shook with laughter.

"I'd better go," she said after a moment, and he dipped his head. "Do you know where Row is?"

"He went over to the palace already. He said to tell you they'd be leaving soon."

"Right," she said, shoveling in more eggs and pouring herself a glass of lukewarm chai before she drained half in one gulp. "What are you going to do while we're gone?"

"Do my best to keep the monsters off the streets until you return with what I hope is a solution."

She scanned the length of him in his Khada uniform. He wore it well. "I'm proud of you," she said, and he blinked. "You've given so much of yourself to this cause. I think you also have a lot of courage, Aarav."

This time, he seemed to be the one at a loss for words. Finally, he pressed his hands together in front of his heart. "Thank you, Zarya."

She pushed up to stand and turned to leave. Before she did, she turned back to ask, "Do you ever think about that night? When Row... killed your friends?"

Aarav gave her a pensive look, the lines in his forehead pleating.

"Every single day," he said.

"Me too." She put her hands on her hips and let out a deep breath. "I'm sorry. I never meant for that to happen."

"I know you didn't," he said. "I'm sorry, too. I should never have blamed you for it."

They stared at each other for a moment.

"Did we just... kind of make up?" Zarya asked, and Aarav snorted.

"Kind of. But let's not let it go to our heads, hey?"

She smiled and nodded. "Good idea."

"Be careful," he said. "Don't get yourself killed out there."

"I'll do my best." Then, she pressed her hands together before her heart, dipped her head, and turned to leave the haveli.

As the door closed behind her, she hoped she would be coming back. There was no pretending everything would be okay in Dharati anymore. Either they found a solution, or they would all die. There was no in-between. Everyone's hopes were riding on it.

She hung a left, entering through one of the palace gardens, wanting to inhale the fresh scent of roses one last time. She was being maudlin, and she knew it, but a worrying premonition that nothing would ever be the same again hovered like a rain cloud overhead.

She stopped at the sound of raised voices, recognizing that low, deep timbre that had haunted her dreams last night. Peering around a bush, she caught sight of Rabin and Gopal Ravana standing nearly toe to toe, hunched towards one another in aggression.

Gopal said something in a low voice that Zarya couldn't hear, and Rabin's arm struck out, his hand closing around his father's throat. Gopal wasn't a small man by any measure, but Rabin was taller and wider, and Gopal clawed at his throat as Rabin pulled his father off his feet, the nawab's toes tickling the pavers.

His mouth gaped as Rabin's brows lowered.

"This is your one warning, Father," he said, spitting out the last word. Rabin leaned in, hissing in his father's face. "If you touch a hair on her head. If you speak another ill word to her or anyone else. If you think an evil thought. If you so much as breathe in her direction wrong again, I will find out, and I will hunt you to the ends of this earth, and I will tear every one of your limbs from your fucking body before I send each one to a different corner of the continent."

Rabin squeezed as Gopal's mouth opened like a beached fish, sweat streaming down his face. The loathing in his eyes was palpable. When he didn't answer, Rabin cracked his head against the stone pillar behind him.

Gopal groaned.

"Is that understood?" Rabin asked, and slowly, Gopal nodded.

"Say it."

"How dare—" the nawab got out before Rabin squeezed his father's neck again, choking off his words.

"Don't," Rabin said. "Don't you fucking dare. Do you understand me?"

"Understood," Gopal finally gasped, glaring at his son with naked rage. Rabin held on for a few beats before finally releasing his father and stepping away.

"Don't think you have any control over me or my life, Father. You have no right or say in anything I do. You lost that privilege years ago."

Gopal clutched his throat, bending double as he coughed and sputtered.

"You got your crown," Rabin snarled over his father's hunched form. "Be content with that."

Frozen in place, Zarya squeaked when Rabin's gaze flew up to her.

"Fuck," he breathed, running a hand down his face, before he stormed towards her, grabbed her arm, and started dragging her away.

"What was that about?" she asked as she scurried to keep pace with his furious strides.

"Nothing."

"Obviously," she answered, but she kept her mouth shut as she took in the rage simmering in his expression and the tension in his jaw. When they'd cleared the garden, he released his hold.

"What are you wearing?" he asked, and she blinked at the abrupt change of subject.

"I... What?"

"This. What are you wearing?" he gestured to her.

"I bought this in the city," she said, smoothing her hands down over her stomach. His eyes tracked her every movement, and she couldn't figure out his problem now.

"It's useless," he said, waving a hand. "This won't protect you against anything. It just looks nice."

She had no idea how to respond to that. "Okay? It's too late for me to go shopping now. Gods, you can't help but be an ass, can you?"

He glared at her before he turned away, rubbing his hand against the back of his neck.

"Are you okay?" she asked. In spite of herself, she was concerned about the conversation she'd just witnessed. What had they been arguing about? Rabin had said something about leaving "her" alone. Who was the "her" in this scenario? Zarya recalled the mention of a sister and wondered if that might be it.

Rabin eased out a low growl before turning around to face her, his gaze scanning her apparently useless armor once again.

"I will be." Then, he jerked his head. "We should get going. They'll be waiting for us."

* * *

The Chiranjivi waited with Vikram and Yasen in the courtyard, shaded under the canopy of Amrita's branches.

Dhawan and Suvanna had their heads bent together, conferring on how they would make their way to the nearest Bayangoma grove.

Rabin stalked past her and paced along the far length of the space, clearly trying to calm his festering temper.

"Zee," Yasen said, and she turned to find him approaching. He stopped and scanned her from head to toe with a quizzical look.

"What?" she asked, looking down at herself. Was he going to comment on her attire, too?

"You got laid," he said, and her mouth dropped open.

"What?"

"I can tell. You have a glow," he said, coming closer and then leaning down before he sniffed. "Plus, you reek of Commander Rabindranath Ravana."

Yasen grinned as she tried to find her voice around her flustered tongue.

"What happened? I want every detail."

She looked around, checking to see that no one was listening before she stretched up on her tiptoes and whispered everything in Yasen's ear.

When she pulled away, he was beaming. He slapped her on the back so hard she nearly stumbled. "Glad you finally got some tongue, Swamp Girl. Maybe you won't cry so much now."

She rolled her eyes. "Maybe."

"Are you ready for this little adventure?" he asked.

"I think so. I wish you were coming, too."

He would remain here with the army as its commander. She still hadn't coaxed him into sharing his feelings regarding his new position, but when she returned, she intended to sit him down and make him spill his thoughts.

She'd cry if she had to.

Zarya had heard many speculative rumors through the palace wondering if Rabin would be resuming his role, but given the way Vikram was glaring at his brother right now, she didn't think that seemed very likely.

Yasen snorted. "And have to watch you and Rabin make 'fuck me' eyes at each other for the next week? No, thank you."

Zarya made an indignant sound. "We are not doing that!"

Yasen gave her a pointed look and then glanced across the courtyard where Rabin stood, giving her what really did look like "fuck me" eyes, apparently taking a break from his brooding.

Zarya huffed and turned to Yasen. "Fine, stay here and protect the queendom." They both glanced at the man in question, who was still watching her with that same hunger.

"Besides, I'm still angry at him. I'm making him work for it," she said. "After everything he put me through."

"Are you?" Yasen asked, clearly skeptical.

"Yes. Kind of. Mostly."

"That's my girl," Yasen chuckled, wrapping her in a hug. "We've never been especially close, Rabin and I, but we did spend many years living under the same roof. Those who served under him still respect him. Including me. I just hope he isn't as scary when you kiss him."

"I haven't let him kiss me yet," she said, weirdly proud of that.

Yasen whistled. "Wow, playing hard-ass. I can respect that."

Rabin's fierce intensity didn't exactly frighten her, but there was nothing subtle about his attention.

"Be careful, Zee. Okay?"

Zarya got the sense he didn't just mean on the journey.

"I will be," she said. "We'll be back as soon as we can."

He wrapped her in a hug and squeezed her tight. "I'll miss you. This place won't be the same without you."

"I'll be back. I promise," she whispered, hoping that was true.

TWENTY-FOUR

"Everyone ready?" Row called to the group, and they all exchanged wary looks. They were as ready as they'd ever be. Everyone nodded before mounting their horses and heading out of the courtyard.

As they passed through Dharati, Zarya studied the ruined buildings. Everything was hollow black ash, the air heavy and distended with an unnatural silence.

Zarya kept in step with Row.

"We're going this way?" she asked.

"The Bayangoma grove is on an island off the southern coast. We have to go through the swamp. From the coast, we'll take a boat to Ranpur Island."

"Can't you use magic to get there and skip the swamp?"

"I can transport one, maybe two other people at a time, depending on their size, but transporting you all wouldn't save much time."

Zarya took a deep breath as they passed the city walls. The gates had crumbled in the last attack, leaving a pile of rubble, reminding them all this was a queendom teetering on the edge of ruin.

Row pulled ahead, and Zarya hung back as awareness pricked up the back of her scalp. She hadn't ventured into the swamp since the night of the ajakava attack. Not since she'd embraced her sixth anchor.

Was she imagining things, or did it feel... different?

As they crossed into the blight, she swore she could hear the sound of heartbeats and rattling breaths buried within a soft whisper. Did the ghost army still linger in this place? Or was the swamp more alive than she'd ever given it credit for? She scrubbed the back of her hand across her eyes, trying to dispel this foreign tension that wound up her spine.

"Are you okay?" came a deep voice, and Zarya looked over to find Rabin trotting beside her.

"I'm fine. This place is just... unsettling."

They traveled slowly, their horses hampered by the bog sticking to their horses' hooves.

"What about you?" Zarya asked. "Do you want to talk about what just happened with your father?"

"No," he said, the firmness in his tone clear.

"Okay," she said before he cut a glance to her, his gaze softening.

"I'm sorry. That wasn't your fault. He just"—he let out a low growl—"pisses me the fuck off."

"I understand. He seems like he would have been a warm kind of father you could really look up to."

That almost elicited a smile, the corner of Rabin's mouth twitching reluctantly.

They continued riding as everyone fell into silence, clearly sensing the wrongness of this place, too. Zarya did her best not to steal a thousand looks in Rabin's direction. Sitting on his horse in his black armor that formed to his muscles, his midnight hair gleaming in the sunlight, he was like some dark god chiseled from the ruins of sin. But the last thing he needed was anything else to inflate his ego.

"I have a question," she asked after they'd been riding for a while. "The day the blight attacked Dharati, you talked me through how to use Aazheri magic, but the day you fixed the rift by the palace, you said your magic was different from mine. How did you know what to do?"

He shrugged one of his broad shoulders.

"I've always had a keen interest in magic. I've read a lot about Aazheri, so I have some idea of how it works."

"So, why didn't you show me when I tried to fix the rift?"

Rabin looked away and ran a hand along the top of his head. Was he blushing?

"Maybe I was trying to show off?"

Zarya barked out a laugh that echoed through the silent swamp.

"That's cute," she said as Rabin glared at her. "I was *very* impressed, Commander."

"I am not *cute*, Spitfire," he growled.

Zarya batted her eyelashes, and he continued scowling as she laughed.

"So, do you believe this is the darkness, then?" Zarya gestured to the decay surrounding them.

He flicked his reins as he surveyed their surroundings. "Power, magic—they aren't inherently evil. They are simply tools. What matters is how they're used. It's just a name. The darkness isn't any more evil than water or air."

"Do you really think so?"

"The darkness is another way to define the limits of magic. Much like your spirit anchor, it simply offers added leverage to wield power. Everyone puts too much stock into trying to define it as an antithesis to other types of power. It isn't good or bad, nor is anyone who possesses it. The only thing that locking it away achieved was to limit the extent of what's possible."

Rabin gave Zarya a careful look then, and she wondered if, somehow, he had gleaned her secret. Could she tell him? Zarya didn't trust him enough for that yet, but a sharp and jagged piece shook loose inside her. At least Rabin might not condemn her for this thing she carried inside her.

"When you held my hand during the blight attack," she said, "I felt my magic grow more powerful."

He blinked, a line forming between his brows.

"I know. I felt it, too," he said, giving her another meaningful look.

She'd given a lot of thought to the idea that he might be her paramadhar. Did that mean he would also be forced to align with the darkness? Would he balk at the idea if he didn't view it as an evil entity like everyone else?

"Do you think that means something?" she asked. She didn't know how common knowledge of paramadhar was. She'd considered asking Dhawan, but after he'd rebuked her for asking questions about the vanshaj, she'd been wary of speaking with him. Plus, she had a weird feeling he'd been trying to prevent her from unlocking her nightfire after that useless lecture about blocks of magic.

"It might," he said. "Do you have a theory?"

She shook her head. "No. I don't."

Rabin scrutinized her, but she turned away before they continued riding.

"Is it my turn to ask a question?" he asked.

"Yes?"

"Why didn't you tell Row I lifted the binding curse?"

Zarya rolled her eyes at Row's back. "He doesn't need to know everything."

Amusement sparked in Rabin's gaze. "You told Yasen, though. About us?"

"There is no 'us,'" she said pointedly, but all he did was give her a knowing smirk. She sighed. "He dragged it out of me. The forest. All of it."

"You've become close friends."

Zarya smiled. "We have. I don't know what I would do without him now."

"I've always thought he was too good for this miserable family."

"Well, your family sure is something," Zarya said as Rabin tossed her a rueful smile.

"Maybe now is a good time to tell me what sort of relationship you have with my brother?"

Zarya wrinkled her nose. "Do we have to talk about that?"

"Vik and I haven't spoken in years, and I know I have bridges to mend."

"I don't think what we did last night will help you on that front."

"Tell me," he said with that same authority that had made her crumple like a dried leaf last night.

She sighed before she answered.

"He was one of the first people I met when I came to the city, and he was kind to me. I thought he was handsome, and I enjoyed his attention." She shrugged. "I don't have much experience with relationships, but I did know what I felt."

"Which was?" he asked, his voice a low, irritated snarl.

"Gods, don't get all possessive on me. I didn't even know you existed then."

"Yes, you did. When did the dreams start happening?"

"Okay, fine, but I didn't know if you were real then."

"Fine," he said, and she rolled her eyes.

"Anyway, we got to know one another, and I thought we were heading towards something special, but he hadn't told me about Amrita and what his future meant."

Rabin blinked. "He didn't tell you any of that? He just... lead you on?"

Zarya narrowed her gaze. "I really don't think you're one to be criticizing anyone in this context."

His nostrils flared, but he didn't respond, clearly conceding her point.

"When I found out, that changed things for me. It's not that I didn't have feelings for him, but I had no desire to be a part of a relationship that had to be hidden. So, I told him as much, and that was that."

"That was that?" Rabin asked.

"Sort of," she said. "He was still interested in pursuing things and has said so several times, but when you found us, I'd just told him it was over for good."

Rabin sighed.

"So, if you're looking to mend fences, pursuing something with me might not be the way to go about it."

"Hmm," he said as his gaze swept over her, a hungry look in his eyes.

"Why are you looking at me like that?"

This time, she was rewarded with a smug smile.

"I was thinking about what happened last night."

She pressed her lips together. "Well, don't. That was... nothing."

"You're the one who brought it up."

"Because I was trying to explain..." she trailed off at his grin. He was clearly riling her up. "Stop it."

"I can still taste you," he said in a low voice that carried softly over the space between them. "And, fuck, the way it felt to have my fingers inside you. I'll carry that to the end of my days."

She pretended she hadn't heard him, flicking her reins and doing her best not to react. Was it possible to die from this curl of desire that was squeezing around her heart?

"I can't *wait* to get you alone again and feel you come on my cock, Spitfire."

That got her attention.

"Will you shut up?" she said. "Someone is going to hear you."

"So?"

"So, that isn't going to happen," she said, though she was already sure this was a losing battle. Why was she pretending?

"Yes, it is," he said with such certainty that she either wanted to smack him or hold out for eternity just to prove him wrong. But who would she be punishing then?

She shifted her gaze away when her attention caught on a tree she was sure she recognized. She looked around, seeing the boggy lake where she used to lie in wait, hunting for naga.

Prickly, uncomfortable heat flushed up her neck at the realization.

Her breath started to come in tight knots that wedged in her throat.

She didn't know why this hadn't occurred to her. They would need a place to sleep tonight, and there was nothing else out here.

There it sat, visible between the trees. Its white walls and thatched roof. Its border of greenery protecting it from the blight.

That day, when she'd felt the wind in her hair and the taste of freedom burning like coals on her tongue, she had vowed never to set eyes on this place again.

Her seaside prison.

TWENTY-FIVE

Every memory she'd been suppressing for months came rushing back with the force of a tidal wave, knocking the breath out of her lungs.

Everything was exactly as she remembered it. The crash of the ocean on the shore. The bright flowers in bloom. The weighty sense of oppression that made it feel like she was trying to inhale sand while she was drowning.

She brought her horse to a stop as she stared at the line of rune-marked trees—the glowing etchings that had been the source of her protection and the limits of her cage. Row's magic had continued to hold the blight back through all these months.

Sliding off her horse, she clutched the saddle as she watched the others approach the house, her heart galloping in her chest.

Rabin looked over his shoulder and pulled his horse back around, dropping onto the ground beside her.

"This is where he kept you, isn't it?" he asked.

She nodded and pointed to a spot nearby. "And that was the spot where I'd black out if I wandered too far away."

Rabin growled low in his throat as they watched Row's retreating back.

She was cemented to the earth, too numb to move. What if she were somehow trapped here again? Now that she knew what lay beyond this place, she would die if the world was ever taken from her again.

Rabin moved closer to Zarya. "Do you want to spend the night somewhere else?"

She turned to him, wondering at his motives, but only found sincerity and the obvious desire to protect in his fierce gaze. "Where? With the swamp monsters?" she asked.

Zarya shook her head. "No, I can do this."

She straightened her shoulders and willed her feet forward.

As the house came into clearer view, she thought of the day she'd leaped on Row's horse and escaped into the forest— that first moment of freedom so bright and sparkling and clear.

"I thought I'd left this place behind forever."

Her voice was as wooden and hollow as the space behind her heart.

Rabin's hand settled on the small of her back, her heartbeat instantly settling. She frowned at him. Did he do that on purpose?

He bent his head and whispered in her ear. "No one is going to keep you here against your will ever again. If Row tries anything, I'll slit him from ear to ear with a fucking smile on my face."

A snort burst out of Zarya's mouth, and she covered it as her body shook. She had no idea why that was so funny right now. His eyebrow arched at her reaction.

"Something amusing, Spitfire? That's not the usual reaction when I threaten to kill a man, though I have to admit your obvious taste for violence is kind of hot."

He winked, and she smiled. He was so damned sure about everything that it was easy to believe everything he said.

"Thank you," she said, meaning it. "That helped."

"I'll tie the horses up." He paused and then added, "But I'm here if you need me."

He shook his head as though he wasn't sure why he'd said that before he walked away. She watched him and then approached the front door.

With a hand on the doorknob, she watched as everyone settled themselves, some claiming the sofas, others unfurling bedrolls on the floor. Food was taken out of packs and passed around.

Not saying anything, Zarya walked past and to her little bedroom at the back of the house. She ran her hands over the dusty bookshelves, visiting her oldest and most loyal friends. On the bed was the rumpled black salwar kameez with stars she had worn her last night on the beach, waiting for Row and Aarav never to return.

Sinking to the floor, she leaned against the bed, her arms braced on her knees and her head tipping back. A tear funneled from the corner of her eye, slipping down her cheek as she spiraled into the memories of the past.

The heaviness squeezed her ribs until it felt like they'd collapse under the weight.

She hated this place. No matter what pockets of comfort this room and her books had brought her over the years, they had been only a bandage over an open wound. This had been her cage, nothing more. She sniffed and rubbed her nose with the back of her hand.

"Why are you crying?" came a soft voice, and she looked up to find Row hovering in the doorway.

"Why shouldn't I be crying?"

He came in and sat on a chair in the corner with a weighty sigh.

"Zarya, I will forever regret the choices I made in regard to your upbringing. I should have been honest with you, at the very least. You deserved that much."

"Yes, I did. I deserved a lot more than that."

He nodded, and she'd never seen him look so... worn. "I hope one day you'll find some way to forgive me. Seeing how you've grown in such a short time, I realize how much I underestimated you. How much I didn't understand who you are. But you're just like your mother. Strong and brave, and scared of absolutely nothing. She would have loved you to her very core."

Zarya caught the wistful expression in his eyes that seemed to burn with a thousand haunted memories of her loss. He really had loved her.

"As you grew up, you began to resemble her so much. There were days I could hardly look at you. It hurt. It was a constant reminder of the woman I'd lost."

She opened her mouth to reply when Row raised his hand.

"None of that was your fault. Not one moment of that was your doing. I knew that, but I was heartbroken, and I am ashamed. I thought too much of myself and too little of you. I'm sorry, Zarya. I'm so sorry."

The warmth of tears ran down her face, and she let them fall.

"Thank you for telling me that. I'm not ready to forgive you, though.

"But I am trying," she added, softer.

He dipped his chin. "I understand. I will do whatever is in my power to show I am worthy of your forgiveness. I know it will take time, but know this is my greatest wish for us. For you."

He slapped his knees and then pushed himself up, giving her one final lingering look before he walked out. Zarya flopped her head back against the bed, looking at the ceiling. Between Aarav, Row, and Rabin, there a lot of apologies and personal reckonings going on in her life. This was getting exhausting.

The tiny room suddenly became cloying and oppressive, and she got up, stalking back through the living room.

Zarya headed outside and into the garden where she'd spent so many hours. She stood at the water's edge, staring at the sea. How often had she fantasized about diving into it and swimming to freedom?

An echo of time found its way into her subconscious. That night when she'd ruined Aarav's life, too. She still heard the screams of Aarav's friends as Row hunted them down. Why had Row deemed her worthy of such protection? Because he loved her mother? Maybe a part of her hoped that he loved Zarya, too.

Suddenly, that mattered for the first time in her life.

The evening was starting to cool, and she wrapped her arms around herself as the wind tossed her hair. She closed her eyes and inhaled the smell of the sea. This had always been one joy she could cling to.

Zarya dropped onto the sand, wiping her eyes.

Someone came up behind a moment later, wrapping a blanket around her shoulders.

Rabin sat down beside her. "I thought you might not want to sleep in there tonight."

"That... was very thoughtful," she said, realizing it was the quilt from her bed.

"I can be very thoughtful," he said, and she snorted.

"I hope you brought something to drink, though."

"Obviously." He produced a bottle of cashew feni, and she reached for it as he pulled out the stopper and handed it over. She took a long swig of the botanical spirit, tipping her head back and savoring the burn down her throat.

Then, she returned it and wiped her mouth with the back of her arm. He chuckled and took a swig of his own.

"Do you want to talk about it?" he asked.

She shrugged, not saying anything for a few moments.

"Sometimes, I can understand why he did it," Zarya said finally. "Why he thought he was doing the right thing by keeping me hidden. Maybe it did save my life. But I can't understand why he had to lie about it. Why couldn't he have told me the truth? Would that have been so hard? I would have understood. It would have changed everything if I'd known."

Rabin sat back, stretching his legs out and leaning against a log. He folded his hands and crossed his ankles.

"Sometimes, truth is difficult. Even when you know it's right, it gets stuck inside you and claws away at you. Sometimes, it can be the hardest thing to reveal."

"Hmm," Zarya said, scooting back next to him and tucking her knees up. They sat in silence, watching the waves gently lap the sand.

"I'm not defending Row, but perhaps what he gave you was his own truth," he said.

"What do you mean?"

"Look at you—you spent your entire life on this tiny spit of land, and yet you emerged not as a meek, cowering woman, afraid of the world.

"That sword you use with such strength; he gave you that. I've been a soldier my entire life, and I've seen what happens when people learn to protect themselves. They become something else entirely. Confidence can be earned. I know part of that was already in you, Zarya, but Row said he couldn't give you your magic, so instead, he gave you that."

Zarya stared at the man sitting next to her.

"Or, if I'm out of line and you want me to shut up, I will."

She smiled. "No, that actually makes sense."

He leaned in, stopping just short of their arms touching. "I can be surprisingly insightful, too."

She rolled her eyes. "I'll try to remember that." She looked back at the house and then at him. "You were right. I don't want to sleep in there tonight."

"Then don't. Sleep out here. It's a beautiful night. I'll stay with you if you like."

Her gaze narrowed with suspicion.

"What?" he asked.

"Don't get any ideas. If I let you stay, then it's only so the demons eat you instead of me."

He lifted his hands in surrender. "Oh, I have all kinds of ideas." The meaning in his tone was clear. "But I'll keep them to myself tonight."

"See that you do."

He handed her the bottle of feni. "More?"

"Absolutely."

She grabbed it and took another swig as together they watched the distant setting sun.

TWENTY-SIX

A small blue and white tugboat bobbed in the water as Zarya opened her eyes the next morning. She rubbed them, wondering if they were playing tricks on her. Where had a boat come from?

Then, she realized she was completely draped over Rabin, his arm wrapped around her, and their legs tangled together. She went completely still. When they'd fallen asleep on her blanket, she'd been sure to keep at least two feet of space between them.

She slowly looked up, praying he wasn't awake and could extricate herself without being noticed. But she was met with a pair of dark, golden-flecked eyes dancing with amusement.

"Comfortable, Spitfire?"

She squeaked and scrambled away, crawling backward on her hands like a crab until she hit the sand and plunked onto her butt. Rabin sat up with a smirk.

"Was it good for you, too?" he asked.

"Shut up."

She was no stranger to sleeping on the beach, but she'd

never slept as well as she had last night. There was no way she was admitting that, though.

The door to the cottage slammed, and they looked over to see Row striding out. He paused as he took in Zarya and then Rabin, a deep furrow creasing his brow. She knew that look all too well and wasn't having *this* conversation right now.

She leaped up and pointed to the boat bobbing happily in the water. "Where did that come from?"

"It's always been there. I took away the cloaking spell," he said in a very matter-of-fact way, like she should have known that all along.

Zarya sputtered, choking out an incredulous laugh. "There was a *boat* there all this time? Just sitting there?"

"Sorry," Row said, his expression apologetic. She didn't know why this annoyed her so much—it's not like she would have known how to steer it, but an escape route had been there all this time? She pinched the bridge of her nose, glaring as Row walked towards it. Being here, surrounded by the artifacts of her former captivity, was proving to be a lot to handle.

"I hate boats," Rabin mumbled, his eyes dark. Zarya remembered when Yasen had told her that rakshasas avoided the water.

"Don't tell me Daragaab's greatest commander is afraid of a little water," she said, and Rabin frowned up at her. She was learning to read these frowns and their various subtexts. There were the truly angry ones, the slightly irritated ones, and ones where he was mostly faking it. This frown seemed to be of the annoyed variety.

"I'm not afraid. I just don't like the water. There's a difference." Then, he narrowed his eyes. "Why are you smiling at me like that?"

"It's nice to know there's *something* fallible about you."

He gave a derisive laugh. "I promise there are many things fallible about me. Never forget that."

Suvanna, Kindle, and Apsara filed out of the cottage as Koura and Row readied the boat for departure.

Zarya walked along the small dock and hopped aboard. Rabin stood at the end, one foot resting on the planks, eyeing the boat with mistrust. Suvanna cackled behind him before she slapped him on the back and shouldered past. With a few long strides, she sprung up onto the prow, flung out her arms, and then dove into the water in a graceful arc.

"Come on," Zarya said, waving him on as he reluctantly stepped into the hull. Benches lined the stern, and they all found a spot. Zarya sat next to Rabin, who leaned forward, his elbows braced on his knees, his head hanging down.

Suvanna surfaced from the water a moment later, and the boat shot forward, cutting effortlessly along the frothing white waves.

"Are you going to make it?" she asked Rabin, whose skin had taken on a delicate shade of green. As much as she wanted to give him a hard time right now, he looked absolutely pathetic with his head between his knees.

"I'm fine," he replied in a clipped tone. He ran a hand down his face. "Sorry. I'm a little anxious."

"It's okay," she said, but decided she would try to distract him. He'd supported her inner spiral last night, and she wanted to return the favor.

"So, tell me why they still call you commander," she said, leaning her elbows on her knees and her face in her hands. "Yasen once mentioned Daragaab's former army commander, who expanded Rani Vasvi's territory and ensured its enemies were few. I assume he meant you."

He looked up at her with a crease between his brows. "Guilty. And because that's who I used to be to many of them. Most of those people served under me. I was their commander for almost a hundred and fifty years. I suppose old habits die hard."

"How old are you, anyway?" Zarya asked, the true depth of immortality weighing on her.

"About two hundred. After a certain point, you kind of lose track. It doesn't really matter anymore."

"What about Yasen and Vikram?"

"Ah, just over a hundred. They're close in age. My father is around five hundred."

Zarya was quiet for a moment. She'd always considered her existence in the context of a normal human lifespan, but now the future spread before her with endless possibilities.

"You'll be there before you know it, too. Life, even an immortal one, moves swiftly."

"It's hard to comprehend."

Rabin smiled at her, still leaning on his elbows. "Thank goodness you'll have more time than that."

He gave her a significant look that she chose to ignore. They could be friendly, but he was still on the road to groveling back into her good graces.

"What was it like being Daragaab's commander for all that time?"

He stretched his neck, clearly considering his words.

"Bloody and brutal," he says. "But it also made me feel alive."

There was a rawness in his voice as he stared into the distance, the horizon of Daragaab's shore fading away.

"Will you come back?" she asked. "I don't think Yasen wants the job."

Rabin's gaze flicked to her. "Why not?"

"I'm not sure, but I don't think that was ever his ambition. I don't think he likes being in charge."

Rabin let out a long breath. "I don't think Vik would choose me. There's probably some noble whose favor he needs to curry, who will serve as a more diplomatic choice."

Zarya raised a brow. "That seems like a dubious reason to select someone to lead your army."

Rabin shrugged. "Such is the way of royals and courts." His words bore an edge of bitterness.

"Why did you leave?" she asked. Maybe this was none of her business, but she was burning with curiosity. His gaze shifted to her. She couldn't describe what she read on his face. Too many conflicting emotions flashed in his eyes.

"That's a long story," he said, a bite still in his words.

"Does it have to do with your father?"

"In part," he said, but he didn't elaborate.

"I understand what it's like to carry the pain of those who try to control you."

"How do you know that's what he did?" he asked.

She shrugged. "You said that to him. That he had no control over your life anymore. When I overheard you in the garden."

"One day... I'll kill him," Rabin said with a deadly edge to his voice, and she had no doubt he meant that. "I will make him pay for every hateful thing he's done."

"I wouldn't judge you."

He stared at her as if trying to parse out the sincerity in those words. She didn't know why she said it. Why would he care if she judged him? But she understood that raw need for vengeance.

"Thank you," he said.

"For what?"

"For trying to distract me."

"Did it work?"

"I'm always distracted by you, Zarya. I thought I made that clear."

He gave her a heated look that had warmth crawling through her stomach and dryness coating her throat. He leaned back and chuckled.

"What are you laughing at?"

"You keep pretending you don't want it, but I can read it in every line of your face."

She shook her head. "Just when I was starting to dislike you a little less, you have to go and open your big mouth and say something arrogant."

He laughed again, but it was cut short as he was hit with a wave of nausea, and he buried his head in his hands and groaned. She decided he deserved it and was done trying to make him feel better.

She reached into her bag, pulling out her mother's notebook. Leaning back, she flipped through the pages. She was slowly working through her mother's careful research, treasuring every loop and scratch of ink and its mere presence, knowing she had created these words.

"Where did you get that?" Row sat down on her opposite side.

Zarya opened the book to the picture of her mother and passed it to him.

"I stole it from your study," she said matter-of-factly. She no longer felt guilty about taking it. He should never have kept this from her, but she didn't have the energy to remind him of that. The look on his face suggested he'd already realized it.

He took the book and traced the image of her mother's face. "I haven't looked at this in ages. She was so beautiful."

He looked at Zarya, blinking heavily.

"Have you read it?" she asked.

He shook his head. "I couldn't translate it."

"What do you mean you couldn't?"

"I mean, it never changed for me." He gave her a sharp look. "Why? Have you? How?"

"I saw Dhawan translate a book in the library, so I just tried the same thing. A bit of my blood and some spirit woven with fire and earth."

That made Row's face pull into a frown. He handed it to her.

"Show me."

"Sure," she said, pulling out the dagger from her belt and performing the same spell again. "It's my mother's notebook," she said once she was done. "It outlines all kinds of history and knowledge about Aazheri and their magic. Where did you get it from?"

"When your mother was pregnant with you, I took it as a souvenir before I left Gi'ana," Row said, conflict passing over his expression as he stared at the page now open across her lap.

Zarya smirked. "So, you stole it, too?"

Row smiled slightly. "I guess I did." He opened his mouth and then closed it. "May I see it?"

"Of course," Zarya said, handing the book over. He flipped through the pages, going back and forth as the line between his brows grew deeper and deeper.

"What is it? What's wrong?" she asked.

"Zarya, this isn't your mother's handwriting." He looked up at her. "It's been many years, but I would know his mark anywhere. This notebook belonged to your father."

TWENTY-SEVEN

"Are you sure?" Zarya asked, peering at the page. The words somehow looked different now. Less like a warm hug and more like a snarling monster with teeth. The soft curves and swoops she'd traced so many times with her fingers morphing into harsh points and slashes. A pen carved into paper with brutal force.

Row rubbed two fingers to his forehead and blew out a breath.

"I'm sure. He must have given it to your mother."

"Or she stole it, too," Zarya said, and Row nodded.

"Or that."

"Why couldn't you translate it?" she asked.

"Because he enchanted it to reveal its pages only to someone who shared his blood. When I couldn't translate it, I had already surmised that was the reason, though, like you, I assumed it was your mother's."

"His blood," she said, and Row looked at her. Any lingering doubts that his theories about her parentage hadn't been entirely accurate evaporated at that moment.

"So, it wasn't hers." Zarya grabbed the book back, flipping through the entire thing, hoping she'd find something that indicated her mother had used it, too. But it had all been written in the same hand.

"I thought it was hers," she whispered, choking on the words. She didn't know why she was so upset, but it felt like she'd just lost another piece of her mother.

"I'm sorry," Row said. "But you'll always have her necklace. That was hers."

Zarya touched the pendant that hung around her neck, and Row gave her a small smile.

"I'm sorry that it's all I can give you of her."

"It's okay," she said, wiping the corner of her eye with the back of her hand before the tear welling in the corner could fall.

"Row?" Zarya asked the man who was the closest thing she could claim as a father.

"Yes?"

"Could you tell me all your stories of your time together? You must have a lot. How long were you together?"

"Many years," he said and then swallowed hard, the apple in his throat bobbing. "And of course. That would give me great pleasure to share everything with you, Zarya. An honor."

Her heart clenched at the glimmer of hope in Row's eyes. She would try to forgive him. She was so tired of being angry.

They sat together in comfortable silence as they continued sailing over the sea. Soon, the sun began to set, the ocean sparkling with light.

Apsara stood and pointed in the distance. Zarya followed the line of her finger, squinting into the falling night.

"There it is," Apsara said.

Zarya could make out the buildings lining the coast, golden and gilded against the setting sun.

"Ranpur Island."

The boat docked, bumping against the shore before they hopped off. Rabin stumbled his way onto the ground, falling to his knees and pressing his forehead to the earth. He sucked in several deep breaths as everyone gave him a moment to recover.

Other than Suvanna, everyone seemed to sympathize with his plight.

"Is he going to be okay?" Zarya asked. "Why does he react so strongly?"

"His magic is deeply tied to the land," Kindle said. "I'm the same way in the cold."

"And I struggle with heat," Apsara added. "Our gifts bind us closely to our homes."

"Does your magic change the further you are away?"

"Yes," Kindle said. "That's why you don't find many who live outside their natural homes. Only Aazheri have the freedom to move about without similar restraints."

"Fascinating," Zarya said as Rabin pushed himself up. He ran a hand over his head, shaking off the last of his nausea.

"What are you all looking at?" he grumbled. "Let's go."

They all turned and headed out of the harbor into one of Ranpur's bustling streets.

"We'll need horses," Row said.

"Where are we going next?" Zarya asked.

"To the city of Premyiv," he answered. "It's at the heart of the island. That's where we'll find the grove."

They set out on their journey, stopping to rest for the night when the sun had set.

Zarya lay awake, listening to the soft snores surrounding her, thinking of her conversation with Row on the boat and the notebook that belonged to her father. Would she ever meet him in real life? Did she want to?

She twisted the turquoise jewel that hung around her neck between her fingers, thinking about her mother. She recalled the image in the book with the swirl of magic surrounding the pendant, and on instinct, she floated a tendril of spirit out. Was there any way to feel the heartbeat or the echo of the woman this had once belonged to?

She watched as the pale light surrounded the stone and then sunk into the surface.

Zarya. A woman's soft voice.

She sat up, looking around, searching for the source. Row, Rabin, Apsara, and the rest all slept quietly.

"Who's there?" she whispered into the silent dark.

Her hand had wrapped around the stone, and she pried her fingers open, sending another tendril of spirit into it with more force.

Zarya. The voice came again.

She continued feeding magic into the stone, her heart thundering in her ears.

If you're hearing this, then you've found a way to unlock your magic. I knew one day it would happen, but I tried to protect you for as long as I could.

Zarya's heart seized behind her ribs. *This* was her mother. It had to be.

Your father will come for you. Whether it's soon or many years from now, he will find you. The day the oracle foretold your coming was a death sentence for both of us.

"Mother?" Zarya whispered as the briny sting of tears seared her eyes.

I don't have much time, but no one else knows everything the prophecy said. The oracle chose it for my ears alone. Only I know it in its entirety, and now you will, too.

> *To the queen of the west, an heir shall rise.*
> *Gifted of fire to tame the night skies.*
> *For the people caged by the stars after the fall,*
> *She will be the one to free them all.*

Zarya. Know that I loved you. That I always will. That I had no choice.

Zarya had stopped breathing entirely, her head swimming with the lightness of confusion. She gasped, sucking in a lungful of hollow air as the light around the stone died.

"Mother," she whispered, calling up another tendril of spirit. The same message repeated itself. There was nothing else to draw out, but it was already more than she could have ever imagined.

She listened to it over and over, and only after she'd tasted every syllable in the cadence of her mother's voice did she finally take a magnifying glass to the words.

The first two lines were clearly about nightfire. That part she already knew, but the rest. The *rest*.

To the people caged by the stars.

That could only mean one thing.

She looked into the distance where she knew the rest of Rahajhan lay.

Punished for a thousand years for the actions of two fabled kings.

She had felt the power in Meera's markings—the affinity between their magic.

She inhaled a sharp breath, feeling it like a rib-shattering kick to the chest.

She will be the one to free them all.

TWENTY-EIGHT

When they entered Premyiv the following day, the sun was setting over a crystal blue lake stretching so far into the distance that the other edge was lost to the horizon. Their destination was another island at its very center where the Bayangoma grove resided.

After Zarya's incident with her mother's necklace, she'd lain awake until she'd finally caved to sleep. But she'd dreamed of dark, ancient things for which she had no name. The arrival of morning had been a relief, and she couldn't get the loop of her mother's words out of her head.

What did any of it mean?

"We'll find a hotel for tonight," Suvanna said. "Tomorrow, we'll hire a boat to take us across the lake."

"Why not tonight?" Zarya asked, attempting to focus on the task at hand. She was here to help fulfill this mission. After they returned, she'd have time to dig into the layers of what the prophecy had meant.

"The Bayangoma are only awake for one hour at midday," Kindle answered to her left. "There would be little point in heading there now."

"Besides," Apsara said, gesturing to a massive barge in the middle of the water, "it's Diwali tonight, and they won't let any boats out due to the fireworks. I think we could all use a comfortable bed tonight, anyway. It's been a hard few days."

Zarya couldn't disagree with that as she stretched her stiff neck and watched Rabin eye the water with mistrust. She wondered why he didn't just transform and fly his way to the island.

Suvanna argued with one of the dock hands, and Zarya was impressed the man hadn't melted into a puddle while being subjected to the focus of her ire. He gestured one last time and turned before she stormed back towards them.

"We're set for tomorrow," she said. "He wanted to pilot the boat for us, but I am not allowing some yokel to tag along with us under any circumstances. This mission is too important. *I* will steer the boat."

"Well done," Apsara said with a slight smirk. "We appreciate your... determination."

Suvanna huffed and allowed herself to be dragged into the city's heart, where they found a hotel for the night, everyone looking forward to a warm shower, hot food, and a proper bed.

"Let's all meet for dinner in an hour," Koura said. "I spoke with the hotel manager, and we can find food and drink at the nearby street festival. It will be a chance to enjoy the celebrations."

Everyone nodded and then headed up to their rooms.

A large canopy bed covered in blankets and pillows of pink and orange and green, embroidered with gold, dominated one wall of Zarya's chamber. The spacious room opened out to a small round balcony overlooking Lake Madhy. Zarya squinted into the distance, but the enormous lake stretched out, too large for her to see anything but its smooth, glassy surface. Her room also offered a view of the fireworks barge where people scurried about, setting up for tonight's promised show.

Zarya entered the bathroom to wash off the dirt and dust of travel. This far south of Daragaab, the evening was warmer, and she changed into a lightweight dress of sage green silk, the bodice decorated with golden swirls of beads. The skirt fell to mid-shin, and the thin straps left her shoulders bare.

A knock sounded at her door as she was putting on some finishing touches to her makeup.

She opened it to find Rabin leaning against the frame with his thick arms crossed. He was also freshly showered—and devastating—in black pants and a sleeveless white kurta that hugged his chest and showed off the swell of his biceps.

"Yes?" she asked as his gaze raked over her, making her skin flush.

The past two days had been an exercise in strategic maneuvering as she'd done everything she could to avoid getting too close to him. But he'd made that nearly impossible with his heated looks and constant innuendoes. She was ready to climb out of her skin if she didn't give in to this swirl of fire practically roasting her from the inside out.

"I thought we could skip dinner with the others," he said, looking as sure as the devil standing over his firey dominion. "And go somewhere alone?" He smiled, a dimple popping in his cheek that practically shredded her heart.

"Where?" she asked, hating how thrilled she was by the suggestion.

He shrugged his impressive shoulders. "I found a place. Private. Discreet."

She wanted to say yes, but she was trying to think with her head and not her heart or her... more inconstant body parts because they continued to betray her at every moment, no matter how many times she told herself she would make him wait.

"Coming?" Row said as he appeared in the doorway, an imperious look moving between her and Rabin. For once, she didn't object to his interference. This was the rescue she needed from making a bad decision.

"Yes," she said, closing the door behind her and brushing past both men before she hurried down the stairs to find the others waiting in the lobby. She resisted the urge to turn back and supervise whatever interaction was now happening between Row and Rabin.

Suvanna was a vision in a fitted dress made of light blue silk, her blue-green hair pulled into a high ponytail, the curling tendrils brushing the tops of her narrow shoulders. Apsara had cast off her usual white jacket, leaving only a sleeveless top, the shapely cut of her arms, and her feathered wings attracting plenty of attention. Zarya noted the sweat beading on her brow, remembering what Apsara had told her about the heat.

Outside, they were greeted by the sights and sounds of the festival already in full swing. They joined the crowd, finding an endless line of food stands serving everything from kachori to lassi to every flavor and variety of chaat one could imagine.

The cheerful stands were garlanded with bright orange marigolds and curls of gold ribbons. Lining the sidewalks were large terracotta pots filled with more bright flowers, wrapped with strings of twinkling lights.

It was a burst of color against the dark night. A bright spot in the looming threat they'd all been living under. How could people be so carefree and happy when their world was crumbling at the edges? She was happy to see this, though. Relieved to find a place the blight hadn't reached yet, and she tried not to think about what might happen to these people if they failed tomorrow.

They couldn't. They had to figure this out, not only for the citizens of Daragaab but for every person who might come under its shadow next.

Once they each chose a dish or two, they gathered at one of the dozens of tables that sat on an elevated boardwalk overlooking the lake, a wooden railing running along its length. Koura arrived a moment later with a large jug of beer in each hand and set them down.

The mood was light as they shared their food, tasting bites of earthy chole bhature or a nibble of sweet, syrupy malpua. It was obvious how badly they'd all needed a break from the constant worry of the blight. They had a job to do, and everyone was counting on them, but even wayward heroes needed a moment of rest.

Well, everyone was enjoying themselves, save a certain dark-haired rakshasa who stood with his elbow planted on a high table while he sipped at a glass filled with something that looked strong.

She felt his gaze on her and applauded herself for sidestepping his earlier invitation. He might have wanted things to go a different way tonight, but he could wait. He had made this bed, and now he could lie in it.

She ran a hand down her face with a sigh.

Don't think about him in bed.

As the evening wore on, the celebration swelled in a crescendo of dancing and music, and Zarya lost herself in its carefree rhythm.

Eventually, she found herself seated next to Apsara, who leaned back in her chair with a foot kicked up on another. She held a cool glass of water to her forehead as she watched Suvanna converse with Koura, who towered over her slight, delicate frame.

Zarya's gaze wandered to Rabin lost in a discussion with Kindle. She mentally traced the contours of his profile—the sharp slope of his nose and the curve of his lips. The way his dark hair spilled over his shoulders like rivers of shadow. The lines of his shoulders and the slight flex of muscle in his forearm as he lifted his drink.

"So. Rabin, hey?" Apsara said, tearing through her thoughts.

The winged woman now sat with her arms folded on the table, leaning towards her.

"What?" Zarya asked, pretending like she hadn't just been dissecting him piece by piece.

"Don't play dumb," Apsara said, arching an eyebrow. "You think we can't all see how he's obsessed with you?"

She snorted. "He's not obsessed with me. He's just angry he can't have what he wants."

"What does he want?" Apsara tipped her head in question.

"I don't know. He wants..."

"To fuck?" Apsara asked with a grin as Zarya choked on her drink, "That much is obvious but beyond that?"

"That's what I don't know."

Apsara pressed her lips together. "Fair enough." She appraised Rabin from head to toe. "No one would blame you if you want to"—she swirled a hand in the air—"try out the horse. So to speak. Especially when it looks like that."

As if sensing he was the subject of their conversation, Rabin's gaze turned to them, his glass pausing in midair. Zarya burst out laughing, covering her mouth with her hand. His eyes narrowed into knife-sharp slits.

"Ooh, that's his scary face," Apsara quipped. "You're in trouble now."

"Me?" Zarya laughed. "You're the one who called him a horse."

Apsara grinned—it was nice to see her loosen up.

"Keep up the interrogation, and I'll turn it back on you."

Apsara blinked, keeping her face neutral. "I don't know what you're talking about."

"Oh, please. Like everyone hasn't seen you and Suvanna getting cozy."

It was Apsara's turn to glare.

"Ooh, now there's *your* scary face," Zarya teased, which

forced a smile from Apsara. They both looked at Suvanna, who was still talking to Koura.

"Suvanna... doesn't do relationships," Apsara said eventually like it was something she'd repeated to herself many times. "It would never work, anyway. We're from two very different worlds. Wings and water don't mix."

As if to make her point, she ruffled them softly.

"Do you love her?" Zarya asked.

Apsara's jaw tensed. "That's a very personal question."

"It is, isn't it? Sorry, I grew up in a prison, so I'm not the best at social cues."

Apsara laughed and took a drink of her beer.

"Now I see why Yasen always calls you weird," she said, and Zarya made a high-pitched sound of indignation.

"He does *what*?"

"Just a few times," she said with a chuckle as Zarya huffed.

* * *

It was getting late. The others had wandered off to explore the festival, and Zarya found herself alone, standing at the railing overlooking Lake Madhy, staring at the stars.

She felt a presence behind her, and a pair of strong arms she was all too familiar with landed on either side of the railing, caging her in. She braced herself for the inevitable.

"You've been avoiding me," Rabin said in her ear.

"I've been busy," she replied before feeling the breath of his low laugh spread across her shoulders. He moved closer, and she resisted the urge to lean into his heat, knowing she couldn't hold out against his attention for much longer.

"Did you brush me off for dinner because Row showed up or because you didn't want to be alone with me?"

She inhaled a deep breath. "It's not that I don't want to be alone with you," she said. "I'm just..."

She didn't want to admit she was afraid of what might happen.

"I was hoping to 'apologize' to you again," Rabin said, his voice rough and his meaning clear. He lifted a curl of her hair off her shoulder, twisting it in his fingers, before pressing his nose to it.

Good gods, why was that so hot?

No. She wasn't ready to crumble for him yet. First, she had some things to get off her chest.

She whipped around to face him.

"Let's talk about what *exactly* you need to apologize for."

His lips pressed together. "Give it to me, Spitfire."

Zarya scoffed. She held up a hand, counting his offenses.

"First. You accosted me at the joining ceremony and then yelled at me."

Rabin's throat rumbled, and he stepped closer, an intense look of regret on his face.

"Did I hurt you?"

"No," she admitted. "But you frightened me, and you were such an ass."

She counted off another finger.

"Two. You continued to be an ass when you *accused* me of spying on you."

"Zarya—"

"No, I'm not done yet."

She counted a third finger.

"You stole my book like a *child* and refused to return it."

The corner of his mouth tipped up. "But I had to know what was happening inside that head."

"Fourth. You sliced open my leg when we were sparring."

He snorted. "I'm not apologizing for that. You drew blood first. I thought you were a warrior."

"Is this you being sorry?" she asked, and he gave her a

knowing smile. She would never have respected him at all if he'd gone easy on her.

"Don't pretend you didn't give as good as you got."

"Fourth—"

"You already did number four," he said, moving closer, crushing her against the railing and his hard chest and his infuriating hips. "Five."

Her nostrils flared in irritation.

"Five," she spat. "You touched me and then abandoned me in the forest."

He opened his mouth, but she didn't let him finish.

"Six. You claimed you felt nothing in that forest, and *you* are a fucking liar. You made me feel like a fool!"

His hand slid off the rail and clamped around her hip. A sharp jolt of heat speared between her thighs, making her nostrils flare. She was only dimly aware of the busy street churning in the distance. Right now, it felt like they were the only two people in the world.

"Zarya," Rabin said. "I'm sorry. I am the fool. When I arrived in Dharati, I wasn't expecting to find you at the palace. Then, I saw you in the vicinity of my father, and I jumped to so many conclusions that I regret."

He took her hand, lifting it to his mouth before pressing his lips against it.

"Let me make it up to you. Let's start over. I will never give you a reason to doubt me again. I swear it."

He dropped her hand, once again caging her in his arms. Hard lines met soft curves, and it was driving her to the edge of madness.

"Please," he said, and there was so much sincerity buried in that single syllable that she finally felt the seams of her resolve weakening.

"I'm not very experienced with this," she said and then

winced. She hadn't meant to say that. But if she were being honest, some of her hesitation hadn't only been about her anger with him.

He pulled back with a confused look. "Is that what this has been about?"

"When I told you the other night that I'd done that loads of times, I might have been lying. I mean, I've had sex in the most basic terms, but it wasn't very memorable, and it was only that. None of the... flourishes, if you will."

She was speaking a mile a minute now, feeling her face heat with embarrassment.

"You and Vik didn't—" He stopped, cutting off the thought as Zarya shook her head.

"No! We just kissed a few times."

Relief crossed his expression to be replaced with a dark look. "I admit I'm thrilled I don't have to compete with my little brother. Or that I have to kill him for touching you."

She let out a wry laugh and shook her head, knowing she was probably about to regret her next words.

"There was no contest. There never was," she admitted as a smug grin crept to his face. "From the moment I stepped into that forest..."

He nodded. "Me too."

His hand returned to her hip before he squeezed it.

"Zarya, your level of experience is inconsequential to me. In fact, I rather enjoy the idea of being your first."

"You aren't my first," she said. "Let's make that clear. Don't get any notions of staking your claim or some other alpha bullshit."

He grinned as his fingers dug in.

"No, but I will be your best."

"Do you ever give it a rest?" she asked, and he grinned.

"When I'm done, that asshole who had the audacity to skip

eating you out when he had the chance will be a forgotten memory."

Zarya huffed out a laugh, trying to hang on to some semblance of the upper hand.

"There you go, thinking so much of yourself," she said, but the words were too breathless to have their intended impact, and he knew it. It was obvious he was finally inching over the battle line of their clashing wills.

His thumb swept out, caressing the plane of her stomach, sending her into freefall.

"Let me show you everything," he said with a nearly bestial growl, making liquid heat pool in her stomach. "I want to pleasure you, Zarya. I want to spread you out and fuck you until you see stars."

"What about the biting?" she asked, remembering the conversation with Yasen and Vikram outside Jai Mahal all those months ago.

Rabin's eyebrows rose, and the corner of his mouth ticked up.

"That's part of it—if you want." Zarya nibbled on her bottom lip as she caught a flash of his sharp white canines. "I'll show you that, too. I'll show you whatever you want."

His fingers continued to trace idle circles along her ribs as he pressed into her harder. She felt the unmistakable evidence of how this conversation was affecting him.

"Have you thought about me? When you're alone?" he whispered in her ear.

"Yes," she said, and he grinned against her cheek.

"Did you touch this pretty pink pussy?" he asked, his hand sliding down to cup between her legs. She gasped as she clung to him for support.

"I did," she whispered.

"Did you put your fingers inside yourself as you thought about me?"

"The night we danced in the forest," she said as his hand tightened against the back of her neck. "And the night you abandoned me. And maybe some other times, too."

A low growl rumbled in his chest.

"I want to watch you," he said. "Will you touch yourself for me while I watch, Spitfire?"

Her gaze met his, and the hunger and earnestness in it dissolved any lingering feelings of shame or embarrassment. She was gone. Every argument she could fathom had dissolved into a pile of dust at her feet.

"If you want," she said, and light sparked in his eyes.

"Let me kiss you," he breathed, his mouth so close that she tasted the brush of his breath. It was warm and smoky, like the liquor he'd been drinking, and the burning edge of desire curling between them.

"Yes," she replied. He tipped her head back, the gleam in his eyes so damn satisfied. She moaned as he kissed her; his hands and his mouth burned like sunbaked sand. He kissed her with abandon, his lips firm and demanding. He wasn't just kissing her—he was consuming her. Drowning her in a river of heat and lust that had been cresting for months.

It was every lingering look and gentle touch. The way he'd held her hand as she'd fallen asleep. The way he'd come to her rescue, releasing her from her bound magic. The way he'd saved her, plucking her out of the sky like a falling star. The connection they shared, even if she wasn't ready to name it yet.

Her arms looped around his neck as his hands slid up her ribs, his thumbs sweeping out to caress the arcs of her breasts. He moaned into her mouth, and the sound sent a lightning bolt of desire straight to her throbbing clit.

"Are you done with the fireworks?"

Had they started? She looked up as a cascade of light rocked overhead, flooding the world in blue, red, and yellow. She hadn't heard a thing.

"What fireworks?" Zarya asked, and Rabin smiled against her mouth.

"Then let's get the fuck out of here."

TWENTY-NINE

Rabin took her hand, and they pushed through the crowds. More fireworks detonated in showers of light as they made their way back to the hotel and up to Zarya's room.

The door nearly ripped off its hinges when Rabin slammed it behind them and pressed her into the wall, his hands roaming over every inch of her body. There was decadence in the relief of finally giving herself over to this. Being angry. Being skeptical. It was exhausting. But this was like finding a breath at the bottom of an ocean.

"If I do anything you don't want, tell me, Zarya," Rabin said as he slid the straps of her dress down her shoulders. "Promise me."

"I want everything," Zarya replied, meaning it with every bursting chamber of her heart. She wanted to be consumed by him until there was nothing left but a smile on her face. "Don't hold anything back."

He pressed his hands against the wall and leaned towards her. "You're sure about that? Because, gods, the filthy things I want to do to you."

"I am," she said, sliding her hands under his kurta, exploring the exquisite ridges and dips of his muscles. He felt exactly like she'd imagined so many times she'd lost count. He went still with his eyes closing as she ran her fingers over his chest and stomach and then up his back. He shivered as if he, too, was finally catching his breath.

His eyes opened, and he reached behind his head, yanking off his kurta, allowing her unfettered access to the topography of his skin.

When it seemed he could no longer cling to his composure, he made a ragged sound as he crushed himself against her. The feeling of his warm skin was like being dipped in liquid silk.

Slowly, he pushed down her dress, sliding it over her hips and letting it fall to the floor. He stopped and backed up, rubbing his chin as his gaze rolled over her like a burning flame held to her skin or a match sparking against dry kindling.

Her legs shook, not from fear or nerves but from heady, breathless anticipation. She'd dreamed of a moment like this for so long. With someone just like this. A handsome warrior like the ones in her stories. Someone who would wake her up from her daydreams and remind her she was real.

He continued his slow, hungry perusal before claiming her lips, his tongue plunging into her mouth, his hands cupping her ass before he explored the curve of her throat and the swoop of her collarbone. A hand slid up, cradling her breast before he squeezed it, pulling out a moan. He teased her nipple, rolling it and pinching the sensitive tip hard enough to make her gasp.

Her head fell back as he explored the terrain of her skin with his fingers and his lips.

"I need to taste you again," he said. "It's all I've been able to think about. I'm going to eat you out until you have to beg me to stop, and then you'll come on my cock. Do you understand me, Spitfire?"

He said it in that authoritative voice she couldn't resist, not that she wanted to. She tried to answer him, but whatever response crowded her throat died as he fell to his knees and pressed his nose between her thighs.

"Fuck, you're fucking perfect," he said with a rumble. His finger hooked into her underwear, drawing them down her legs. Then, he stood up and scooped her into his arms before carrying her to the bed.

He laid her down and then unbuttoned his pants. Zarya leaned up on her elbows to watch him undress, riveted to all six-plus feet of his fierce male beauty. Her gaze fell on his thick cock that stood hard and erect, her eyes widening at the sight. He was... big. A lot bigger than she had imagined and definitely very different from the fishing boy in Lahar.

"You look worried," he said with a smirk as he climbed over her.

"I... What... Is that going to fit?"

He chuckled softly. "It will fit."

She nodded with a knot lodged in her throat. "If you say so," she whispered.

He lowered himself onto her, his delicious weight pinning her to the mattress. He kissed, and she squirmed beneath him, craving friction between her damp thighs. He made a low, throaty laugh, sensing her impatience.

"Are you ready for another apology?" he asked, and she blew out a shaky breath.

"Yes, please."

"I knew I'd wear you down, eventually."

She breathed out a laugh. "Don't push your luck."

His soft but insistent lips trailed over her skin—her breasts and her ribs. Her stomach and that sensitive spot under her navel. Lower, he moved until he slid off the edge of the bed.

"Here I am, once again on my knees for you," he said.

He lifted her leg and kissed the inside of her thigh as he moved towards the apex before he shifted to the other leg. She made a sound of impatience, and he looked up with a wicked gleam in his eyes.

Then, he bent down and sucked on her clit so hard that her entire body bowed up. She gripped the bedsheets as he thrust his tongue inside her, his hands gripping her thighs as though he was holding every part of himself back.

He moaned as he swirled his tongue and hummed into her. Her limbs liquefied as her vision blurred out into a wash of white noise as she fought for a sliver of oxygen.

"Fuck, you taste like magic," he murmured as he slid a finger into her and then licked her again until she was teetering on the edge, ready to plunge.

"Oh, Commander," she groaned, and then she shattered apart, breaking into a thousand points of nothing. Zarya cried out as fireworks lit the sky through the windows, ribbons of blue and purple and red and green bathing their flushed, naked skin as her brain seemed to forget where it was, and it took several long seconds to catch up to the present.

"You know," Rabin said, still kneeling between her legs. "When you say it like that, I don't mind that name." She let out a breathless laugh, still floating at least six inches off the bed.

He nipped kisses along the insides of her thighs, crawling back up the length of her body, trailing more kisses, each one like a brand staking his claim.

"You're forgiven. Just don't fuck up again," she said, and this time he laughed, the sound clear and light, and she loved that sound probably more than she should. She still wasn't entirely sure what he wanted beyond this night, but she was doing her best not to get into her head about it. That bottomless feeling in her stomach was nothing to be concerned about, right?

As he stretched over her, she reached down, circling her hand around his cock. Squeezing it gently, she slid her hand up and down, exploring the length and weight of it. Each prominent vein and the way it pulsed with every languid stroke.

His hips thrust, and she loved the sound of his tortured groan. He'd spent the last several days trying to undo her—break down her walls—and now it was her turn to exact a dose of revenge.

She maneuvered herself out from under him and pushed him on his back, straddling his hips. He gripped her thighs, looking up with an expectant expression. She'd never done this before, but she'd read about it enough. She was confident she could manage. How hard could it be? Though as she took him in her hand again, she wondered if she'd make that fit, after all.

Well, Zarya was always up for a challenge.

"What's going through that head?" he asked, and she crooked up the corner of her mouth as she stroked him with a firm grasp. His eyelashes fluttered as his fingers dug into her thighs, the pressure bordering on the edge of bruising.

"It's my turn to 'apologize,'" she said.

"You don't have anything to be sorry for."

"Pretend that I do," she said, and his eyes darkened.

"Then apologize away, Spitfire. I'm furious with you."

She snorted a laugh and then bent down, sucking on the curve of his neck as she continued stroking his cock, feeling it grow thicker and harder under her touch. She took her time, exploring every inch of his torso, using her tongue to trace outlines against the bricks of his chest and the ladder of his stomach, the testaments of his bone-crushing power.

She slid lower, finding those delicious planes of muscle that arced along the front of his hips, slowly dragging her mouth over the left and then the right as his breathing shortened, his chest heaving in and out.

"Zarya," he said with that commanding tone in his voice but restrained like he was doing everything he could to keep from snapping in half like a brittle twig.

"Hmm?" she asked as she swirled her tongue again.

"Be a good girl and suck on my cock," he growled as his

hand slid into her hair before he gripped it and tipped her head up. "I want to see how you look with it in your mouth."

Zarya swallowed as heat bloomed in her stomach, and she found herself nodding. She had no capacity to resist when he spoke that way. It penetrated the flesh of her burning heart, rendering her his willing servant. She'd move mountains for him when he spoke like that.

He guided her head down, and she gripped him again, licking the tip. He shuddered out a deep moan before she drew an inch between her lips.

"Yes," he said. "Just like that."

She channeled him in deeper, slowly, and with purpose, loving the way he tasted, like warm breezes and the roots of the earth. Right now, she was in control. With her hand and her mouth, she stroked and sucked, feeling like a warrior staking her flag on the mountain of his ragged, helpless moans.

He gripped her hair tight as he thrust his hips, hitting the back of her throat.

"Fuck," he gasped as he pumped, and she held on, letting him guide her movements. A moment later, he stopped, his short breaths serrating from his chest.

"I need to come inside you," he said, and, without warning, pulled her up and flipped her onto her back. He moved on top of her, crushing her with his weight.

"I need to fuck you, Spitfire. It's consumed my thoughts since the day I met you."

Then, he positioned himself at her entrance, and she felt the probing heat of his tip as it spread her apart, dipping slowly into her body. She gasped, clutching at the bedsheets, at his arms, at anything that would stop this freefall before he held still, waiting for her to adjust to his presence.

"Are you okay?" he asked as he backed up onto his knees and then thumbed her clit, sending shocks across her skin. She nodded as he kissed her again, slowly teasing her as he slid in inch by glorious inch, touching every dark corner and shadowed recess. Not just of her physical body but of every lonely night she'd spent by the sea. Of every moment, she'd wished for something more.

"So fucking hot and tight," he murmured into her skin. "Fuck—you were made for me."

He pushed in further, stretching her with small, careful thrusts until he was fully seated. Zarya's shaky breath tore through her lungs, snagging on the corners of her ribs.

"Good?" he asked, and she nodded as he slowly drew out and then pushed back in. She could already feel her stomach tightening, that burning sensation waiting to break free. He churned his hips, thrusting in and out as he placed wet, open-mouthed kisses along her neck.

The edge of his knife-sharp canine grazed the delicate pulse of her throat. His tongue slipped out, licking the spot.

"Ready?" he asked as he closed his mouth over her skin and *sucked*.

"Yes, show me everything you promised," she gasped.

He drove into her with force, his teeth sinking into her flesh, sending a bolt of exquisite pain straight to her clit. She clung to him, the pain dissolving into melted sunshine mixing with her blood. It carried through her limbs, making her fingertips grow warm and her heart squeeze in her chest. He sucked on her neck while he fucked her harder and harder, pressing her into the mattress.

She'd never felt so many different things all at once.

Like she'd been doused in flames, burning her from within, gilding her organs and her bones, turning them into burnished gold. Her thighs quivered, and an ache twisted in her core, and then she fell apart, curving off the bed as her release spread through every cell, cleaving them into scattered pieces.

Rabin pulled his teeth away and then leaned up, hooking a hand under her leg as he pounded into her, losing control.

Together, they stared down at the spot where he moved in and out. He let out a guttural moan and then a growl as she felt him thicken and then release. His gaze never wavered from hers as the tendons in his neck pulled tight until he had emptied every last drop.

Then, he collapsed on top of her, kissing her fiercely before he found her neck and swirled his tongue over the marks left by his teeth.

"That was..." Zarya said. "I... think I've forgotten how to speak."

He chuckled low and softly as he pressed a kiss to her lips.

"That was fucking incredible," he said.

"It was okay?" she asked, still feeling somewhat self-conscious about her lack of real-world experience.

He growled and pulled her in close. "Zarya, there is nothing you could have done that wouldn't have made that the most mind-blowing moment of my life." He hooked up an eyebrow and gave her a mischievous smile. "But *where* did you learn how to suck on a man's cock like that?"

Zarya blushed, overwhelmed by his declaration and slightly embarrassed by the question. She cleared her throat.

"You read those lines from my favorite book," she said. "Row never paid much attention to what he brought me. Anything I learned, I learned from them."

Rabin smirked. "I should have known. Remind me to thank him next time I see him."

Her eyes widened. "Don't you dare."

Rabin chuckled softly, and then he kissed her again.

THIRTY

When Zarya awoke the next morning, Rabin lay asleep on his stomach with his arms under his head. She nestled against his side, staring at his face in a way that might have been a little invasive if he were awake. Maybe it still was, but he was so... beautiful. She couldn't help herself.

With the usual hard lines and planes softened, he appeared gentle and so much more vulnerable, traces of the fearsome warrior wiped away. She loved how he commanded a presence in every room, but something about this version of Rabin felt like a secret only for her. She sensed he didn't reveal the man she'd seen last night to many people.

Rabin had "apologized" three more times until Zarya had to beg him to stop. He'd taken her from behind with her lying on her stomach and with her riding him as he let her take control, seeking her pleasure how she wanted it.

He'd only relented when she'd sworn she'd finally forgiven him.

The smile of satisfaction on his face had definitely been worth holding out for so long. Though it really hadn't been that long, but she was ignoring that fact. He had been very persuasive, and she was just one woman with needs—how was she supposed to resist?

Eventually, they'd finally fallen asleep, though that couldn't have been more than an hour or two ago. It was going to be a long day in more ways than one.

Her hand slid over the swell of his shoulder and across his back, where she noticed a tattoo between his shoulder blades. A flower about the size of a lemon with six wide petals wrought in black ink so dark it seemed to absorb the light. Five of the petals were intricately decorated, but the sixth was left blank. When she looked closer, she noticed that each one represented a form of elemental magic—one for the earth with leaves and vines and another with flames for fire.

She traced the circumference with a light touch over curlicues of air, swirling waves of water, and points of light, pausing on the empty one. She recalled his words as they'd passed through the swamp.

Power, magic—they aren't inherently evil. They are simply tools. What matters is how they're used. It's just a name. The darkness isn't any more evil than water or air.

Who *was* this man?

"Mmm," Rabin's sleepy voice said. "How do I ensure I get woken up like this every morning?"

She smiled at the rumbling drowsiness in his voice. "Perhaps you could fall asleep next to me every night."

His eyes peeled open, and he stared at her before she leaned down and pressed her lips to the strange tattoo before trailing a line of kisses down his spine, taking in every line of perfection. He shifted, and the sheet covering his hips tugged down, exposing a mass of scars on his lower back.

Not ordinary scars.

But jaggedly carved letters—angry and violent.

The raised flesh spelled "Freak".

"Who did that to you?" she demanded as she sat up.

"My father," he answered, the tone wry with derision.

"Why? Why did he carve the word 'freak' into you?" Her voice was stretching into panic. She would destroy Gopal Ravana.

His lips pressed together. "Because of my dragon." The words struggled out of him like he was trying to shove through a wall.

She shook her head. "I don't understand."

Rabin sighed. "You remember when Dhawan said to be dragon-born is a gods' gift? Well, he was fucking wrong."

"Explain this to me. Please," she said. She couldn't stand the idea of anyone hurting him; a fierce need to protect him swelled in her chest.

"As the professor said, I'm the only living dragon shifter, and my father believed me to be an aberration," Rabin said. "He nearly killed me the first time I turned."

"How old were you?" she asked, placing a hand on his arm, barely able to get the words out.

"I don't remember exactly, but I was a child. Maybe six or seven."

"That monster," she hissed.

"He beat me every time I shifted, but when our magic is young, we don't always have the best control over it. I tried so hard to please him, but nothing I did worked."

"Why did he hate it so much? Why is being the only dragon so bad?"

"Because it made me stand out, and therefore drew negative attention to our family. My father is obsessed with appearances and proving to everyone the Ravanas are the most powerful and influential rakshasa family. But dragons aren't creatures of the earth, they're creatures of the sky. He said it tainted me and, in turn, our entire legacy."

"You know that's not true," she said.

His answer was a rueful look. "It took me a very long time to realize that. I think he might have been jealous because it proved that I'm stronger than him. It did make me stand out. It has made me different, and he never liked that I had more magic."

She ran her fingers gently across the letters, and he flinched.

"Sorry," she said, pulling her hand away. "I didn't mean..."

He shook his head. "I'm just not used to anyone touching me there. It's not exactly the most pleasant thing to look at."

"I'm not afraid," she said. "It's a part of who you are."

"Are you sure about that?"

"I am," she said. He took her hand and placed it on his back, his jaw hard but his eyes brimming with something that felt like trust. She accepted the invitation, tracing the ridges and grooves, feeling the echoes of his pain at her fingertips.

"When did it happen?" she whispered, watching a shiver roll down his spine.

"I was about twelve and was finally learning to control it," he said. "But I had to shift regularly, or it would start to eat at me, clawing to get out. I also loved flying. It was the only time I felt free. One night, I snuck out and spent hours in the sky, stretching my wings and soaring as high as I could.

"When I came back, my father was waiting."

Rabin stopped for a moment, gathering himself.

"He'd been drinking, and I was already lost before I even said a word. He forbade me from ever allowing anyone to see my dragon, and I tried to explain that was impossible, but he wouldn't hear it.

"He called for his guards and told them to strip off my clothes and pin me to the floor. And that's when he did this." He flicked his head towards his back. "He carved each letter slowly, making sure they were deep enough to mark me forever. I remember just *screaming*.

"When he was done, he decreed that no one was allowed to heal my wounds, and then he left me there. Lying on the ground, alone, afraid, broken. If I didn't have the gift of rakshasa healing, then it would probably have killed me. Instead, I was left with this."

Zarya's mouth opened with a breath.

"That's horrific," she said, and he shrugged, but the gesture felt forced.

He sat up and held out his arm, showing her the ladder of scars she'd seen that night in the forest.

"I tried desperately to control it," he said. "After that, whenever I felt the need to shift coming on, I'd cut myself. The release of blood helped ease the pressure, but the shift was inevitable. The only thing it did was delay it until it almost drove me out of my mind."

She wrapped her hand around his wrist and held it.

"As soon as I was old enough, I joined the army just to put some distance between us," he said.

"Is this why you didn't change when we were on the boat? I was wondering why you didn't just fly yourself over the water."

He ran a hand down his face.

"I don't... like showing that side of myself to others."

"You did it when you saved me that night."

"I did," he replied.

"What about when Amrita was taken?"

"It was just you and Yasen, and I didn't want those things anywhere near you. I'd do it a thousand times again if it kept you safe."

"Is this why you left Daragaab?" she asked, tucking away that heartfelt admission to examine later.

"Eventually, yes."

"I'm so sorry," she said.

He grunted something that sounded like "whatever" and rolled off the bed. Then, he dragged her towards him, scooping her into his arms.

"What are you doing?"

"You need a rinse," he said, carrying her into the small but opulent bathroom. "You were a very dirty girl last night, and I need to clean you up."

She huffed out a somewhat mortified laugh as he carried her into the glassed-in shower. He placed her on her feet and started the water before tugging them both under. She could take the hint—he wanted to change the subject.

The hot stream sluiced over their skin, and he reached for the soap and the sponge, lathering it up before he started cleaning off her shoulders and arms, running it down her back and the curve of her ass.

Her arms looped around his neck as they kissed slowly, their tongues probing and sliding, luxuriating in a deep, languid clash of their mouths.

Rabin flipped her around so her back was against his chest, one arm banded around her waist, as he slid the sponge over her breasts as soapy water coasted down her stomach and legs.

"Hmm," he rumbled, speaking into the curve of her neck. "This is everything I need. You wet and glistening, making those sexy little noises I will never get enough of."

He circled the sponge over her sensitive nipples, the rough material making them peak. The hand around her waist slid down and between her thighs. He used the soapy water to circle her clit with a finger as her head fell back against his chest.

"Are you sore?" he asked into her throat, and she nodded.

"A little, but I don't mind."

"That's my girl," he said as he slid a finger inside her, making her gasp. He pumped his hand slowly, gently rubbing her swollen bundle of nerves, bringing her closer and closer to the edge. She rode the crest, her toes stretching as she pressed against his hard body.

He pulled his hand away, and she made a sound of disappointment before he backed her against the wall and lifted her, wrapping her legs around his waist.

"Don't worry, Spitfire, I'll never leave you wanting," he said before he guided his hard cock towards her entrance, sliding into her slowly. She moaned at the fullness of it, still not entirely used to it. He sunk deep, sucking in a breath as they melded together, becoming one.

He leaned down and kissed the spot behind her ear. "This pussy is mine now, do you understand?"

"Yes," she whispered, somehow knowing it was true. Something had brought them together. Something had made them find one another in those dreams.

When could she reveal her suspicions about what they might be to one another? He'd already spurned her once, and while he was doing everything to prove himself, she was still trying to be on her guard. He was making it very difficult, though.

With one hand around the back of her neck and the other gripping her hip, he churned into her, her back pressed against the shower-warmed tiles. He fucked her slowly and with purpose, dragging out each swing of his hips before he slid back in.

It didn't take long until she felt a buildup of tension deep in her core. His movements picked up as she clung to his shoulders, their low moans and grunts echoing in the swirling steam. Zarya cried out as she came, and he followed closely after, warm water bathing them as they rode out their release.

When they were done, they finished washing up and returned to the bedroom. He fell on top of her, kissing her deeply.

"Why did we wait so long to do this?" he asked.

"Are you for real?" Zarya asked. "That is entirely your fault."

"I know. I'm an idiot."

She laughed and then shoved him off her. "You said it, not me."

Rabin groaned as she shifted and attempted to wiggle out from under him.

"Where are you going?" he asked.

"We need to get ready to leave," she said as he yanked her back with an arm banded around her waist.

"Tell them to go without us. Let's just stay here forever. I'm only getting started."

She laughed again. "While that's very tempting, it wouldn't be very heroic of us."

Rabin flipped her over onto her back again, rolling on top of her, propping his elbows by her head.

"Never make the mistake of thinking I'm a hero, Spitfire."

Zarya rolled her eyes. "I forgot you're a tough guy," she said.

His eyes lit with amusement before he kissed her, his mouth devouring hers with a bone-deep longing. Her legs wrapped around his waist, wishing they *could* just stay in this bed forever.

Finally, she pried herself away and scooted off the bed, but not before barely evading another snatch of Rabin's hand.

"Come back here," he demanded, using that same voice that had wilted her resolve more than once, but she stood firm against it.

"Fine," he grumbled as he stood to retrieve his clothing. She watched him, entirely distracted by the works of art that were his rounded butt and strong thighs.

"Keep looking at me like that, and you're the one who's going to make us late," he growled as he pulled up his pants.

She blinked and gave him an innocent smile. "Perhaps I was too hasty."

"You're the responsible one," he said, coming over and grabbing her chin before he kissed her deeply. "Don't tempt me to blow this whole operation off."

She didn't answer as he tugged on his kurta and shook out

the length of his damp hair before he pulled her up to stand and kissed her again, his hand squeezing her ass.

"Thank you for an incredible night," he said, touching his forehead to hers before he turned towards the door.

"Rabin," she said. He stopped and turned. "Just... don't break my heart, okay?"

He lifted the corner of his mouth into a smile before towing her in with an arm around her waist.

"Never," he growled. "You have mine in the palm of your hand now. Just try to take it back."

She followed him to the door, and he swung it open. Zarya let out a yelp when she saw Row on the other side, his fist poised to knock.

"Row," she said, suddenly conscious of the fact she was wearing only a towel and both hers and Rabin's hair was wet from the shower. They couldn't be more obvious if they'd painted a sign in bold, glittering letters and marched it through the streets. "What are you doing here?"

"I came to see if you were okay," Row said, eyeing Rabin with deep mistrust. "You disappeared from the festival last night."

Zarya smoothed back her hair, trying to come up with some reason for her absence that didn't include telling him the truth.

"I... We..." She blushed to the roots of her scalp as he stared at her and then at Rabin.

"I'll see you soon," Rabin said to her, and then he pushed past Row into the hallway and clapped Row on the shoulder. "I owe you a thank you."

"For what?" Row asked, a deep groove creasing between his brows.

Rabin just smiled, winked at Zarya, and then walked away like he didn't have a care in the world.

When he was gone, Row turned his dark glare on Zarya,

who was now gripping the door handle so hard her fingers ached.

"I'm just going to get dressed," she said. "I'll see you downstairs."

She flipped him a half-hearted wave and then closed the door on his thunderous expression.

THIRTY-ONE

After Zarya was dressed, she prepared to leave, half expecting to find Row standing on the other side of the door with his arms folded and a disapproving scowl on his face. When she entered the empty hall, she breathed a sigh of relief.

In the lobby, the others were already gathered, and Rabin's gaze found her immediately, his dark eyes burning with what felt like a secret fire just for her.

"Okay, let's go," Suvanna said, tucking some coins into the belt around her waist. "The boat should be ready for us."

"Great, another boat," Rabin said with a grumble as they exited the building and made their way through the streets. "And why are you wearing that again?" he demanded, scanning Zarya up and down.

"Because it's the only thing I brought for travel," she snapped.

He murmured something under his breath she didn't catch. She offered him an arch look that made the dimple pop in his cheek. Gods, she'd never be able to stay mad at him when he flashed that thing at her. When had she become so... malleable?

When they arrived at the docks, Suvanna traded a few more

coins with a man before she leaped aboard the deck of a small sailboat. As Zarya passed her, Suvanna smirked before her gaze flicked to Rabin.

"Have a good night?" she asked, mirth dancing in her eyes. Zarya was sure she'd never seen the merdeva this cheerful before.

"Maybe," Zarya said as Suvanna barked out a laugh and then spun on her heel and ran to the front of the boat, hopping up onto the prow.

"Let's go!" she shouted as everyone followed onto the vessel one by one.

Between Apsara's wind magic and Suvanna's water magic, this was sure to be a swift journey. Zarya noted the lake was still, smooth like glass, the morning sun reflecting off its surface.

As she peered overboard, she noted the fish and sea life moving about in the crystal-clear water where she could see straight to the bottom and to a bed of soft sand. She took a seat next to Rabin, who was already looking a little peaked, before the boat sprung to life, skimming over the water.

"Are you okay?" Zarya asked. He looked only slightly less pale than during the journey across the Dakhani. He nodded and leaned back, closing his eyes.

"I know you don't like changing in front of others, but is this better?"

With his eyes closed, he heaved out a long breath. "It freaks everyone out."

"Don't tell me you care about scaring anyone?" she joked.

His hand found hers on her lap, and he squeezed it. "I'd rather stay here with you."

The earnest way he said those words made her heart twist.

She leaned in, speaking close to his ear. "Well, that's very sweet, but you don't need to put yourself through this for my sake."

"Zarya, may I have a word?" She turned to find Row

hovering over them, that frown she knew so well on his face. Row's gaze flicked to Rabin, who had managed to open his eyes. Despite his nausea, Rabin hooked up an eyebrow, clearly demonstrating he wouldn't be intimidated.

Zarya did *not* want to have a word. Not at all. But she supposed the conversation was inevitable. Still, she'd been hoping Row would at least wait until they were both alone.

"Now. Please."

He said it in a way that brooked no argument, so Zarya huffed out a breath and nodded. He turned then and walked to the other end of the boat, clearly expecting her to follow. At least they'd have *some* privacy.

"I think I'm in trouble," Zarya whispered under her breath. Rabin's eyes had drifted closed again, but he reached out and squeezed her knee.

"Don't take any of his shit, Spitfire."

Zarya snorted and stood, crossing the boat where Row stood staring out over the water. At her approach, he turned and gestured to a bench.

"Will you have a seat?"

She rolled her neck and, feeling like a chastised toddler, settled next to Row with a heavy sigh. This felt very familiar— like the time they'd sat together in the garden before Row had disappeared from her life all those months ago.

That conversation hadn't ended well, either, and she didn't have high hopes going into this one.

"Zarya, I want to caution you on the relationship you seem to be forming with the commander," Row said, his tone careful.

Though she'd expected it, she couldn't help her annoyance. She ran a hand down her face. "Why?"

"It's just—I've known Rabin a long time."

"And?"

"And, I'm not sure this is a good idea. No one knows where he's been all this time, and I don't understand his intentions in returning to Daragaab now. You are inexperienced in these matters, and I want you to be cautious..."

Row trailed off, his gaze flicking to her as he pressed his hands between his knees.

"I assume you know I'm not interested in hearing this, and that's why you look so nervous right now?" she asked.

His shoulders dropped, and he rubbed his temples. "Just take things slowly. You've only known him for a few weeks. He's lived a long time, and I'm sure he has many secrets."

Zarya took a deep breath and closed her eyes, realizing she had caused this, in part. By not divulging the full story, she had inadvertently prejudiced Row against Rabin.

"I guess that's what this must look like," she said slowly.

"What do you mean by that?"

"I haven't only known Rabin for only a few weeks. I've known him for longer than that."

"How is that possible?" he asked.

She then confessed the truth about the dream forest and Rabin's hand in releasing the binding curse. Of course, she left out a few key details about appearing half-naked and the almost kiss, and *all* the kisses that did come after that, as well as the inscrutable sense of wonder she experienced during every moment in his presence.

"I see," Row said after she'd finished. "Neither of you is controlling the visions?"

"Apparently not. He was convinced it was me, but as far as I'm aware, it isn't."

"And Rabin severed the curse? Alone?"

"Yes." Noting Row's pensive expression, she asked, "Why?"

"I wasn't aware rakshasa magic was capable of that." Row rubbed his chin. "He's always been powerful, but I suppose it goes deeper than I realized."

Zarya spread her hands. "All I know is he helped me when

no one else could. And since then, that's all he's done. Made me feel safe and protected."

Row rubbed a hand along the back of his neck. "I appreciate the explanation, but still, a few months isn't enough to truly know someone."

"I know that, Row. I may be inexperienced, but I'm not stupid."

"That's not what I was implying, Zarya. But—"

"But nothing." She cut him off. "None of this is actually any of your business. You aren't my father."

Zarya knew it was a low blow, and the look on Row's face confirmed it. She immediately regretted her words.

"I'm sorry. I didn't mean it like that. But I'm an adult now, Row. Maybe I am being impetuous, and maybe I don't have a wealth of knowledge, so the only thing I have to go on is my instincts. But this feels right. *He* feels right. And if I am wrong, then I need to be allowed to make my own mistakes."

Row's nose flared. "You've always been one to run two feet first into everything. Even when it couldn't take you very far." Zarya wasn't sure if he meant that as condemnation or praise. "But I suppose you're right. I need to let you live your life. You may not be my daughter by blood, but I hope you understand my desire to ensure you're safe and protected. It's all I've ever wanted for you."

"Thank you," she said as they both fell silent.

"I read about something in my father's notebook," she said, and Row turned to look at her. "About paramadhar. Have you ever heard of them?"

Row nodded, confusion crossing his expression.

"I have, but they're very rare. Only the most powerful Aazheri have ever been known to bond with them."

Then, his eyes widened.

"Do you think that Rabin is—"

"I don't know," she said. "I've been wondering if that's what created the forest. Would that make sense?"

Row rubbed his chin, his gaze wandering to the far side of the boat where Rabin sat, his eyes still closed as he tried to keep very, very still.

"That could be a plausible explanation. Have you told him of your suspicion?" he asked.

"No, I wanted to know more about it before I did." Zarya looked at Rabin and back at Row. "Have you had one?" She wrinkled her nose. "Oh gods, it's not Aarav, is it? All this time, you had some mystical bond?"

Row shook his head, chuckling. "No. I do not have a paramadhar."

"Thank gods," Zarya said.

"It does stand to reason, given your gifts, that you should find yourself with a paramadhar," Row said. "You will need to tell him. To complete the bond and use it to its full potential, you must both inscribe twin marks on your skin. The binding is irreversible and will tether his life to yours while stabilizing and protecting your magic."

"What if we don't complete it? Is that a choice we get to make?"

Row shook his head. "It is, but I don't know what happens if you don't. My knowledge of paramadhar is limited."

"I don't know if I can ask him to do that, anyway," she said. "Give his life for mine? What does that make him to me? A kind of servant?"

Row canted his head. "In essence, yes. It's like a knight's squire or a queen's advisor, though obviously, it goes much deeper than that."

"I don't know," she said. "If we're... *involved*, that seems like it could get complicated."

Row nodded. "Paramadhar were far more common before the Hanera Wars when Aazheri magic was strongest. Personal relationships beyond the bond were generally discouraged for those reasons."

"Nothing is simple here on the outside, is it?" she asked, and Row chuckled.

"I don't want to say 'be careful what you wish for'"—Zarya shot him a dark look, and he raised his hands in surrender—"so I won't."

"Good," Zarya said, folding her arms and sitting back.

"You will need to tell him," Row said after a moment. "If he really is your paramadhar, then he has a right to know and a right to choose if he will serve in that role."

She nodded. "I'll talk to him when we get back."

"I know you'll do the right thing," he said, patting her on the knee before he stood, moving to the side of the boat to converse with Kindle and discuss whatever it was they had in common.

Zarya watched Rabin for another moment before she made her way back to his side of the boat. He'd moved, leaning forward with his elbows on his knees and his head in his hands. She sat down and rubbed his back, hoping to offer some relief.

"How did it go?" he asked, turning to look up at her.

"It's fine." She waved her hand.

"He hates me, I suppose."

"Do you care if he does?"

"No, I don't. Unless that creates a problem for you."

"He doesn't hate you. He's just being protective."

Rabin sat up and leaned back, taking her hand and placing it on his heart.

"Let him be a little protective, Zarya. That's his job in what-ever parent-type role he plays in your life. You're fortunate to have that."

She considered his words, knowing he was right. Given Rabin's relationship with his own father, he'd probably welcome what she had with Row.

She'd wanted a family, and he was offering her one. The

only one she was punishing by refusing to forgive him was herself. Mistakes had been made, and Row had apologized. No one was perfect, and she would make the choice to move past it once and for all.

Zarya sat back, chewing on the nail of her thumb before she looked over at Rabin's beautiful face.

"I can't believe you actually thanked him this morning," she said.

He laughed darkly, squeezing her hand tighter.

"Well, I was *extremely* grateful."

THIRTY-TWO

It took another hour to cross the massive lake. Zarya sat with her legs draped over Rabin's lap and her head pressed to his shoulder. Row knew the truth, and there was no need for pretenses anymore.

She was flipping through her book, reading more about paramadhar and the twin markings Row had told her about. She looked up at Rabin, whose eyes were closed, and studied his face. What would it be like to be tethered to him? If he agreed to become her paramadhar, how could she live knowing his life was forever tied to hers?

If she died, so would he. But if he died, nothing would happen to her. It didn't feel right. Rabin's hand rested on her knee, his thumb rubbing the inside of her leg. Even that benign touch was enough to make her stomach burst with butterflies.

When today was over, she would tell him and ask what he wanted to do. If his desire was to walk away from whatever this was between them, then it might break her heart, but she would also understand.

She returned to the book, flipping through the pages, landing on the image of her mother where the prophecy about her nightfire had been written. But it only contained the first two lines. Her mother's message had been clear that no one else knew the rest.

She will be the one to free them all.

What exactly did it mean, and how would she even begin to do that?

She continued reading, hoping for a clue, when she landed on a page about the Jai Tree and the day it had been planted a thousand years ago. It wasn't just a tree—it was a seal.

"Row," she said. "Do you know about this?"

She crossed the boat and sat down next to him, showing him the passage. Apsara stood over them a moment later.

"What's going on?"

"Did you know that Amrita is a seal?"

"For what?" she asked.

Zarya pointed to the page. "It says the Jai Tree was used to contain the darkness."

"I've never heard of this before," Row said. "Why is this not more common knowledge?"

"It was a long time ago, I guess," Zarya said. "Did Rani Vasvi ever try to overpower it? Fight against it or push it back down or something?"

"She tried a few times," Apsara said. "But nothing happened."

"If Amrita dies, what would happen without an heir to take her place?" Zarya asked.

Row scanned the page as he shook his head. "This suggests that if anything happened to her permanently, the consequences could be so much worse than losing Daragaab to the blight."

"Worse... as in the darkness would be freed completely," Zarya said as grim silence permeated the air.

"What else does it say?" Apsara said. By now, everyone was

listening to their conversation, save Suvanna, who was in the water directing the boat.

Row skimmed the page. "The original yakshi who took up the Jai Tree used an amplifier to help close the seal."

"An amplifier?" Apsara asked, and Row shook his head. "It references a chain of magic."

"What sort of chain?"

"I don't know. That's all it says."

As the boat cut through the water, everyone contemplated that information.

"It does explain a few things," Kindle said. "If the Jai Tree is the seal, then it makes sense that this dark magic would have manifested itself in Daragaab first."

"It does," Row agreed.

"So now we're looking for whatever this chain is?" Apsara asked. "This was a wasted trip?"

"Maybe the Bayangoma can shed light on this question," Row said. "We've come this far. We might as well finish the journey."

Just then, Zarya noticed the smell of smoke. It seemed everyone else did, too, because their gazes all turned in the direction they were traveling. Apsara and Kindle walked to the edge of the boat, staring into the distance. A mountain range loomed on the far side of the lake, and Suvanna steered the boat left.

Zarya stood up to get a better look. A plume of smoke drifted into the sky, hovering over the center of the island where they were headed. As the boat rounded the mountains, the lake opened onto a wide bay with a narrow beach and dense jungle lining the shore. They docked against the sand before Kindle and Row jumped off, securing it with stakes and ropes.

As the rest disembarked, a sense of foreboding hung in the air, as heavy as dusty velvet curtains.

"The grove," Apsara said as everyone exchanged wary glances. "We should hurry."

They formed a line and plunged into the dense brush. The island was quiet as ash drifted on the breeze, peppering their clothes and hair. Using their weapons, they hacked through the tangled mess of vines and branches.

Sweat was beading on Zarya's brow as they pushed through the dense foliage, the unrelenting sun pummeling them like falling rocks. Finally, they emerged into a clearing to find a ring of charred trees, the tips of the branches glimmering with embers and tendrils of smoke curling off them.

The Bayangoma grove had been destroyed.

Everyone paused in stunned silence before they slowly approached. Dozens of Bayangoma birds sat petrified amongst the branches, their mouths frozen open in a soundless, eternal song.

Zarya surveyed their surroundings, walking the perimeter of the fire line that formed a perfect circle around the trees.

"Did someone cause this?" Row asked, noticing the same thing. This hadn't been a natural fire.

Rabin drew his sword from his back as the zing of weapons filled the air.

Zarya bent down, frowning at the dead grass. She touched the line where the fire had stopped, her fingertips coming away covered with flakes of yellow dust.

She sniffed them, something tickling the back of her memory. She'd seen this substance before. She walked along the circle, noting more of it mingling with the ash.

My flowers are very precious to me.

"Zarya, what are you doing?" Row called.

"When did Professor Dhawan come to Daragaab?" she called over her shoulder.

"Shortly after we did," Apsara said. "After Rani Vasvi asked for the Chiranjivi's help with the blight. Why? What does that have to do with anything?"

Before Zarya could answer, a rustle in the trees hooked their attention.

"It's a trap," Rabin said, his shoulders stiffening as he turned to face the sound. A moment later, as if by magic, dozens of armed bodies melted through the leaves. They wore dark brown leather armor draped with deep red swaths of fabric around their hips and shoulders.

"Kiraaye Ka," Kindle said. "What are they doing this far south?"

"Who are they?" Zarya backed up.

"Hired thugs who reside in Bhaavana," Rabin said. "Not quite a trained army, but close enough. Loyal to no one and nothing other than the highest bidder."

Rabin's hand circled her arm as more Kiraaye Ka emerged from the trees surrounding them on all fronts.

Row addressed Rabin from her other side.

"You care for her?" Row asked.

Rabin's stance was challenging as he gave Row a sharp nod. "Of course I do."

"Then help me protect her."

"I can protect myself," Zarya said, pulling her arm from Rabin's grasp and backing away. Rabin stepped closer, his hand cupping the back of her neck as he pulled her towards him.

"I know that, Zarya," he growled. "But you've never faced an army organized and designed to kill.

"Stay near me or Row. I'm not asking you to sit out. I know you can fight. Just let us help protect you. We are vastly outnumbered." He paused as he searched her face like he was trying to commit every piece of her to his memory. "*Please*."

It was the 'please' that moved her. The torment in his voice. The shedding of his outer carapace to reveal the sliver of softness that lay within.

Zarya had no choice but to relent.

With a nod, she pulled her sword from her back. "Okay. But don't get in my way."

Rabin smirked. "I wouldn't dream of it, Spitfire."

There was no more time to think because all at once, the army of Kiraaye Ka roared and charged. When Rabin had claimed they were outnumbered, it hadn't been an exaggeration. Hundreds of heavily armed fighters stood against their tiny battalion of seven.

Steel met steel in a ringing clash as the foreign army descended, assured of their unbalanced victory.

But the Kiraaye Ka consisted mostly of humans, and no one could have understood the full extent of the ancient magic that joined the Chiranjivi. A power so old and so lost to time not even the history books remembered its existence.

Their group was forced to stand back-to-back in the center of the burned clearing as seven warriors were called by something so venerable, so primal, that each of them felt the shift deep in their souls. United, their strength multiplied, forging a bridge between them that was infinite and almost unbreakable.

As the horde crashed upon the Chiranjivi, they didn't stand a fucking chance.

Apsara rained down shards of razored ice; like messengers from the sky, they speared into the enemy as they scrambled for cover. She pierced through backs and throats with vicious mercilessness as their bodies collapsed to the earth.

Kindle sent out waves of fire that melted skin and hair and bone and teeth until there was nothing left but husks of ash, black smudges smearing the grass. Row whirled down lightning and vengeance while Koura and Suvanna became blurs of light and steel and rage, felling soldiers like limp rag dolls.

Commander Rabin Ravana's unholy wrath was a reminder of just why they still fell to their knees when they whispered his name in the streets of Dharati.

Vengeance and fury and something more bottomless than the depths of the earth burned in his eyes. He split the ground beneath their feet, the world tearing apart in a thunderous roar as it swallowed the soldiers like nothing but insignificant dust.

Boulders the size of elephants dropped from the sky, crushing mercenaries in their wake, while the jungle sprung to life, vines reaching out like long arms to circle their throats, cutting off the last of their terrified screams.

Zarya fought with every skill Row had drilled into her from the day she'd been old enough to hold her talwar. Nightfire flooded through the trees as bodies were torn apart, their cries echoing in the air. Tears blurred her eyes, but she fought them back, knowing it was this or die. She had never killed another human until that moment, and the reality of the power she held in her hands made her heart tremble with a deep-seated fear of the destruction she could wield if given the right motivation.

What their magic didn't finish off, their weapons did, blades flashing in the light. It might have taken hours or minutes, but as the Chiranjivi's power sang through the clearing, it forged a link that an army of a thousand couldn't have stopped.

As the last few skirmishes tapered out, Rabin stalked over to a Kiraaye Ka writhing on the ground before plunging a sword through his heart. He then grabbed another man by the collar and pulled him up, dragging him to the center of the clearing before he threw him to the ground at their feet.

"Who sent you?" Rabin asked the trembling soldier, who raised his hands and pressed them together, tears leaking down his blood-stained cheeks.

"Please. I don't know. I'm but a lowly soldier hired to join this mission."

"You don't ask questions about the people who hire you to kill?" he snarled. "You just take their money?"

The man was too scared to answer, his eyes spreading wide.

"It was Dhawan," Zarya said as Rabin held his sword to the man's throat.

"What are you talking about?" Apsara asked. Her white wings and fighting leathers were painted with crimson.

"The yellow pollen that started this fire. It's all around the clearing. I saw him using it at his cottage. He said it could be used to control lines of flame. He uses it for gardening. I found the same thing all over my clothes after the fire that killed Rani Vasvi. I didn't connect them at the time, but it's too much of a coincidence not to mean something."

"Why?" Row asked. "I don't understand. Why would he do this?" He gestured to the surrounding massacre. "He's been the one helping us."

Zarya shook her head. "I don't think he has. He killed Vasvi and found a way to get us out of Dharati. And he tricked me into suggesting this idea. He's the one who told me the grove was close to Dharati."

"He knows," Apsara said, exchanging glances with Row. "He knew she was the seal all this time, and if Amrita dies, then..."

Her voice trailed off.

"We must return to Dharati immediately," Row said.

"What if we're already too late?" Kindle asked, voicing the dire question they were all thinking.

"I don't know," Zarya whispered, fear for her friend swelling in her chest.

"I can take you," Rabin said, his shoulders tight. "I can get there faster if I shift. I should be able to carry two more without it slowing me down too much."

Row nodded. "Then Zarya, you go with Rabin. Koura and Kindle, you go, too. Apsara can fly as well, and I can take Suvanna. It will be a drain on my strength, but I'll do the best I can."

"Just get me to the shores of the Dakhani Sea," Suvanna said. "I can swim to Daragaab, and you'll travel faster alone."

Everyone nodded, preparing to leave. Rabin gave Zarya a look that conveyed so many things he couldn't say. She knew he hated changing with an audience, and she wondered if there was some way she could help him work through this thing that kept him from embracing all of himself. Even the most confident warrior needed someone in his corner.

With grim determination, Rabin stepped away as the air shimmered around him before he dissolved into a puff of black. Before their eyes, he transformed, and a towering, iridescent black dragon stood in the clearing, his scales radiant in the sunlight.

She stared up in awe. This was the first time she'd been able to truly appreciate the magnificence of his dragon form. He was rippling strength and sinuous elegance as his massive black head turned towards her. She saw him in the deep wells of his eyes, and a thousand questions ran through her head. She approached and reached out to touch him—his scales were slick and cool—like oiled steel.

He was larger than life. Larger than anything.

Lowering his head, Rabin gestured to his back. Zarya, Koura, and Kindle clambered on, using his leg for leverage.

Zarya took the front seat, gripping the scales that covered his neck, hoping she wouldn't slide off while noting the mesmerizing shift of color from green to purple to blue against the black.

As his wings picked up, the air around them bent and buckled before he let out a roar to shake the sky.

Then, he took a few running steps and launched himself into the air.

THIRTY-THREE

Apparently, Zarya was afraid of heights. Terrified, in fact. As Rabin soared across the sky, wings flapping steadily, her stomach bottomed out, tinging the edges of her vision with green. Every beat crashed with the air in a resounding thump, like sails catching the wind. She clung to his neck, trying not to look down, willing this to be over as quickly as possible.

The winds ripped through her, chilling her skin as she did her best not to scream. She chanced a glance over her shoulder at Kindle and Koura. The former looked as uncertain as she felt, and the latter maintained his usual calm disposition true to form.

Zarya clung tighter to Rabin, her body flattened against him, her hands growing numb the longer they flew.

He wouldn't let me fall.

She repeated the mantra to herself over and over. Of that, she was sure. But the thought still did little to quell the spinning pit in her stomach.

As night fell, they approached the northern coast of Ranpur Island. Rabin descended, landing on the earth with a gentle thump. A journey that had taken them days over land was crossed in mere hours on his back. Zarya, Koura, and Kindle slid off, shaking the icy tingling from their feet and hands.

Rabin remained in his dragon form as his giant head flopped to the ground and his eyes closed, his labored breaths kicking up clouds of dust.

As Rabin rested and the others rubbed feeling back into their limbs, Apsara appeared from the sky, followed by Row with Suvanna in tow, the pair materializing out of thin air.

The unrelenting day of travel had left everyone spent.

"We'll rest for a few hours," Row said. "Leave at the first signs of light."

Zarya nodded and peered in the direction of Dharati, wishing they didn't have to stop. But they would be no use to anyone if they arrived dead on their feet. No one spoke much as they passed out food and water before they prepared to spend another night sleeping under the stars.

The sound of rustling drew Zarya's attention to where Rabin was dragging his massive body deeper into the trees. He dropped to the ground before his eyelids slid into sleep. Once Zarya had eaten, she wiped her hands and approached on gentle steps, trying not to disturb his rest.

She listened to the deep tumble of his breaths and then ran a hand down his neck. His scales were warmer now, like they'd been toasted under the sun. She kneeled on the ground and curled into the spot where his neck met his body, resting her cheek against his side. He shifted, and a magnificent wing stirred before it descended over her, enveloping her in the cocoon of his heat.

With a sigh, she fell asleep against him.

When her eyes peeled open to the sound of Apsara's voice, it felt like it had been only minutes since she'd closed them. Rabin had returned to his rakshasa form, and he cradled her from behind, his arms wrapped around her and their legs tangled together.

"Morning, Spitfire," Rabin mumbled into the back of her neck, his face buried in her hair. She shivered at the warmth of his breath down her back.

Zarya rolled over to face him, cupping his cheek with her hand, savoring the prickle of his stubble against her palm.

"How are you feeling?" she asked. "You were so tired last night."

"You slept next to me," he replied.

She frowned. "Of course I did. Why wouldn't I?"

He tucked a lock of hair behind her ear. "I was worried I might frighten you like that. You've never been that close to my dragon before, and—"

His words cut off, and he shook his head. She'd never seen him like this—exposed and vulnerable like a raw nerve at the end of a splinter. He cleared his throat, rolled away, and then jumped up.

"I'll get you some breakfast," he said, leaving her staring after him, that brief moment of openness wiped away. She tried not to let that bother her. He'd let down his guard last night, but Row's words repeated themselves in her head. She didn't really know all that much about him, and he'd already broken her trust once.

She stretched her arms and examined the knee of her pants. They'd taken some damage during the scuffle with the Kiraaye Ka in the form of a small rip.

"I told you those were useless," Rabin growled, handing her a bowl filled with rice, channa, and mint yogurt. "And why are you looking at me like that?"

She wrinkled her nose. "Sometimes, I'm half expecting you to begin pretending I don't exist again."

His face darkened.

"I suppose I deserved that," he said.

"Hmm," Zarya replied.

"You forgave me, remember?"

"Only under duress."

"Don't pretend you didn't love every moment of it."

She shoved him away playfully. "I kind of did."

His answering smirk was all too smug.

"And what is your problem with my outfit?" she demanded. "I think it's nice. What has it ever done to you?"

"It's useless," he said, waving his hand. "All flash, no substance."

She narrowed her eyes. Given the leather had torn, and his armor didn't appear to bear a single scratch, she conceded he was probably right, but she wasn't about to admit that.

"Besides, you're way too fucking distracting in that."

"Oh?" she asked, raising an eyebrow. "Is that a problem?"

"Yes."

She barked out a laugh. "Why are you so upset about it?"

He dug into his food, hunching his shoulders, and shrugged.

"I'm a little bit obsessed with you," he said in a growly voice that did scandalous things to her insides.

"Only a little?" she said, pretending to be offended.

He smiled with a crooked tip of his mouth.

"Okay. Very obsessed. And I don't want to see you get hurt walking around in that crap they sell in the market."

Zarya looked down at herself. "Well, I'm sorry your big dumb man brain can't handle multiple emotions at once."

That earned her a wicked grin. "You're going to pay for that comment later."

"How?" she asked, genuinely curious. Would there be ropes and spanking? She'd read about that in her books, and it sounded... interesting.

"Gods," he groaned as his gaze slid to the others chatting quietly over their food. "Don't make me say it, or we're never leaving here."

He took a bite of his food and then pointed his fork at her.

"Now, you're looking at me like *that*," he snarled.

"A gentleman might not point it out."

"When did I ever give you the impression that I'm a gentleman?" he asked as he leaned over and bit her earlobe, sharp enough to make her gasp.

"My mistake," she said.

They continued eating in silence, and she looked over at him.

"Have you ever heard of something called paramadhar?" she asked. Maybe now was not the time for this conversation, but she couldn't keep the words in anymore. It was like the tether that connected them was dragging them to the surface.

He frowned. "I haven't. What is it?"

"I came across it in the notebook of my father's." She pulled it out of the bag at her hip and flipped to the page. The effects of the translation had worn off, and it was currently unreadable.

She touched the page and then went on to explain what she'd read about them, including her hunch about what had caused the dream forest. When she was done speaking, his face was expressionless, and she had no idea how to decipher what he was thinking or feeling.

"You think you and I—"

"I know it sounds ridiculous," she said, regretting that she'd brought this up now. "Forget I said anything." She went to stuff the book away when Rabin grabbed her wrist.

"It's not ridiculous," he said. "It actually explains a lot."

He said it with curiosity and a hint of wonder, and the tightness in her chest loosened.

"Does that scare you?" she asked.

"Not at all." He said it with his usual confidence, and suddenly, she didn't feel as insecure about the idea. "Zarya, there's something else we should talk about first—"

"Let's get moving," Row called across the clearing, interrupting whatever Rabin was about to say next.

"What is it?" Zarya asked, glancing at Row.

"It's okay. We need to go. We'll talk about it later," Rabin said, and Zarya nodded.

They all packed up, preparing for the journey back to Dharati.

Suvanna stalked towards the beach, clearing the treeline and vanishing into the ocean without a backward glance. Row readied himself to leave as Apsara departed on white feathered wings. Rabin transformed into his dragon in a puff of black smoke before Zarya, Kindle, and Koura climbed aboard.

Zarya was a little more comfortable with the altitude today, knowing beyond a doubt that Rabin would never let her fall. She forced herself to take in the scenery as they shot out over the bright blue waters of the Dakhani. It was breathtaking, flying over the frothing waves as Daragaab came into view.

As the ocean melted beneath them, they careened over the blackened swamps of the forest that had been Zarya's companion for so much of her life. She could make out the small patch of green and the small white cottage that had once been her home.

From this vantage, Daragaab's devastation was rendered in stark relief. What had once been endless miles of verdant forest and jungle were gone. Dead and black and dry.

In the distance, the kingdom of Svaasthy lay to the west, a yellow patch of desert sands sparkling against the sunlight. It would only be a matter of time before the blight began its march into the home of spirit magic and Niramaya.

The edges of the blight escaped in every direction, like paint spilled on a canvas, and nothing would evade its grasp. The swamp's quiet call didn't reach Zarya in the skies, but it was hard not to notice how it had grown outward from the shore.

From that place where Zarya had spent her entire life.

Kindle cried out, and she looked over her shoulder to find him pointing in the distance.

Along the eastern coast sat six enormous warships with black sails, bobbing in the turquoise waters several miles south of Dharati. Where had they come from? Had Dhawan orchestrated this part, too?

As Rabin's large head swerved to take in the view, their altitude dropped, Zarya's stomach climbing up her throat. It felt far too much like the night the kala-hamsa had flown her over Dharati. He recovered quickly, and then, with a resounding boom of his wings, they shot forward, picking up speed.

If Dhawan was responsible, he must have moved these ships in after they'd traveled through the swamp five days ago. A carefully orchestrated plan, where they had been too far inland to see the ships amassing on the shore and already too far away to realize troops had moved into the city. He had played them all like puppets on iron cables.

The assault at the grove had clearly been intended to annihilate the seven members of Chiranjivi, and they were never meant to return. Their only hope now was to arrive in time to interrupt Dhawan's plans. If he hurt a single leaf on Amrita's head, Zarya would personally make it her mission to gut him and skin him to his bones. The duplicitous old fool. So many lies. So many endless secrets. He had looked her in the eye and pretended he was her friend.

Before long, Dharati appeared in the distance. The southern span of its blackened walls signaled a warning to anyone daring to enter. Rabin coasted over the city towards the palace, where Zarya could see the courtyard's doors had been sealed shut, catching Daragaab's army off guard and leaving them locked outside. Everyone had been looking outwards towards the swamps, preparing for danger. No one had expected the threat to come from within.

As Rabin soared lower, she saw them preparing a battering ram to break down the Jai Palace's beautiful blue gates.

He cleared the wall and dropped into the middle of the

courtyard before Zarya, Kindle, and Koura slid off. She surveyed the scene as dread soured the back of her throat.

Hundreds of Kiraaye Ka swarmed the courtyard, an invading army of disease crawling over Amrita's trunk and slithering through her branches as they performed their gruesome task.

Axes. Hundreds of axes.

Sunlight glinted off their razored edges as they hacked into Amrita's trunk, sending splinters of pale white wood spinning in every direction. Where they struck, grey patches formed, leaving her surface mottled and bruised like an abused peach. More Kiraaye Ka straddled her branches with hacksaws in their hands, working their way through the wood, rough sounds poisoning the air.

Thousands of flower petals rained from the sky, creating a conflicting contrast of serene beauty, backdropped by the queen's destruction. They were killing her. Slowly and painfully and without a shred of mercy.

"Someone open the gate!" Rabin called, now returned to his rakshasa form, his sword gripped in his hand. "Why is no one opening the fucking gate!"

Several of the palace soldiers, fighting off the Kiraaye Ka, spun around at the sound of his voice before about a dozen sprung for the exit.

"Just one of you!" he roared before they finally figured themselves out, and the gate started to creak open.

Zarya went on the offensive, knocking Kiraaye Ka out of the way as she approached the tree, ducking at the sound of an overhead crash right before a thick branch thundered down, ripping flowers and small branches with it.

Knowing her magic couldn't harm the Jai Tree, Zarya gathered her nightfire and blasted a group of Kiraaye Ka dangling from a lower branch. They screamed as their perch exploded in a shower of splinters, scattering across the sky.

Zarya screamed, too, dropping her hands. That wasn't supposed to happen. Her body trembled as she stared at her palms.

"How did it...? Magic isn't supposed to affect her!"

Rabin watched her with an inscrutable gaze before he tipped his head with a curious look.

Zarya turned back to the Jai Tree, noticing a large patch of dead grey bark spreading where the nightfire had hit. Zarya wanted to crawl into herself and wither away.

Magic couldn't harm Amrita, but for some reason, hers could?

She was poisoned to her very core, and soon, everyone would realize it.

"Kill them with your sword, Zarya," Rabin said, grabbing her chin and forcing her gaze on him. "You cannot stop. Amrita needs you. You're so much more than just this power. Never forget that."

Zarya nodded, her eyes lining with tears. She could do this. For Amrita, she would pull herself together. Rabin turned back to the courtyard where Daragaab's forces were finally streaming in.

They formed a line, facing Rabin with their fists pressed to their hearts.

"Commander Ravana," shouted a soldier at the front. "We await your orders."

Rabin studied the soldier. "Who's in charge here? Where's the steward? Or Commander Varghese?" he asked, scanning the area.

"Sir, we aren't sure," the soldier replied.

Zarya's breath hitched as she squeezed the hilt of her sword. She'd burn down the world if anything happened to Yasen.

Daragaab's former commander hesitated, conflict swirling in his eyes before he turned to Zarya.

"Be careful. If anything happens to you now, I won't survive it."

Then, he reeled her in for a fierce, bruising kiss. As he pulled away, a moment of indecision flickered in his expression before it morphed into steely resolve. He turned to face the soldiers lined up in neat rows and began shouting orders before they stirred into action.

As he took control, she watched him, knowing something was changing. This tangle of feelings was solidifying into a warm pulse beating under her ribs that she'd soon have to reconcile with.

At last, Row appeared out of thin air, and Apsara landed inside the courtyard on one bent knee with a delicate whump, her chest heaving with effort. They all looked towards the palace, where Suvanna came storming through the doors, dripping with water and her hair sparking around her like ribbons of thunder clouds.

They were together again, and now, they could stop this. They had no choice. If they lost Amrita, not only would Zarya lose a friend, but they'd lose their last line of defense against the blight.

A grinding clash of swords and axes ensued as the Chiranjivi and Daragaab's soldiers descended on the Kiraaye Ka. But they were outnumbered, and more grey patches bloomed on Amrita's surface as life slowly drained away from the queen. If she held still, Zarya thought she heard a distant, agonized scream.

A bow lay at Zarya's feet, the quiver still attached to its dead owner. She picked it up and fired arrow after arrow at the Kiraaye Ka in the trees, each shot aimed with deadly precision. Rabin was right. For her friend, she could do this.

They fought furiously, picking off the Kiraaye Ka, but Amrita was still suffering. Grey patches streaked up her trunk as branches quivered high above their heads. It took a moment to feel it. The ground beneath their feet trembled. The sounds of steel meeting bark vibrated under the surface.

"Her roots," Row said, taking off at a run. Zarya followed behind, with Koura and Kindle on her heels. She heard Rabin rattle off a series of commands to the soldiers, ordering them to proceed underground.

"How do we get down there?" Zarya asked as they entered the palace.

"This way," Row replied. "There are tunnels running below the building."

At that moment, Zarya caught sight of Vikram running towards them, surrounded by guards.

"What happened?" she asked as he came to a stop. He had a black eye and a bleeding cut on his cheek.

"Dhawan locked us up," he said. "Me and the rest of my family. We had to fight our way out. What happened to you?"

Row quickly recounted the events on Ranpur Island as Vikram's eyes widened with alarm.

"What about Yasen?" Zarya asked. "Where is he?"

"He was trapped with us, too," Vikram said. "He went underground with a squadron after we escaped."

"We're heading there now," Row said. "Everyone else is in the courtyard."

Vikram nodded and turned towards Amrita as Row led the rest through a door and down a stairway that spiraled into the earth, the air growing cool as the sounds of metal striking wood echoed louder the deeper they went.

Zarya emerged behind Row, peering over his shoulder to a scene of even more Kiraaye Ka hacking away at the thousands of roots that grew beneath the surface of Jai Mahal.

She choked back a sob at the horror of the sight.

A jumbled maze of tunnels and caverns and bridges all formed a breathing system that kept the Jai Tree alive. It was now easy to see why a mere fire hadn't finished Rani Vasvi off immediately. Here, life flowed as solid as the earth itself. But that life was being choked away. This time, Dhawan clearly meant to finish the job once and for all.

Roots, some as fine as hairs and some as thick as a human body, shuddered with every chip of the axes. Amrita's cries of anguish rang out louder and clearer as a thousand limbs were cut off at once.

Mercenaries spread in every direction, hundreds of them swinging their axes with indiscretion. But Amrita's root system was a living thing, and the tunnels formed beneath the surface were sentient; they moved and shifted, closing off one opening and surrendering another. It was a mass of confusion as soldiers dispersed, the pathways changing, the cavern alive and breathing.

Zarya began attacking Kiraaye Ka, some so focused on their task that they didn't notice until she was right behind them. It didn't take long before the roots shifted enough that Zarya found herself separated from the others. She approached a broad man with a thick beard, hacking away at a frantic pace.

Zarya was nearly on him when he saw her. He swung his axe, but it was a large and clumsy thing. The momentum of his swing went wide, causing him to nearly stumble into the wall. As he recovered, she slashed at his leg, a deep slice opening on his thigh. He stumbled as he attempted another turn with the axe, this time gripping it with both hands and tossing it at her with all his might.

Zarya ducked, the axe clattering against the wall behind her. The Kiraaye Ka pulled out his sword as a wicked gleam formed in his eyes. Two more Kiraaye Ka noticed them and approached, their weapons drawn. Zarya was surrounded on three sides, the living wall of Amrita's roots at her back.

She wouldn't risk her nightfire as much as she needed it right now. Not after what she'd seen it do above. She would not be responsible for causing any more harm to the queen.

Their swords clashed as the first soldier lunged, the sound echoing through the tunnels. On her left, another Kiraaye Ka advanced at the same time. Afraid to use any of her magic now, Zarya risked only a tendril of air, tangling it through his legs, knocking him to the ground.

On the right, a female Kiraaye Ka charged at Zarya. She ducked, sending the woman flying overhead and landing on the ground on her back, the wind knocked out of her. Zarya plunged a dagger into her heart, and the woman gurgled as her life drained out with her blood.

The first man advanced, his sword lashing out and biting into Zarya's thigh. Blood blossomed as pain radiated through her leg. Swinging at him, they fought, their swords clashing against the walls, the space too tight for anyone to get in a proper hit.

She didn't notice the second soldier coming up behind. He'd retrieved his axe and was swinging it wildly. It caught her in the side, its sharp edge slicing through skin as she fell to her knees. She pressed her hand against the gushing wound, trying to stand up as the man with the axe came in for another swing. Zarya closed her eyes. This was it. She was going to die. At least this time, she'd been properly kissed.

"Stop," a voice called. "She lives. Dhawan just gave the order—she's to be brought to the courtyard."

It was the only distraction Zarya needed.

She leaped up, pouncing on the back of the bearded man who had turned away, her dagger slicing across his neck. At the same moment, Zarya blasted wind at the other two Kiraaye Ka, wrapping them together. She squeezed with all her strength until they finally collapsed.

She once again found herself alone.

Stumbling along the path, she fell to her knees and then dropped onto her hands, panting as the ground spun beneath her.

THIRTY-FOUR

The wound in Zarya's side throbbed as her breath rattled out in gasps. She touched it gingerly, wincing at the blood soaking the leather. She needed help but was surrounded by endless shifting tunnels, silence stretching in every direction.

With a hand pressed to her ribs, she dragged herself along the wall, leaving a trail of blood with every step she took. She resisted the urge to call out for help, worried about bringing attention to herself in a weakened state. She was done if one of the Kiraaye Ka found her like this.

Her side continued dripping blood, pain drilling into her bones with each halting step as black spots burst in her vision, the corners smearing together.

These tunnels were endless, folding in on themselves every time she rounded a corner. This was getting her nowhere. She stopped both to catch her breath and to listen for sounds of the battle but found only a yawning silence.

"Fuck," she mumbled under her breath as she convinced herself to take a few more steps.

Finally, she turned a corner and stumbled into a large cavern hewn from the rock. Roots had pushed through the stone walls, tendrils forming a pattern almost like a mural hung to admire. Rows of torches lined the space, flames flickering and casting shadows into concealed corners. If she listened, she imagined she could hear the waves of the ocean rolling in the distance. She hoped the torches suggested she was close to an exit.

Taking another moment to catch her breath, she leaned against the wall as her legs gave out, and she slid to the floor. Still clutching her side, blood oozed between her fingers as her eyelids grew heavy. In her hazy thoughts, she wondered where Rabin had ended up and what had become of Yasen.

She sucked in mouthfuls of air, her limbs and lungs shaking with the effort. Her entire side had gone numb, her wound pulsing like it had its own heartbeat. Just another minute, and then she'd get up. She had to find a way out of here and get help. No one would know where to find her, and she was losing too much blood.

Footsteps echoed in the distance, someone running down a different tunnel leading into the cavern. She tensed, scrambling against the wall, attempting to get up. If it were an enemy soldier, she'd have no chance of fighting them off.

When a familiar figure appeared, she choked on a shuddering sob of relief.

"Yasen," she whispered as he stumbled into the room with blood coating his uniform and his talwar raised. "You're okay."

"Zee," he replied, his voice hoarse and filled with just as much relief.

Yasen ran to her, skidding on his knees as he wrapped his arms around her, pulling her in for a hug. "I was so worried. Dhawan appeared with his army, claiming you were all dead and that he was taking over the palace. They started killing anyone who tried to stand up to them."

She clung to his clothing, sobbing into his chest. "It was a trap. Dhawan sent us out there to be slaughtered, but they failed. When we realized we'd been tricked, we came back here as fast as we could. Vik told us what happened to you..." She dissolved into a fresh wave of tears, and Yasen rocked her, running a hand down the back of her head.

"It's okay," he said. "I'm okay, and you're going to be okay."

They sat that way for another few seconds before he asked, "But what's going on? Why did Dhawan try to kill you, and why is he chopping down the queen?"

Zarya recounted what they'd discovered about Amrita, her role in containing the darkness, and what they all now suspected about Dhawan.

"That bastard," Yasen said, his jaw tightening. "I'll kill him."

"Get in line," she said and then winced at a stab of pain. "I'm killing him first."

"Shit," Yasen said. "You're bleeding. A lot."

She nodded, closing her eyes and leaning her head against the wall.

"Always the master of observation, aren't you?" she said as she felt him moving around her. "I don't feel great."

"You don't look great," he said, not missing a beat.

"Shut up," she huffed and then winced at another shot of pain.

Yasen helped Zarya lie down before he stripped off his coat and started tearing it into ribbons. She listened to the jagged sound of fabric ripping as she drifted in and out of consciousness.

"Remember that day in the swamp, Zarya? When the naga attacked you?" Yasen asked before tearing more strips from his jacket.

She almost smiled at the memory. "No, I'd almost forgotten the day I was nearly eaten by a sock with teeth."

Yasen snorted and then peeled away the bottom edge of her leather top, slicing it apart to access her wound.

"You were so ridiculous, leaping out to try and save us, nearly getting yourself eaten. I had to save you that day, too."

He wrapped the torn strips around her midsection, gently lifting her up to feed them around her back. She could feel the tremble of his practiced hands, so different than all those months ago when he'd bandaged her in the swamp.

Zarya groaned as he shifted her to her side. "You didn't save me. How dare you?"

Talking was becoming harder, so she watched his face, noting the tightness of his smile and not missing the fact that he was attempting to distract her.

"Then, you swept into all our lives, and nothing has ever been the same since," he said softly before he shook his head. Finished with wrapping her stomach, Yasen tucked a piece of hair behind her ear. "And I think we're all the better for it."

Tears pooled in her eyes, threatening to drown her. She grabbed his hand, pressing it against her heart. "You did save me, Yas. You saved me in so many ways that I will be forever grateful for. In every way that truly matters. Thank you for taking care of me. I love you. You have no idea how much you mean to me."

Panting from the effort of speaking, she sat back again.

"I love you, too, Zee." His voice caught, and he swallowed, the knot in his throat bobbing. "You're a really amazing second-best friend."

"I take it back. I hate you," Zarya said quietly, her eyes closing.

Yasen snickered. "And you're not going to bleed to death on me. We need to get you out of here. Let's get you to the infirmary and find Koura."

She nodded, her eyes still closed. Yasen scooped her up, and she felt him crossing the cavern when a voice broke through the cloudy fog of her drifting thoughts.

"What do we have here, then?"

Her eyes snapped open to find Professor Dhawan at the opposite end of the cavern, surrounded by a group of massive soldiers wearing black leather armor.

Flanking them were two small ajakava tied to glittering leashes that must have been some type of magic. They were being held by two soldiers, their pincers snapping and as ghastly and hideous as she remembered. Their feet clicked against the stones as their bronzed shells gleamed in the low light.

Yasen slid Zarya's legs to the ground before he pulled his sword from its sheath.

"Dhawan," Zarya hissed. "What have you done?"

His hands spreading in a magnanimous gesture, Dhawan replied, "Why, my dear, only what I had to."

She growled low in her throat. "I don't understand. Why?"

She eyed the ajakava pacing along on the stones with confusion and trepidation. How was he controlling them?

Dhawan tilted his head, his gaze moving over Yasen and Zarya. "I don't think I need to answer that right now, but in due time, you will understand, Zarya."

Dhawan gestured to his soldiers to move, and they drew their weapons as they advanced.

"They were supposed to capture you at the Bayangoma grove and return you to me. But it seems I underestimated the power of the Chiranjivi." He peered at her, clearly angry about that fact. "How did you manage to best such a formidable army? None of you should have walked away from that."

She narrowed her eyes, not about to reveal anything. He hadn't known then what would happen when the seven of them joined together. An advantage that had saved all their lives.

When she didn't answer, he gave her a cold, dead smile.

"Seize her," he said, gesturing to two of the soldiers. "I'll extract the rest of her secrets in due time."

The soldiers approached Zarya, grabbing her by the arms and

dragging her to Dhawan whose expression dripped with oily satis-faction. Both twice her size, Zarya's attempts to resist were futile. The other two soldiers seized Yasen, who struggled like a caged wild animal. A soldier drew a khanjar, pressing it against his throat, and Yasen went still as a line of blood trickled down the side of his neck.

Dhawan produced a small vial filled with clear liquid from the folds of his cloak, holding it up to the light.

"Open up, my dear," he said.

"I am not your *dear*," Zarya spat at him.

Dhawan tutted. "To think you were such a nice girl when I met you."

"I'm not *nice*." She hissed the word, not sure why it offended her so much to hear him say that.

He made a fake pout.

"That snarl is quite unbecoming," he said. "You're so much lovelier when you smile."

As Dhawan advanced, Zarya shook her head, trying to back away, but the soldiers held her firmly in their grip. There was nowhere she could go.

Lifting the vial, Dhawan brought it to her lips. Zarya clamped her mouth shut so hard she tasted iron. Dhawan signaled to one of the soldiers, who then smashed a massive fist into her stomach, forcing her knees to buckle as fresh, warm blood leaked down her side.

Suspended between the soldiers, she fought for air as one roughly grabbed her chin and pried her mouth open before Dhawan tipped in the contents of the vial. She gagged on the invasion, trying to spit it out, but a guard fisted her hair and wrenched her head back before the other slammed her chin with such force she felt her teeth rattle. She sputtered as it went down before the guard released her chin.

Instantly, Zarya felt the effects of the potion. The flame inside her heart withered, shrinking to a point of nothing. The bright and glittering presence that had become her constant companion winked out. Her magic was gone.

Zarya's heart stuttered in panic, especially at the sight of Dhawan's cold, benevolent smile. It set every hair on her body at attention.

"Trust me when I say this is for your own good, Zarya."

Dhawan pulled out two more vials and handed them to one of the soldiers.

"That should hold her until you reach Andhera—I gave her a strong dose—but keep these with you. Give her another in seven days' time, regardless. I don't know the limits of her ability yet. She has been lying to everyone about her power, haven't you, my darling Zarya?"

Zarya's sense of self was rapidly draining away, but she summoned a look so scathing it could melt through steel. "What do you want from me?"

"You will find out soon enough. Once I finally deliver you home."

"Home? What are you talking about?"

Home. Andhera.

Lingering on a tenuous edge of consciousness, something important wedged itself into the smoke of her thoughts, but she couldn't focus on it. It hung there like a carrot on a string, just barely out of her reach.

"What about this one?" asked the guard holding the dagger at Yasen's throat.

With a cold gleam in his eyes, Dhawan glanced at Zarya as her stomach plunged to her feet.

"He means a lot to you," Dhawan said with a concerned furrow of his brows, but she heard the implied threat.

"Please," she begged. "I'll go with you. Don't hurt him."

"Zarya, no!" Yasen said, growling at her.

Dhawan rolled his neck and then flicked a hand.

"I have no use for the bastard," Dhawan said. "Let the ajakava deal with him."

"No!" Zarya said, a sob escaping. "Please, no."

"And tie him up first. I don't want him following us."

Zarya bucked against her restraints, kicking and fighting, dragging up the last fragments of her waning strength. "You monster! I'll destroy you!"

The soldiers forced Yasen to the ground, pressing his cheek to the stone with a boot planted in his back, while the other tied his wrists together. Their eyes met, but she could barely see through the haze of her tears. She refused to accept this was goodbye.

"No!" Zarya screamed, again trying to free herself, but it was no use.

"Come." Dhawan gestured to the four soldiers. "You need to leave now. Get her away from here as fast as possible."

Zarya still fought, bucking and kicking and screaming with whatever small bit of strength she had left. Begging and pleading for Yasen.

"No! No! No!" she repeated over and over again. "Please, no! Yasen!"

Dhawan snapped his fingers, and the ajakava sprung loose from their leashes before they circled around Yasen. He struggled against the bonds, eyeing his sword lying just out of reach. He rolled to get closer to it, but the monsters blocked his way.

Her mind dissolving, she screamed so loud it clanged off every surface, echoing in her ears like she was falling into an endless, shapeless void.

"Yasen! No! Yasen!"

And the last thing Zarya saw before she was dragged from the cavern was the sight of two bronze demons lunging for her best friend.

THIRTY-FIVE

Zarya sobbed so hard she felt fissures forming in her chest. Blood and dirt and tears blinded her to everything as she sagged, her soul ripped out and shredded to dust.

"No," she murmured over and over as her heart squeezed so hard it felt like it was turning to nothing but bloody, amorphous pulp. "Yasen. Oh, gods. No."

They dragged her through the tunnels before they let her go, her knees striking the stone floor with a crack. She felt nothing as she wrapped her arms around herself and repeated "no" over and over again, willing this to be a nightmare she would wake up from soon.

"Take her to the wagon," Dhawan ordered.

Two soldiers grabbed Zarya from either side, hauling her from under her arms as she blacked in and out of consciousness. Half dragging, half carrying, they emerged from the depths of the palace into the empty, sunlit garden.

The sounds of the battle in the courtyard rang in the distance.

No one knew they were taking Zarya away.

"We'll follow once we're done here," Dhawan said. "Don't

let her die. I need her alive." Despite the mysterious concern for her mortality, she heard the promise of something sinister in his words.

Zarya was tossed in a heap into the back of a small closed wagon, landing on her injured side. Blinding white light flared in her vision as she almost passed out from the pain. The doors slammed shut, plunging her into darkness, where she continued to weep for Yasen.

The wagon lurched to life, jolting Zarya back and forth like a rag doll until, finally, the pain towed her under like a riptide, and everything went black.

She wasn't sure how much time had passed when she awoke to the lurching, clumsy sway of the wagon. It bumbled along slowly, tipping to the left and right at an alarming slant. They clearly weren't traveling down any road designed for a vehicle.

She blinked, but her cage was a curtain of deep, impenetrable black. Holding out her hand, she tried to make out the lines of her fingers, but there was nothing to see. She winced at the pulsing pain in her side, touching the bandages Yasen had so lovingly tied around her, sobbing at the memory. She'd lost him —her first real friend. Someone who had come to mean everything to her, and he was gone. How could she go on without him?

Her fingers came away slick, and she shuddered on a ragged breath, attempting to organize her thoughts.

Dhawan wanted her alive.

He'd said they were sending her *home*.

The potion dampening her magic would last until they arrived in Andhera, and it was then the pieces slid together, forming the picture of his deception.

Dhawan was sending her back to the man who had fathered her—the one who wanted to steal her magic for himself.

The king knew, then.

He knew Zarya existed and that she bore the gift he'd coveted for so long. The magic he'd sought as his own. There would be nowhere she could hide ever again. She heard her mother's voice through the necklace, reminding her this was already a foregone conclusion. That the prophecy had been a death sentence for them both.

Dhawan hadn't just attempted to seal all of Rahajhan's fate —he'd also sold Zarya out for some unnamed ambition. She could only imagine what sort of devious bargain had landed her in the back of this wagon.

Though the darkness threatened to drown her, Zarya's eyes finally adjusted, and she made out the bright edge of the doors where sunlight filtered through the narrowest of gaps. She crawled over, trying to ignore the pain attempting to drag her under.

Dhawan would pay for what he'd done to Yasen.

For what he had done to Rani Vasvi and Amrita.

She had to get out of here to avenge her friends and stop Dhawan from delivering her to Raja Abishek. Once they got her onto one of those boats, she'd be trapped with nowhere to run. Her route to freedom was now or never.

The carriage hit a bump and nearly toppled, tossing Zarya against the wall. Pain flared in the recesses of her soul as she shuffled towards the doors, slamming her feet against the surface. They held fast and the action sent a bolt of agony ripping through her. Zarya struggled to her knees, hands skimming along the doors, hoping to find a latch. Her fingers met with the cold touch of smooth steel. Zarya slumped back down, hopeless and defeated, willing herself not to pass out.

Hunched over on her hands and knees, she squeezed her eyes shut, trying to come up with a plan. In through her nose and out through her mouth, she dragged in slow, long breaths.

And then she felt it. So small. So insignificant it would have been easy to miss. Black dots swirled in her vision as she swayed on a teetering point of consciousness. She shook them away, forcing herself to focus.

It was there—a spark. Her star. Her anchors. The light that had lived inside her since the day Rabin had released her from the binding curse.

The magic that had changed everything, bestowing a history and a past she had never dreamed possible.

Zarya dug into it, coaxing the ember as it flickered to life, so feeble and weak. Dhawan's potion had erected a shield blocking her from its source, but it was still *there*. She concentrated harder, willing her magic free from his trap.

This was just another prison. Another noose. Another person trying to cage her, and she was fucking sick of it.

With her teeth gritted, she willed the jagged blade of her mind inward, finding the outlines of the shield, and *there* was something tangible she could tear down. She prodded at the surrounding blackness, testing its limits, searching for weaknesses in its armor.

Her anchors glowed softly, swirling to life, magic fortifying her limbs. She tried to grasp them, like pinching a molten thread of glass between her fingernails. With a soft pull on her spirit, the shield began to crumble, bit by bit, pieces breaking away in silvery splinters. Her spark flared brighter, spreading out at the edges. Zarya pulled again, the shield flaking away as the glittering presence inside her grew and grew.

Dizzy with effort, she sat back as the carriage bumped along the ground. She was sure they must be somewhere in the swamp, heading for the ships they'd seen from Rabin's back.

How much longer did she have? There would only be one chance to make this work, and if they were too close to the shore, they'd see exactly what she'd done. How many guards escorted her now? With so many unknowns, every move was a gamble with infinite stakes.

But she had to try.

With her eyes closed, she focused again.

Zarya's pain melted away as magic pooled into her cells and pores. It flowed from her heart, racing along her limbs, drenching her in its power. She dug into it. Willing it to the surface. Like that day in the crumbling streets of Dharati when she had tamed the blight with Rabin's hand around hers, filling her with strength.

He wasn't here to help her now, but it was his face she saw. His velvet eyes, his demanding mouth. She thought of the moment he'd finally admitted he felt something, too. How her heart had almost split when he'd kissed her. Of the night they'd spent in Premyiv when he'd made Zarya feel worthy of something.

When he'd kissed her, his touch had been full of a promise she didn't quite understand yet. But she desperately wanted to explore where it led.

Zarya bundled the strength he'd given her, the strength she'd always known she had, and balled them into her heart.

Then, she thought of Yasen. Dhawan had murdered him. Taken away his light. His grin. His irreverence and that unmistakable essence that had made him. Dhawan ended the one thing that had kept Zarya grounded through every soaring victory and every crumbling defeat.

Her power and strength grew brighter and brighter, fueled by the pure and uncomplicated love she felt for Yasen. For what he'd done to Yasen, Zarya would find Dhawan and tear him limb from limb if it took every last dying breath.

This was her vow to her first best friend.

If there had been a window in the carriage, the guards might have seen it. Might have noticed the light and the radiance that filled the dark space.

If they'd been paying attention, they might have felt her awakening.

She was strong and ready and whole.

With her palms flat against the walls of the carriage, Zarya closed her eyes, pulled on her magic, and then... she exploded.

Nightfire erupted, blasting and searing, the walls shattering to pieces as she clung on with her fingertips. A roar tore through the air as the world ripped apart. The carriage shattered, and she flew, landing in a heap on the earth. Cool mud pressed between her fingers and against her cheek as she lay on the ground, panting. She blinked at the bright blue sky, noting the smell of burning flesh and the heaps of smoldering wood and metal surrounding her.

Somehow, she'd survived, and she would keep on surviving.

Slowly, she pushed herself up, surveying the damage, hearing only the wind in the trees. Almost nothing remained of the carriage. Her nightfire had obliterated it, leaving a circle of torched emptiness around her.

They were deep in the swamp, but had anyone seen the blast? Were they on their way already? Neither Dharati nor the warships were visible from where she sat. Maybe there was still a chance, but she had to get back to the city.

No longer distracted by the need to escape, her pain returned, and she clutched the wound at her side, blood soaking through the makeshift bandages. She struggled to her feet, sucking in a deep breath and willing herself not to faint.

A groan caught her attention. A soldier lay partially submerged in the muck of the swamp, half his face burned away, leaving a ruin of blood and blackened skin. He looked up at her, misery in his remaining eye, his soul barely clinging to life.

Zarya reached down, pulling the sword from his sheath.

"I should leave you here to suffer," she said, her voice filled with sadness.

He made an agonized sound in response, pleading with his eyes. *Please.*

She already knew she'd never choose to be the one responsible for any more pain. Maybe none of this had been his fault. Maybe Dhawan had lied to him, too. With both hands, Zarya raised the sword high above him and dropped it down, spearing it through his heart as his body jerked and then went limp.

She choked on a sob, sparing only a second for him before she hobbled away, heading north towards Dharati. The effort of walking was monumental, and she had to rest every few steps, using the sword for support. It was going to take her days to get back to the city at this rate, if she even survived that long.

Her toe caught on a root, and she went sprawling face-first in the mud, agony cresting in white hot sheets. Tears escaped her eyes as she lay on the ground, gasping for breath, unable to muster the strength to lift herself up again.

She felt for her magic, wondering if there was some way it could help, but it flickered weakly like a candle held up to a strong breeze. Whether from the explosion or the lingering effects of Dhawan's potion, it fluttered dimly in her chest. She had to get up, but she was so tired and heavy. She needed a few moments to rest.

If she slept for just a bit... Zarya's eyes closed, exhaustion making her muscles seize.

A soft whinny came from her left, and she felt a caress of warm air as a velvety nose brushed against her cheek. Her eyes struggled open.

"Ojas," she breathed, recognizing Row's horse that had abandoned her all those months ago. How could he still be alive? "You stupid horse, you left me."

Ojas huffed out a loud breath, shaking his head in response.

"Don't blame me. I didn't know those things were going to attack us."

He let out a whinny as if telling her she should have known better.

"I need your help, Ojas," Zarya said, tears coming again as she carefully lifted herself up. The horse looked a little worn out but mostly healthy. Row's saddle was still strapped around his middle, though Zarya's bags were long gone.

With a groan, she limped over to Ojas, pulling herself up on the saddle with a staggering effort. Once she was seated, she leaned forward, wrapping her arms around his neck.

"Take me to the city, Ojas. You abandoned me once. Now's your chance to redeem yourself."

The horse whinnied one more time, turned around, and began trotting in the direction of Dharati.

THIRTY-SIX

She felt him before she heard him. His wings stirred the surrounding atmosphere, ruffling her hair and cooling her skin as her eyes peeled open. For some reason, she was lying on the ground.

Ojas probably had done his best to get her back to Dharati, but she must have fallen off as she had slid into unconsciousness.

The earth vibrated beneath her as Rabin landed with a great thump, all sinuous limbs and gleaming scales.

Zarya watched him from where she lay on the ground, dazzled as his skin reflected in the sunlight, shifting from violet to teal to indigo and then black as he morphed into his rakshasa form on a curling puff of smoke.

She whimpered as he ran towards her.

"Zarya," he growled, gently rolling her over.

Though she could barely move, she managed a small smile, loving how he said her name, like casting the world with the brightness of wildfire.

He scooped her up, cradling her in his arms as her head fell against his chest. He was so warm and solid, and she swore she could feel her heartbeat aligning with his as they fell into a parallel rhythm.

Thump, thump. Thump, thump.

"What happened?" he asked.

"It was Dhawan," Zarya managed to croak around her dry throat. "He captured me so he could send me to Andhera—he must have told my father about me."

Rabin's arms stiffened beneath her, his grip tightening on her thighs. He placed a kiss on the top of her head. "You're safe now. I won't ever let anything happen to you. I swear it."

"It hurts so much," Zarya whispered, clinging to him, "I think I'm dying."

"You are *not* dying," he replied with a ferocious snarl.

Rabin lay her back down as she stared at the sky, inhaling wheezing breaths. As her heartbeat slowed, she felt herself slipping away.

Rabin placed his large hand against her stomach, where her wound throbbed, warmth flowing from his touch and into her. She whispered a breath of surprise as the pain trickled away, just for a moment, before it flooded back, ricocheting through her limbs. She jerked at the impact and groaned.

"I'm sorry," Rabin said.

Her limbs were so heavy. Her eyelids fluttered open and closed, sound rushing through her ears, white and indistinct and roaring. Whatever waited for her on the other side of this life called to her—beckoned her with its soothing embrace. All she had to do was... let go.

"Zarya!" Rabin said. "You will hang on. Do you hear me?"

"What did you just do?" she whispered. "Did you feel that?"

Paramadhar.

She was more sure than ever now. He had started to heal her, and it had to be because of their connection.

"I did," he said, and then he gave her a significant look that told her everything. While they hadn't been given the opportunity to discuss it yet, his expression said it all. They were destined, and he was all in.

"Can you... fix it?"

"I don't know," he said, and then he placed his hands on her again, and she felt that same warmth stir to life, filling her with calm before it blew out like a match against a thunderstorm.

"*Fuck*," Rabin swore, a sound of despair tearing from him. "I'm not strong enough to heal you alone. Zarya, I need you to help me. You can do this."

He took her hand and crushed her fingers with his while he kept the other pressed against her wound. He stretched out next to her and whispered in her ear.

"You can't die, Spitfire. I have waited too long for you."

She heard him over the buzzing in her ears, feeling the earth-shattering plea in his voice. These words sang to her, lighting up that empty space that had always lived behind her heart.

"Tap into your magic, Zarya," he said. "I need you to use it. Join your anchors. Just a little bit. Please. You can't die. Do you hear me? You cannot fucking die."

Zarya did as he asked, vaguely aware she would do anything he demanded of her. She was willingly at his mercy, like a disciple finding their god.

Dimly, her anchors flickered.

All six of them rose to her call, but the darkness didn't offer seduction today. Today, it offered a lifeline.

She was dying. And she wasn't ready to die yet. Her life had only just begun.

Rabin had said it wasn't evil, and the darkness was only a form of strength and power. Strength she needed right now if she was going to avenge Yasen. If she was going to answer the promise of this connection between her and this man who'd swept into her life and changed everything.

Zarya pulled them all, light bursting in her chest. Rabin made a strangled noise in his throat as the warmth at her side glowed again. She felt the tingle of flesh knitting and blood clotting as heat suffused her skin. It simmered through them both, bright and glittering like a rainbow of stars.

Her magic erupted with one last gasp and then died out.

But it was enough for now. She blinked at the sky, knowing something had just happened.

"Thank fucking gods," Rabin sighed, dropping his face against the curve of her throat as his body shook. Then, he framed her face with his hands, smoothing back her hair as he kissed her gently.

"You did it," he said.

"No. *We* did it."

Their gazes met, and she remembered the moment when she'd first known he was a path she could never turn back on. She felt that now, knowing that no matter what happened, this connection between them had been destined from the very start.

Rabin stood and scooped Zarya into his arms. "We need to get you to Koura. I don't know how long this will hold."

Ojas still lingered nearby, munching on a patch of black grass. Rabin grabbed the horse's reins, helping Zarya up before he settled into the beaten saddle. Zarya leaned against his chest. He was so warm and solid and comforting. She sighed against the familiar smell of falling rain and fresh-tilled earth.

Zarya wasn't sure what to call this glowing thing she felt for Rabin yet, but for now, he was as he had been from the first day she'd met him—her safety, her protection, her lifeline, and maybe so much more.

He directed them towards Dharati, one of his arms wrapped across her waist.

When they entered the courtyard, it was to a scene of chaos as the battle for Amrita's life continued. Whatever magic they had conjured together was enough for Zarya to keep her eyes open. Row and Apsara ran towards them as they helped her down from Ojas.

"I found your stupid horse," she croaked as Row set her on her feet.

He laughed, placing a hand on her head and sweeping her hair from her forehead.

"So you did, my girl." There was such affection in his voice that her stomach twisted. Not her father, but he, too, had become someone important.

"Where's Dhawan?" she asked, and Row shook his head.

"We haven't been able to locate him yet."

"He tried to take me," she said as alarm crossed Row's expression. "He was sending me to Andhera." Row's alarm turned to confusion as Rabin scooped Zarya up from behind, and she started kicking.

"Put me down. I need to find Dhawan," she said. Now that her life no longer hung in the balance, her only goal was vengeance.

"You're in no condition to hunt down that mad Aazheri. Rest a moment," he said.

She glared, glad to have some of her usual energy back.

"Where's Koura?" Rabin asked Row, ignoring her. "She needs healing."

"He's in the tunnels trying to ease some of Amrita's pain," Row replied. "Watch yourselves."

Rabin gave a grim nod and proceeded to stalk through the courtyard.

"I can walk," Zarya said, squirming in his arms.

Soldiers turned to stare at their fearsome commander carrying her like she was a fragile doll.

He growled, his grip tightening.

"You almost died. I'm carrying you."

Zarya glared at him again, but she was still weak, and it

didn't have much force behind it. With a smirk, Rabin hoisted her against him and kept walking.

"Koura!" Rabin shouted once they entered the dim tunnels. "Koura!" His rough voice skittered through the halls. Rabin wandered the maze through tunnels and arches, twisting in and out. It was a wonder anyone ever made it out of here.

Zarya was losing consciousness again. The bleeding had stopped, but her entire side was both numb and aching.

"Hang on," Rabin whispered, looking down at her. "I'm going to take care of you."

"Koura!" he called.

Finally, Koura stepped out from a tunnel and ran to them, worry in his kind eyes.

"Put her down," Koura said.

Zarya grabbed his arm with her flagging strength.

"Just enough so I don't die. Save your strength for Amrita. Promise me," she whispered.

The healer paused, his lips pressing together before he nodded, laying his large hands on her side. Zarya gasped as a tingle washed over her like being dipped in a hot bath after coming in from the cold. Koura's golden healing light filled the cavern, flowing all through her body, finding each laceration and coaxing it back to life.

Rabin held her hand before his gaze flicked to Koura. Then, he leaned down to kiss her, his hand wrapped around the back of her neck, infusing it with longing and hope and the shape of a promise. He pulled away, his gaze searing into hers.

"Don't scare me like that again." His voice was thick with an emotion he was choking back. "And we're getting you some proper armor after this is over."

Zarya glanced at Koura and almost laughed out loud as he stared intensely at a random spot on the wall, clearly trying to give them privacy in the confines of the cramped tunnel. She looked down at the ruined fighting leathers she'd so proudly purchased and huffed out a laugh.

"Fine," she said as a shout echoed through the cavern, and three Kiraaye Ka rounded the corner.

"Excuse me a moment," Rabin said before he jumped up and launched himself at the fighters.

As Koura worked, she felt tissue and skin grafting together, sealing the wound as his healing light flowed over her skin.

"It's a deep cut," Koura said after another minute. "It's not fully healed, but that should hold, at least for now. Try not to move too much."

"Thank you." Zarya lay back, taking several long, slow breaths of relief. She felt a little better. At least the numbness was gone, and she'd stopped gushing blood.

Koura helped her stand. "You need to rest. Get yourself to the infirmary where they can bandage you up properly."

Zarya shook her head.

"No, I have to find Dhawan first."

Koura's nose flared. "Zarya, this isn't wise. The wound isn't healed. If you let me use more power..."

"No," she said, grabbing his forearm. "I'll be fine. Save your strength, and please help my friend here." She gestured to the roots around them. "Amrita cannot die, or we are all lost. The darkness will win, and you know that cannot happen. I have to finish this. For Amrita."

Koura nodded slowly and placed a fist over his heart.

"For Amrita. For Daragaab. May the stars light your way, Princess."

"I'm not a princess," Zarya said.

"Perhaps not yet." Koura smiled.

She returned it and ran off in the direction Rabin had taken, but the tunnels had shifted again, and he was gone. Zarya rounded corner after corner, searching for him, his kiss still warm on her lips.

She ran through the tunnels, her movements fueled by the adrenaline firing in her veins. As two Kiraaye Ka appeared, she swung at them, barely pausing as she gutted one with her knife and swung her sword, slicing the other in the side of the neck, blood pouring from the wound.

She didn't have long before her body would give out again, but for now, Zarya moved like nightfire itself, with vengeance in her blood and love in her heart.

THIRTY-SEVEN

Her voice echoed through the tunnels as Zarya called for Rabin, but the shifting labyrinth had swallowed him up. She raced through the underground, dispatching any Kiraaye Ka who crossed her path.

But she was wasting time looking for him, and she ground to a stop. She was sure he would find her, but *she* had to find Dhawan. He was the goal right now. The prize she sought.

She found a staircase that wound up, reasoning Dhawan probably wasn't camped out amongst Amrita's roots. The stairs deposited her into a quiet, empty hallway she wasn't familiar with.

The surf pounded outside, gently vibrating the floors as she walked slowly down the pristine hall. Colorful marble gleamed brightly in the afternoon sun as her blood- and dirt-caked boots left a trail of grime.

Her strength continued to wane as her wound throbbed, causing her to stumble over her feet, catching herself just before crashing to the hard floor. The near miss impressed upon her the little time she had left. All she could do was press forward and hope she survived this.

But the palace was enormous. Finding Dhawan would be impossible. What if he'd already left? He'd told the soldiers he'd be along behind them. But he'd soon discover Zarya wasn't on the boat, and then he'd return for her. Besides, surely he wouldn't leave before securing Amrita's death. He must still be here somewhere. She would accept nothing else.

Her crusted bandages were wet with blood again, and she heard Koura's warning. She should have listened to him, but she had to finish this. Zarya uttered a quiet sob as she unloaded her weight against a wall, blood smearing on the priceless hanging tapestry, but she didn't have the energy to move away.

Footsteps sounded down an adjacent hallway, and a familiar figure appeared before her. Aarav approached, covered in blood, his sword raised.

"Aarav," she breathed. "I'm so happy to see you."

It was true, she realized. After everything, it was finally true.

"I was looking for you," he said. "I wanted to help."

She winced at a stab of pain in her side. "I think I need to see a healer."

"Let's get you to the infirmary," he said, wrapping an arm around her waist and helping her off the wall. She limped as he ushered her slowly along.

"What happened?" he asked.

She tried to explain everything that had transpired since they'd left for the Bayangoma grove a few days ago. "Aarav, Dhawan killed Yasen," she said, her voice sticking in her throat. "The last I saw of him—"

She couldn't speak.

Aarav's mouth pinched together.

"He was a good man," Aarav said. "I feel lucky to have called him my friend."

"Me too," she said and then bent over as another wave of pain seized through her side.

"Would it help if I carried you on my back?" he asked.

She sucked in a breath through her nose and out through her mouth. "I'm not—"

BOOM.

The ceiling shattered, a hail of marble raining over their heads as Aarav shielded her with his body, bearing the impact. They hacked on the dust that clogged their eyes and noses, waiting for it to settle.

When the haze cleared, she saw Professor Dhawan at the end of the hallway with his fingers linked in front of his chest, wearing an ugly sneer on his ugly face.

Zarya and Aarav drew their swords as Dhawan approached, his boots clicking ominously against the tiles.

"How did you end up back here, girl? It seems I have greatly underestimated your abilities." He stopped a few feet away, studying her. "I don't understand—how did Row keep you so well hidden all that time? I spent twenty years searching for you, and I never caught a hint of your presence until you showed up on my doorstep. An Aazheri with your gifts should have been more detectable even when veiled by magic."

Zarya took a step back, her sword raised. Aarav, jaw set, walked next to her. Finally, her protector and companion. Her family.

Zarya stared at Dhawan, willing his words to make sense. "What do you mean, you spent twenty years searching?"

The corner of his mouth turned up in a cold smile as he took another step.

"I knew your mother's secret. I knew who her lover had been and whose child she was carrying."

Zarya backed up as he took another step, wanting to maintain as much distance from him as possible.

"You said her name the first time you saw me."

With his fingers pressed to his lips, Dhawan nodded.

"Asha was an enchanting woman. Beautiful. Cunning.

Ambitious. Sometimes, I wonder if she intended to use you herself. Even without the prophecy, she might have caught Abishek's eye, given the depth of her power.

"It was pure chance I discovered what she was hiding, but when I did, I used magic to ensnare her mind. Trick her into trusting me. She must have discovered it because she deceived me, too. She gave birth and secreted you away before I could intercept. Quite the little actress she was."

Something unfocused lingered in his gaze before he snapped back to Zarya with knife-sharp clarity.

"I assumed Asha must have given you to Row—he was the only one she would have trusted. But he disappeared, too, didn't he? That's when I knew for sure. He abandoned everything, including Raja Abishek, his master. I traveled the continent trying to find him, but no one saw him for years.

"But then, a few years ago, the Chiranjivi were called to help with the blight in Daragaab, and noble Row, of course, couldn't refuse the call. I made my way to Dharati as quickly as I could. A retired old professor from Gi'ana seeking a quiet life in the forests of the south? Who would be worried about me? In fact, they quickly turned to me for guidance and advice."

Zarya bared her teeth. He had tricked them all.

"But Row surfaced alone. No young woman next to him. Where had he hidden you? Had he sent you away somewhere? It was a mystery. But I waited. A year feels like a sneeze when you're as old as I am. And my patience was rewarded tenfold when you appeared on my doorstep, all innocent-eyed and filled with longing. And a fair bit of rage, conveniently enough.

"I recognized your mother in you. I knew it had to be you. You trusted me because you thought I knew your mother. But it wasn't with fondness that I remembered her. That witch paid for what she did."

His smile was as frigid and brittle as an arctic breeze.

Something rose in Zarya's chest. Anger, but also a crushing

sense of loss. It hadn't been out of love or wonderment that he'd said her mother's name. He'd hated her.

"Did you... hurt her?"

"I didn't," he said. "But fate caught up with her all the same."

"Why? What did you want with me? What was the point?" Zarya asked, putting aside questions about her mother for now. Despite the itch in her hand to cut out the man's heart, Zarya knew she had to keep him talking, or *her* secrets would die with him and be lost forever.

"Well, that was the question, wasn't it? Given your lineage, you should have been quite powerful, but by all counts, it seemed that you couldn't even light a candle. Your mother's binding spell was nearly impenetrable."

He tilted his head, studying her carefully. "But you were keeping secrets of your own, weren't you? How did you break the curse, Zarya? I've been dying of curiosity. I should have known then you were also a good little actress. The rotten apple never falls far from the tree."

Zarya firmed her grip on her sword as she exchanged a wary look with Aarav. It was clear what a shock this information was to him, too.

"When the kala-hamsa attacked, you revealed what you were capable of, and all my searching, all that waiting finally paid off. Here you were. The wielder of nightfire, exactly what had been promised."

Dhawan rocked on his heels as he clasped his hands behind his back.

"Though I briefly thought my plans had been foiled when Commander Ravana showed up at the same moment."

Those words settled over her, stilling her like a statue.

"What?" she asked in a whisper.

"No one has known where he's been these past years, but I know. While I've been wearing myself thin tracking you down, the commander has been cozy at Raja Abishek's side. From what I hear, he thinks of Abishek almost like the father he never had."

Zarya swayed on her feet as the world shrunk to a point and then detonated like a dying star in her chest.

Rabin had been with her *father* all this time? That couldn't be true.

"You're lying," Zarya said, her voice hoarse and her limbs and fingers tingling with the cold numbness of betrayal.

Dhawan *had* to be lying.

Rabin would have told her. He wouldn't have deceived her like this. She understood his heart and his mind; she would have *known*.

With a tut, he tilted his head. "I know, my dear, it must feel terrible knowing the man you fell for is working for the man who wants to enslave you. He was only using you to climb his way up to more power. Raja Abishek rewards loyalty, after all."

Zarya's entire body throbbed, her heart pulsing somewhere outside of her body.

Had Rabin lied to her, too? Promised her something on the edge of transcendence designed to deceive Zarya and manipulate her desperate need to be loved?

Then, she remembered Rabin's words earlier this morning. That he had something he had to tell her. What if this had been it?

A hot, bitter tang filled her mouth. How could he have been pretending? Row had been right. Zarya knew nothing about Rabin, and she'd walked right into this trap like the foolish little girl she'd always been. Gods, she was so stupid.

A tether snapped, loosing her from the earth like a shot fired into the sky. Pain and rage and fury exploded inside her chest, her blood boiling as she turned her burning anger on Dhawan. Zarya would end this monster if it was the last thing she did.

Nothing mattered anymore. She'd lost everything today. It was as if she'd never left the seaside cottage at all.

Yasen was gone. Amrita almost dead. Rabin had betrayed her. Her family didn't want her. Zarya was trapped in an endless cycle of deception and half-truths.

Now, she had become something truly dangerous because she had nothing left to lose.

With a roar, Zarya raised her sword and ran at Dhawan. She would cut him limb from limb. She would destroy him. She would make him hurt until the world burned down around her.

Pain seized in her chest, squeezing her heart, and she tumbled to the floor, rolling over and over. It wasn't the same searing pain of the axe wound at her side, but crippling, aching pain, like someone was trying to pull her bones out through her skin. She writhed on the ground as agony shot through every sinew, her back arching as she tried to claw away from it.

Aarav charged after her, but Dhawan raised an arm and drove him into another mess of twisted limbs at her side.

Dhawan stood over them, smiling. "I forget you have a small drop of power as well," he said, considering Aarav like he was a worm curling over his toe.

"You're fortunate I need you alive," Dhawan said to Zarya as she gnashed her teeth against the onslaught. "The king's rewards may be withheld if I return only with a body. You're not much use to him dead. But you've already proven you won't come quietly."

Zarya strained against Dhawan's vise, shaking as he twisted his magic, forcing a scream to rip from her throat.

A moment later, she felt a pulse against her skin, and the atmosphere shifted as a wave of power cascaded over Zarya, slamming into Dhawan's chest. The ancient Aazheri flew in the air, landing on his back with a muffled thump as his grip on her released. Dhawan scrambled to his feet, his eyes lit with panic before he shook it off.

"Nice trick. But it's not going to be that easy," he sneered.

Zarya had no idea what had just happened, but she used the opportunity to gather a thin stream of nightfire. Her magic fluttered weakly, and Dhawan deflected it with ease, sending it ricocheting off the ceiling. More marble rained down over Zarya and Aarav's heads.

Dhawan threw the magical vise against Zarya and Aarav again. It wrapped around them, closing in, agony tearing their limbs and bones and skin. But the same mysterious force reacted a second time, flaring out and throwing Dhawan's magic back in his face.

Again, the professor went flying, crashing into a wall before sliding to the floor. Now, dreadful uncertainty filled his gaze, his confidence dripping away.

She still didn't understand what had happened, but Zarya rose to her feet and smirked at him, anyway, stalking towards him with every intent to cut him off at the knees.

Aarav called a warning.

"Zarya!" She looked over her shoulder to find a row of Kiraaye Ka, armed to the teeth, blocking the far end of the hallway.

"Deal with them," Dhawan ordered, some of his previous bravado returning. "Bring her to me. Kill the other one."

Without missing a beat, the soldiers charged, crashing upon Zarya and Aarav in a ringing of blades. Zarya screamed with the rage that boiled the blood in her veins as she attacked the Kiraaye Ka without mercy, hacking them down like paper dolls.

Rabin had lied to her and tricked her. He had broken her heart, shattering it into splinters of glass that shredded under her skin. He wasn't her paramadhar. He was nothing but another fucking *man* in her life, using her and making a fool out of her.

She sobbed as she razed the Kiraaye Ka to the ground,

reveling in the satisfaction of their blood and their screams. They had fucked with the wrong woman today.

Before long, Aarav and Zarya stood amongst a heap of bodies.

She spun around to face Dhawan, whose smile had slipped from his face.

"You!" Zarya hissed. "You're next! Do you hear me!"

She prowled towards him, her blade gripped in her hand. He flung out a blast of magic, but anger had cleared her head, and now she could focus. She lifted her arm, pulling on a thread of spirit and fire, erecting a shield as she batted his magic away.

Dhawan backed up as he tried again, but she flung out a blast of air, knocking him back. He groaned as he slid along the floor before he scrambled onto his hands and knees.

His hand flung out again, narrowly missing her as fire singed the tip of her braid, and then, like the gutless weasel he was, he ran.

"Get back here, you coward!" she screamed.

"Zarya!"

She turned to find another flood of Kiraaye Ka spilling into the hallway. At least a dozen spotted Zarya and Aarav, and they came barreling down the hall. Zarya turned back towards Dhawan, but he'd disappeared.

"Run!" Aarav called, and they both pumped their arms and legs, skidding around corners, trying to lose the Kiraaye Ka, who stayed close on their heels. Zarya cried out and stumbled as a blade nicked her calf.

Aarav grabbed her by the arm, hauling her back up as they continued running.

"We can't outrun them," Aarav said. "Go and find Dhawan. I'll deal with them."

"You can't do this alone!"

"I'll distract them," Aarav yelled as they hooked around another corner. "Go after Dhawan. I'll take care of this."

"Aarav, no."

"Zarya, go. Let me do this for you. Find Dhawan and kill him, and then go and find your father and kill him, too. Let me protect you now as I should have been doing all these years."

He cast a quick glance in her direction as he reached out and took her hand, squeezing it.

"I owe you that."

Then, he shoved her down a hallway through a set of doors, slamming them behind her. She spun around and crashed against them as she heard the lock click.

"Aarav!" she screamed, pounding on the door. "Don't do this!"

"Get out of here! Tell Lekha I love her!" he shouted through the wood before she heard his cry of rage and then the clash of steel against steel.

For several long seconds, she stared at the door, blinking furiously.

But she had to keep moving before the soldiers came through the barrier and before Aarav's sacrifice had been in vain.

She pressed the tips of her fingers to her lips and floated a kiss towards the door—a final goodbye as a tear dripped off her chin.

"Goodbye, Aarav. Thank you."

And then she turned around and ran.

THIRTY-EIGHT

The fire continued to burn in her limbs as she honed in on her desire to find Dhawan down the endless halls. She spotted a trail of blood, crimson footsteps smearing together, and smiled to herself. She searched, continuing around corners as the tracks grew closer together.

Given the amount of blood, he must have been quite badly injured. Zarya tried to conjure up the slightest ounce of sympathy and found none.

The footsteps led through a set of double doors that entered a large ballroom. Zarya eased herself around the one standing slightly ajar, catching sight of a giant map of Rahajhan hanging on the wall.

She squinted in the dim light that filtered through a round window cut into the ceiling. Pain gripped her heart as she entered, sending her to her knees. Dhawan was trying to bind her magic again, his power enclosing the star in her heart, trying to seal what Rabin had freed.

Rabin, who had given her back her magic so he could turn her over to the king of Andhera. It all made sense now. That's why he had helped her and why he'd appeared out of thin air.

How could she have been so blind? Why had she trusted anything he'd said?

Zarya grunted as her ribs twisted on the verge of cracking, and just when she was sure she couldn't take it anymore, that same mysterious force crested out like a shockwave, peeling away Dhawan's magic and flinging it back at him. It sent him flying into the wall with a hard crack. He groaned, sliding to the floor.

Zarya struggled to her feet, barely able to stand, before she limped over.

Dhawan croaked, lifting a hand as if to fend her off as a pool of blood congealed under him. He'd hit the wall hard enough to shatter it, cracks snaking up from where he lay. He flung out his magic, but she batted it away.

"How are you doing that?" he asked, referring to that strange magic that continued to react without her influence.

She ignored the question. Even if she knew, she wouldn't tell him.

"Tell me why," Zarya demanded, pointing her sword at his throat, violence and adrenaline the only things keeping her upright anymore. "Why do you care if my father has me? Why are you working for him?"

Dhawan cowered against the wall, but the loathing in his eyes was as steady as marble.

"Because he cast me out," he spat. "I made one little mistake, but he refused to listen to reason. He threw me aside like I was no better than a filthy vanshaj."

Zarya pressed the tip of her sword into the flesh of Dhawan's neck, pulling up a bead of crimson that trickled down the line of his throat.

"I groveled. I begged for centuries. But he wouldn't forgive me. Not like Ravana, who walked in like the world owed him everything."

Zarya reacted to Rabin's name as Dhawan's words speared through her heart.

"You are my path to redemption and a place at the king's side, once again."

He glared up at Zarya as though all of this had been her fault. She pressed the blade harder, and he sucked in a gasp, scrambling against the wall at his back as though he could melt right through it.

"Why Amrita? And Rani Vasvi? What did they have to do with this?"

Now, his angry expression morphed into one of smugness.

"Oh, that wasn't for me. That was for you, my dear. For you and your father."

His smile grew wider as Zarya's brows knit.

"You're a smart girl. Surely, you've realized by now that *you* are responsible for all of this? That the darkness lives in you? Why do you think the swamp grew on the shoreline where you spent your entire life? Why do you think the king covets your nightfire so much? With the darkness set free, the possibilities are limitless. *You* started all of this—I was merely helping it along."

Zarya let out a pained breath. For months, she'd suspected it. Ever since the night of the kala-hamsa attack, she'd known she was tainted. She took another step forward, pressing the sword tip into Dhawan's throat harder. He wheezed against the pressure, fear spreading into his eyes.

"What does that mean?" she asked.

Dhawan began blubbering, pressing his hands together in a plea as if detecting a chink of mercy in her armor.

"My dear girl. You may be strong beyond comprehension, but I have lived so long, and I have so many secrets. I can tell you so many things. With me and your father at your side, you can do anything," Dhawan scrambled to his knees, his hands still fused with hope. "You could rule the continent with that much power in you. Spare me, and I will help you. The darkness, Zarya—it is yours to command. If you learned to use it properly, no one could *ever* make you a prisoner again."

"But my father wants to steal my magic for himself," she said.

Dhawan shook his head. "No. They're all lying to you. Don't you see? They're just holding you back from everything you could be."

Zarya considered his words. His offer. His promise. Rabin had told her it wasn't evil, but he had lied about everything.

Dense black ribbons of magic curled in her chest, seducing her with whispered nothings. Crawling shadows unfurling from dark corners. A tender hope pushing through soil to greet the sun.

To never be caged again.

That's all anyone had tried to do to her from the day she was born. Her mother had stolen her magic. Row had locked her away. And her father? Could she place any trust in Dhawan's words?

She imagined what it would be like to never be vulnerable or at anyone's mercy again.

She stared down at Dhawan, who now seemed so small as he trembled at her feet.

But even if her father wasn't trying to use her, Zarya did not want to become a creature molded of fury and vengeance. She did not see a future built on the ashes of darkness. What she saw was light. The brightness of the life she'd found here. Her friends. Her family.

She would not become the thing everyone feared.

That, too, would be its own kind of prison.

With a deep breath, Zarya shoved the darkness back into its cave and locked it away, where she would keep it contained forever.

This was a promise to *herself*.

"No," she said, shaking her head as the temporary light reflecting in Dhawan's eyes flared out. "You killed my friends. And that will never be what I want."

As tears slid down her cheeks, she pressed the point of her blade into the soft flesh of his throat, using the weight of her body to drive it home. Blood trickled down his front as he gurgled, his eyes wide, and then he slumped over dead.

The blade clattered from her hands, and she inhaled a ragged gasp like someone had been holding her head underwater.

Stumbling back, she reached for something to steady herself, but there was nothing, only empty space as she tripped, crashing to the floor as the world faded away.

THIRTY-NINE

Hurried footsteps sounded in the distance as Zarya's eyes fluttered open. She studied Dhawan's cooling body, lying a few paces away as blood pooled underneath him. She had done that. Killed him. Exacted her revenge for everything he'd done, but for the briefest of seconds, she'd considered the opposite.

She didn't know if she could ever reveal the shame of how she'd wavered to anyone—even if it was only for a moment. But her only witness was dead now, and so Zarya would add another secret to her growing collection, hoping she wouldn't break under their weight. The footsteps drew closer, and she groaned. She couldn't fight anymore. Her body had turned numb from the inside out. She wasn't sure how she was even still conscious.

Row and Apsara burst into the room, and Zarya choked on the taste of her relief.

Their eyes flicked to Dhawan's slumped form crumpled on the floor. Apsara kneeled and smoothed Zarya's hair back, squeezing her shoulder.

"Hang on," Apsara said. "Help is on the way."

Kindle and Suvanna entered the room, and Zarya squeezed

her eyes shut as Vikram arrived and kneeled before her. He gently took her hand as she noted the purple and black bruises covering his face and his torn clothing streaked with dirt.

"Yasen," Zarya said, twisted with an agonized sob. "Dhawan killed him. He's gone. Someone needs to find him. He was in a cave in the tunnels."

Vikram's fingers tightened against hers as his eyes shone with tears. He nodded, ordering a pair of guards who stood near the door to search for his body. Then, he clutched her hand as he slumped to the ground, tears streaming down his face.

"I'm so sorry." Her voice shook. "I couldn't stop him."

"It wasn't your fault."

He glared at Dhawan's prostrate form.

Finally, Koura jogged into the room.

"You again?" he asked softly, crouching next to her.

Zarya opened her mouth, and Koura raised a hand. "I know. I am helping Amrita, but it seems you are also a hero in this story."

He gestured to Dhawan, and Zarya offered him a weak smile.

Koura set to work, using his magic to piece her seams back together. The room held still and silent for several long minutes as Koura's magic restored her damaged body.

Another set of footsteps echoed at the end of the room, and Zarya looked up, feeling her heart fold itself over inside her chest. Rabin looked at Dhawan before his gaze drifted to Zarya, his bloody sword clutched loosely in his hand.

The look on his face was one of pure, unfiltered relief as he approached, but the sight of him made her grow hot and cold all over as her heart raced and the ceiling began to spin. She struggled to push herself up.

"You should rest," Koura said, but she waved him off, lurching to her feet on trembling legs.

"Is it true?" Zarya asked Rabin, her voice cracking. "Were you lying to me?"

His gaze shifted away, guilty truth written all over his face.

No. She hadn't wanted to believe it. She would give anything for Dhawan to have been lying.

"Is it true?" she asked louder. "Tell me what he said was a lie!"

Hysteria clawed up her throat, threatening to drown her in a sea of simmering rage. Rabin looked down and then back at Zarya.

"What is it?" Row asked, coming to stand next to her. "What's going on?"

Swaying on her feet, she reached for him, holding his arm to steady herself.

"Dhawan claimed he's been with Raja Abishek all these years." She dropped the accusation at his feet, hoping he'd kick it away.

Zarya couldn't take her eyes off Rabin as he stared at her.

"What?" Row asked with disbelief in his voice.

"Deny it, Rabin! Tell me it isn't true. Please tell me it isn't true." Her voice broke apart on the words like waves crashing into jagged rocks.

"Zarya, I was going to tell you—" he started, stepping closer.

She held out a hand, stilling him in his tracks.

"But you didn't. You lied to me! Just like all of them. You're the same as everyone else! You found me, and you wanted to use me!"

"Zarya, no," he said, his deep voice vibrating through her chest. "That's not what it was. I swear to you, I had no idea who you were until Row revealed the truth. That isn't why I sought you out. That *isn't* why I came here."

She closed her eyes, swaying dangerously on legs like rubber, clinging to Row as a jagged slash ripped through her chest.

When she spoke, her voice was as raw as broken glass.

"I *gave* myself to you, body and soul. I told you the hardest thing to stomach was the lies, and you sat there, and you listened to me, and you said nothing. You let me believe you cared about me." She dragged in a shaky breath.

Rabin's gaze turned fierce, the gold flecks in his eyes burning like falling embers.

"I meant every single thing I said, Zarya," he said, sinking to his knees. "It was all real. Nothing about what I feel for you is a lie. I didn't tell Abishek about you, and I wouldn't have, not until you were ready. I'd never do anything to hurt you. You're wrong about him."

She shook her head, tears clogging the back of her throat.

"You hurt me, Rabin. Hurt me more than all of the other lies combined. I trusted you. I believed in you. In *us*. I thought —" Zarya broke off, pain shearing her heart, crushing the words to ash in her mouth. "You promised not to break my heart!"

"Don't do this. Let me explain, please. Zarya, please, I'm falling in l—"

"No!" Zarya shouted so loud it practically shook the crystal chandeliers as she choked on great hiccupping sobs. "Don't you dare say that. Don't make this even worse. You have no right to say that to me!"

Rabin rose to his feet, moving closer to her. "Tell me what I can do to fix this, Spitfire. I will do anything."

Steely resolve settled in his jaw, but Rabin's unwavering confidence wouldn't work for him this time. She was too broken to even look at him—this wound cut too deep, where light couldn't reach.

She shook her head. "I can't trust you. Leave. I don't want to see you ever again."

Rabin's jaw turned to stone as he stood before her, not moving, refusing to accept her words.

"Get out!" Zarya screamed at him, feeling herself boil over, her skin hot, her blood molten in her veins.

It was then that Rabin's expression finally shattered, his shoulders collapsing and his posture curving into defeat.

"Very well," he said. "If that's what you want."

Zarya's heart cleaved in two as he turned and strode out of the room, the bruise on her lungs so heavy her breath stopped.

Silence followed his retreating footsteps as Koura guided Zarya back to the floor and began to heal her again. She turned on her side and sobbed into her arms as Row gently rubbed her back.

Then, every eye in the room turned to the ceiling as the anguished roar of a mighty dragon rang out over the city so loud it shook every star in the sky.

FORTY

Hours later, Zarya rested in bed, listening to the sounds of the ocean. After Koura had healed the worst of her injuries, she'd taken a bath and changed into clean clothes, but nothing could wash away the stain in her heart.

Limbs sticking straight out like a starfish, Zarya stared at the underside of the canopy, blinking away a never-ending stream of tears. Still feeling Rabin's kiss from that morning, Zarya touched her bottom lip, trying not to spiral into the yawning cavern of his betrayal.

It felt like it had all happened a million years ago. How could so much have changed in less than a day?

She missed Yasen with every fiber of her soul. She couldn't stop thinking of him. And of Aarav and the way he'd given up his life for hers. They had spent every day at odds, and just when they'd finally forgiven one another, he'd been whisked away forever.

It all left a hollow ache in her chest, like a lonely echoing pit.

A knock came at her door, and Row's head poked inside. She sat up and brushed the tears from her cheeks.

"How are you feeling?" he asked, pulling up a chair to sit at her bedside.

She shrugged. "A little weak, but I'll survive. What about you?"

Row gave her a sad smile. "I've been better. Will you tell me what happened with Aarav?"

She nodded and then explained what had transpired in his last stand with the Kiraaye Ka. "We made up at the end," she said, wiping another tear from her eye with the corner of her blanket. "We both apologized and forgave one another for everything."

Row let out a heavy breath. "You know, that makes me very happy to hear." He leaned forward and clasped his hands. "Are you ready to talk about what happened with Rabin?"

Zarya shook her head. "I don't know what there is to say. You were right about him, and I was wrong."

He made a wry face.

"I didn't want to be right," he said. "I hope you know that."

"I do," she said. "But how did no one know that's where he was?"

"Abishek has always been very secretive. Andhera is difficult to get to, and news rarely travels outside its borders. If he wanted to keep it a secret, then it wouldn't have been hard."

"So, Rabin was keeping it a secret."

Row spread his hands. "I can only assume so."

"Why?"

"That, I can't answer, Zarya. I wish I could."

She rubbed her hands down her face. "It doesn't matter. It's over. I can't trust him again."

Row reached over and clasped Zarya's hand in his before he squeezed it.

At that moment, another knock came at the door, and Row stood to answer it, speaking with someone on the other side before he turned to Zarya.

"I do have a surprise that I think should help cheer you up."
His eyes twinkled as he smiled.

"What?" she asked, frowning at him.

"Come with me. I promise you it will be worth it." He cocked his head and gestured for her to follow.

"Just tell me," Zarya said. She was not in the mood for any more surprises right now.

"No. Now, I'm going, and you can follow me, or you can stay here, but I think he'll be pretty disappointed if you don't come and see him."

The corner of Row's mouth ticked up in a smile as she let those words sink in.

"What?"

Immediately, she jumped up and winced at the twinge in her side.

"Are you okay?" he asked, concern furrowing his brow.

"I'm fine. Show me."

Row held out an elbow, and Zarya looped her arm through his. Slowly, he directed her down the hall, matching her halting pace. Zarya heard a groan from a room a few doors down and then an indignant voice.

"Ow! That hurts!" it said.

She inhaled sharply. She *knew* that voice.

"Oh," she whispered, pressing her fingers to her mouth as tears filled her eyes. Row smiled down at her before Zarya took off running, all her aches and pains forgotten. She skidded into the room where Yasen lay in bed while a healer attempted to change the bandages on his arm.

"Yasen!" She ran across the room and leaped onto the bed, collapsing on top of him and squeezing him tight.

"Ahhhhh!" he cried. "Gentle! I almost died!"

"You're alive," she cried. "You're alive."

"Well, I won't be much longer if this butcher has his way,"

he said, and the healer rolled his eyes before he started to pack up his tools.

"He meant to say thank you. Right, Yasen?"

Yasen cocked a brow, offering the healer a grin.

"He knows I was kidding. Right?"

The healer bowed. "You're welcome," he said and then left.

Zarya threw her arms around Yasen's neck, peppering his cheeks with sloppy kisses.

"Stop that," he grumbled, pretending to wipe them away, but she saw the glimmer of fondness in his eyes. She knew him too well now.

"How are you alive? I saw those things lunge at you."

"Because I have many, many talents," he said.

She narrowed her eyes. "You were literally tied up."

Yasen shrugged. "It was Rabin. He found me a few minutes after Dhawan left with you. He freed me, and then we killed those hideous things. I was in rough shape, but I made him leave and go after you."

"That's how he knew to find me in the swamp," she said, and Yasen nodded.

"He went out of his mind when he heard Dhawan had taken you away," he said quietly. "I'm sorry he isn't who you thought he was."

She waved a hand, pretending she wasn't bothered. "It doesn't matter. You're alive, and that's all I care about right now."

Zarya hooked her arm into his, sliding down and placing her head on his shoulder.

"I heard Aarav took on a battalion of Kiraaye Ka, too," Yasen said. She tensed for a moment and nodded.

"He went down fighting for me."

Yasen whistled. "Woah."

"He called you his friend."

Yasen said nothing for a moment and then replied, "Well, now I feel like an asshole."

She shrugged against him. "He didn't make it easy, did he? But it turns out he wasn't such a bad guy."

"That idiot," he said with a touch of reverence in his voice, and Zarya laughed.

Row leaned in the doorway with his arms crossed as he watched them.

"How's Amrita?" she asked him.

"Koura is doing what he can, but she continues to live in a lot of pain."

"Have you all discussed what we learned from my father's journal and the Jai Tree being the seal for dark magic?"

"We have," Row said. "And we think we finally have a solution."

"It's us, isn't it?" Zarya asked. "The 'chain' my father referred to? Amrita needs the magic of the Chiranjivi to contain the darkness."

"That's the same conclusion we came to," Row said.

"Dhawan asked me how we survived the Kiraaye Ka, and it was clear he didn't know how potent our combined powers would become."

Row blew out a breath. "So, despite everything, he did us a favor by forcing us together like that."

"So it would seem," Zarya said. "I want to go and see her." She shuffled off the bed and glanced at Yasen. "Can you walk?"

"Of course, I can walk." He swung his legs over and stood, wavering for several seconds before he steadied himself. "But let's walk slowly."

Zarya smiled and held out a hand for him. The trio made their way through the quiet halls of the palace, where signs of the battle were visible everywhere. As they neared the court-yard, the halls fared worse and worse. Chunks were carved out of every surface, scratches marred the floors, and there was blood, so much blood.

They exited into the courtyard, where they found Apsara, Koura, Kindle, and Suvanna. Apsara was holding one of Koura's hands as he pressed the other to Amrita's bark. Koura's light flared as it shot up the trunk, returning it to glistening white. Light filtered through her branches and spread, flowers blooming as his magic traced along Amrita's damaged limbs.

"How did you do that?" Zarya asked. Koura's healing magic typically only offered some relief but couldn't actually heal the queen. However, Zarya thought of the way her nightfire had shattered Amrita's branches during the battle, and it was clear some types of magic could work on her.

Dark circles ringed Koura's golden eyes, and he looked like he must have been working around the clock. Amrita had healed considerably, her shining white bark restored in many places. Patches of black and grey marred some of her trunk, while bare branches, stripped of their flowers, reached into the sky.

"We figured out that if we use the chain of our Chiranjivi power, it works on Amrita," Apsara said. "With our help, she can heal much more quickly."

"That's incredible," Zarya said. "So, what do we do about the blight?"

"Let's go in," Apsara said, and they all filed into the Jai Tree where Vikram sat quietly next to the shadow that was Amrita.

"We've spoken with Her Majesty," Apsara said. "It will require her strength to push the blight back, but we do not know what it might cost her."

Everyone's attention turned to Vikram. "Once fully healed, she is prepared to do whatever is necessary. She is not afraid. She is a queen, and if this is her destiny, she is willing to shoulder whatever burden is required."

"Are we certain we're the 'chain' Abishek referred to in his notebook?" Suvanna asked. "Why are we so sure he was right about this?"

"Abishek has been alive for a very long time," Row said. "He knows more than most people have forgotten. And what else can we do but try?"

"But now we've lost one," Kindle said. "We are only six."

"I'm sorry," Zarya said. "Maybe I shouldn't have made him leave."

"No," Row said firmly. "He lied to all of us. You were right to do what you did."

"If only that made me feel any better."

Zarya looked up. If she'd been hoping to see a huge black dragon soaring across the sky, she found herself disappointed.

"You really think it will work?" she asked.

"The chain still works when there are only two of us linked," Apsara said. "With six of us, it will have to be enough. And as Row said, all we can do is try."

Zarya nodded. "There's another thing I don't understand. Dhawan was trying to use some kind of binding trick on me. I could feel him trying to tie up my magic so he could take me back to Andhera, but something strange kept happening. A power that knocked him back, but I wasn't controlling it."

Puzzled looks greeted her, and then Row reached out, running his finger under the thin golden chain around her neck. The translucent turquoise stone caught the light as he freed the necklace from under the fabric of her kurta.

"Your mother loved you. Asha had no choice but to give you up, but had she lived, she would have thought about you and regretted the choice she had to make every day of her life. She told me to give this to you and never to let you take it off."

Zarya reached up to grasp the stone, remembering the words she'd unlocked that night on Ranpur Island. This gift had followed her throughout her life without her even knowing it.

"Asha was a very powerful Aazheri in her own right. A

protection spell. Something to keep you safe even when she couldn't be with you."

Zarya might never get to meet Asha, but she had this. The unchangeable proof that someone had loved her as a parent should love their child. She looked at the man who had been given the unenviable task of being her keeper. Love comes in many forms, even if it's not one you immediately recognize.

"Row," Zarya said. "Thank you. For doing what she asked. For keeping me safe. I know it wasn't an easy choice for you, either. And I'm sorry I made it so hard."

He took a deep breath and blinked watery eyes; this warrior who had never shown her an ounce of emotion until a few weeks ago. Or so she had always believed. Row wasn't entirely the man—the villain—she'd created in her head. Without the tint of her rage, she was finally seeing him for who he really was.

Stern. Yes. A bit grumpy. Sometimes. Brave and strong and good. Definitely.

"Thank you." He grabbed her and pulled her in close, wrapping his arms around her. "Thank you."

And a father. Maybe that, too.

For a moment, she hesitated, still unused to affection from Row, and then she laughed and hugged him back, freeing herself from the last shackles of her anger.

He might not be her real father, but for now, she'd have to accept that Row would be the closest thing she would ever have.

And she couldn't have asked for anyone better to fill the role.

FORTY-ONE

Aarav was buried at sea. Barges carried the dead, floating in the waters of the Nila Hara laden with flowers and surrounded by hundreds of coppery lights bobbing amongst the waves.

Zarya found Lekha standing on the beach, surrounded by her family, tears shining on her cheeks. At the sight of Zarya, she broke down into a fresh wave of sobs, and Zarya went over to embrace her.

"His last words were about you," Zarya said. "He wanted you to know that he loved you."

Lekha's body shook as she cried on Zarya's shoulder.

"I'm so sorry," Zarya said, squeezing Lekha tight. "If it's any consolation, it was a noble death."

"He would have wanted that," Lekha whispered.

"I agree."

They clung to each other for another moment, and then Lekha pulled away. "Thank you for telling me."

"Of course. Keep in touch. I'd love to see you again."

Lekha wiped her cheek. "Yes. I'd like that."

After another hug, Lekha returned to the embrace of her family, and Zarya wandered down the beach, finding Yasen staring into the distance. She looped her arm through his, and they watched the current take Aarav, along with those who'd lost their lives in the fight for their queen, away.

Copper light imbued the evening sky, guiding the dead towards the afterlife, where their next journey would await. Zarya hoped Aarav's next life would bring him the peace he'd sought in this one. Beautiful and tragic, the circle of life would continue.

"You know, I kind of miss him," Yasen said.

"Me too." Zarya rested her head on Yasen's shoulder. "Can you believe that?"

"Not really." His voice was soft.

Silently, they watched as Kindle cast ribbons of fire towards each barge, engulfing them in flames that crackled in the air.

"How are you feeling?" Yasen rested his cheek on Zarya's head. She shrugged.

"Like I've been cut into pieces and restitched by a blind-folded tailor. I miss him, Yas. Maybe I shouldn't, but I do."

"For what it's worth, I don't think Rabin was faking what he felt for you. I've known him a long time, and I've never seen him smile like that. I don't think I've ever actually seen him smile, come to think of it. No one is that good an actor."

Hope tickled in her chest, still overshadowed by betrayal, a wound still too raw to bear. Zarya squeezed Yasen's arm tighter and sighed.

Aarav continued to burn, the orange flames mingling against the brilliant hues of the setting sun like the world was on fire.

It was a glorious sight. A fitting end for a hero.

"Farewell... friend," Yasen said as Aarav disappeared over the horizon.

* * *

Supported by the chain of the Chiranjivi's magic, Amrita made a full recovery. Koura worked through every root and knot until the Jai Tree's bark shimmered, and Amrita's canopy of flowers grew lusher and more beautiful than ever.

They now had one more task to complete.

Zarya clutched her father's notebook to her chest. Somehow she'd managed to hang on to it through all the chaos.

"You have the power to seal in the darkness, Amrita. The book claims your roots are the key. They are what keeps the darkness at bay."

"She is ready," Vikram replied before he looked at everyone. "Before we begin, we have an announcement we'd like to share."

Everyone turned expectantly to Amrita.

"We've decided to release the seed Amrita had implanted after the joining, and she is currently with child. After such a near miss, we decided not to delay."

Zarya opened her mouth, not entirely sure how to respond. *How* had they released the seed? She thought it was probably better not to know.

A chorus of congratulations erupted, hugs going all around. For a moment, Vikram looked shell-shocked, and then he grinned as his face lit with joy.

"I'm going to be a father!" He threw his arms wide, and they all laughed and congratulated and hugged him again. Perhaps a child would stave off the strange loneliness of Vikram's life and give him something else to focus on.

Whatever animosity had lingered between them had been stuffed away for now. She hoped he wasn't harboring any ill will towards her, and in time, maybe they could be friends again. He'd been burdened with choices that weren't his own, too.

"She is ready," Vikram said, and everyone went quiet, watching Amrita.

"Does she know what to do?" Yasen asked.

Vikram nodded. "She's been testing it on her own, but it requires a great deal of strength. She wouldn't be able to do it without you."

"Are we sure this is going to work with only six of us?" Zarya asked just as a set of sharp footsteps drew everyone's attention to the Jai Tree's door.

Rabin strode across the tiles as the breath in Zarya's lungs seized. She didn't know where he'd gone after she told him to leave, and she hadn't been prepared to see him again now.

Wary looks were shared around the circle, and Zarya caught Yasen's eye, his expression asking if she was okay. She nodded. Helping Amrita was far more important than her silly, broken heart.

"There are seven of us now," he said.

"Excellent," Kindle replied after a brief pause. "Then, let's proceed. We were all using some form of our magic that day in the grove."

Everyone nodded as they stirred up their magic in their own unique way. Kindle held a small flame in his hand, while a breeze whipped around Apsara, churning up her hair and the feathers on her wings. Zarya formed a small ball of nightfire and let it hover over her head.

She felt it almost immediately, the way the seven of them connected like a ribbon had tied them together—whole but also separate. It was different than the connection she'd experienced with Rabin—that had been a consuming wave she'd felt right into her very marrow. In those moments, they'd become one.

She did her best not to look at him, but her inconstant gaze faltered. When she found him watching her, she inhaled a sharp breath before she looked away, focusing on Amrita.

"We're ready," Kindle said.

"She is starting," Vikram replied.

At first, it seemed like nothing was happening.

Amrita's eyes fell closed, her expression calm as her leaves swayed on an invisible breeze. But then Zarya felt it over the miles: that connection to the darkness, to the blight that had plagued Daragaab for years. Dhawan had told her she had been the one who'd drawn the blight out, and maybe he was partly right.

Wherever the truth lay, she felt it now.

"It's working," Zarya said.

She *was* connected to this darkness, but soon, it would be banished to where it had come from. Soon, it would never bother her again.

Vikram's eyes were closed, too, and his face scrunched together. "She is struggling. It is too much. She cannot hold on."

Amrita began to shudder and shake, her wood creaking like the masts of a ship caught in a storm, her face screwed against the strain.

"She needs more from us. Try joining hands," Row said, reaching to his left and right.

Zarya hesitated, wondering if her presence would help or hinder Amrita's efforts. But today, her sixth anchor lay quietly where she'd stowed it away. She would never release it again.

The Chiranjivi linked themselves into a glittering chain of magic. Situated at the ends, Zarya and Row placed their free hands against Amrita, their magic flowing into the queen. Light pulsed in invisible waves on a sea of power.

She felt the crest of their strength, the way each piece aligned together.

Would this work? They had only a few scribbled notes and a well of hope to cling to. If Zarya hadn't found that book and realized she could translate it. If Dhawan hadn't sent them to that grove where they'd discovered their nearly unstoppable power, then Dharati might have been lost. Fate had maneuvered to give them an answer, and it had come just in time.

Amrita's power swept through Daragaab, touching the darkness and forcing it back. Hemmed in and pushed down, it drowned into an abyss, sealed into its prison, deep, deep into the blackest recesses of the earth.

Cheers erupted through Dharati as the blight receded from the city. People chased after it, tears of joy in their eyes. It swept over the land, leaving behind the desiccated ruins of a queendom once under siege. But they would recover.

They would rebuild, and Daragaab would be stronger than ever.

Magic swept over the miles, taking the demons that did not belong to this world with it. Screams of anguish rang out as Amrita's magic sealed them back into the darkness forever.

Over the cadaverous forest, it swept towards the ocean, racing against the earth, reclaiming the miles that had been lost. The rivers, the trees, the towns it had devoured. They were gone, but they would come back. They would find a way to reclaim their lives once again.

What was dead would live again. What had been taken would regrow in time. Hope replaced the darkness as it was once again buried deep beneath the Jai Tree. Light and love and joy flowed over the land, over the hills, through the forest, and through the hearts and minds of a people who had almost lost everything.

As the darkness was pushed further and further down, it finally met its end, receding from the shore and away from the small whitewashed cottage that sat quietly by the sea.

FORTY-TWO

With the blight contained, it was time for the Chiranjivi to return home. Apsara stood in the courtyard, her snowy white wings sparkling in the sunlight. She embraced Zarya, squeezing her tight.

"I'll see you soon," she said, clasping her hands.

"Promise me that," Zarya said. "Have you said goodbye to Suvanna? Will you see each other after this?"

Apsara sighed. "It seems the timing isn't right for us. Yet again. Perhaps in the next life."

"I'm sorry," Zarya said.

"I'll be fine. You take care of yourself." She gave Zarya a small smile, and they embraced again. After they pulled apart, Apsara flapped her wings, rising into the air and disappearing into the clouds.

Next, Kindle said his goodbyes as he shared a brotherly moment with Row.

"See you around, old friend," Kindle said, clasping elbows with Row.

"We always manage to run into each other eventually, don't we?"

Kindle nodded, bowing to Zarya. "Take care of him, will you? We can't go losing him again."

"Of course I will." She grinned, and in a swirl of flame, Kindle disappeared.

"Okay, well, see you," Suvanna said, saluting to everyone. She took off running through the palace and towards the sea, leaping into the air and gracefully diving into the waves in a flurry of blue and green.

Finally, Koura gave one gentle pat to Amrita, kissing his fingers and placing them on the bark. "Take care, lovely queen," he said.

He shook hands with Row and turned to Zarya.

"And you take care, Princess," he said, bowing to her. She hugged him before he pulled himself onto his horse and trotted out of the courtyard.

Row then turned to Zarya. "I guess it's you and me now."

"I guess."

"Zarya, I'd like for us to be a family. Try to find the happiness I could never give you. We can both move into the haveli. Start over."

"You promise never to make me return to the cottage again?"

"I promise," Row said with a smile. "I'll burn the damned thing down if you want."

She laughed at that, linking her arm with his.

"I'd like that, Row. All of it."

Once everyone was gone, they walked back to the haveli, navigating the bustling street.

"Zarya," came a deep voice that brought her to a stop. She looked over her shoulder to find Rabin. "Can we please talk?"

She tightened her hold on Row and looked up at him. He laid a hand over hers.

"Do you want me to give you some space?"

"No," she said. "Stay with me, please."

He nodded.

"I have nothing to say to you," she said, turning to Rabin.

"Please," he said. "I want to explain—"

"I don't really want to hear it right now."

"Then when?"

"I don't know."

Then, she turned back to Row, and they walked away.

"I'm not giving up on you!" Rabin called through the crowd, and she resisted the urge to turn back, straightening her shoulders and pretending her heart wasn't oozing out between her ribs.

* * *

A few days later, Zarya stood on the edge of the Nila Hara Sea, the sun high and the waves lapping the sand, the hole inside her gnawing away.

"Zarya," came Row's voice, and she turned to face him. "What are you doing?"

She sighed. "Row. I think... I have to leave."

His shoulders dropped, disappointment crumpling his expression. She opened her mouth, already prepared to argue her case, but he raised a hand, silencing her.

"I expected as much," he said.

She approached him. "I'm sorry. It's not that I don't want to live with you and get to know you better. It's just that I have to find them."

"Your family," Row said, and she nodded.

"I know what you said—that they wouldn't welcome me, but I can't continue living here knowing they're out there without even trying to meet them."

Row ran a hand down his face.

"Besides, if Dhawan told Abishek where I am, I'm not safe

here anymore. I can hide myself in Gi'ana until I figure out what to do about him."

"Zarya, I think it would be better if you went back into hiding. He's going to find you."

"No." She shook her head. "You know I'd never agree to that. I will never be locked away again."

"I do understand that," Row said. "But he *will* find you."

"Then I'll deal with it," she said. "But I will face it on my own terms."

"Let me come with you, then," he said. "I can protect you."

"No. I need to do this alone. I have so much growing to do, and I need to figure this out by myself."

She twisted the stone of her mother's necklace between her fingers. Her mother had said no one else in the world knew, but Zarya knew she could trust Row with this.

"There's something else I need to show you," she said as she sent out a ribbon of spirit, twisting around the stone. "Listen."

Row leaned forward as her mother began speaking before he nearly fell over in shock. Asha repeated the same words Zarya had listened to so many times she could recite them by heart.

It was the last two lines of the prophecy she couldn't get out of her head.

> *To the people caged by the stars after the fall,*
> *She will be the one to free them all.*

After her mother's words fell silent, Row stared at Zarya.

"Did you know it could do that?" she asked, and he shook his head.

"No. I suspect it would only work for you, though."

"Did you know about the second half of the prophecy?"

"No. I've never heard of such a thing."

"What does it mean?" Zarya asked, hoping he could arrange this puzzle into something recognizable.

"The vanshaj," Row said. "Free them? *You* will free them?"

"That's what I thought, too, but it's too wild to consider, isn't it?"

Row sighed heavily. "I... I'm not sure."

"The first part came true."

"It did." He gave her a wary look.

"And I think I have to figure out what the rest means. And I have to go to Gi'ana for that."

When he looked like he wanted to continue protesting, she said, "You owe me this. After everything, this is what I need you to do for me. I forgive you for everything, but I'm asking you to let me go and to trust me."

Row nodded slowly, staring at the stone hanging around her neck.

"Your mother was full of more mysteries than I ever imagined."

Then, he opened his arms and drew her into a long hug.

"You're right. Just, please be careful," he finally said.

"I will. And I will come back. I promise."

He cupped the back of her head and nodded against her temple.

"I'm holding you to that."

She squeezed him and then let go.

"I'll write, too," she said.

"Thank you."

* * *

Zarya finished packing her bags but knew she couldn't leave without doing something first. She ran downstairs and opened the door to find Yasen coming up the front walk.

"Hey," he said.

"Hi. I was just coming to look for you."

"What's up?"

She was suddenly overcome with the idea of losing him. "I'm leaving."

He nodded. "I thought that might be the case, eventually."

She snorted a laugh. "Apparently, I'm very predictable. Row said he knew, too."

He let out a sigh. "The way you've been sitting out on that balcony staring at the water like you want to jump in and swim away forever was my first clue."

She huffed. "I guess I have been doing that."

She looked at the water and then back at him.

"What would you have done if I had?"

He gave her a crooked smile. "Jumped in after you, Zee. Surely, you know that by now."

Tears burned her eyes. "I'm going to Gi'ana to find my family."

"I figured that."

"I'm going to miss you," she said.

"No, you're not."

She frowned at him.

"Because I'm coming with you."

"You are?"

He shrugged. "Someone needs to look out for you, and I'm guessing you already turned Row down for the position."

She blinked, her heavy heart already growing lighter.

"You would do that for me?"

"Yeah. Of course."

"What about your position as commander? What about Vikram?"

"I just resigned," he said. "I never wanted that to be my life. As for Vik, he's got enough to keep him busy for now, and I think that maybe it's finally time for me to live my own life. You know?"

She gave him a watery smile. "I do know."

"And we'll be back, right?"

"Of course," she said.

"So, what are we waiting for?"

She grinned and then burst out laughing. "I'm going to cry," she said. "So much. But it's all your fault you're making me cry."

"I know you are." Then, he cocked his head. "But I'm still coming."

She released the hold on her tears as she threw herself against him, hugging him tight. "I love you, Yas."

"I know you do. I'm very loveable."

She snorted a laugh, sniffling and then wiping her nose with the back of her sleeve.

"Disgusting," Yasen said, curling his lip.

"Let me go get my bag. I'm already packed."

He nodded, and then she ran up the stairs. She picked up her bag and hoisted it over her shoulder as she stared about the room.

A few months ago, she'd arrived here a very different person, and she would miss this place. She would miss Row.

She then pulled a book out of her pack—her favorite romance that she'd read so many times it was practically falling apart. She walked over to the desk and laid it down. This would be her promise to Row that she would return someday. A piece of herself left behind in Dharati.

Looking up, she caught sight of herself in the nearby mirror, and she studied herself. These last months had changed her physically. She looked older and more confident. More sure of herself. She was ready for whatever life had to throw at her.

As she stared at her reflection, something shifted behind her eyes. She blinked, suddenly a bit dizzy as her image blurred, revealing a face she didn't recognize. A man with a dark beard and glittering black eyes, his expression serious.

She watched as his eyes turned into fiery red pits.

"Zee!" Came a voice, tearing her away from the image. She heard Yasen coming up the stairs and looked back at herself, but the image had returned to normal.

"You coming? What's taking so long?"

"Yeah," she said. "I'm ready."

After one last glance at the mirror, she took his hand, blaming her overactive imagination for whatever that had been.

"Let's go."

Then, they headed downstairs and into the bustling streets of the city, marching towards whatever destiny waited for them.

A LETTER FROM NISHA

Dear Reader,

I want to say a huge thank you for choosing to read *Heart of Night and Fire* and its sequel *Dance of Stars and Ashes*. If you enjoyed them and want to keep up to date with all my latest releases, just sign up at the following link. Your email address will never be shared, and you can unsubscribe at any time.

www.secondskybooks.com/nisha-j-tuli

If you loved *Dance of Stars and Ashes*, please consider leaving a review on your favorite platform. And if you'd like to get in touch, I love hearing from readers! You can join my Facebook reader group, send me an email on my website, or message me on Instagram.

Love,

Nisha

KEEP IN TOUCH WITH NISHA

www.nishajtuli.com

facebook.com/NishaJT
instagram.com/nishajtwrites
tiktok.com/@nishajtwrites

PUBLISHING TEAM

Turning a manuscript into a book requires the efforts of many people. The publishing team at Bookouture would like to acknowledge everyone who contributed to this publication.

Audio
Alba Proko
Sinead O'Connor
Melissa Tran

Commercial
Lauren Morrissette
Jil Thielen
Imogen Allport

Cover design
Andrew Davis

Data and analysis
Mark Alder
Mohamed Bussuri

Editorial
Jack Renninson
Melissa Tran

Copyeditor
Angela Snowden

Proofreader
Catherine Lenderi

Marketing
Alex Crow
Melanie Price
Occy Carr
Cíara Rosney

Operations and distribution
Marina Valles
Stephanie Straub

Production
Hannah Snetsinger
Mandy Kullar
Jen Shannon

Publicity
Kim Nash
Noelle Holten
Myrto Kalavrezou
Jess Readett
Sarah Hardy

Rights and contracts
Peta Nightingale
Richard King
Saidah Graham

Milton Keynes UK
Ingram Content Group UK Ltd.
UKHW041102130224
437765UK00004B/172